Gay Conversion Practices in Memoir, Film and Fiction

Library of Gender and Popular Culture

From *Mad Men* to gaming culture, performance art to steampunk fashion, the presentation and representation of gender continues to saturate popular media. This series seeks to explore the intersection of gender and popular culture, engaging with a variety of texts – drawn primarily from Art, Fashion, TV, Cinema, Cultural Studies and Media Studies – as a way of considering various models for understanding the complementary relationship between 'gender identities' and 'popular culture'. By considering race, ethnicity, class and sexual identities across a range of cultural forms, each book in the series adopts a critical stance towards issues surrounding the development of gender identities and popular and mass cultural 'products'.

For further information or enquiries, please contact the library series editors:

Claire Nally: claire.nally@northumbria.ac.uk
Angela Smith: angela.smith@sunderland.ac.uk

Advisory Board:

Dr Kate Ames, Central Queensland University, Australia

Dr Michael Higgins, University of Strathclyde, UK

Prof Åsa Kroon, Örebro University, Sweden

Dr Andrea McDonnell, Emmanuel College, USA

Dr Niall Richardson, University of Sussex, UK

Dr Jacki Willson, University of Leeds, UK

Published and forthcoming titles:

The Aesthetics of Camp: Post-Queer Gender and Popular Culture
By Anna Malinowska

Ageing Femininity on Screen: The Older Woman in Contemporary Cinema
By Niall Richardson

All-American TV Crime Drama: Feminism and Identity Politics in Law and Order: Special Victims Unit
By Sujata Moorti and Lisa Cuklanz

Are You Not Entertained?: Mapping the Gladiator across Visual Media
By Lindsay Steenberg

Bad Girls, Dirty Bodies: Sex, Performance and Safe Femininity
By Gemma Commane

Conflicting Masculinities: Men in Television Period Drama
By Katherine Byrne, Julie Anne Taddeo and James Leggott (Eds)

Fat on Film: Gender, Race and Body Size in Contemporary Hollywood Cinema
By Barbara Plotz

Fathers on Film: Paternity and Masculinity in 1990s Hollywood
By Katie Barnett

Film Bodies: Queer Feminist Encounters with Gender and Sexuality in Cinema
By Katharina Lindner

From the Margins to the Mainstream: Women On and Off Screen in Television and Film
By Marianne Kac-Vergne and Julie Assouly (Eds)

Gay Pornography: Representations of Sexuality and Masculinity
By John Mercer

Gender and Austerity in Popular Culture: Femininity, Masculinity and Recession in Film and Television
By Helen Davies and Claire O'Callaghan (Eds)

Gender and Early Television: Mapping Women's Role in Emerging US and British Media, 1850–1950
By Sarah Arnold

The Gendered Motorcycle: Representations in Society, Media and Popular Culture
By Esperanza Miyake

Gendering History on Screen: Women Filmmakers and Historical Films
By Julia Erhart

Girls Like This, Boys Like That: The Reproduction of Gender in Contemporary Youth Cultures
By Victoria Cann

'Guilty Pleasures': European Audiences and Contemporary Hollywood Romantic Comedy
By Alice Guilluy

The Gypsy Woman: Representations in Literature and Visual Culture
By Jodie Matthews

Male and Female Violence in Popular Media
By Elisa Giomi and Sveva Magaraggia

Masculinity in Contemporary Science Fiction Cinema: Cyborgs, Troopers and Other Men of the Future
By Marianne Kac-Vergne

Positive Images: Gay Men and HIV/AIDS in the Culture of 'Post-Crisis'
By Dion Kagan

Postfeminism and Contemporary Vampire Romance
By Lea Gerhards

Queer Horror Film and Television: Sexuality and Masculinity at the Margins
By Darren Elliott-Smith

Queer Sexualities in Early Film: Cinema and Male-Male Intimacy
By Shane Brown

Screening Queer Memory: LGBTQ Pasts in Contemporary Film and Television
By Anamarija Horvat

Stand-up Comedy and Contemporary Feminisms: Sexism, Stereotypes and Structural Inequalities
By Ellie Tomsett

Gay Conversion Practices in Memoir, Film and Fiction

Stories of Repentance and Defiance

Edited by James E. Bennett and
Marguerite Johnson

BLOOMSBURY ACADEMIC
LONDON · NEW YORK · OXFORD · NEW DELHI · SYDNEY

BLOOMSBURY ACADEMIC
Bloomsbury Publishing Plc, 50 Bedford Square, London, WC1B 3DP, UK
Bloomsbury Publishing Inc, 1359 Broadway, New York, NY 10018, USA
Bloomsbury Publishing Ireland, 29 Earlsfort Terrace, Dublin 2, D02 AY28, Ireland

BLOOMSBURY, BLOOMSBURY ACADEMIC and the Diana logo are
trademarks of Bloomsbury Publishing Plc

First published in Great Britain 2024
This paperback edition published 2026

A catalogue record for this book is available from the British Library.

Library of Congress Cataloging-in-Publication Data

Names: Bennett, James, 1964- editor. | Johnson, Marguerite, 1965- editor.
Title: Gay conversion practices in memoir, film and fiction : stories of repentance
and defiance / edited by James E. Bennett and Marguerite Johnson.
Description: London; New York: Bloomsbury Academic, 2024. | Series: Library of
gender and popular culture | Includes bibliographical references and index.
Identifiers: LCCN 2023053404 (print) | LCCN 2023053405 (ebook) |
ISBN 9781350289833 (hardback) | ISBN 9781350289871 (paperback) |
ISBN 9781350289840 (ebook) | ISBN 9781350289857 (pdf)
Subjects: LCSH: Conversion therapy in literature. | Conversion therapy in motion pictures.
Classification: LCC PN56.C677 G39 2024 (print) | LCC PN56.C677 (ebook) |
DDC 809.935–dc23/eng/20240214
LC record available at https://lccn.loc.gov/2023053404
LC ebook record available at https://lccn.loc.gov/2023053405

ISBN: HB: 978-1-3502-8983-3
PB: 978-1-3502-8987-1
ePDF: 978-1-3502-8985-7
eBook: 978-1-3502-8984-0

Series: Library of Gender and Popular Culture

Typeset by RefineCatch Limited, Bungay, Suffolk

For product safety related questions contact productsafety@bloomsbury.com.

To find out more about our authors and books visit www.bloomsbury.com
and sign up for our newsletters.

To all those who survived conversion practices
and
In memory of those who did not

Contents

Part 3 Memoir, Film and Fiction

Figures

Series Editors' Introduction

Many of the books in this Library explore issues of sexuality. The representation of non-binary sexuality is found in film from the early part of the twentieth century, as Shane Brown's *Queer Sexualities in Early Film* (2016) explores, and continues to be celebrated in popular television and film, as Anamarija Horvat's *Screening Queer Memory* (2021) shows. However, what Bennett and Johnson's edited collection reveals is an ongoing and perhaps increasing rejection of gay identities in society. Emerging from collabarative research and teaching by Bennett and Johnson at The University of Newcastle, Australia, this book explores a world where dangerous conversion practices damage and traumatize those who experience them as part of a populist shift away from liberal politics, and the rise of an associated Christian Right.

This collection explores how conversion practices are represented across a range of genres, challenging the notion of 'conversion' and 'therapy' along the way. The idea of 'converting' a gay person into a straight person is critiqued throughout the book. The damage and trauma that this causes is all the more galling as it is closely linked with the religious notion of 'conversion' and therefore clearly aligns with the Christian Right. Religion, particularly Christianity in the United States and Australia, is at the heart of many of the chapters in this book, and the editors have provided a helpful overview of the context for this in their Introduction.

The use of 'therapy' is challenged, as it is certainly not a therapeutic treatment that would be acknowledged by any reputable counsellor or clinician. To ameliorate this, the editors offer a compromise of 'conversion practices', which avoids the pseudo-medical connotation of 'therapy'.

The inclusion of memoirs is particularly devastating, with the voices of those who have been affected by these practices showing how they were not only unsuccessful in 'converting' gay to straight, but led to depression, self-harm and even suicidal thoughts. This makes this collection particularly important, as it allows the voices of those affected by these practices to be heard, aside from the mediated voices in films and other fictional works.

While the majority of those subjected to conversation practices are gay men, what this book offers is an insight into how these practices include women and trans people. More recent films have started to deal with issues of trans conversion practices, and this is discussed in this book.

While there is much in this book that could lead the reader to despair at the traumatizing and dangerous conversion practices so clearly described, there is also hope in the form of resistance and celebration. The book offers an interesting mix of memoir and fiction which allows for a more open discussion of the issues it raises.

Claire Nally and Angela Smith

Foreword

This powerful and profound edited collection brings together and interweaves the voices and stories of survivors of gay conversion practices in Australia and the United States. Spanning multiple forms and genres of storytelling, this book makes clear the damage done by these discredited practices. At the same time, storytelling emerges here as a vitally important way to publicize and push back against these dangerous practices.

Written by survivors and scholars, the book's Introduction and individual chapters are deeply informative. They examine and explain what gay conversion practices are and how they emerged in Christian churches in the context of the modern gay and lesbian movement of the 1970s and after. The misnomer that 'practitioners' apply to what they are doing is 'conversion' or 'reparative therapy'. But this book makes clear that they are not practising 'therapy' at all and, in fact, all mainstream professional medical, psychological and psychiatric organizations repudiate these practices. Moreover, these practices do not 'convert' anyone from gay to straight as the leaders of the 'ex-gay' movement claim. Nor do they 'repair' anyone but, in fact, do great harm.

Giving voice to these truths in this book are actual people and characters based on actual people who experienced and survived gay conversion practices, as well as entirely fictional characters. Factual, first-hand accounts of growing up gay and Christian in Australia and the United States over the second half of the twentieth century and into the twenty-first inform all of the stories told here. The memoirists tell of the devastating pressure – both external and self-inflicted – to suppress their gay identity to conform to conservative religious beliefs. The gay conversion practices they were subjected to were not just ineffective but incredibly dangerous, leading to depression, self-harm and suicidal thoughts and actions. There are other voices here too, both real and fictionalized, including former leaders and ministers of the ex-gay movement who engaged in and now repudiate these practices, as well as a few figures who still support and promote them.

However, it is the voices of survivors that are most prominent in these pages, and they are conveyed in a variety of forms. The memoirists provide a direct, meaningful connection to the reader, sharing the emotional conflicts and costs of all they experienced, and how they came through to create better lives for themselves and to contribute to a better world. Their stories are expressed in their own words and writings, presented in documentary films, and fictionalized in novels and feature film. All these forms of storytelling are crafted and shaped by the authors and filmmakers. Yet they differ in nature, purpose and audience expectations and allow the stories of survivors to be told in different ways.

In the case of film, documentaries are factual and expository, presenting persuasive evidence and argument, while feature films are fictional and dramatic, offering compelling plot and characters. With both filmic forms, the process of putting personal stories on screen is not simple or straightforward, and filmmakers must make choices. For the documentary filmmakers, informing and opening up public debate about gay conversion practices requires explanation and contextualization. For the feature filmmakers, the priority of entertainment edges out education. They need to decide whether to convey complexity or simplify stories and characters – and how – influencing what audiences are likely to take away from viewing. Such decisions are explored here and can be especially fraught for filmmakers adapting a novel or memoir for the screen. Genre conventions further inform such decision-making. How these stories are told differ whether the genre is a YA novel, teen comedy, adult drama, or biopic.

While the scholarly contributors to this book consider what is gained and what is lost in telling different kinds of stories about experiencing and surviving gay conversion practices, they agree these are examples of 'new storytelling'. New storytelling is a powerful means to express deeply personal life stories, particularly for marginalized individuals and groups in society. It allows for the personal expression of hard truths and, in turn, for audiences to identify with and make their own interpersonal connections to the storyteller and stories. New storytelling is also associated with new technologies with the core print or film text augmented by paratexts and extratextual events. Media coverage, blogposts and podcasts surrounding or in conjunction with these books and films inform and extend their meaning for audiences. In this way, new storytelling can be considered a genre in its own right, reflecting and affecting the content, style, structure and reception of these personal stories.

At the same time, this new storytelling of encountering and enduring gay conversion practices often mirrors a classical narrative three-act structure of conflict, crisis and resolution. Whether a first-person account or fictional narrative, the conflict between survivors' religious and gay, lesbian or queer identities leads to great anguish and distress that builds and builds until reaching a crisis. That critical moment changes the memoirist or protagonist and their lives: the breaking point is a turning point. Changing their lives does not necessarily mean abandoning their religious beliefs, however. Instead, many turned to seeking out churches that welcome and embrace the LGBTQ+ rainbow community.

They also turn to public engagement, political activism and professional careers to push back against gay conversion practices. In the two memoirs that open and lay the foundation for this book, Stuart Edser becomes a psychologist, Anthony Venn-Brown pursues service and activism for the rainbow community, and they both write ground-breaking books that they draw on for their chapters. With a few exceptions discussed here, former leaders and ministers of the ex-gay movement similarly work to end these practices. Indeed, these practices, particularly for minors, are successfully being banned around the world. By sharing these stories, the memoirists, authors, and filmmakers discussed in this book have made the personal public and political.

We can surely hold out hope that these stories of defiance and repentance, as the co-editors so aptly call them, will be heard by current practitioners and leaders of the ex-gay movement. For the rest of us, may these life-affirming stories continue to educate and empower readers and viewers to challenge and change these damaging practices to allow everyone to find themselves and flourish in our communities.

Jennifer Frost
Associate Professor of History
University of Auckland

June 2023

Acknowledgments

James and Marguerite's collaboration spans over two decades with a shared interest in representations of gender and sexualities. Their joint projects began with the Gender Studies conference at the Ourimbah campus of The University of Newcastle, Australia in 2002 and has ranged from a variety of public engagement events to publication of their research findings in the form of both peer reviewed journal article and short form writing for *The Conversation*. One of their career highlights was designing and teaching a History undergraduate course called Sex and Scandal in History, which was the starting point for an important dialogue, first with each other, then with their students, on conversion practices.

That conversation required engagement with the lived experience of conversion survivors and led us in turn to two key contributors to the book, Anthony Venn-Brown and Stuart Edser. We thank Anthony for his generosity in talking with our students, sharing his profound knowledge of the topic with public audiences in Newcastle, including the Newcastle Writers' Festival, his unstinting support of our project and for facilitating so many of the vital contacts that we made to expand and deepen our own research on this book. We are indebted to him for his wisdom, advice and good humour, which provided us with the necessary insight and confidence to design and execute a project that constantly revealed itself in new layers of challenge and complexity. We also thank Stuart for a generous spirit in sharing both his personal and professional experience at the Newcastle Writers' Festival as well as in the book. Stuart and Anthony's chapters provide the structural foundations of the book and the vital platform on which Parts 2 and 3, dealing with representations of conversion practices, are laid.

We warmly acknowledge the many students who enrolled in our Sex and Scandal course for stimulating – as well as sometimes difficult – conversations on the topic and thank them for their deep engagement with course themes. We are particularly appreciative of one – Tom

Sharples – who began his own form of conversion journey with us as an Ancient History major, before writing a research essay on conversion practices as a third year History student, then pursuing this further as a PhD thesis. We express our gratitude to him, not only for agreeing to produce a chapter, but for doing so at short notice while juggling full-time employment commitments. Apart from Stuart, Anthony and Tom, we thank our other contributors – David Coon, Jessica Ford, Annika Herb and Scott McKinnon – from whom we could not have expected more as editors.

The US and UK reviewers of our book proposal are owed a special vote of thanks for their enthusiastic embrace of the project and careful reading of the proposal. Their many helpful suggestions have been put to good use in crafting the structure and content. The review process was also instrumental in our efforts to secure one of the contributors to the project, David Coon, whose input we have valued greatly.

Various journalists contacted us over a period of several years about faith-based conversion practices or about the earlier history of failed medical experiments in the twentieth century that were designed to change or suppress gay and lesbian people's sexual orientation. They are Giselle Wakatama (ABC Newcastle); Steve Kilgallon (*Sunday Star Times* and stuff.co.nz, NZ) and journalists at *The Conversation* (Australia). We thank them for their interest in our work and for bringing it to the attention of a wider public as we do the organizers of the Newcastle Writers' Festival, notably its founding director, Rosemarie Milsom, who made possible our 2019 panel session, 'Lives Erased: The history of LGBTQI conversion therapy'.

James extends his appreciation to documentary directors, Daniel Karslake and Heather Corkhill, for engaging with questions about their respective productions, *For They Know Not What They Do* and *The Cure* as well as their generosity in sharing images, and to Richard Yeagley for facilitating access to his documentary, *The Sunday Sessions*.

Several audiences listened to presentations dealing with themes covered in the book and I thank them for their excellent engagement with, and insightful responses to the ideas in these papers. Specifically, these audiences are my panel session at the Australian and New Zealand Society of the History of Medicine (ANZSHM) Conference at the University of Auckland (December 2019), the History Seminar Series in the School of Humanities at the University of Auckland (May 2023) and the Newcastle Booklovers Group at Cooks Hill Bookshop (April 2023).

I thank colleagues at the University of Auckland for their support and feedback, notably Linda Bryder, Jonathan Scott, Jennifer Frost, Malcolm Campbell, Kim Phillips and Derek Dow. My New South Wales-based friends and colleagues – Lyndall Ryan, Troy Duncan, Margot Ford, David Betts, Jude Conway, David Blyth, Beans Goodfellow, Juan Carlos Lilø and Den Milenkovic – all showed interest in the project and made a range of helpful suggestions. I greatly appreciate the intellectual stimulation from, and synergy with Chris Brickell at the University of Otago. Lastly, and most importantly, I acknowledge an intellectual debt to my dear friend and colleague, Marguerite, without whom this book would not have materialized. I have profited from her skill and generosity as an interdisciplinary scholar in all our intellectual endeavours. The whole has most definitely been greater than the sum of its parts.

Finally, I acknowledge my partner, Raihan, and my nonagenarian mother, Bernice Bennett, for their love and support.

Marguerite extends her warmest thanks to her wonderful friend and co-researcher, James, whose intellectual rigour and dedication has meant all of their projects have always gone without a glitch and, quite surprisingly, a disagreement. She is also indebted to her partner, Leni and their two children, Jack and Kate, who always believe that her work is worthwhile and who ground her in all that she does.

Lastly, both James and Marguerite thank Bloomsbury Academic for their support and belief in the project, particularly the commissioning editor, Anna Coatman. We are also grateful to Judy Tither and Merv Honeywood at Refinecatch for their efficient copy editing and seamless management of the production process respectively. This book had a very long gestation period, disrupted by the Covid-19 pandemic as well as a raft of other unanticipated issues that confronted us. Such an experience makes both of us cherish the result even more.

Abbreviations

ACT UP	AIDS Coalition to Unleash Power
AIDS	Acquired Immune Deficiency Syndrome
APA	American Psychiatric Association
APS	Australian Psychological Society
DOMA	*Defense of Marriage Act* (USA)
DSM	Diagnostic and Statistical Manual (American Psychiatric Association)
FRC	Family Research Council
GLEH	Gay & Lesbian Elder Housing
HIV	Human Immunodeficiency Virus
HV	Homosexual Visibility (novels)
LIA	Love In Action
MCC	Metropolitan Community Church
NARTH	National Association for Research & Therapy of Homosexuality
PFC	Prefrontal cortex
POV	Point of view
PTSD	Post Traumatic Stress Disorder
SSA	Same-sex attraction
UCLA	University of California, Los Angeles
YA	Young Adult

Introduction

James E. Bennett and Marguerite Johnson

This collection began as an expanded response to the editors' role in organizing a panel for the 2019 Newcastle Writers' Festival, called Lives Erased: The History of LGBTQI Conversion Therapy. The panel comprised four contributors to this book: the two editors and chapter authors, Marguerite Johnson (host) and James Bennett (panellist), and two chapter authors, Stuart Edser and Anthony Venn-Brown (panellists). The panel centred on Australia, as both memoirists, Edser and Venn-Brown, are Australians, and both scholars, Bennett and Johnson, were then employed at an Australian university, The University of Newcastle, Australia, and have focused their research on the topic largely within an Australasian context.[1] The concept for the panel was threefold: the (then) recent release of the films, *Boy Erased* and *The Miseducation of Cameron Post* in 2018; the inclusion of material relating to gay conversion practices in the editors' jointly delivered undergraduate course at The University of Newcastle over several years; and the aftermath of the *Marriage Amendment (Definition and Religious Freedoms) Act 2017*, passed by the Australian Federal Parliament.

The panel attracted a 'full house' of around sixty attendees. This was particularly pleasing in view of its role as the first panel of this kind to feature in the festival; indeed, it was the first of its kind for the New South Wales region of Newcastle and the Hunter Valley.[2] Panellists Edser and Venn-Brown each presented a raw account of their experiences as survivors of conversion practices and the anguished and confronting process of writing their memoirs (for example, Venn-Brown spoke powerfully about the writing process as a re-traumatizing act). Audience members were invited to ask questions after a fifty-minute presentation, and there were many questions – in fact, far too many for the remaining ten minutes.

The experience inspired the four panel members, especially the editors of this collection, to take the topic further to begin a wider conversation about the process of narrating survivor testimonies and the outcomes – both written and filmic – of these accounts (autobiographical, semi-autobiographical and fictional). This process is reflected in the approach or methodology undertaken herein; namely, the chapters privilege an interdisciplinary approach to the topic as well as one that extends authorship beyond the traditional academy.

Terminology

The phenomenon involving attempts to change a person's sexual orientation or gender identity is beset with a quagmire of terminology, some of it quite misleading. We need, therefore, to shine a light on the wide variety of contemporary and historical usage to bring the frame of reference for this collection into sharp focus – and to contest some of the popular terminology surrounding it. As one of our contributors, Venn-Brown, reminds us, anecdotally it is commonplace to encounter surprise from casual observers that 'conversion therapy' persists to this day. However, this is to confuse more recent faith-based conversion attempts with historical medical interventions that sought unsuccessfully to 'cure' or at least suppress non-normative sexual orientation through such brutal and invasive techniques as aversion therapy, chemical castration, electric shock treatment and even lobotomies, practices that reached their peak in the mid-twentieth century.[3] A rich historiography exists on these long discredited medical interventions in the United States and the United Kingdom, and while in some contemporary contexts they may form part of a cocktail of measures designed to alter sexual desire or gender identity, 'conversion therapy' was not the nomenclature used for these practices and they are not within the remit of this book.

The use of psychoanalysis, on the other hand, to inform efforts to reorient homoerotic desire has endured in the United States where a collective of fringe professionals coalesced in 1992 to form the National Association for Research & Therapy of Homosexuality (NARTH).[4] Although ostensibly secular, NARTH, co-founded by the late Catholic psychologist Joseph Nicolosi, allied itself to a range of religious organizations. Popularly dubbed 'conversion therapy' or 'ex-gay therapy' – a pseudoscientific practice condemned by all contemporary major mental health and medical organizations – 'reparative therapy' (from the verb 'to repair') based around psychotherapy techniques, is the term favoured by NARTH and its affiliates and one that is in wide circulation in the United States.

Ranging from 'conversion therapy', a term bestowing respectability on a phenomenon that raises many ethical, consensual and mental health issues, at one end of the spectrum, to epithets like 'bigoted quackery'[5] expressed by indomitable opponents, the popular usage cannot go unchallenged. Analyzed separately, neither word in the semantic conjugation 'conversion therapy' bears scrutiny. As the discussion above indicates clearly, historical experiments to convert or suppress orientation (as opposed to the far more superficial and transient concept of sexual *behaviour*) were a rank failure that caused – and continue to cause – great human damage (see Chapters 1 and 2 of this book). Of course, it is also germane to this study to note that the word 'conversion' in the phrase 'conversion therapy' is decidedly religious in connotation, reminding one of the concept and practice of religious *conversion* as the acceptance of a new faith-based identity, or the adoption of a new religion. In the context at hand, 'conversion' signposts the aim of 'treating' an individual until they accept a new sexuality and/or gender identity. Turning to the second word – 'therapy' – and in the words of another of our contributors, Edser, this is a dangerous misnomer; to take up his argument, he considers it to be 'anti-therapy', and in diametric conflict with his own approach as a practising clinician.[6]

To navigate this semantic minefield is not easy. In the end we have been guided by the term favoured by survivors, namely *conversion practices*. Despite its inadequacy, 'conversion' does at least have the advantage of being a universally recognizable term, while 'practices' captures the breadth of techniques that underpin faith-based attempts to alter or suppress sexuality, including spiritual endeavours (ranging from prayer to exorcism), 'ex-gay' programmes as well as 'coerced heterosexual marriage and rape'.[7] In some contexts, we have retained the term 'conversion therapy', particularly when appearing in a quoted passage or where it is consistent with the interpretation or emphasis of the contributing author.

Similarly, a broad spectrum of terms has been used historically to express the concept of same-sex attraction (SSA). No single word is favoured in this collection as homoerotic desire and responses to it have varied significantly over time and space. As editors, we have tried to limit the usage of behavioural and medicalizing terms such as 'homosexual' in favour of gay, lesbian and same-sex attracted (sometimes expressed negatively by pro conversion forces as 'unwanted SSA') or, where a more inclusive term is appropriate, 'queer'. When referring to the rainbow community in all its diversity, we have opted for the standardized abbreviation, LGBT+.

The relationship between conversion and a range of theologies and religious practices introduces a further complication to the semantic terrain. First, we need to establish a clear correlation between conversion practices and particular denominations in the Christian community. While Christians do not by any means have a monopoly on the phenomenon of conversion, the experiences narrated in this collection are all co-extensive with the Christian faith.[8] According to a report released in 2020 by the Williams Institute at the UCLA School of Law, seven per cent of LGB Americans aged eighteen to fifty-nine have been subject to conversion practices and over eighty per cent of the reported cases were undertaken by religious leaders.[9] Many of these practices are concealed within evangelical spaces, and are typically 'pushed out through a thriving network of courses and mentors in the borderless world of cyberspace, cloaked in the terminology of "self improvement" or "spiritual healing"'.[10] To return to an earlier point, while there is some evidence of residual use of historical techniques by healthcare providers, contemporary conversion practices are overwhelmingly faith-based in origin and motivation.

In this collection, many of the contributing authors use a variety of appellations to reference conservative Christian theology. While distinctions can certainly be drawn between conservative denominational expressions of the Christian faith, such as Catholicism and Protestantism, orthodoxies of fundamentalism and evangelicalism, and practices that may extend to Pentecostalism and 'born-again' expressions of faith, they are all underpinned by belief in the 'supreme authority of Scripture'.[11] Many of the specific examples introduced to narrate conversion experiences are evangelical in origin, 'a transdenominational trend in theology and spirituality', and a very broad umbrella category that defies easy categorization. By way of example, evangelicalism in the United States today is 'composed of several institutions, churches and a network of largely conservative spokespersons', including Baptists, Methodists as well as the mega-church, Hillsong, located in both Australia and America.[12] With some differences in emphasis from other denominations, Pentecostals are also part of this trans-denominational trend. Politically, evangelicals have been a mainstay of support for the Republican Party since the 1980s and share common cause in their opposition to marriage equality and abortion, all the while advancing 'family values'.[13] This political alliance appeared to reach its apotheosis during the Trump years from 2017 to 2020.

In an Australian context, religious history scholar Stuart Piggin notes the splintering of evangelicalism into three camps by the late twentieth century: exclusive conservatives; inclusive progressives, and Charismatics and Pentecostals. Tensions between conservatives and progressives were sharpened in response to the expanding influence of ultra conservative Sydney Anglicanism, led from 2001 by the 'conservative exclusive evangelical' Anglican Archbishop of Sydney, Peter Jensen. Both Sydney Anglicans and Hillsong expanded globally in the early twenty-first century, and the Sydney Anglican worldview received strong endorsement from some quarters internationally, nowhere more so than from African provinces.[14] While evangelicalism remains inherently fractured as a movement, as Piggin observes, same-sex attraction functioned as a cultural lightning rod:

> The Sydney Anglicans used the vexed issue of homosexuality to leverage even greater support. Indeed, only this issue was big enough to garner the support of the most progressive evangelicals in the West as well as evangelicals in the developing world. It was this issue which distinguished nearly all evangelicals from liberals and galvanized them again into one movement.[15]

Alister McGrath notes that evangelicalism is based around four major assumptions, one of which is the need for personal conversion.[16] Researcher Tanya Erzen's insightful ethnographic study of New Hope, a non-denominational ex-gay ministry near San Francisco, using extended participant observation and interviews, illustrates vividly the desired fusion of religious and sexual conversion:

> Change is a conversion process that incorporates religious and sexual identity, desire, and behavior. Sexual identity is malleable and changeable because it is completely entwined with religious conversion. A person becomes ex-gay as he accepts Jesus into his life and commits to him.[17]

Geographical scope

When pitching the book proposal, the editors were regularly asked about the focus on Australia and the United States. Surely, reviewers enquired, conversion practices are a global phenomenon? Indeed, they are. However, in collecting material, a particularly poignant statistic was uncovered; namely, written and filmic accounts of conversion practices are overwhelmingly from Australia and the United States. As discussed above, Edser and Venn-Brown are among the few authors, to date, who have committed such stories to writing. The fact that both are Australian men is another interesting statistic. On this topic, it could be speculated that there is an environment of freedom of speech in Australia that caters for such memoirs, especially when compared to the experiences of survivors of the same practices in, for example, Africa and the Middle East. In the United States, the First Amendment guarantees the right of free speech and this, in conjunction with the country's film industry and its scale – both Hollywood as well as independent companies – must surely go a long way in explaining, once again, this collection's focus on America. Therefore, necessity has governed content in this instance, although where other countries and cultures have contributed to narratives of conversion practices in memoir, film and fiction, the editors have ensured these accounts are included.[18] What this limitation by necessity has revealed, however, is the need for more voices to come forward, for more challenges to the practices to be made as loud and as public as possible, and, in the most general and urgent sense, for the lives of all queer people globally to be recognized and made safe.

Historical overview

Timelines tracing the significance of moments or events in the making of the modern gay and lesbian movement often demarcate the Stonewall Inn, New York in 1969 as its birthplace. As a popular emblematic moment in the long struggle for equality, Stonewall's pre-eminent place is frequently acclaimed whilst overlooking important precursors.[19] Historians observing underlying processes that explain important shifts in the progress of human society look further back in time to the unrivalled transformational power of the Second World War. For the first time ever, same-sex attracted men and women, often hailing from rural communities with limited or no experience of others like them, were suddenly thrown together in all-male or all-female wartime communities. As gender studies scholar Chris Freeman notes, the changed wartime context offered likeminded men and women many opportunities to find each other. Rather than returning to their pre-war rural communities, many resettled in cities after the war, the first sites of gay community in the United States and other combatant countries.[20]

The early post-war years saw the rise of the first homophile organizations, notably the Mattachine Society and Daughters of Bilitis in the west of the United States during the 1950s, spreading to other parts of the Anglophone world in ensuing decades. These organizations sought tolerance and understanding through public awareness and education and engaged supportive professionals with a public profile, including liberal members of the clergy, to further their agenda of limited reform. The hostile Cold War environment (particularly in the United States) coupled with a repressive legal and social context, significantly constrained their progress.[21] It was the homophile groups nonetheless that laid the essential foundations for the gay liberation movement, which came of age in the 1970s. Gay liberation shunned the moderate, respectable profile and strategy of its precursors, adopting instead an activist stance that embraced radical, and frequently confrontational, tactics.[22]

Australian historian Graham Willett refers to 'the three pillars of ignorance' that liberationists railed against. Legal, medical and religious institutions were all deemed to be 'keystones of homosexual oppression'.[23] The criminalization of consenting same-sex acts by adult males can be traced back to the colonial period in the British world (in contrast, for example, to the French legal code) and, in combination with other factors, continues to leave a long shadow in many developing countries whose legal systems inherited British common law.[24] The limited case for decriminalization in the United Kingdom was set out in the 1957 Wolfenden Report, but not enshrined in law for another decade until the *Sexual Offences Act, 1967*. Identifying a single date when these laws were repealed in the United States and Australia is impossible as both have federal systems of government in which the carriage of such laws is devolved to individual states and territories. It is though salutary to note that in the birthplace of gay liberation, only one American state – Illinois in 1962 – moved in advance of the British to strike out this legislation. Even more noteworthy and perhaps little known outside the United States is that it required an activist Supreme Court as late as 2003 in Lawrence v. Texas to rule that 'sodomy' laws were unconstitutional. At the time of the Court's ruling, fourteen states still retained this offence on their statute books, and twenty years later, at the time of writing, still awaits formal repeal by the Texas legislature.[25] Progress towards nation-wide decriminalization in Australia, although not as protracted, was nevertheless a process that took over two decades from the first jurisdiction – South Australia in 1975 – to Tasmania in 1997.

The American Psychiatric Association's (APA's) removal of homosexuality from the second edition of its influential *Diagnostic and Statistical Manual* (DSM) in 1973 is a landmark and celebrated moment in the history of gay liberation.[26] This was clear recognition that medicalization had contributed significantly to social stigmatization. Indeed, the power of psychiatry in defining 'sickness' and its popular influence in classification of sexuality on the basis of psychological type is hard to overestimate in this era. It was a measure of the significance gay liberation attached to the influence wielded by this branch of medicine that the Gay Liberation Front in Melbourne included a Counter Psychiatry Group, which polemicized psychiatrists as 'High Priests of Modern Society ... reinforcing, under the guise of scientific objectivity, primitive Judeo-Christian morality'.[27]

Notwithstanding this, the popular and celebratory gay liberation narrative requires some qualifications. First, as Willett points out, many gay people were either oblivious to, or defiant in their response to 'expert' medical opinion even at the high point of psychiatric interventions in the 1950s and 1960s.[28] Second, while the APA's initiative represented a critical shift, and its normalizing view came to represent mainstream scientific authority on the issue in America and other Western countries, a significant minority nevertheless dissented. Even in professional communities, the notion of 'normal' continued to be the subject of intense debate and disagreement, particularly around sexual behaviour.[29] This was particularly the case in the United States where theoretical positions were deeply entrenched.[30] It was not until

1991, for example, that the American Psychoanalytic Association made a major policy revision in the same direction, a position not accepted by a fringe group of practitioners led by psychologist Joseph Nicolosi, the most prominent advocate of 'reparative therapy'.[31] Third, at the same time historically that the APA liberalized its policy and many practitioners began moving away from 'treatment' of same-sex attraction, faith-based churches and ministries moved in to fill the void.[32]

As David Coon, one of our contributors, astutely observes in Chapter 6 of the book, the popular view that Christianity and the gay movement were implacable foes locked in a binary oppositional struggle manifestly oversimplifies a complex relationship and speaks to the effectiveness of the rhetorical strategies employed by activists on both sides of the debate.[33] These tensions occurred against the backdrop of a rupture in American Protestantism, which saw a shift towards non-denominationalism and a splintering into smaller churches.[34] Coon further notes that notwithstanding the radical tactics employed by gay liberation aimed at the 'traditional enemy' – religion – many gays and lesbians embraced religious organizations rather than turning away from them. The Metropolitan Community Church (MCC), formed in the late 1960s, which sought common ground between Christianity and queer people, is a pathway that some took.[35] Others, like prominent ex-gay leader and later staunch critic of conversion practices, Michael Bussee, as discussed in Chapter 3, worked with peers to build a support group for gay Christians that paralleled existing collectives in their megachurch. Erzen notes in this regard a rise in the phenomenon of parachurches in which networks would develop between churches across denominations on particular social issues, including same-sex attraction.[36] It was this very process that led to the emergence of the ex-gay movement, located firmly within the Christian tent. The birth of Exodus International at a conference in California in 1976 was a foundational moment in that trend.

The success of ex-gay ministries began to stall by the 1980s: there had been some high-profile defections from its ranks; gay people had become more visible in society, and gay liberation had played an important role in breaking down social stigmatization. Then the AIDS crisis intervened, creating conditions ripe for revitalization of the ex-gay movement; after all, the wider socio-political context was fertile ground to opportunistically promote an ex-gay lifestyle as a refuge at the same time as the Religious Right manipulated the meaning of AIDS to claim the disease was God's punishment of homosexuality.[37] The Religious Right is a loose coalition of 'political actors, religious organizations, and political pressure groups' emphasizing traditional family values that emerged in the United States in the 1970s. Holding broad appeal to conservatives across the Judeo-Christian religious divide, its principal support base was 'white evangelical and fundamentalist Christians'. In the 1990s and 2000s, some groups in the Religious Right changed approach, moving beyond their limited membership base to reach a wider audience in more sophisticated ways.[38] This included an alliance with the ex-gay movement in the late 1990s to promote an anti-LGBT+ advertising campaign, intensifying an existing climate of fear and hate.[39]

Marriage equality – or same-sex marriage – became the defining issue of the early twenty-first century for the gay movement on one side of the contentious debate and religious conservatives on the other. The battlelines were drawn federally in the United States with the passage of *DOMA (The Defense of Marriage Act)* in 1996, defining marriage in wholly traditional terms as 'a legal union between one man and one woman'. In a pre-emptive move against same-sex marriage, the legislation provided that no state was required to recognize the marriage seal of another state.[40] DOMA would later serve as political inspiration for conservative Australian Prime Minister John Howard whose government secured passage of the *Marriage Amendment Act, 2004*. Under the leadership of Alan Chambers from 2001, Exodus International became actively engaged in the politics of marriage at both state and federal levels, lobbying on the basis that marriage equality is not legitimate as gay people *choose* a false identity that disqualifies their entitlement to marriage as a right. Consistent with evangelical Christian practice, the anti-marriage equality arguments advanced by Exodus rested significantly on testimonial narrative, asserting the role of individual transformation through a personal relationship with God: in effect, to be born again.[41]

This brief historical survey of the modern gay movement and responses to it is intended to highlight the challenging and complex terrain on which many queer lives were lived out – and continue to be – as attested in the narratives that form this collection. Returning to Willett's three pillars of ignorance, while much remains unresolved for transgender people in respect to their sexual citizenship, the relationship between legal and medical institutions, and gays and lesbians, has transformed significantly over time. Religion, at least of the conservative, scriptural literalist variety – the prime source of sustenance for conversion ideology – remains an obstinate outlier. Marriage equality may represent the high point of the gay movement's claims to equality, but like any rights fought for and won through sustained activism, it can also be undone by reactionary collective action undertaken by conservative political and religious interests, the more so given the significance of this reform as a socially transformative agent in contemporary society.[42] Given the immutability of knowledge systems upon which these interests base their utterances and actions, there can be no suggestion that conversion practices and the ideology underpinning them will fade in the foreseeable future. And yet, a central idea posited by this belief system – that there is something fundamentally wrong about being gay or having a gender diverse identity – demands never-ending vigilance for this is the fodder that feeds conversion practices.[43]

Gender

In several chapters of this collection, there is reference to the alleged links between same-sex attraction and so-called gender identity disorder (see, for example, Chapter 5). Such links are, of course, established and often underpin two principal strands of conversion practices: pseudo-scientific psychoanalytic 'treatment' and religious-based 'therapy'. Often, as in the case of Nicolosi,[44] psychoanalysis and 'praying the gay away' (in this instance, 'repairing' a 'symptom' of same-sex attraction in the form of perceived gender incongruence) are inextricably intertwined (or, in the words of André P. Grace, – 'when medical science beds religion').[45] Likewise, 'treatments' for transgender individuals to 'cure' 'gender identity disorder' (only removed from the APA's DSM in 2013), focus on intervention models to redivert the 'patient' to identifying with their sex at birth.

It should come as no surprise that the apparently 'vexed' and 'troublesome' issue of gender identity underpins the ex-gay movement, as well as the politics of the Christian Right. In short: females must be feminine, and males must be masculine. Of course, what defines femininity and masculinity is a matter of social constructionism (a social structure, as per Barbara J. Risman)[46] that is subject to variables based on environment and culture, as well as historical specificities. While contemporary queer politics, as well as various public entities or institutions, now acknowledge and endorse non-binary and gender-fluid identities, supporters of conversion practices and the ex-gay movement rigidly adhere to outdated, essentialist Western expressions of femininity and masculinity. Godly masculinity (manhood) and femininity (womanhood) are the rarefied and idealized goals of the Christian Right, firmly based on heterosexual marriage and the family as the ultimate earthly achievement.[47] Gary Yagel, former Presbyterian pastor, and Executive Director at Family Builders Ministries, Inc. (Maryland), a conservative Christian advocate of Godly or Biblical manhood (and, less urgently, by default, Godly or Biblical womanhood) defines gender through the orthodoxies of fundamentalism and evangelicalism, underpinned by biblical literalism, accordingly:

Masculine Orientation	Feminine Orientation
To initiate	To respond
To lead	To assist
To provide	To nurture
To protect	To beautify[48]

As with the work or ministry of Yagel, many other promoters of conservative Christian values tend to focus on males in discourses about gender expectations and ex-gay ideology. Women, while far less a concern, are, according to Jennifer Terry, 'implicated in every mention of male homosexuality' in 'much of Christian anti-gay discourse'.[49] Terry exemplifies this position in her extensive references to Nicolosi and his male-centred universe of sexual 'therapy' and 'healing' in which:

> women are simultaneously exalted as the bastions of moral virtue and yet demonized as smothering or negligent mothers responsible for the pathological imbalances of their sons. While fathers are also blamed in the more recent models of homosexuality-as-psychopathology, mothers continue to be blamed for their overbearing and emasculating desires. The virtuous woman, in both Nicolosi's and the Promise Keepers' vision, is the understanding or forgiving wife and the patient girlfriend, whose main role is to abet the spiritual, moral, and psychological healing of men. But she cannot heal her man alone.[50]

In Nicolosi's influential system of gender identity (read, masculinity), his 'gender deficit' or 'gender-identity deficit' model is defined accordingly:

> Male gender-identity deficit does not mean simply that this man fails to fit into his culture's image of masculinity. The heterosexual may have an artistic nature and enjoy theater, art, and cooking; on the other hand, the homosexual may be a rodeo rider or professional football player. Rather, it refers to an inadequacy in the inner sense of maleness or femaleness. Gender-identity deficit is the internal, private sense of incompleteness or inadequacy about one's maleness, and this is not always evident in explicit effeminate traits. Some outwardly masculine homosexual men have carefully cultivated their outer images as an armor against inner anxieties of masculine inadequacy.[51]

Despite Nicolosi's mild or half-hearted protestations, he does consider a stereotypical form of effeminacy a key component of male gender deficit and is overt in his 'clinical' observation that such a 'syndrome' is an integral part of male homosexuality. To wit, in Nicolosi's surrealist system, the male homosexual seeks to overcome the deficit and become whole again through gay relations.[52]

As Nicolosi has virtually no interest in discussion of same-sex attracted women,[53] we must turn elsewhere for discussion points around the ex-gay movement and lesbians. C. M. Robinson and S. E. Spivey are useful in this regard, especially on the interwoven subjects of anti-gay ideology and gender prescripts (unsurprisingly the prescripts advocated by the Christian Right): 'Antigay bias is also highly correlated with a belief in sharply differentiated gender roles and the subordination of women to men.'[54] That lesbians are seen to be in active rebellion against the subordination of women to men, in conjunction with other forms of gender insurgence, such as (masculine) appearance and (masculine) performativity,[55] they must be tamed. Conversion practices not only seek to make men into men, but to make women into women – thus transforming the deviancies of homosexuals who are also, by default and inherently, gender traitors.

Discussions of conversion practices and the focus on men should not deny the presence of both same-sex attracted women and trans people who have also been subjected to such 'therapies'. Indeed, a more intersectional approach to the practices overall is needed, expressly by writers, journalists and academics. One area in which intersectionality has been addressed to some extent is in documentary films, such as *For They Know Not What They Do*, discussed in Chapter 3. Therein, the families and individuals who feature include Victor Baez, Annette Febo and their gay son, Vico (a Puerto Rican and Catholic family); Coleen and Harold Porcher and their transgender son, Elliot (a mixed-race family); David and Sally McBride and their transgender daughter, Sarah (a Presbyterian, white family); Linda and Rob Robertson and their gay son, Ryan (a white, evangelical family). While this high-level synopsis unfortunately risks reducing the participants to race, religion, sexuality and gender, it is intended as a shorthand to emphasize the significance of the intersectional voices employed in the film.

Trans people

In her ground-breaking book, *Banning Transgender Conversion Practices: A Legal and Policy Analysis*, Florence Ashley makes the vital statement: 'Academic scholarship, especially in law, has tended to focus on sexual orientation to the exclusion of gender. There is a dire need for more scholarship and especially legal scholarship on the matter.'[56] The words and imperatives voiced by Ashley became louder and louder as this collection took shape, and we extended our research to track the history of transgender conversion practices. We discovered, as Ashley has strongly communicated, that there is a dearth of anecdotal and scholarly material on the topic of transgender people and conversion practices; to date, for example, we do not have such narratives in memoir or fiction, although as Chapter 3 reveals, those voices are beginning to emerge in the documentary genre and, at the time of the finalization of this book, a horror film set in a conversion camp, *They/Them* (i.e. *They Slash Them*) (2022), includes Jordan, who identifies as trans and non-binary, and Alexandra, who identifies as trans. Slowly, the landscape is changing with the publication of 'Association Between Recalled Exposure to Gender Identity Conversion Efforts and Psychological Distress and Suicide Attempts Among Transgender Adults'.[57] In combination with the work of Ashley, this research has revealed significant data, including the fact that out of the participants surveyed (a cross-sectional study of 27,715 American transgender adults), 63.4 per cent of transgender women and 56.5 of transgender men stated that they have been subject to efforts by professionals to make them identify only with the sex assigned at birth.[58] While there has been success in the fight against such practices in relation to the transgender community, such as the removal of 'gender identity disorder' from the APA's DSM in 2013, pro-conversion lobby groups throughout the West maintain the rage, with ongoing culture wars being waged over sexuality and gender identity, with particular focus on the transgender community in the wake of marriage equality victories for same-sex partners. The point here is the rise of the conservative backlash throughout the West where marriage equality has won the day, with legislation and political sabre-rattling targeting LGBT+ rights in the workplace, in health care, and in educational institutions. In that sense, transgender people are the latest – and most vulnerable – targets in reactionary collective action designed to wind back rights.[59] In short, the conservative and Religious Right may acknowledge losing one major battle (marriage equality) but not the LGBT+ culture wars.

New storytelling

As this book is the first to address the representation of conversion practices in cultural forms through the media of memoir, film and fiction, it acknowledges and seeks to further exemplify (through the case studies or chapters herein) the research of both Ken Plummer[60] and Christopher Pullen[61] on the power of new storytelling in both factual and fictional forms. The term 'new storytelling' refers to a narrative that began to make its presence increasingly felt in, roughly, the last two decades of the twentieth century.[62] Plummer discusses the development of the genre by drawing attention to its early phase when, in the 1970s, second wave feminists wrote on rape through the hybrid lens of analysis and personal anecdote,[63] and explains how it later extended in the 1980s and 1990s to include 'coming out' lesbian and gay stories'[64] as well as 'recovery tales'[65] on 'all manner of new sufferings'.[66] Pullen develops Plummer's work, particularly his 'telling sexual stories',[67] and focuses on queer stories, expressly gay and lesbian identity, writing:

> I argue that the social agency of new storytellers offers a collaborative matrix of political possibility, which through audience identification, bonds individuals and groups, holding political ideals together. The power of new storytelling is that in contemporary social settings, it offers identity connections to a fragmented and dispersed gay and lesbian populace.[68]

Like Plummer, Pullen acknowledges the power inherent in new storytelling, emphasizing the importance of its role in un-silencing and un-shaming the traditionally silenced and shamed, and, in so doing, providing options for 'spaces to open up' through 'a politics of possibilities'.[69] While a memoirist like Venn-Brown writes in Chapter 1 that engaging with new storytelling is not necessarily cathartic but rather traumatic in its re-traumatizing,[70] he also acknowledges the widespread, positive impact his book has had on those who have been through conversion practices. Like Venn-Brown, Edser writes in Chapter 2 of the impact of his new storytelling project – not only on readers, but on himself – lighting a fire of activism that has sustained him throughout his life since the publication of his memoir.[71] It is in stories like those by Venn-Brown and Edser as well as Conley's *Boy Erased* (see Chapter 8) and, in the medium of film, the humble and humbling short film, *Michael Lost and Found* (2017) (see Chapter 4), that we see the profound possibilities of new storytelling. In the words of Pullen, they show 'the power of life stories, which (on varying levels of engagement) offer narratives of change.'[72]

Of course, there are more stories than the ones discussed herein, and these need to be acknowledged as contributing to the growing canon. Among the most compelling are Peter Gajdics's *The Inheritance of Shame: A Memoir* (2017)[73] and Alex Cooper, with Joanna Brooks's *Saving Alex: When I Was Fifteen I Told My Mormon Parents I Was Gay, and That's When My Nightmare Began* (2016).[74] Both offer first-hand accounts of conversion practices, which are different to those discussed in this collection: Gajdics experiences a reprobate psychiatrist and a cult-like environment, while Cooper's account deals with her attraction to other females within a traditional Mormon family.

Thematic strands

This collection of eight chapters is divided into three sections: Part 1: Memoirs and Memoirists (i.e., primary literary sources); Part 2: Stories of Repentance and Defiance in Documentaries and Biopics; and Part 3: Memoir, Film and Fiction. Within this structure, there are at least seven thematic strands with each chapter forming connections with others as a dialogue on conversion practices in memoir, film and fiction unfolds. The two chapters that open the conversation are by the authors, Venn-Brown (Chapter 1) and Edser (Chapter 2), who reflect on the process of writing on their experiences with conversion practices. From this 'raw' or primary material, the second section examines another expression of personal experience in the form of expository documentaries (Bennett), and biopics, personal and promotional films (Johnson). The third section consists of four chapters on filmic treatments of the subject, addressed chronologically by year of release. In Chapter 5, Tom Sharples discusses the cult comedy, *But I'm a Cheerleader*; David Coon analyses the drama, *Save Me* in Chapter 6; Jessica Ford and Annika Herb explore the novel-into-film, *The Miseducation of Cameron Post* in Chapter 7; and, similarly, in Chapter 8, Scott McKinnon writes on the literary memoir and filmic versions of *Boy Erased*.

These high-level chapter synopses demonstrate that each contribution, albeit revolving around the same theme, is extremely diverse and varied (comparatively speaking). This is testimony to the wide-ranging approaches employed by writers and filmmakers and to the individualization inherent in every story of conversion practices – real, semi-fictionalized and fictionalized. It also reflects the interdisciplinary approach to the topic, which extends to the inclusion of contributions that lie outside of the academy as it is traditionally defined (Chapters 1 and 2). This has ensured that the collection is not one of repetitions, but one of nuances and multiple shades, linked by its overarching agenda. These shades also speak to the power of approaching conversion practices through the lens of storytelling, particularly new storytelling, which brings with it an acknowledgement of, and engagement with the complexities of narrative genres.

Accordingly, the ideology underpinning conversion practices and multiplicity of ways in which it circulates, is an issue addressed by various authors in the collection. As a social phenomenon, conversion is predicated on the emotions of shame, guilt and fear.[75] Venn-Brown offers a rich exploration of these feelings in the context of post-war

Sydney, celebrated as a gay mecca in more recent times, but in the context of his youth was the capital city of a state that created what some believe to have been the world's only experimental prison designed to incarcerate, segregate and medicalize homosexual men.[76] By detailing his personal experiences, Venn-Brown also conveys a strong sense of tactics employed by evangelical churches to maximize shame and maintain it as a powerful force in his life, notably through the forced confession of his sexual 'fall' to a large church congregation. This public confession of 'sins' as a cleansing act is paralleled by Love in Action participants, discussed by McKinnon in Chapter 8 who, like Bennett in Chapter 3, contextualizes it within Foucault's system of sex, institutions and power.[77] Like Venn-Brown, Edser outlines his personal experience of growing up in New South Wales. As a clinician, he points to the sickness model intrinsic to traditional psychoanalytic views, underpinned by shame and upheld by conservative religionists as an article of faith in conversion ideology.[78] Johnson observes in Chapter 4 that this ideology is disseminated through a culture of scriptural literalism. While most commonly associated with what Edser refers to as the 'sledge-hammer' biblical texts, Johnson's analysis highlights its elusive seeping nature in the contemporary world via mass media and technology.

Religion and politics are deeply implicated in each other on LGBT+ issues and conversion practices are no exception. In his discussion of two documentaries in Chapter 3, Bennett draws our attention to the entrenched role of the ex-gay movement in the politics of marriage equality and, via director Daniel Karslake's argument in *For They Know Not What They Do*, that it is impossible to disentangle their mutually reinforcing influence when analyzing the origins and persistence of conversion practices. Edser makes a similar point, noting that the battle for marriage equality in Australia – and particularly the 2017 plebiscite that featured a 'Yes' and a 'No' campaign – became a platform for public abuse of LGBT+ people with opposition emerging from both religious and political sources. The entangled influence of religion and politics has been at the vanguard in prosecution of the culture wars and, as

Bennett observes, transgender people have become the new target. Johnson's case study of Matthew Grech's televised evangelism and responses to it highlights a specific example of a culture war framed around the rhetoric of conversion ideology. This discussion brings to light the broader point that religious 'freedom' (read, the right to discriminate) – increasingly tied to freedom of speech – is a central element of the culture wars.

The memoir is an important but sometimes overlooked voice for human rights, particularly LGBT+ rights. In the context of the themes of this collection, the memoir has been, and continues to be a powerful means to communicate the widespread emotional, psychological, and spiritual damage wreaked by conversion practices. The privilege of reading the words of two memoirists, Venn-Brown and Edser, who write first-hand accounts of the experiences leading up to the personal and political imperatives to share their stories, emphasizes the impact of words that challenge injustice. These two chapters also reveal the personal cost to the individual who braves the journey of memoir – often described as a healing or cathartic experience, but uncommonly characterized as (also) traumatizing. Within the pages authored by Venn-Brown and Edser, there is also the complexity and emotional turmoil or entanglement of exploring their deep, personal faiths as well as their same-sex attraction amid the experiences of conversion practices that brutally endorse the former and demonize the latter. McKinnon interrogates the process of translating such works from page to screen in his chapter on *Boy Erased: A Memoir of Identity, Faith, and Family* by Garrard Conley, published in 2016 – a best-selling literary memoir[79] made into a motion picture in 2018. What emerges from the memoirs, including the film version of *Boy Erased*, is the challenge the narratives make to ex-gay testimonies by voicing queer survivor counter testimonies that speak to the power of both written and filmic media to affect change.

For those working on the topic of conversion practices within the parameters of narrativization, it is difficult not to explore the multiple examples of the paratext that surround the work(s) and, at times, the extratextual stories of activism – both of which inform the principal text. In Chapter 4, which examines three films of different genres, *I am Michael* (2015), *Michael Lost and Found*, and *Once Gay - Matthew and Friends* (2019), the extensive paratext and transmedia stories that lay waiting online for curious film audience members are shown to provide additional information and counter-narratives. McKinnon's chapter also includes the 'extras' that come with, in particular, the film version of *Boy Erased*, quoting, for example, writer and director, Joel Edgerton's reflections, which provide supplementary insights into the memoir and the film for those who wish to extend their understanding of both. Such approaches to interpreting text can also extend to the scholar and/or writer accessing information on the institutions represented in narratives of conversion practices, such as Love in Action, which features in Conley's story and is the subject of one of the documentaries analyzed by Bennett in Chapter 3, *This is What Love in Action Looks Like* (2011). Bennett and McKinnon also discuss the extra-narrative effects of written and filmic stories in terms of their power to affect change as activist texts. McKinnon examines Conley's extratextual activism linked to *Boy Erased*, while Bennett considers activist filmmaker, Morgan Jon Fox, director of *This is What Love in Action Looks Like*, as well as Kristine Stolakis, director of *Pray Away*, and the intent behind the pairing of her documentary with online resources. Likewise, Coon discusses storytelling as a form of activism to affect social change, and includes the case study of Mythgarden, the independent production company responsible for *Save Me*.

The clash between Christian and queer identities and resulting cognitive dissonance experienced by those with a conservative faith is a central theme of this collection. That conflict between feelings and faith frames the opening of *Save Me*, a fictional film that in Coon's analysis makes a timely intervention by building a reconciling counter-narrative to the received story of mutual hostility between queer people and Christianity, traditionally leaving no space for a dialogue. For Ryan Robertson in *For They Know Not What They Do*, discussed in Chapter 3, it remained an unresolved conflict, leading eventually to fatal consequences. Another version of that clash emerges in *Boy Erased*, the final chapter of the collection, when a minor, the son of an evangelical pastor, is forced to attend a conversion camp. The visceral, tormented personal accounts of Edser and Venn-Brown in the first two chapters of the book can leave us in no doubt about the high stakes involved for ardent adherents of evangelical theology who must also wrestle with their queer selves. Both ultimately resolved the clash in different ways but not without great personal cost. Edser's experience as a survivor who later took up the role of clinician, encountering many gay Christians over a long period in his professional capacity, mirrors the background of Paul Martin, a talking head in *The Cure*, discussed in Chapter 3. As a qualified health professional, Edser is ideally situated to present his reasoned scientific analysis of why conversion practices are ineffective, unethical and harmful.

Several of the works examined herein point to some of the core issues or themes underpinning the tenets of conversion practices, including distorted definitions of gender that privilege essentialism. In texts that feature female protagonists, such as the film, *But I'm a Cheerleader* as well as the 2012 novel and film adaptation, *The Miseducation of Cameron Post*, there is decidedly overt messaging about the reprogramming of same-sex attracted women to present as traditionally cisgendered ultra feminine heterosexuals. The absurdity and inherent outrageousness of such tenets make them ripe for satire, as evident in *But I'm a Cheerleader*, which uses colour to emphasize gender stereotypes and lambasts programmes on rediscovering one's gender identity, as Sharples discusses in Chapter 5. The film also mocks attempts to reorient one's gender through performance, as the facilitators at the fictional True Directions conversion camp preach against males who avoid sport and females who like fixing cars. On a more serious and sombre note, as discussed by Ford and Herb in Chapter 7 on the novel and film, *The Miseducation of Cameron Post*, such tenets and practices are predicated on the falsity that non-normative gender identities are a pathway to sexual perversion – expressly, queer and homosexual 'lifestyles'. The theme is also present in *Boy Erased*, and McKinnon discusses an extension of it – a variation on a theme – by noting so-called practitioners' pop psychology approach to allegedly bad parental role models in the form of weak (read, feminine) fathers and domineering (read, masculine) mothers. Apparently, such poor and gender-confused parents can breed deviants! Bennett also discusses gender, particularly through his interrogation of Nicolosi's psychobabble on alleged gender deficits, featured in the documentary, *Pray Away* (2021).

Genre is a significant consideration in several chapters, with form influencing content in memoirs, novels and films. As discussed by Ford and Herb, for example, Emily M. Danforth's novel, *The Miseducation of Cameron Post* is both Young Adult fiction as well as queer fiction, the former reflecting readership age more so than genre. It is also, as the authors acknowledge, a Bildungsroman and, as such, lends itself well to the narrative expectations of a coming-of-age narrative so suited to the subject matter that defines it. Translated into a teen film, the essence of the novel is preserved in a genre that can, as Ford and Herb note, express deep-seated and vital social concerns. The potential dangers of films that embrace the genre of queer cinema is a key consideration of McKinnon, who is sensitive to, and critical of the film version of *Boy Erased* due to its indulgence of the trope of the tragic queer in its portrayal of Cameron, one of the camp attendees. The three films – *Boy Erased*, *The Miseducation of Cameron Post*, and *But I'm a Cheerleader* – have been clearly written and directed by individuals who have thought long and hard about the role of humour and satire as appropriate inclusions. While there are moments of absurdist levity in *The Miseducation of Cameron Post*, its complete absence is conspicuous in *Boy Erased*, as McKinnon discusses. Genre, humour and/or satire, and the theme of conversion practices are potential filmic dynamite, liable to blow-up and backfire. And this is a major topic in Sharples's examination of *But I'm a Cheerleader*, a film he is critical of for what he regards as misplaced, ill-timed, and poorly judged use of comedy to narrate tragedy. This is not to characterize Sharples as a humourless wowser, but to draw readers' attention to a counterargument to those who cherish and laugh along with a film that has achieved cult status.

Finally, this brief discussion of genre demonstrates the complexities inherent in cultural artefacts such as memoir, film and fiction. As many of the chapters show, genre is also unwieldy and multi-faceted and, at times, boundaries are blended, as one category of creative form bleeds into another, producing hybrid models of storytelling. This contribution to the study of the scourge that is conversion practices celebrates the occasions of narrative fusion and paratextual 'contamination', regarding them as integral to the topic at hand, with all its humanness and chaos. Therefore, not only are memoir, film and fiction treated as storytelling, but also documentary and biopics, with the anticipated outcome that more formats – from fine art to journalism – will be collectively analyzed to continue to tell such important tales.

Notes

1   Denoting Australia and New Zealand. See, for example, J. Bennett and C. Brickell, 'Surveilling Minds and Bodies: Sexualities, Medicine and the Law,' *Journal of Australian Studies*, 46:3 (2022): 273–7, DOI: 10.1080/14443058.2022.2095728, and J. Bennett and M. Johnson, 'Teaching Entangled Australian Sexual Histories: Pedagogy and Approaches,' *History Compass*, 19:10 (2021): 1–9. DOI 10.1111/hic3.12690.

2   'Lives Erased: The History of LGBTQI Conversion Therapy' is available as a podcast; see, https://soundcloud.com/nwfpodcast/lives-erased (accessed 4 April 2023).

3   A. Venn-Brown, 'Tasmania to Ban Conversion "Therapy",' *The Big Smoke*, 16 September 2022. https://thebigsmoke.com.au/2022/09/16/tasmania-to-ban-conversion-therapy/ (accessed 4 April 2023).

4   See M. Forstein, 'Overview of Ethical and Research Issues in Sexual Orientation Therapy.' In *Sexual Conversion Therapy: Ethical, Clinical and Research Perspectives*, eds A. Shidlo, M. Schroeder and J. Drescher (New York: Haworth Press, 2001), especially 168.

5   A term used by Daniel Andrews, Premier of the state of Victoria, Australia. See A. Carey, 'Victoria to Ban Conversion Therapy,' *The Age*, 3 February 2019.

https://www.theage.com.au/national/victoria/victoria-to-ban-gay-conversion-therapy-20190203-p50vdn.html (accessed 3 April 2023). Similarly, when signing into law a bill to outlaw conversion practices on minors, California Governor Jerry Brown proclaimed: 'These practices have no basis in science or medicine and they will now be relegated to the dustbin of quackery.' W. Buchanan, 'State Bans Gay-Repair Therapy for Minors,' *SFGate*, 29 September 2012. https://www.sfgate.com/news/article/State-bans-gay-repair-therapy-for-minors-3906032.php (accessed 5 April 2023).

6 S. Edser, 'Being Gay, Being Christian': The Professional Reflects.' In *Gay Conversion Practices in Memoir, Film and Fiction: Stories of Repentance and Defiance*, eds J. E. Bennett and M. Johnson (London: Bloomsbury, 2024), 89. The term is dismissed by experts who point out that it has no scientific underpinnings. See M. Roberts, 'Analysis,' in '"Gay Conversion Therapy" to be Banned as Part of LGBT Equality Plan,' *BBC News*, 3 July 2018. www.bbc.com/news/uk-44686374 (accessed 5 April 2023).

7 T. W. Jones, J. Power and T. M. Jones, 'Religious Trauma and Moral Injury from LGBTQA+ Conversion Practices,' *Social Science and Medicine*, 305 (2022): 4.

8 Initial research by Jones et al. in Australia suggests conversion practices are also commonplace in conservative Muslim, Jewish, Hindu and Buddhist communities. See T. W. Jones, A. Brown, L. Carnie, G. Fletcher and W. Leonard, *Preventing Harm, Promoting Justice: Responding to LGBT Conversion Therapy in Australia*, Melbourne, GLHV@ARCSHS and the Human Rights Law Centre, 2018, 11.

9 'LGB People who have Undergone Conversion Therapy almost Twice as Likely to Commit Suicide' (press release), Williams Institute, UCLA School of Law, 15 June 2020. https://williamsinstitute.law.ucla.edu/press/lgb-suicide-ct-press-release/ (accessed 22 January 2024).

10 F. Tomazin, '"I am Profoundly Unsettled": Inside the Hidden World of Gay Conversion Therapy,' *Sydney Morning Herald*, 9 March 2018. https://www.smh.com.au/national/i-am-profoundly-unsettled-inside-the-hidden-world-of-gay-conversion-therapy-20180227-p4z1xn.html (accessed 9 April 2023). On the influence of the self-help and recovery movements on ex-gay philosophy, see T. Erzen, *Straight to Jesus: Sexual and Christian Conversions in the Ex-Gay Movement* (Berkeley: University of California Press, 2006), especially 9 and 121–2.

11 A. E. McGrath, *Christian Theology: An Introduction*, 2nd edn (MA, USA and Oxford: Blackwell, 1997), especially 121, 123, 569 and 571. See also T. Shoemaker, 'Understanding Evangelicalism in America Today', *The Conversation*, 4 August 2021. www.theconversation.com/understanding-evangelicalism-in-america-today-164851 (accessed 7 April 2023).

12 Shoemaker, 'Understanding Evangelicalism in America Today'. See also Religions: Pentecostalism. BBC. www.bbc.co.uk/religion/religions/christianity/subdivisions/pentecostal_1.shtml (accessed 7 April 2023).

13 Shoemaker, 'Understanding Evangelicalism in America Today'.

14 S. Piggin, *Evangelical Christianity in Australia: Spirit, Word and World*, 3rd edn, (Melbourne: Acorn Press, 2012), 1, 3-4, 10.

15 Piggin, *Evangelical Christianity in Australia*, 12.

16 McGrath, *Christian Theology*, 121.

17 Erzen, *Straight to Jesus*, 6.

18 See, for example, the references to Ireland and Malta in Chapter 4.

19 See, for example, H. Lemney, 'Party and Protest: The Radical History of Gay Liberation, Stonewall and Pride', *The Guardian*, 25 June 2020, https://www.theguardian.com/world/2020/jun/25/party-and-protest-lgbtq-radical-history-gay-liberation-stonewall-pride (accessed 1 September 2023).

20 K. Brekke, 'How WWII Started the Modern Gay Rights Movement', *Huff Post*, 13 October 2015 [updated 4 April 2017]. https://www.huffpost.com/entry/modern-gay-rights-movement-wwii_n_561d103ce4b0c5a1ce607d4b (accessed 10 April 2023).

21 'Before Stonewall: The Homophile Movement', LGBTQIA+ Studies: A Resource Guide, *Library of Congress*, https://guides.loc.gov/lgbtq-studies/before-stonewall (accessed 10 April 2023). 'The Homophile Movement.' *Making History Project*. https://info.umkc.edu/makinghistory/the-homophile-movement/ n.d. (accessed 10 April 2023).

22 'The Gay Liberation Movement', *Making History Project*. https://info.umkc.edu/makinghistory/about-this-project/ n.d. (accessed 10 April 2023).

23 G. Willett, *Living Out Loud: A History of Gay and Lesbian Activism in Australia* (Sydney: Allen & Unwin, 2000), 92.

24 See, for example, J. Keating, 'British Colonialism and Anti-Gay Laws', *Foreign Policy*, 19 June 2012. www.foreignpolicy.com/2012/06/19/british-colonialism-and-anti-gay-laws/ (accessed 11 April 2023).

25 'Milestones in the American Gay Rights Movement,' *PBS*. www.pbs.org/
   wgbh/americanexperience/features/stonewall-milestones-american-
   gay-rights-movement/ (accessed 10 April 2023). N. Lakhani, 'Effort to
   Repeal Texas Sodomy Law Advances with Bipartisan Support,' *The
   Guardian*, 7 April 2023. www.theguardian.com/us-news/2023/apr/06/
   texas-sodomy-law-repeal-bipartisan-support (accessed 10 April 2023).

26 The World Health Organization used a parallel and far less commonly
   cited system known as the International Classification of Diseases (ICD).
   Same-sex attraction was not removed from the World Health Organization
   (WHO) manual until 1990.

27 Willett, *Living Out Loud*, 102.

28 Willett, *Living Out Loud*, 102.

29 P. Cryle and E. Stephens, *Normality: A Critical Genealogy* (Chicago and
   London: University of Chicago Press, 2017). See especially Chapter 9.

30 G. Willett, 'Psyched In: Psychology, Psychiatry and Homosexuality in
   Australia,' *Gay and Lesbian Issues and Psychology Review*, 1 (2005), 53–7.

31 J. Drescher, 'Can Sexual Orientation Be Changed?' *Journal of Gay &
   Lesbian Mental Health*, 19 (2015): 86.

32 See Jones et al., *Preventing Harm*, 4.

33 D. Coon, '*Save Me*: Reconciling Queerness and Christianity.' In *Gay
   Conversion Practices in Memoir, Film and Fiction: Stories of Repentance and
   Defiance*, eds J. E. Bennett and M. Johnson (London: Bloomsbury, 2024),
   190.

34 Erzen, *Straight to Jesus*, 24.

35 Coon, '*Save Me*' 191. A more recent example of a Christian organization
   that embraces LGBT+ Christians, providing pastoral support, is Diverse
   Church, which originated in the United Kingdom. For further details, see
   www.diversechurch.website (accessed 17 May 2023)

36 Erzen, *Straight to Jesus*, 24.

37 W. Besen, *Anything but Straight: Unmasking the Scandals and Lies Behind
   the Ex-Gay Myth* (New York: Harrington Park Press, 2003), xvii, 81, 99.

38 M. J. McVicar, 'The Religious Right in America,' *Oxford Research
   Encyclopedias*, 26 February 2018 [first published 3 March 2016] https://
   oxfordre.com/religion/display/10.1093/acrefore/9780199340378.001.0001/
   acrefore-9780199340378-e-97 (accessed 8 April 2023).

39 Besen, *Anything but Straight*, 211.

40 'Milestones in the American Gay Rights Movement.' For an analysis of
DOMA, see N. Cott, *Public Vows*, revised ed. (Boston, Harvard University
Press, 2009), chapter 9.

41 T. Erzen, 'Testimonial Politics: The Christian Right's Faith-Based Approach
to Marriage and Imprisonment,' *American Quarterly*, vol. 59, no. 3 (2007):
992, 996–9.

42 On this point, see D. Betts and J. Bennett, 'Resurgent Prejudice: Responses
to Marriage Equality in Australia,' *Australian Journal of Social Issues*, 58:4
(2023): 732–46, DOI: 10.1002/ajs4.279.

43 See, for example, L. Suckling, 'Uncovering Gay Conversion Camp,'
New Zealand Herald, 18 March 2015, https://www.nzherald.co.nz/
lifestyle/lee-suckling-uncovering-gay-conversion-camp-video/
R3U4PKW6YWGOAOXNH7V2QWRN3U/ (accessed 13 April
2023).

44 On the deception underpinning Nicolosi's promotion of NARTH 'as a
secular, scientific guild for reparative therapists' when in reality it is 'a
"smokescreen" for conservative religious beliefs,' see C. M. Robinson and
S. E. Spivey, 'Ungodly Genders: Deconstructing Ex-Gay Movement
Discourses of "Transgenderism" in the US,' *Social Sciences*, 8 (2019): 10.

45 A. P. Grace, 'The Charisma and Deception of Reparative Therapies: When
Medical Science Beds Religion,' *Journal of Homosexuality*, 55, no. 4 (2008):
545–80.

46 B. J. Risman, 'Gender as a Social Structure: Theory Wrestling with Activism,'
Gender & Society, 18 (2004): 429–50.

47 See, for example, J. Rigney, '7 Important Lessons about Masculinity,'
Crossway, https://www.crossway.org/articles/7-important-lessons-about-
masculinity/ (accessed 10 April 2023); G. Yagel, '7 Reasons Boys Must
Understand Godly Masculinity,' *The Ministry of Gary Yagel: Igniting Men to
Action*, https://www.forgingbonds.org/blog/detail/7-reasons-boys-must-
understand-godly-masculinity (accessed 10 April 2023).

48 G. Yagel, 'Biblical Manhood,' https://www.forgingbonds.org/study-topics/
biblical-manhood/ (accessed 13 April 2023).

49 J. Terry, *An American Obsession: Science, Medicine, and Homosexuality in
Modern Society* (Chicago: University of Chicago Press, 2010), 383.

50 Terry, *An American Obsession*, 383. Terry defines Promise Keepers as 'an
evangelical Christian-based men's movement with alarmingly negative

implications for women' (383). The organization is still active. See: *Promise Keepers: Men of Integrity*: https://promisekeepers.org/ (accessed 15 April 2023).

51 J. Nicolosi, *Reparative Therapy of Male Homosexuality: A New Clinical Approach* (Maryland: Jason Aronson Inc., 1991), 64–5.

52 Nicolosi, *Reparative Therapy of Male Homosexuality*, 73.

53 In *Reparative Therapy of Male Homosexuality*, for example, there is not one reference to lesbians (title withstanding), although, as Terry has stated, women are present through default as wives and helper maidens; see, Terry, *An American Obsession*, 383.

54 C. M. Robinson and S. E. Spivey, 'The Politics of Masculinity and the Ex-Gay Movement', *Gender & Society*, 21, no. 5 (2007): 650–75. See also, C. M. Robinson and S. E. Spivey, 'Putting Lesbians in Their Place: Deconstructing Ex-Gay Discourses of Female Homosexuality in a Global Context', *Social Sciences*, 4, (2015): 879–908.

55 In the Butlerian sense, see, J. Butler, 'Performative Acts and Gender Constitution: An Essay in Phenomenology and Feminist Theory', *Theatre Journal*, 40, no. 4 (1988): 519–31.

56 F. Ashley, *Banning Transgender Conversion Practices: A Legal and Policy Analysis* (Vancouver, B.C.: University of British Columbia Press, 2022), 175. See also F. Ashley, 'Interrogating Gender-Exploratory Therapy', *Perspectives on Psychological Science*, 18, no. 2 (2023): 472–81.

57 J. L. Turban, N. Beckwith, S. L. Reisner and A. S. Keuroghlian, 'Association Between Recalled Exposure to Gender Identity Conversion Efforts and Psychological Distress and Suicide Attempts Among Transgender Adults', *JAMA Psychiatry*, 77, no. 1 (2020): 68–76. Prior to this study, see also T. Wright, B. Candy and M. King, 'Conversion Therapies and Access to Transition-related Healthcare in Transgender People: A Narrative Systematic Review', *BMJ open*, 8, no.12 (2018): e022425. Wright et al. also conclude: 'Although there has been considerable research into conversion therapies in LGB people, much less is known about what such therapies in the UK and elsewhere may entail for TGD people, and how widespread such practices might be'.

58 Turban et al., 'Association Between Recalled Exposure to Gender Identity Conversion Efforts', 70 (Table 1). Professionals included psychologists, counsellors, as well as religious advisors, 71. Ashley notes that 13.5–18 per

cent of transgender people in the United States and 11–19 per cent of trans people in Canada have experienced a form of conversion practice (*Banning Transgender Conversion Practices*, 70).

59 Betts and Bennett, 'Resurgent Prejudice.'

60 K. Plummer, *Telling Sexual Stories: Power, Change and Social Worlds* (London: Routledge, 1995).

61 C. Pullen, *Gay Identity, New Storytelling, and the Media* (Basingstoke: Palgrave Macmillan, 2009).

62 Plummer, *Telling Sexual Stories*, 50.

63 See Plummer, *Telling Sexual Stories* on Susan Griffin, 'Rape: The All-American Crime,' *Ramparts Magazine*, 10, no. 3 (1971): 1–8. Plummer comments that Griffin 'captured the blend of personal and analytic' (67) on the subject of rape. Griffin continued to experiment with and develop the style of new storytelling in *Rape: The Politics of Consciousness* (New York: Harper & Row, 1979); on this, see Plummer, *Telling Sexual Stories*, 51–2.

64 Plummer, *Telling Sexual Stories*, 52–4.

65 Plummer, *Telling Sexual Stories*, 54.

66 Plummer, *Telling Sexual Stories*, 54.

67 The title of Plummer's book, and discussed by Pullen, *Gay Identity, New Storytelling*, 5.

68 Pullen, *Gay Identity, New Storytelling*, 11.

69 Pullen, *Gay Identity, New Storytelling*, 162.

70 A. Venn-Brown, '"A Life of Unlearning": The Author Reflects.' In *Gay Conversion Practices in Memoir, Film and Fiction: Stories of Repentance and Defiance*, eds J. E. Bennett and M. Johnson (London: Bloomsbury, 2024), 41.

71 S. Edser, '"Being Gay, Being Christian": The Professional Reflects.' In *Gay Conversion Practices in Memoir, Film and Fiction: Stories of Repentance and Defiance*, eds J. E. Bennett and M. Johnson (London: Bloomsbury, 2024), 69.

72 Pullen, *Gay Identity, New Storytelling*, 7.

73 P. Gajdics, *The Inheritance of Shame: A Memoir* (Long Beach, CA, Brown Paper Press, 2017).

74 A. Cooper with J. Brooks, *Saving Alex: When I Was Fifteen I Told My Mormon Parents I Was Gay, and That's When My Nightmare Began* (San Francisco: HarperOne, 2016).

75 On the role of churches in perpetuating shame in contemporary society,
   see D. Marr, 'Christian Schools Hang on for Dear Life to the Shame of
   Homosexuality,' *Guardian Australia*, 26 February 2023 https://www.
   theguardian.com/commentisfree/2023/feb/26/catholic-schools-hang-on-
   for-dear-life-to-the-shame-of-homosexuality (accessed 26 February 2023).

76 On Cooma gaol, see L. Featherstone and A. Kaladelfos, *Sex Crimes in the
   Fifties* (Melbourne: Melbourne University Press, 2016), especially 178–86,
   and G. Nunn, 'Cooma Jail: Prison that was Once "World's Only Jail for Gay
   Men"', BBC News, 24 April 2022 www.bbc.com/news/world-
   australia-61006503 (accessed 18 April 2023).

77 See D. J. Kinitz and T. Salway, 'Cisheteronormativity, Conversion Therapy,
   and Identity Among Sexual and Gender Minority People: A Narrative
   Inquiry and Creative Non-fiction,' *Qualitative Health Research*, 32, no. 13
   (2020): 1965–78: 'Sexual and gender minority (SGM) people experience
   *structural systems of oppression that reify cisgender and heterosexual norms
   as the dominant status quo* (i.e., cisheteronormativity) throughout their
   lives' (1965) (our italics).

78 For insights about the role of guilt and shame historically in male patients
   presenting to psychiatrists, see for example D. J. West, *Homosexuality: A
   Frank and Practical Approach to the Social and Medical Aspects of Male
   Homosexuality* (Harmondsworth: Penguin, 1960), 47–8.

79 Distinguishing between memoir and literary memoir is difficult, partly
   because it involves the hermeneutics and genre theories of literary
   criticism. For the purposes of this project, literary memoir is made distinct
   from memoir per se by virtue of its closeness to the novel; for example, in
   G. Conley's *Boy Erased: A Memoir of Identity, Faith, and Family* (New York:
   Riverhead Books, 2016), the structure, while basically chronological,
   includes non-linear aspects that extend to flashbacks, movements away
   from the main narrative arc, biblical metaphors and stories-within-stories,
   as well as characterization and development.

Bibliography

Ashley, F. *Banning Transgender Conversion Practices: A Legal and Policy
Analysis*. Vancouver, B.C.: University of British Columbia Press, 2022.

Ashley, F. 'Interrogating Gender-Exploratory Therapy.' *Perspectives on Psychological Science*, 18, no. 2 (2023): 472–81.

'Before Stonewall: The Homophile Movement,' LGBTQIA+ Studies: A Resource Guide.' *Library of Congress*. www.guides.loc.gov/lgbtq-studies/before-stonewall. n.d.

Bennett, J. and C. Brickell. 'Surveilling Minds and Bodies: Sexualities, Medicine and the Law.' *Journal of Australian Studies*, 46:3 (2022): 273–7, DOI: 10.1080/14443058.2022.2095728.

Bennett, J. and M. Johnson. 'Teaching Entangled Australian Sexual Histories: Pedagogy and Approaches.' *History Compass* 19, no. 10 (2021): 1–9. DOI 10.1111/hic3.12690.

Bennett, J., S. Edser, M. Johnson and A. Venn-Brown. 'Lives Erased: The History of LGBTQI Conversion Therapy.' *Newcastle Writers Festival*. [Podcast]. 27 June 2019. https://omny.fm/shows/newcastle-writers-festival/lives-erased-the-history-of-lgbtqi-conversion-ther#description

Besen, W. *Anything but Straight: Unmasking the Scandals and Lies Behind the Ex-Gay Myth*. New York: Harrington Park Press, 2003.

Betts, D. and J. Bennett. 'Resurgent Prejudice: Responses to Marriage Equality in Australia.' *Australian Journal of Social Issues*, 58:4 (2023): 732–46. DOI: 10.1002/ajs4.279.

Brekke, K. 'How WWII Started the Modern Gay Rights Movement.' *Huff Post*, 13 October 2015 [updated 4 April 2017]. https://www.huffpost.com/entry/modern-gay-rights-movement-wwii_n_561d103ce4b0c5a1ce607d4b.

Buchanan, W. 'State Bans Gay-Repair Therapy for Minors.' *SFGate*, 29 September 2012. https://www.sfgate.com/news/article/State-bans-gay-repair-therapy-for-minors-3906032.php

Butler, J. 'Performative Acts and Gender Constitution: An Essay in Phenomenology and Feminist Theory.' *Theatre Journal*, 40, no. 4 (1988): 519–31.

Carey, A. 'Victoria to Ban Conversion Therapy.' *The Age*, 3 February 2019. www.theage.com.au/national/victoria/victoria-to-ban-gay-conversion-therapy-20190203-p50vdn.html

Conley, G. *Boy Erased: A Memoir of Identity, Faith, and Family*. New York: Riverhead Books, 2016.

Coon, D. '*Save Me*: Reconciling Queerness and Christianity.' In *Gay Conversion Practices in Memoir, Film and Fiction: Stories of Repentance and Defiance*, eds J. E. Bennett and M. Johnson. London: Bloomsbury, 2024. 187–201

Cooper, A. with J. Brooks. *Saving Alex: When I was Fifteen I Told My Mormon Parents I was Gay, and That's When My Nightmare Began*. San Francisco: HarperOne, 2016.

Cott, N. *Public Vows*, revised ed. Boston: Harvard University Press, 2009.

Cryle, P. and E. Stephens. *Normality: A Critical Genealogy*. Chicago & London: University of Chicago Press, 2017.

Drescher, J. 'Can Sexual Orientation Be Changed?' *Journal of Gay & Lesbian Mental Health*, 19 (2015): 84–93.

Edser, S. 'Being Gay, Being Christian': The Professional Reflects.' In *Gay Conversion Practices in Memoir, Film and Fiction: Stories of Repentance and Defiance*, eds J. E. Bennett and M. Johnson (London: Bloomsbury, 2024), 67–92.

Erzen, T. *Straight to Jesus: Sexual and Christian Conversions in the Ex-Gay Movement*. Berkeley: University of California Press, 2006.

Erzen, T. 'Testimonial Politics: The Christian Right's Faith-based Approach to Marriage and Imprisonment.' *American Quarterly*, vol. 59, no. 3 (2007): 996–9.

Featherstone, L. and A. Kaladelfos. *Sex Crimes in the Fifties*. Melbourne: Melbourne University Press, 2016.

Forstein, M. 'Overview of Ethical and Research Issues in Sexual Orientation Therapy.' In *Sexual Conversion Therapy: Ethical, Clinical and Research Perspectives*, eds A. Shidlo, M. Schroeder and J. Drescher, 167–79. New York: Haworth Press, 2001.

Gajdics, P. *The Inheritance of Shame: A Memoir*. Long Beach, CA, Brown Paper Press, 2017.

Grace, A. P. 'The Charisma and Deception of Reparative Therapies: When Medical Science Beds Religion.' *Journal of Homosexuality*, 55, no. 4 (2008): 545–80.

Griffin, S. 'Rape: The All-American Crime.' *Ramparts Magazine*, 10, no. 3 (1971): 1–8.

Griffin, S. *Rape: The Politics of Consciousness*. New York: Harper & Row, 1979.

Jones, T. W., A. Brown, L. Carnie, G. Fletcher and W. Leonard. *Preventing Harm, Promoting Justice: Responding to LGBT Conversion Therapy in Australia*. Melbourne, GLHV@ARCSHS and the Human Rights Law Centre, 2018. https://www.ohchr.org/sites/default/files/Documents/Issues/SexualOrientation/IESOGI/Academics/Equality_Australia_LGBTconversiontherapyinAustraliav2.pdf (accessed 12 March 2021).

Jones, T. W., J. Power and T. M. Jones. 'Religious Trauma and Moral Injury from LGBTQA+ Conversion Practices.' *Social Science and Medicine*, 305 (2022). DOI: 10.1016/j.socscimed.2022.115040.

Keating, J. 'British Colonialism and Anti-Gay Laws.' *Foreign Policy*, 19 June 2012. www.foreignpolicy.com/2012/06/19/british-colonialism-and-anti-gay-laws/

Kinitz, D. J. and T. Salway. 'Cisheteronormativity, Conversion Therapy, and Identity Among Sexual and Gender Minority People: A Narrative Inquiry and Creative Non-fiction.' *Qualitative Health Research*, 32, no. 13: (2020): 1965–78.

Lakhani, N. 'Effort to Repeal Texas Sodomy Law Advances with Bipartisan Support.' *The Guardian*, 7 April 2023. www.theguardian.com/us-news/2023/apr/06/texas-sodomy-law-repeal-bipartisan-support

Lemney, H. 'Party and Protest: The Radical History of Gay Liberation, Stonewall and Pride,' *The Guardian*, 25 June 2020. https://www.theguardian.com/world/2020/jun/25/party-and-protest-lgbtqradical-history-gay-liberation-stonewall-pride

'LGB People who have Undergone Conversion Therapy Almost Twice as Likely to Commit Suicide.' [Press Release]. Williams Institute, UCLA School of Law. 15 June 2020. https://williamsinstitute.law.ucla.edu/press/lgb-suicide-ct-press-release/

Marr, D. 'Christian Schools Hang on for Dear Life to the Shame of Homosexuality.' *Guardian Australia*, 26 February 2023. https://www.theguardian.com/commentisfree/2023/feb/26/catholic-schools-hang-on-for-dear-life-to-the-shame-of-homosexuality

McGrath, A. E. *Christian Theology: An Introduction*. 2nd edn MA, USA & Oxford: Blackwell, 1997.

McVicar, M. J. 'The Religious Right in America.' *Oxford Research Encyclopedias*, 26 February 2018 [first published 3 March 2016.] https://oxfordre.com/religion/display/10.1093/acrefore/9780199340378.001.0001/acrefore-9780199340378-e-97

'Milestones in the American Gay Rights Movement.' *PBS*. www.pbs.org/wgbh/americanexperience/features/stonewall-milestones-american-gay-rights-movement/

Nicolosi, J. *Reparative Therapy of Male Homosexuality: A New Clinical Approach*. Maryland: Jason Aronson Inc., 1991.

Nunn, G. 'Cooma Jail: Prison that was once "world's only jail for gay men".' *BBC News*. 24 April 2022. www.bbc.com/news/world-australia-61006503

Piggin, S. *Evangelical Christianity in Australia: Spirit, Word and World*, 3rd edn, Melbourne: Acorn Press, 2012.

Plummer, K. *Telling Sexual Stories: Power, Change and Social Worlds*. London: Routledge, 1995.

Promise Keepers: Men of Integrity. https://promisekeepers.org/

Pullen, C. *Gay Identity, New Storytelling, and the Media*. Basingstoke: Palgrave Macmillan, 2009.

'Religions: Pentecostalism.' BBC. www.bbc.co.uk/religion/religions/christianity/subdivisions/pentecostal_1.shtml

Rigney, J. '7 Important Lessons about Masculinity.' *Crossway*. n.d. https://www.crossway.org/articles/7-important-lessons-about-masculinity/

Risman, B. J. 'Gender as a Social Structure: Theory Wrestling with Activism.' *Gender & Society*, 18 (2004): 429–50.

Roberts, M. '"Gay conversion therapy" to be banned as part of LGBT equality plan.' BBC News, 3 July 2018. www.bbc.com/news/uk-44686374

Robinson, C. M. and S. E. Spivey. 'The Politics of Masculinity and the Ex-Gay Movement.' *Gender & Society*, 21, no. 5 (2007): 650–75.

Robinson, C. M. and S. E. Spivey. 'Putting Lesbians in Their Place: Deconstructing Ex-Gay Discourses of Female Homosexuality in a Global Context.' *Social. Sciences*, 4, (2015): 879–908.

Robinson, C. M. and S. E. Spivey. 'Ungodly Genders: Deconstructing Ex-Gay Movement Discourses of "Transgenderism" in the US.' *Social Sciences*, 8, no. 6 (2019): 1–28. DOI: org/10.3390/socsci8060191.

Shoemaker, T. 'Understanding Evangelicalism in America Today.' *The Conversation*, 4 August 2021. www.theconversation.com/understanding-evangelicalism-in-america-today-164851

Suckling, L. 'Uncovering Gay Conversion Camp.' *New Zealand Herald*, 18 March 2015. www.nzherald.co.nz/lifestyle/lee-suckling-uncovering-gay-conversion-camp-video/R3U4PKW6YWGOAOXNH7V2QWRN3U/?c_id=6&objectid=11419149

Terry, J. *An American Obsession: Science, Medicine, and Homosexuality in Modern Society*. Chicago: University of Chicago Press, 2010.

'The Gay Liberation Movement.' *Making History Project*. https://info.umkc.edu/makinghistory/the-gay-liberation-movement/ n.d.

'The Homophile Movement.' *Making History Project*. www.info.umkc.edu/makinghistory/the-homophile-movement/ n.d.

They/Them [Film] Dir. J. Logan, USA: Blumhouse Productions, 2022.

Tomazin, F. '"I am Profoundly Unsettled": Inside the Hidden World of Gay Conversion Therapy.' *Sydney Morning Herald*, 9 March 2018. https://www.smh.com.au/national/i-am-profoundly-unsettled-inside-the-hidden-world-of-gay-conversion-therapy-20180227-p4z1xn.html

Turban, J. L., N. Beckwith, S. L. Reisner and A. S. Keuroghlian. 'Association between Recalled Exposure to Gender Identity Conversion Efforts and Psychological Distress and Suicide Attempts among Transgender Adults.' *JAMA Psychiatry*, 77, no. 1 (2020): 68–76.

Venn-Brown, A. 'Tasmania to Ban Conversion "Therapy".' *The Big Smoke*, 16 September 2022. https://thebigsmoke.com.au/2022/09/16/tasmania-to-ban-conversion-therapy

Venn-Brown, A. "A Life of Unlearning': The Author Reflects.' In *Gay Conversion Practices in Memoir, Film and Fiction: Stories of Repentance and Defiance*, eds J. E. Bennett and M. Johnson. London: Bloomsbury, 2024, 41–66.

West, D. J. *Homosexuality: A Frank and Practical Approach to the Social and Medical Aspects of Male Homosexuality*. Harmondsworth: Penguin, 1960.

Willett, G. *Living Out Loud: A History of Gay and Lesbian Activism in Australia*. Sydney: Allen & Unwin, 2000.

Willett, G. 'Psyched In: Psychology, Psychiatry and Homosexuality in Australia.' *Gay and Lesbian Issues and Psychology Review*, 1 (2005): 53–7.

Wright, T., B. Candy and M. King. 'Conversion Therapies and Access to Transition-related Healthcare in Transgender People: A Narrative Systematic Review.' *BMJ open*, 8, no.12 (2018): e022425.

Yagel, G. 'Biblical Manhood.' *The Ministry of Gary Yagel: Igniting Men to Action*. n.d. https://www.forgingbonds.org/study-topics/biblical-manhood/

Yagel, G. '7 Reasons Boys Must Understand Godly Masculinity.' *The Ministry of Gary Yagel: Igniting Men to Action*. n.d. https://www.forgingbonds.org/blog/detail/7-reasons-boys-must-understand-godly-masculinity

Part One

Memoirs and Memoirists

1

'A Life of Unlearning': The Author Reflects

Anthony Venn-Brown

The young lady in the third row raised her hand, eager to ask her question at the end of my presentation. Possibly a budding writer, I thought.

'Was it cathartic writing your autobiography?' she asked.

It's a question I get almost every time I speak. I think most people would assume the answer is 'Yes'. There was a time I would have thought the same. My experience taught me differently.

'No, it was actually the opposite. It was re-traumatizing,' I replied and began to explain.

I'll need to backtrack here.

I've written my autobiography three times. A strange thing, I know. Let's go back further to the story itself.

Every story has a beginning

I was born in Sydney in 1951 to a typical post-war Australian family, the youngest of three children, the first and only son. The following year, something happened that would determine the course of the next thirty-nine years of my life.

The American Psychiatric Association published the first Diagnostic and Statistical Manual (DSM1) in 1952, which listed all the conditions psychiatrists considered mental disorders.[1] Homosexuality was classified as a 'sexual deviation' within the larger 'sociopathic personality disturbance' category of disorders. The sexual deviation diagnosis included 'homosexuality, transvestism, paedophilia, fetishism and sexual sadism'. Before I knew who or what I was, I had been classified as sociopathic and deviant.

At this time, post-war Sydney had a slightly more relaxed view of morality. Previously, gay men had connected at dinner parties, secret events, private balls and hanging out with the bohemian elements of society.[2] In fact, after the war, some hotels and public areas became known for homosexual rendezvous. Although clandestine, as long as they kept to themselves, homosexuals were being tolerated by *some* Australians, mostly those living in capital cities, like Sydney and Melbourne. On the other hand, there were those who saw this as a growing social problem that had to be eradicated. The New South Wales Police Commissioner, Colin Delaney, a friend of my father, called homosexuality Australia's 'greatest menace'. As a newly appointed Commissioner, he stated his two goals were to 'reduce the road toll' and to 'fight the growing cancer of perversion'.[3] During the 1950s, a moral panic was fuelled regularly in the media. Sensationalist headlines, such as 'Sex Perverts Flood Sydney' and 'Shocking Male Vice Must Be Wiped out in Sydney' were common.[4]

The media not only reported regularly on the 'growing menace' but helped instil the fear that young men such as me could be 'infected'. Comments such as Delaney's – 'I cannot stress too strongly the dire need for parents to exercise the closest control and supervision over their children, particularly young boys' – were sobering warnings to parents with sons; especially sons who were sensitive, artistic, effeminate and did not like sport.[5] The media commentary was vile and relentless. My parents, along with society, were fed a constant diet of ignorance, stereotyping and fear of homosexuality, which would have influenced their relationships with their children for decades to come.

Sexuality awakens

As sexual awareness awakens, it seeks to be expressed and explored. This can only happen with connection and experimentation. Something inside told me I might find what I was looking for on the streets or in parks late at night. This was not a conscious thing, but very real all the same; an urge I could only describe as an inner knowing. When I found the sites, I knew it was what I was looking for and the only places a gay teen in the 1960s could explore those urges. It became a pattern.

With the constant threat of imprisonment or institutionalization, these were dangerous times, not only for homosexual men, but for young gay boys like me. The culture of secrecy and shame meant we were vulnerable to bad people and terrible experiences. During those mid to late teen years, I was robbed, raped and bashed, but never arrested. These things were the price we paid in a hostile world that either did not understand homosexuals or hated us. It could have been worse. I could have been murdered. Many were.[6]

By the final year of high school in 1968, it felt like my life was out of control. The shame and secrecy led to depression and an attempt to take my own life. I needed help. I began having sessions with a psychiatrist. My sessions comprised lots of questions and note taking by the psychiatrist. In other suburbs of Sydney, gay men were being treated with electric shocks and aversion therapy.[7] After a series of sessions, my psychiatrist told me it was a stage I was going through. He recommended I work on a closer relationship with my father. He also suggested I no longer have any contact with a school friend who I confessed I had become sexually involved with. If only it were that easy. I tried. I so wanted to be 'normal' and for the nightmare to end.

No matter how hard I tried to change, my thoughts, feelings and habits were stronger, and once again I found myself lurking in dark places, parks and public toilets, having meaningless, brief sexual encounters with strangers. Sometimes these lasted mere seconds with no conversation, intimacy or affection. The brief moments of release were soon overcome with feelings of shame, guilt and that gnawing question, 'Why me?' I was angry at God. I was angry at life.

Jesus and the Devil

Our family were dedicated Anglicans. In my formative years, family life revolved around the church, but as a teenager in the 1960s, I had rejected it all as archaic and irrelevant. However, on one summer holiday, I was asked to help at a young people's Christian camp at a beach south of Sydney. It was a welcome relief from the turmoil of the previous year. I had not expected the time to be anything more than fun camp activities and teaching some Bible stories, as I had done at Sunday School.

The other workers at the camp differed from previous Anglicans I had known. They talked about Jesus, not as a historical figure, but as though He was still alive and a significant part of their everyday lives. The contrast hit me. Maybe this was my answer. A personal relationship with God and Jesus? After all, were not they the source of all forgiveness and miracles? I was acutely aware of how much I needed a saviour and redemption. I was a depraved sinner. Towards the end of the week, after everyone had gone to bed, with the moon as my only light, I walked along the beach. Sitting on a dune, staring at the waves crashing in on the sand, I cried out to God: 'My life is a mess, but if you want it, I'll give it to you.' It was a bargain. Take this curse away and I will do anything you want of me.

I was not conscious of anything supernatural happening. No voices, tingling feelings or flashing lights, but returning to Sydney I felt something had happened. I became a 'born again' Christian[8] with all that entailed, including Bible studies, prayer meetings and taking every chance I could to talk to others about Jesus. It felt like I had found the freedom I had so longed for.

A conversion, by nature, is a life-changing experience, but over a matter of time, the euphoria wears off and one realizes how much of the 'old self' can rear its ugly head. I had not been as transformed as I had initially thought. Now I had an enemy who was out to destroy my soul, and his inroads into my life were through my 'past' homosexuality. I was reminded constantly of the scripture that I was a 'new creation in Christ Jesus. Old things have passed away, behold all things become new.'[9] I had a battle on my hands with the desires of the flesh and the Devil himself. I could not let him win. My eternal destiny, heaven or hell, depended on it.

A new pattern developed in my life. I would be tempted, I would fight, I would resist, I would pray, I would do everything not to 'fall'. It was a four-way battle with myself, God, the Devil and my fleshly desires. When I lost the battle, dark days followed, repenting, asking God for forgiveness, more strength, and promising it would not happen again. But it did, and I would go through the cycle again. David Wilkerson,[10] popular preacher, founder of Teen Challenge in New York and author of the bestseller, *The Cross and the Switchblade* wrote about the way out of homosexuality:

> Desperation is the key that unlocks the door. Then you must learn to hate, despise, crucify and mortify your flesh. You must learn to look into a mirror and honestly say, 'My body, my flesh, is worthless, worm-eaten, and full of decay and death!' Cultivate a shame for your nakedness. Go to the throne of God in prayer and ask for a divorce from the love of flesh that has enslaved you. All your power to bring your flesh under subjection will come through sincere, fervent prayer. Christ has the power to deliver you from the love of flesh. He alone can break the power of this sin in your life.[11]

Self-hatred and self-loathing became developed skills to help overcome the thoughts, feelings and behaviours I struggled to eradicate. God hates sin and I must also learn to hate mine.[12]

My outward, rather dramatic conversion endeared me to some, and my evangelistic zeal on top of an increasing knowledge of the Bible earned me respect among my Christian peers. My personal struggles were just that. I kept them to myself. I had learned early in life to never talk to others about what was happening secretly in my life. Shame kept that door tightly shut.

Devils in Bible College

Ever since my 'born again' experience, I had felt that God was going to call me into full-time service as a preacher, pastor or missionary. I had to ensure that this evil was not just under control but obliterated entirely. At Bible College in 1971, surely, in that completely spiritual environment, it would be easier for me to live free from homosexual desires and temptations? There was only one thing to focus on really – getting closer to God and being trained to serve Him. Like overcoming any addiction, I felt I needed an extended period to get the thing completely out of my system. I became a model Bible College student, throwing myself into the early morning prayer meetings, lectures, off-campus opportunities of preaching and doing children's work, and even became the principal's pet.

What I thought would be easier was actually harder. In that cloistered environment, I was reminded daily of how far from the mark of true holiness I was. When I hit breaking point and disappeared from the college for the day to be alone with God and pray, I caused a panic on the campus. Apparently, in a previous course, another young man had disappeared. His body was found washed up on a nearby beach. The cause of death could not be determined (whether it was suicide or if he had slipped off the rocks and drowned). I have often wondered if he was troubled like me.

Returning to the college, I was ushered into the principal's office to explain my disappearance. The principal kept pressuring me to find out why I was so troubled. I clouded my answers in Christianese. 'I'm struggling with sin.' 'I'm under constant attack from the Devil.' 'No matter what I do, I can't seem to get the victory.' The principal was not satisfied. He kept digging. Eventually I had to reveal the real reason for my turmoil.

'I have a homosexual problem,' I said. It was much more palatable to say a 'homosexual problem' than 'I am a homosexual'. That level of ownership was terrifying. After revealing details of the years of struggle with my 'problem', the principal told me I needed deliverance from an evil spirit that had taken control of my life. It made sense to me. Considering my weakness and lack of control, I had often wondered about that myself. The principal arranged for me to have sessions with a leading exorcist, Neville Johnson, who pastored a Pentecostal church and regularly had visions and talked about seeing angels and demons. It was deeply disturbing, waiting days until I could have my sessions with him, believing I had evil spirits inside me.

Over the next several weeks, I had a number of sessions with Pastor Johnson and associates to release me from my 'bondages'. I say 'a number' because apparently, I had picked up quite a few extra demons along the way, which had all also taken host. We went through an inventory of my pre- and post-Christian sins in order to confess them so as not to leave the door open for demons to return. These included things like my past involvement in the occult, stealing sweets from the local shop and, of course, masturbation (that was a big one). I even had to renounce my father's involvement in the Masonic Lodge, which was believed to trigger a curse that could be handed down to the third and fourth generation.[13] The sessions included physical manifestations of moaning, heavy breathing (hyperventilation) and expelling demons. I did not feel free, just exhausted. Eventually though, they could not find any more devils. Surely now, my life would become easier and hopefully 'victorious'.

My last chance

In 1972, returning to Sydney after college was challenging, and it was not long before I found my old patterns returning. The constant inner turmoil drove me to where I was emotionally and spiritually spent, and I felt close to a nervous breakdown. I knew people who had been institutionalized after breakdowns and I had no desire to be like them. There was a Pentecostal church community in the southern suburbs of Sydney that had grown out of a rehabilitation programme, working with drug addicts, prostitutes and homosexuals. I admitted myself into the residential programme. It was one of only two in the world, the other located in upstate New York.

There were a lot of similarities to the Love in Action programme detailed in *Boy Erased*,[14] as discussed in Chapter 8 by Scott McKinnon.

I was told it would take two years to be completely transformed into heterosexuality. The programme included strong gender role conformity, which not only involved daily 'male' activities but also strict dress standards, including underwear. Prayer and Bible study were daily activities, along with an intense church weekly programme. Living within the 24/7 monitored environment meant I was protected from outside temptations in 'the world' so that I would not 'fall into sin'. This really was my last hope. I had tried everything else.

The leadership was emotionally and mentally abusive, and a series of traumatic events left me drained of motivation. Before the first twelve months were up, I left, believing, and hoping, that somehow God and I could sort out my problem outside the oppressive environment of the residential community. I moved to the country in 1973, away from the familiar places of temptation, and joined a little Pentecostal church. Here, no one would know about my past. I could serve God in the church and begin a new life. Here, my dreams would come true.

Dreams come true

In the small country church, Helen and I were the only single young people, and it seemed inevitable to everyone that we would become a couple. We did. I proposed. She accepted and we got married. You may notice that I never mentioned I fell in love with Helen. Like most gay men who marry women, we do not fall in love with our spouses.[15] We love their friendship, we love their companionship, and we love the idea of being a husband and a father. I thought it was love and that seemed enough. On top of this, Helen, being a committed Christian, wanted to serve God and was willing to support me in my ministry. I told her about my past, but we were simple enough in our faith to believe that our marriage would be the final answer. We had two beautiful daughters, Rebekah and Hannah, who were the joy of our lives.

Feeling the call of God, and towing a huge caravan, we left Orange in 1978 and began preaching from one country church to another. We lived by faith. After several years of itinerant preaching and church planting, we relocated to Sydney in 1983 to begin a national evangelistic ministry. My preaching proved popular, and more and more invitations came from churches around Australia. I was usually booked up six months in advance and preaching regularly in Australia's growing megachurches such as the famous (now infamous) Hillsong Church.[16] My dreams had come true. Well, almost all. Behind the scenes, the battle with my homosexuality continued. Sometimes I would win the battle, other times not. What made it worse than before was that I was being unfaithful to my wife and breaking the vows I had made to her on our wedding day. Also, there was the hypocrisy of being a high-profile preacher with a secret life of sin. As long as I kept fighting it, I justified, God would understand my struggle. Even better, I knew my heart. If I did not give up, one day it would be gone completely. I had to hold on to that.

Coming undone

In 1991, only weeks before my fortieth birthday, I had an encounter with a man in Brisbane, Jason, that brought it all undone. After all the encounters I had gone through, that night was different. In my motel room, I experienced tenderness, affection, devotion and intimacy. The gay self I had tried to suppress and kill for over two decades sprang into life. I did something I had never done before. I agreed to see him a second time. Powerful emotions quickly surfaced. I was thinking of him constantly. I had never considered homosexuality to be about anything else but sex, but now, I wanted to love and be loved by that man. The cloak of denial I had wrapped myself in for years was ripped away and I was forced to face the reality that I was, am, and always will be gay. I knew I could no longer preach or pretend.

I began working on extricating myself from the ministry and planned to just disappear to be with Jason. A crazy plan looking back, considering how well known I was.

However, before I could put my plans into place, the affair was discovered. I resigned and was required to confess publicly in front of a large congregation at the next Sunday service, with my wife and children in the front row. 'Devastating' does not adequately describe what happened. Physically and emotionally, I was broken. I became a zombie and cried for three weeks, knowing I had hurt and humiliated so many people, and lost everything I had worked for and held dear. It seemed like the grief and pain would never go away; I wondered if I would ever recover.

After twelve months, I moved to Sydney, found a job, and Jason joined me. Maybe at last, I would find some peace? But it was not to be. It turned out that Jason was a compulsive gambler, physically abusive and had many unresolved issues. He had also failed to disclose that he was HIV+. My dream had become a nightmare. No matter how many compromises I made, the relationship did not survive the full year.

What about my faith? That had been packed away. Too much pain and too many questions without answers. I thought I would probably go to hell for 'giving in to my homosexuality' as some former Christian friends put it. I had planned to live the next few years as an openly gay man, then commit suicide at fifty before I became old and lost my attractiveness. It had been drummed into me for years that 'all gay men end up sad, lonely, bitter and twisted'. Not me. I was checking out before then.

A story to tell

Why write a memoir? Many people say they will. Most do not. Some write for pleasure, some for fame, some hope their memoir will become a bestseller and make lots of money. I guess others write their memoir for the therapeutic possibilities in devoting days, months or years to reflecting on and documenting their lives. The reason I wrote *A Life of Unlearning* was very specific and quite obscure.

After Jason and I broke up, I discovered the 'gay scene', or as conservative Christians like to call it: the 'homosexual lifestyle'. I danced my little socks off every weekend at nightclubs, bars and dance parties, took drugs and had several short-term relationships. One-night stands and weekend romances filled in the gaps. My fun-filled, hedonistic lifestyle was such a contrast to my previous life of eternal issues and being responsible. I made lots of friends and had a fantastic time.

Alas, my excesses eventually caught up with me after the breakup of my most substantial gay relationship and I ended up in hospital. The wonderful friends I had made shone. They looked after me 24/7 for a couple of weeks. I knew I needed to make some changes.

Time for a turnaround

I came across a personal development programme. Personal development had always been an interest of mine, and I had incorporated many of the fundamental principles into my preaching and youth work. The programme uniquely combined science, philosophy, religion, spirituality, personal growth principles, new age teaching, visualization, the power of thoughts and meditation. It was not long before I realized how much of the teaching was familiar to me. I had built a successful national ministry on many of the universal, or what I had considered previously as biblical, principles. I wondered, had I thrown the baby out with the bathwater?

After a particularly inspiring meeting, alone at home, I prayed for the first time in eight years. 'God, I don't know where this is going or what it all means, but you and I are on speaking terms again.' That was all I needed or wanted to say at that stage.

In 1999, keen to explore more, I withdrew every dollar I had to attend a week's conference on the Yucatán Peninsula, Mexico, next to the Mayan sacred sites and the 1,000-year-old pyramid at Chichén Itzá. The week's programme was inspiring and disturbing, as much of my previous Christian belief system was being challenged. Then something completely unexpected happened. This extract from my memoir explains it best:

> It was extremely hot and cooling off after lunch in one of the five pools at the resort was a welcome relief. I began a conversation with one of the participants from Canada, John, and listened as he shared his life journey, rejecting his Roman Catholic faith and then rediscovering it again with a deepened sense of spirituality. Up to this point, I had found it impossible to make sense of the various experiences of my life; it was like a jigsaw puzzle scattered across a table. I'd had so many wonderful experiences as a preacher and father, contrasted by numerous devastating ones, dark and light pieces that wouldn't match. The picture was not only unclear, it was confusing. I was transported as he spoke and could still hear his voice in the background whilst it seemed I was in another place. Like most, I'd often heard the term 'my life flashed before me' used to describe the experience before death when years are reduced to microseconds. In that moment my past, present and future merged in front of me playing out like a video, every step and experience fitting together perfectly in sequence – my journey finally made complete sense.[17]

In this almost daydream state, three simple statements came to me:

> 'Tell your story.'
> 'Be completely honest.'
> 'It will help many people, and don't worry about a publisher, I'll organize everything.'

That was it. Clear and succinct. It felt like I'd just experienced a life-defining moment.[18]

So, what motivated me to write my memoir? I was told to. Honestly, there was no other reason. You can decide who or what told me. I did not hear an audible voice, but the statements were unmistakably clear.

I had never planned to be an author. I returned to Sydney and began writing. I put an affirmation above my computer that said, 'I am a successful, published author.' Every time I looked at it, I visualized myself at a book launch or walking into a bookstore and seeing a display of my books.

Reliving the past

That was 1999. *A Life of Unlearning* was not published until 2004. Between those years, I stopped and started. There was one big break of over a year. Some would call that writer's block. I realized later it was because the next chapter was going to be the most challenging to write. It was about Jason. Not that the previous ones were not challenging, but maybe my subconscious was saying: 'Not yet. You're not ready for that one.'

To express what happened for the reader, I had to go back to those dark experiences to feel them and relive them. Originally, during the dark moments and experiences, I did not have time to grieve the losses or process any emotions. Possibly, I was incapable of really getting in touch with them as they were so powerful, and maybe, if I really went there, I would be overcome and never emerge from the darkness. It terrified me.

The trauma and grief I had buried kept coming to the surface. While writing, there were times when my eyes filled with tears, and I could no longer see the text on the screen. At other times I would stop, put my head in my hands and weep, and still other times I would just have to get up and walk away from the computer. Sometimes I would bang the keyboard so hard out of anger I was sure it would break. I became a chain smoker, needing something to relieve the tensions that built up.

You can't put on the page what you don't feel in your heart and soul. And sometimes what you feel in your heart and soul can't be expressed adequately on the page.

I had no idea what I was doing to myself. Post-traumatic stress disorder (PTSD) was something veterans experience as far as I knew. I was re-traumatizing myself.

The instructions I received in the pool in Chichén Itzá in 1999, 'Don't worry about a publisher, I'll organize everything,' came to pass. Through a series of synchronistic events that still amaze me today, I had a publisher, contract and advance, with New Holland. And an unfinished manuscript that needed a lot of work. The publisher's deadline fixed that.

Finally . . . it's out in the world

Only an author knows the incredible feeling of holding the first copy of their own book, knowing that what they hold represents incalculable hours of commitment and devotion. I remember opening it up to an embarrassingly revealing part and thought, 'Fuck, what have I done? My mother is going to kill me.' I need not have worried – she never read it. But I had put my life out there, secrets, including my hypocrisy, stupidity and weaknesses, for all to judge. So much I was not proud of. I felt very vulnerable.

Within days, the first email from a reader arrived. I was deeply moved by the profound impact my story had on him:

> I was really blown away by your book. It's been nearly three years since I left the church and became true to myself. Not since then have I come across anybody who I could say I could really empathize with. Your story really touched me because I grew up in a Pentecostal church. I've carried a lot of hurt around and anger towards those who spent my whole life lifting me up and telling me I was loved only to abandon me when I most needed friends and support. The final chapters of your book ruined me, broke my heart! I had to put it down almost every paragraph to refocus my puffy red eyes. But somewhere between you saying in the first chapter, 'Something died in me that day' and the end of the book, I had a moment with the universe where something inside of me wanted not to be broken anymore. For the first time I wasn't convincing myself that I was loved and valued and that everything was OK. I actually knew it.[19]

These dramatic revelations in personal correspondence did not abate over time, as evidenced in the following message:

I just wanted you to know that you are an inspiration to me.

Between fourteen and thirty I tried to get rid of the gay. I did informal programmes with my pastors and AWFUL workbooks. Then I did a six-week camp at Love Wins, a programme of Exodus International. When I turned thirty, I realized the futility of those efforts. Around thirty-two to thirty-three, I became happy that I was gay. I'm thirty-four now. Half of my life does seem wasted.

Reading *A Life of Unlearning* assisted my mental health and acceptance for myself in a tangible way. I used to be on six antipsychotic drugs and now I'm only on one mild antidepressant. Thank you. It truly did help. I've always been taught that God hates me.

I made a lot of friends in conversion therapy. Out of forty, only six are still alive (one died naturally, the rest suicide.) Your book gave me hope and let me see a truer Christ.[20]

My inbox became a daily stream of emails. Some were a simple paragraph or two, others three pages long. Many began with the words 'Your story is my story'. The majority said, 'Thank you for your honesty'. I was reminded once again of what I had been told in Mexico, 'Tell your story, be completely honest, it will help many people.' I did not know how important that honesty was. Readers can tell when the author is holding back. It gave people the freedom to share openly with me.

Many emails were tragically sad. Some writers had attempted suicide more than once, young people had been disowned by their families, others rejected by Christian friends and churches, some had lost partners to suicide because of the cognitive dissonance induced by conversion practices, a phenomenon discussed in Chapter 2 by Stuart Edser. Once again, I cried at the computer, not for my pain this time, but for theirs. The majority were telling me things they had never shared with anyone because they knew I would understand. My inbox had become a microscope for a hidden world of conversion 'therapy' survivors and intense inner conflict over their faith and sexuality. I answered every email. How could I not? These people had taken the time to write, express their gratitude, and pour their hearts out to me. It was impossible to ignore the needs and cries for help.

Sometimes, if people were in Sydney, they wanted to talk more over a cup of coffee; to be with someone in the flesh who really understood their pain. In their presence, I held it together, but walking away, I would often weep. In one way, the tears were good. Since I had walked away from everything, I found I could not really cry any more. At times when I should have cried over the loss of a parent or family member or Jason leaving, I was unemotional, cold, unfeeling. Later, I discovered there was a deep well of tears waiting for release. When it was time, I cried regularly for a year.

Once again, unknowingly, like the effects of reliving the story writing, these tragic stories were affecting me. Sometimes it is labelled vicarious PTSD.

The 2004 first edition of *A Life of Unlearning – Coming Out of the Church, One Man's Struggle* became a bestseller in Australia and sold out.

Creating a monster

Naïvely, I had thought that once the book was written, I could get on with my life and work on my professional coaching business, which was my only source of income. Making money from a book is a misnomer, unless you are a successful author like Stephen King or on the *New York Times* bestseller list. Neither of these is true of me. After nearly two years of responding to readers and trying to run the coaching business, I began a support network called Freedom2b.[21] Chapter meetings and an online forum gave people the opportunity to connect with others of like background and experience. Handing readers over to Freedom2b relieved the burden, but in the process, I had created another monster: a growing lesbian, gay, bisexual, transgender and queer (LGBT+) organization run by volunteers. It all needed managing which, along with my coaching business, had me working eighty- to one hundred-hour weeks. Thank God I lived alone and was single. I did not have to contend with a partner yelling from the bedroom 'Get off that computer and come to bed.' Trying to run the business and Freedom2b, I burnt out a few times and after six years, resigned and handed the organization over to the volunteers.[22]

Let's do it again

As mentioned earlier, when I wrote the first edition in the early 2000s, I had never considered myself to be a writer and had a limited understanding of writing. Emails from readers were often full of compliments, repeatedly disclosing things like they 'couldn't put it down' or they had 'read it more than once'. Understandably, confidence in my writing ability was boosted enormously.

When the first edition sold out, for the second edition, I used the original manuscript and rewrote the entire book from page one. An extra eighty pages were added because of new insights and because my research had given me an even deeper understanding. I spent time giving context to various situations. These included, for example, Exodus International, current international events for readers, conversion 'therapy', and finished with a letter I had written to the Assemblies of God National Executive, summarizing the hundreds of stories I had received.[23] Once again, there were emotional moments in writing. When I finished the manuscript on the publisher's deadline, I went for a walk to get out into the fresh air. I only got to the end of the driveway and had to come back home. I was exhausted. I went to bed and remained there for three days. I was emotionally and physically spent. 'I'll never do that to myself again,' I said to myself. Famous last words!

This second edition was available on Amazon.com which opened it up to an international audience and the print run also sold out. Amazon resellers jumped in and people began paying hundreds of dollars to get their hands on the last few copies or second-hand ones.

The publisher decided not to do a third edition. I believed *A Life of Unlearning* was just as relevant as it was in 2004 and 2007. Maybe more so. Eventually I would self-publish, I thought. By 2015, when the third edition was released, there was an entire generation of LGBT+ youth growing up in churches who were experiencing the same struggles, ignorance and discrimination. While my memoir had changed thousands of lives, the church essentially was in stasis. And then there was the marriage equality battle in Australia we had to endure. Predictably, the opposition came from Christian churches; many I had preached in.

While preparing the manuscript, I realized I had added too much additional information in the second edition that kept taking the reader out of the story. For the third edition, I began writing from page one again and stuck closely to the narrative. In the first two editions, there were some experiences I felt I could not connect with deeply enough. Either too painful or unable to adequately express in words? I dug deeper this time and allowed myself to go there. In the third edition, I tapped into each of those for the reader. The epilogue was completely rewritten and updated, which represented my challenge to each and every one of us to create change. I feel proud of what I produced and with the wonders of modern technology such as print on demand and eBooks, *A Life of Unlearning* will never sell out again.

Lives touched

In writing this chapter, it has been good to put so many thoughts down on the page, and it has also caused me to think about the gifts *A Life of Unlearning* has given me.

By far the most rewarding thing is knowing that my story has helped so many people more than I ever imagined or could count. Not only has it brought healing and reconciliation to LGBT+ people, but also family members, mums, dads, siblings and friends have come to a greater place of understanding and acceptance. Some pastors and church leaders have realized the need to update their beliefs and are now LGBT+ advocates. Some of my readers have become LGBT+ community leaders. A few were at the point of taking their lives and *A Life of Unlearning* saved them. This message came from a young man in the USA through Facebook:

> I read your book when I was sixteen. I kind of stumbled across it in my darkest hour and it saved my life. I grew up in a Pentecostal megachurch in the bible belt. I came out and basically got banished from the church and my family. It broke me the way they treated me I was at the point where I had told myself I'd just end it. No one loved me (so I falsely believed). I had a plan and date but I came across your book. Man did your experience touch me. I made a decision to live and to live life to my fullest potential after that. And I'm doing pretty darn great now. I really believe I would have ended it that day if I didn't come across A Life of Unlearning. I truly believe God used your experience that night. I know you don't really know me but just wanted to say thanks for being brave enough to share your story.[24]

I have developed some very special friendships with people all over the world along the way. Friendships that have enriched my life through encouragement and support.

Another wonderful gift is a greater level of self-awareness. One of those areas of self- awareness was an understanding of how the traumas over the years affected my life.

A revelation

In 2013, I happened on a movie called *Oranges and Sunshine*.[25] A true story, Margaret Humphreys, a British social worker, investigated a woman's claim that at the age of four she had been put on a boat to Australia by the British government under a scheme that finally ended in 1967.[26] Margaret discovered that this was just the tip of an enormous iceberg and 150,000 children had been deported to a 'new life' in distant parts of the British empire. The deported children were promised 'oranges and sunshine' but in fact, for many, it was a life of horrendous physical, emotional and sexual abuse. Margaret unravelled the shocking secret, and it became her mission to reunite these innocent and unwilling exiles with their families in Britain.

Hearing so many horrendous stories, Margaret began having serious mental and physical symptoms. I related totally to what she was experiencing. Every single one of those experiences was familiar to me. Her husband sent her to the doctor, who without hesitation said she was suffering from PTSD. I thought: 'How could she have PTSD just hearing the stories?' Suddenly, the penny dropped. I realized that what had been happening to me was not only about my own buried trauma, but it had also been compounded by the hundreds of tragic stories I had listened to. How could I have gone through all this without being deeply impacted? Could this explain the emotional meltdowns I had experienced from time to time? I booked myself into a psychologist I had previously had a few sessions with. He knew my story.

'Could I have PTSD?' I asked. I was a little taken aback by how amused he was at my question. We had a few more sessions discussing how PTSD happens and its effects, and I came away with a phrase that has stood me in good stead ever since: 'The trauma never leaves you; you just learn to manage it.' It was gold. My initial feelings of peace and resolution back in 1999 were so overwhelming that I thought I was 'healed' of all the hurt and pain. A concept of healing that was a leftover from my Christian belief system.

I relate to Brazilian writer Paulo Coelho, who has been quoted as saying: 'Don't allow your wounds to transform you into someone you are not.'[27]

A happy ending

I am in a good place. Many conversion 'therapy' survivors are not. Conversion 'therapy', whether in formal or informal religious settings is always harmful because it is based on a false premise that if you are gay, lesbian, bisexual, transgender or gender diverse, something is wrong with you; you are broken. There is an abundance of research showing the harms. Many conversion 'therapy' survivors have ongoing mental health issues. Some are on medication and most likely will be for the rest of their lives. Some have regular sessions with a therapist to keep some sort of equilibrium in their lives. I know of some who can no longer work and are on government benefits.

So much damage has been done to countless individuals because of ignorance about sexual orientation and gender identity and religious people doggedly holding onto outdated beliefs about six passages in the Bible.[28] The lives lost so needlessly through suicide is also incalculable.

So, I consider myself blessed and very grateful that somehow, I have survived. I have often wondered if it is because of my personality or make up or that I have learnt to manage PTSD as the psychologist said. One of the key things I believe that has helped me is my connections with personal development principles. Positivity in thoughts and what I say are important, as are future focused goals. I have learnt to revive my sense of humour, which I lost through the intensity of the work with traumatized people of faith. I have learnt to become an observer of emotions and to remind myself that they are simply chemical reactions in the brain. I have become more aware of my triggers and how to avoid them. I have learnt to reframe things so that negativity is removed. Also, I have learnt to laugh at the bigots, homophobes and prejudiced for their stupidity instead of letting them trigger me. I have learnt that words only have the power you give to them. I have learnt to forgive and make peace with my past; to find the good amongst the bad. These are just some of the strategies I have put in place.

I feel very fortunate to have a wonderful sense of accomplishment and achievement, writing my autobiography (three times), founding two not-for-profit organizations and the difference I have been able to make in the world and in the lives of individuals. Being acknowledged by my tribe on several occasions, like twice being voted One of Australia's Most Influential Gay and Lesbian Australians in 2007 and 2009, has been extra special.[29] I guess the *pièce de résistance* was being awarded the Order of Australia Medal (OAM) in 2020, as part of the Queen's Birthday Honours for service to the LGBT+ community.[30] We do what we do, not for recognition or accolades, we do it because the work is important and often lifesaving. I am grateful for the acknowledgments, of course.

I live daily with a strong sense of mission and purpose. *A Life of Unlearning* gave me that.

In closing *A Life of Unlearning*, I summarized what I had to unlearn and what I had learnt. I ended that list with this: 'In life's journey, you are never off the path. Every detour, dead-end, back alley, even road wrecks, looked at with insight, are the journey.'[31] It seems to be that way for me. It has made for a rich life anyway.

The sub-title for this chapter, 'An Author Reflects', is perfect because that is exactly what writing this chapter has caused me to do. Reflect not only on the past, but on the challenging journey of writing and the aftermath … and the gifts. So, the next time you know of a memoir writer who has received awards and accolades, know that behind all that success is another story – one that may never be told, as I have had the fortune of doing here.

The saying often attributed to Joseph Campbell, author and mythologist – 'The cave that you fear to enter, holds the treasure that you seek' – is definitely true for me, both of my sexuality and telling my story.[32]

Notes

1   Committee on Nomenclature and Statistics, American Psychiatric Association, *Mental Disorders: Diagnostic and Statistical Manual* (American Psychiatric Association, Mental Hospital Service, 1952).

2   G. Wotherspoon, *Gay Sydney: A History* (Sydney: UNSW Press, 2016).

3   'Police Fight Against Perversion,' *Sydney Morning Herald*, 2 December 1953: 11.

4   'Sex Perverts Flood Sydney,' *Barrier Miner*, 14 December 1948: 4. 'Shocking male vice must be wiped out in Sydney,' *Truth*, 6 December 1953: 10.

5   'Concern Over Perversion,' *Sydney Morning Herald*, 20 October 1951: 4.

6   A. Benny-Morrison, 'Police to Review 88 Possible Gay-hate Deaths,' *Sydney Morning Herald,* 21 May 2016, https://www.smh.com.au/national/nsw/police-to-review-88-possible-gayhate-deaths-20160519-goz7x6.html (accessed 11 August, 2023).

7   B. Castellari, '"Learning Therapy" A New Hope for Deviates,' *Sydney Morning Herald,* 14 October1966: 16.

8   The term often used by evangelicals to describe the conversion experience. It is a reference to the conversation Jesus had with the Pharisee Nicodemus, who was seeking further enlightenment: 'Jesus answered and said unto him, Verily, verily, I say unto thee, Except a man be born again, he cannot see the kingdom of God' (John 3:3 KJV).

9   'Therefore if any man be in Christ, he is a new creature: old things are passed away; behold, all things are become new' (2 Corinthians 5:17 KJV).

10 David Wilkerson became a popular preacher and author during the Jesus Revolution in the late 1960s and 1970s. His work amongst gangs, drug users, prostitutes, troubled youth, and runaways in New York was documented in the book he co-authored, *The Cross and the Switchblade* (first published in 1963). The book raised his international profile and established Wilkerson as the expert on youth issues. The book became a best-seller, with over 50 million copies in over thirty languages, and is included in Christianity Today's 'Top 50 Books That Have Shaped Evangelicals'.

11 D. Wilkerson, *Hope for Homosexuals* (Brooklyn, NY: Teen Challenge, 1964).

12 'Put to death therefore what is earthly in you: fornication, impurity, passion, evil desire, and covetousness, which is idolatry. On account of these the wrath of God is coming' (Colossians 3:5-6 ESV).

13 '…the iniquities of the fathers are visited upon the sons and daughters – unto the third and fourth generation' (Exodus 20:5 KJV).

14 *Boy Erased* [Film]. Dir. Joel Edgerton, USA: Focus Features, 2018.

15 Anthony Venn-Brown, 'Situational Heterosexuality,' *Ambassadors & Bridge Builders International,* 4 April 2010, https://www.abbi.org.au/2010/04/situational-heterosexuality/ (accessed 11 August 2023).

16 Hillsong Church was founded in Sydney in 1983 by Brian and Bobbie Houston. It experienced phenomenal growth and was famous for its music and worship style and conferences. Hillsong began planting churches

around the world. By 2022, it had churches in over thirty countries as well as many around Australia. The initial scandal was about Brian's father, Frank, who was accused of multiple sexual abuse incidents that went back many years. Brian was accused of mishandling the initial revelation and aftermath. A series of controversies and scandals have continued since then and Brian Houston himself was stood down as leader in 2022.

17 A. Venn-Brown, *A Life of Unlearning: A Preacher's Struggle with His Homosexuality, Church and Faith*, 3rd edn, rev. (Ambassadors & Bridge Builders International, 2015), 262.

18 Venn-Brown, *A Life of Unlearning*, Chapter 20, 'And the pieces finally fit'.

19 Personal communication, 12 July 2004.

20 Personal communication, 12 May 2015.

21 www.freedom2b.org

22 One thing those years taught me was that we could spend the rest of our lives running ambulances down the bottom of the cliff, but we needed to build fences at the top. In 2013, I founded another organization, Ambassadors & Bridge Builders International, which focused on education, resources and reaching out to Christian leaders, churches and organizations to engage them in dialogue about LGBT+ issues, www.abbi.org.au

23 A. Venn-Brown, 'Letter To The Australian Assemblies Of God National Executive', 'ABBI', 3 May 2005, https://www.abbi.org.au/2005/05/assemblies-of-god-homosexuality-2/ (accessed 11 August 2023).

24 Personal communication, 5 September 2016.

25 *Oranges and Sunshine* [Film] Dir. Jim Loach, Australia: Icon Film Distribution, 2011.

26 For more details on the scheme and its implications for Australia, see, for example, C. Dow and J. Phillips, '"Forgotten Australians" and "Lost Innocents": Child Migrants and Children in Institutional Care in Australia' (Canberra: Australian Parliamentary Library, 2009), 1–2. https://www.aph.gov.au/library (accessed 18 December 2023).

27 P. Coelho, 'Quote Fancy', https://quotefancy.com/paulo-coelho-quotes (accessed 11 August 2023).

28 What does the Bible Really Say About Homosexuality, https://www.abbi.org.au/audio-resources/what-does-the-bible-really-say-about-homosexuality/

29 B. Cubby, ‘A Gong for Gay of Influence,’ *Sydney Morning Herald*, 10 October 2007, https://www.smh.com.au/national/a-gong-for-gays-of-influence-20071010-gdrazc.html (accessed 11 August 2023). The year 2009’s SameSame’s 25 Most Influential Gay & Lesbian Australians, ‘ABBI,’ 9 October 2009, https://www.abbi.org.au/2007/10/most-influential-gay-australians/ (accessed 11 August 2023), https://web.archive.org/web/20160319182804/ http://www.samesame.com.au/25/2009/

30 ‘The Queen’s Birthday 2020 Honours List,’ https://honours.pmc.gov.au/honours/awards/2007052 (accessed 11 August 2023).

31 Venn-Brown, *A Life of Unlearning*, Chapter 20, ‘And the pieces finally fit’.

32 See Quote Investigator, ‘The Cave You Fear to Enter Holds the Treasure You Seek,’ 23 May 2013. www.quoteinvestigator.com/2013/05/23/ (accessed 19 May 2023).

Bibliography

Benny-Morrison, A. ‘Police to review 88 possible gay-hate deaths.’ *Sydney Morning Herald,* 21 May 2016. https://www.smh.com.au/national/nsw/police-to-review-88-possible-gayhate-deaths-20160519-goz7x6.html

Boy Erased [Film] Dir. Joel Edgerton, USA: Focus Features, 2018.

Castellari, B. ‘“Learning therapy” a new hope for deviates.’ *Sydney Morning Herald,* 14 October 1966: 16.

Coelho, P. ‘Quote Fancy,’ https://quotefancy.com/paulo-coelho-quotes

Committee on Nomenclature and Statistics, American Psychiatric Association, *Mental Disorders: Diagnostic and Statistical Manual.* American Psychiatric Association, Mental Hospital Service, 1952.

‘Concern Over Perversion.’ *Sydney Morning Herald*, 20 October 1951: 4.

Cubby, B. ‘A Gong for Gay of Influence.’ *Sydney Morning Herald*, 10 October 2007, https://www.smh.com.au/national/a-gong-for-gays-of-influence-20071010-gdrazc.html (accessed 11 August 2023).

Dow, C. and J. Phillips. ‘“Forgotten Australians” and “Lost Innocents”: Child Migrants and Children in Institutional Care in Australia.’ Canberra: Australian Parliamentary Library, 2009, www.aph.gov.au/library

Freedom2b. https://www.freedom2b.org

Oranges and Sunshine [Film] Dir. Jim Loach, Australia: Icon Film Distribution, 2010.

'Police Fight Against Perversion.' *Sydney Morning Herald*, 2 December 1953: 11.

'Shocking Male Vice Must be Wiped Out in Sydney.' *Truth*, 6 December 1953: 10.

'Sex Perverts Flood Sydney.' *Barrier Miner*, 14 December 1948: 4.

Venn-Brown, A. *A Life of Unlearning: A Preacher's Struggle with His Homosexuality, Church and Faith*, 3rd rev edn. Sydney: Personal Success Australia, 2015.

Venn-Brown, A. Ambassadors & Bridge Builders International (ABBI), https://www.abbi.org.au

Wilkerson, D. *Hope for Homosexuals*. Brooklyn, New York: Teen Challenge, 1964.

Wotherspoon, G. *Gay Sydney: A History*. Sydney: UNSW Press, 2016.

2

'Being Gay, Being Christian': The Professional Reflects

Stuart Edser

At the outset of this chapter, I feel that I should say why I have been asked to contribute to this anthology, and what credentials or background I bring to its creation. I am now a man in my sixties. I am gay, cisgendered and married. I am out, both personally and professionally, and am in private practice as an endorsed counselling psychologist in New South Wales, Australia, now in my third decade of clinical work. I have seen many hundreds of LGBT+ people over the course of my career.

In an earlier part of my life, I was intensely religious, being both a minor seminarian in the Roman Catholic Church, even living in a monastery for three years, and later, a leader, elder, teacher, worship-leader and church-founder in the evangelical wing of the Protestant Church. After almost two decades of inescapable cognitive dissonance between my religious identity and my gay identity, occasioned by significant psychopathology, I abandoned the religious path and sought help in therapy. Within a year, I had accepted myself fully and became comfortable in being gay, and within three to four years, had revisited and revised my theology, culminating in the writing of my first book, *Being Gay, Being Christian*.[1] This work brought together my personal experience, my training in science as a psychologist, and my understanding of Christian theology. So, I have first-hand insights into the reality of gay conversion 'therapy', the distress it brings and the harm it causes.

Being gay, being Christian – you can be both

My book came out of my own journey. The history of my own gay sexual identity formation and its interface with my religious identity brought about powerful psychological, relational and epistemological forces to compete in my mind and body. This took place for almost two decades and culminated in a serious deterioration of my mental health, living a life of loneliness, guilt, sin consciousness and mandated celibacy. At the completion of successful therapy where I did in fact learn to accept myself, I returned to my historic religious faith after a couple of years with a view to seeing whether there was anything there worth retaining, only to find that I had changed too much to accept the veracity of that version of faith in my life.

My book, published in 2012, took me four years to write and research. I set about analyzing all the science around human sexuality, its history, and philosophical thought in its involvement with Christianity, the law and the medical field. I looked at the theology of the Christian church, especially the two wings with which I had had immediate experience, the Catholic wing, and the Protestant/Pentecostal wing. This involved examining in detail the Catholic pronouncements around homosexuality, as well as the evangelical treatment of gay sexuality based on face-value readings of scripture, especially the few texts that I called the 'sledge-hammer texts'.[2]

The purpose of *Being Gay, Being Christian* was two-fold. I wanted to speak to the conservative Christian churches to say: 'You cannot keep teaching these unscientific and harmful doctrines about gay people. You need to change. You have changed in other areas; you can change here too'. But further, I wanted to say to gay people of Christian faith: 'Your sexual orientation does not preclude you from pursuing your faith and spirituality if that's what you want to do'. The book is not an apologia for Christianity, nor is it in any way proselytizing. As a matter of interest, I have moved on theologically since the publication of my book and no longer use the appellation of 'Christian' to describe myself.

The book's publication inevitably led me to speak about it publicly. Of course, this turned me into an activist; something I had not clearly anticipated, so by the time Australia was having its public debates about same-sex marriage, I was very vocal and regularly gave my opinion on social media and occasionally in mainstream media. I participated in a New Zealand documentary by Elephant TV in 2012, essentially a discussion by proponents, myself and two others, and opposers, three evangelical Christians. I co-wrote in August 2015 with the Anglican Dean of Brisbane, Dr Peter Catt, a *Sydney Morning Herald* article, 'Christian Australia is Ready for Marriage Equality'.[3]

I was particularly affronted in that debate by the willingness of conservative politics in Australia to submit marriage equality to what was essentially a plebiscite in 2017; essentially, to place the lives and relationships of LGBT+ people into the hands of a public vote with a Yes and No case given moral equivalence. In my view, this was unforgiveable. This state-sanctioned vote on our civil rights placed us in the firing line of every bigoted, homophobic entity in the country as they argued the No case. The invective endured by the LGBT+ community was obscene and most of us will have their personal stories from Facebook or Twitter from that time.[4]

Of course, the outcome is legendary. The plebiscite was carried by almost two-thirds of those who voted (around 80 per cent of eligible voters participated) and a subsequent vote in the Parliament was carried easily. But the cost to the LGBT+ community of conservative politics teaming up with conservative religion to stop a movement of social progress that most of Australia was already behind was a heinous act. The unnecessary plebiscite caused serious mental health issues, divided families, friendships and workplaces. A 2019 study by the University of Sydney captured some of this, finding that increased exposure to negative messages about marriage equality during the Marriage Law Postal Survey increased levels of anxiety, depression and stress in LGBT+ people.[5]

While marriage equality is a reality now in Australia, we are only too aware that when the 'hard right' of politics and conservative religion are given access to the levers of power, the first place they go to is women and queer people. Progressives must maintain a constant vigil lest hard-won rights be swept away by conservative religious and political forces.[6] And as an intellectual exercise, what would we have done, despite the rightness of our cause, had the Australian plebiscite gone the wrong way and forbidden us to marry? How would we have coped had the hard-right conservatives, hard-line religionists and newly-platformed bigots and homophobes won the day? The personal is political and the political is personal.

So then, what do we do when we hear that the future of another beautiful young LGBT+ person is stolen because they have taken their life due to bullying and ostracism at school? How do we contain the confusion and anger when we hear that yet another LGBT+ adult has taken their life, or attempted suicide, or descended into mental illness because of some protected religious conversion programme where false promises are made about becoming straight? This is a point I return to later in the discussion.

The great misnomer

There are major problems with conversion 'therapy', but even before we get into those, I would simply start with the nomenclature itself. You see, it is not 'conversion', and it is not 'therapy'. It is a great misnomer to call it thus. This so-called therapy or ministry originally purported to change a person from gay to straight, and when it was finally figured out that 'conversion' did not actually take place, the goal was adjusted to assisting participants 'to live with same sex attraction' but making survivors deny the agency of that attraction in their lives in perpetuity.

Secondly, it is not therapy. 'Therapy' is a word that is more properly associated with trained clinicians: psychologists; psychiatrists; counsellors. Only after completing years of university training that includes examinations, placements and internships, supervision, 'continuing professional development' and public registration with state-run health bodies, are clinicians best placed to offer therapy to people. Registered clinicians are mandated to follow their professional Code of Ethics.

Conversion therapy proponents in Australia are, with few exceptions, not clinicians. What they offer is not therapy by any standard. Mostly, they are religious folk, some pastors, some working with a dedicated ministry (although these are fewer now) who minister to people beset with confusion or distress due to their same-sex attraction or gender identity. Importantly, the source of that confusion or distress is the teachings of the very churches these susceptible people go to for help. This unfortunate situation sets up massive cognitive dissonance, makes the individuals particularly vulnerable and renders them especially manipulable. It is analogous to a situation of domestic violence where an aggressive partner subsequently hugs the victim, offering comfort and solace after perpetrating violence against them.

Is there a place for government in such situations? I believe so. While I remain a firm believer in the separation of Church and State, I do not believe religions should have unfettered powers over their adherents to the point where people can be harmed. Governments can and should step in. Fortunately, the states in Australia have been looking at this question, often with robust debate, and at the time of writing three of them (the Australian Capital Territory, Victoria and Queensland) have already enacted legislation to ban the practice.[7] Several other jurisdictions, including the states of Tasmania, Western Australia and New South Wales, are now looking to enact similar legislation.

There are three compelling reasons, in my view, why conversion practices should be banned in all jurisdictions. So-called conversion therapy is 'ineffective (it does not work), it is unethical/immoral (it applies outdated pop psychology conflated with religious ideology to convince well but vulnerable people that they are sick) and it is harmful (it causes injury to people psychologically).

Why they do this

Most committed Christians of the evangelical persuasion in 'Bible-believing' churches have a strong belief in 'serving the Lord', to use their language. 'Bible-believing' is a euphemism for churches which take scripture at face value and generally believe that the age of miracles and the supernatural did not end in the first century but still exists today. Serving the Lord amounts to acts of service in his name. Proponents of gay conversion take the teachings around human sexuality as the basis for offering their ministry.

So, what are the fundamental evangelical teachings around human sexuality? Below I enumerate them in précis form:

1. God created humans as male and female only;
2. God's order is that men are attracted only to women and women only to men;
3. Any attraction deviating from this model is therefore not in line with God's natural order;
4. Acting on same-sex attraction is therefore sin and a rejection of God's ways;
5. Sex is only permitted in a marriage between a man and a woman, nowhere else;
6. Same-sex sexual activity is regularly listed alongside such behaviour as fornication, adultery, bestiality, drunkenness and theft;
7. It is to be renounced and repented of, where the supplicant must ask God for forgiveness, and rely on God to stay pure;
8. Purity means the individual must live a life of celibacy or marry someone of the opposite sex.

The above teachings would also all be endorsed by conservative Catholics. For those in the Pentecostal churches, there is often an addendum:

9. Gay people are oppressed (read: possessed) by a demon or demons;

10. These demons must be renounced, and the person must be set free from demonic activity in a ritual exorcism known as deliverance ministry.

Practitioners of gay conversion genuinely believe that what they are doing is bringing freedom to the oppressed in the name of God. They use the above tenets as their non-negotiable foundation in all that they believe and all that they do.

Conversion 'therapy' model of homosexuality

Practitioners of gay conversion 'therapy' believe that homosexuality, historically a medical term, is both a sin and a sickness. They have taught that this 'condition' is reversible. Thus, an ex-gay movement grew where influential thinkers and proponents became famous for leaving the 'homosexual lifestyle', and 'successful' graduates of their programmes became known as ex-gays.

First, the leaders of these ministries see gay sexuality as sinful because they view it as both a choice and a rejection of God's natural order. While science sees sexuality as an emergent quality, typically around the time of puberty, proponents of conversion 'therapy' view it as volitional. The rationale goes like this: If it is an immutable psycho-biologic reality as science observes, then it cannot be changed. There are genetic influences as well as neural circuitry wired into the identity parts of our brain as it develops both before birth and after. However, if it is a choice, like drinking too much or stealing your neighbour's goods, then it *can* be changed. You can choose not to do those things. If homosexuality is in the same order of experience as drunkenness and theft, then it follows, you can choose not to be homosexual. They also rely on a few biblical writings, the sledge-hammer texts, that are contested by biblical scholars and about which I have offered an in-depth analysis in my first book,[8] texts which, they claim, outlaw gay sexuality. Thus, gay sexuality is further confirmed as sin, in their view.

Second, they view it as a sickness. The gay individual is seen as sick and broken. A healthy sexuality is heterosexuality. Conservative religionists have never abandoned the old psychoanalytic views of seeing gay sexuality as a psychopathology, or a red flag for future psychopathology. Thus, it is seen as deviancy, brokenness, failure. There is something deep within the person that is fundamentally dysfunctional and not working. It needs repair. This is the mindset that informed the pseudo-scientific approach of 'reparative therapy' closely identified with its most prominent advocate, American psychologist, Joseph Nicolosi.

What happens

Individual conversion 'therapy', which is what I experienced, and group-based therapy are both premised on the teaching of the conservative church around human sexuality and specific beliefs around homosexuality. It involves prayer counselling, where leaders pray over the individual, wait upon God to give them a word or a scripture verse and use that as the basis for the ministry of that session. God will be asked to intervene in the person's life. Church attendance is a given, as is personal Bible study and personal prayer. Fasting may also be used. Deliverance ministry may be offered where demonic spirits of uncleanness or selfishness are said to be cast out of the person. Prayers of healing will be prayed. In group work, praise and worship singing as well as Bible teaching are part of the platform. There is repentance, forgiveness and entreaties to the Holy Spirit to imbue the person with strength to overcome the evil one, Satan.

However, there are also practical lessons to learn. Gay men are encouraged to go out with women and to date them. They are not to have sex with them, which would be against the biblical injunction, but they are encouraged to go as far as they can without sinning by exploring their desire and their bodies with women. They are also encouraged to eschew so-called effeminate pursuits and to engage with traditionally masculinized endeavours such as cars and engines, football and other sports. Clothing must be masculine, emphasizing darker colours: black, browns, purples, dark blues, dark greens. No yellows, mauves or salmons. In like manner, lesbian women are encouraged to go out with and date men. They are encouraged to eschew rougher pursuits and to engage in traditional stereotyped women's activities such as learning how to apply makeup, cooking, sewing, crafts and keeping house. And of course, they are to dress modestly in more traditionally feminine attire.

Participants are indoctrinated into believing their lives are broken, that their manhood or womanhood is defective and sick, requiring healing. And further, the body is always associated with sin, with 'the flesh', with uncleanness. Desire is not to be given into unless in a heterosexual marriage. You must not give room for desire otherwise. Thoughts, feelings, physical sensations that do not conform to this sole model of sexuality are to be ignored and actively repudiated, without exception.[9]

While some in the ex-gay movement in more recent times accept the existence of gay sexuality, they will quickly say that while the orientation itself may not be a sin, *acting* on it *is* a sin. Therefore, for you to be right with God, you must deny your natural self forever. Never act on it. And if it does manifest, in either thought or deed, you must repent and ask God for forgiveness. Such a twisted view brings about a whole world of pain for the vulnerable conversion participant.

My own experience

For the best part of twenty years, I put myself through an individualized conversion programme where I sought prayer counselling, deliverance from demonic oppression, healing and an empowered ability to walk in God's ways as I was taught them. During 1976, my final year of high school, I left the Catholic Church, the church I was born and thoroughly enculturated into, and joined my Protestant friends as we walked with the Lord according to the typical teachings that you would find in so-called Bible-believing churches.

During this time, I remained doggedly celibate and missed out on the thrill of my twenties as a young gay man. Instead, I threw myself into believing for a miracle, a miracle that would change me into a straight person. I was very naïve at the time and had no understanding of how sexuality works. I had many rituals and many engagements with processes that I deemed spiritual, including the healing of the memories, the healing of my manhood, belief for a wife, attempts at dating girls, the study of scripture, putting on the armour of God, doing spiritual warfare, praying in tongues, having deliverance ministry and prayer counselling, and engaging with visiting high-powered Christian speakers.

As I went about my daily routines, kept secret from the rest of my friends and church folk, I endured heart-aching loneliness as well as a debilitating skin hunger which inevitably led to depression. I longed to be held by a man and to hold him in my arms. I longed to be in love and to feel passion, but such emptiness and depression eventually brought about suicidality, and at twenty years of age, I had a suicide attempt, brought on by the yawning chasm between my religious identity and my sexual identity.

I was slowly being torn in two. My sexuality and emotional life were twisted into a contorted grotesquerie of what they were supposed to be in a fit and healthy youth; and still I practised my daily rituals and held fast to my faith that God would act and change me. The godlier I acted, the more mentally ill I became. The people from whom I sought help all believed the same stuff I did. There was no one there to put me right; trapped within that paradigm, there was no way out.

In the end, I did not have a breakdown, I had a breakthrough. In my early thirties, I found myself on top of a local hill. I was in despair and broke down, but the despair did not last long. In its place, a great rage came up within me. For the first time in over a decade, I was true to myself. I was angry at God and let him know it, full-throated and muscular. I knew that I could not go on the way I was. I knew that I would probably wind up ending my life should my life not change.

In that moment, I had an epiphany where I finally understood that the teachings on human sexuality and homosexuality were 'all bullshit'. I allowed myself the freedom to turn the air authentically blue. If God was not going to change me, then I would have to change things myself. In that moment, I made the decision to go to therapy. And it was in therapy where I learned that I needed to accept myself and jettison the religious judgement I had absorbed over all those years that I was an abomination, a sinner, a rejector of God, and that I was seriously broken. In therapy, I had to find a way to feel comfortable about being a gay man. A huge journey, but ultimately a liberating and life-changing one.

The psychologist reflects – cognitive dissonance

It is at this point that I want to speak from my professional capacity and offer some insights that my decades-long psychological practice has given me. I ended the last section by briefly touching on the deterioration of my mental health that ultimately led me to a breakthrough and a decision to go to therapy. This was brought about by a serious tension that developed between my religious identity and my gay identity.

It was a researcher called Leon Festinger who, in 1957, first talked about cognitive dissonance.[10] This was the concept that suggested a state of psychological and sometimes physical tension is created when holding two competing ideas in the mind at the same time. I want to go for a swim because I feel hot, but I want to go and have coffee with my friend who has just arrived and invited me. Competing cognitions. Competing emotions attached to them. Tension is created. Festinger suggested that the amount of tension created is proportional to the importance you place on each of the incompatible thoughts: not much importance, just a little tension, extremely important, a great deal of tension. We might even call this latter form, distress.

I was typical of many Christian gay people who had accepted intellectually the legitimacy of the traditional Christian teachings about gay sexuality. Inside, however, a war was waging. I was a very committed

Christian, but I had same-sex attraction. And this meant that to remain faithful, there could be absolutely no gay stuff. And not just for a time. But for life. I was either to marry a woman or remain celibate till death.

Opposing this was my burgeoning sexuality. I was in my twenties. I was young and fit. I had the sex appeal of youth. I was horny. I wanted physical touch. And I was lonely. And these feelings would not go away. So, due to my Christian beliefs, I suppressed them. But the more I suppressed them, the stronger they got. I was drowning in cognitive dissonance.

The level of importance I had placed upon the mutually exclusive cognitions was significant. My gay identity was relentless in its insistence to be manifested and reified. Well, of course it was. Desire and erotic neural pathways are wired into our brains and strengthened with repeated firing. The thalamus, hypothalamus, occipital cortex and nucleus accumbens have all been shown to be activated in males in sexual arousal, while working in conjunction with increased activity in the insula, amygdala and anterior cingulate gyrus for general arousal.[11] And we know that our own identity – the memories and reflections of who we are, formed from middle childhood onwards – is located significantly in the medial pre-frontal cortex (mPFC) located in the inside walls of the PFC in both hemispheres as they fork the central fissure between left and right sides of the brain.[12] Our sense of identity as a gay person or a straight person, of how I navigate the world of desire and the erotic, is a complex wiring of circuitry in this region. Trying to suppress or deny that identity is a fruitless and harmful exercise.

On the other hand, I was steeped in both traditional Christian and Pentecostal theology such that my religious identity, too, had been laid down and entrenched in my brain over decades of repeated use, again in an area where self-representation, emotional associations and goal-driven behaviour are significantly located, the ventral pre-frontal cortex (vPFC).[13] I felt that to let go of that whole religious *modus vivendi* was effectively to abandon God, to deny him. In hindsight, if I was possessed by anything, it was not a gay demon but my indoctrination which, at war with my ineradicable sexual orientation, was slowly suffocating the life out of me.

Of course, such deeply felt cognitive dissonance, which persisted for more than a decade, took its toll on my mental health. I had a diagnosable depression. My symptoms included depressed mood, blunted affect, lethargy, initial insomnia, the cognitive symptoms of lack of concentration, fuzzy thinking and some recall impairment. Further, there were feelings of helplessness, hopelessness and worthlessness. Suicidal ideation visited me twice, once, at twenty years of age, resulting in an attempt. Ultimately, I retreated into social isolation and withdrawal, as is common in Major Depressive Disorder. I somehow managed to avoid substance abuse, but many others in my situation did not.

Cognitive dissonance and depression are the inevitable outcomes of the clash of these two worlds. There is no escaping their life-negating clutches when two mutually exclusive worldviews are entrenched neurally, emotionally, cognitively and behaviourally. It is brutal. And it must be obvious to the reader by now why so many people take their lives, attempt to suicide, or harm themselves.

The answer of conservative religion to this turmoil is conversion. However, if conversion 'therapy' is as I say it is, ineffective, unethical and harmful, it would be useful to understand the mechanism of that harm. I therefore want to devote the remainder of this chapter to explaining that harm based on a model – Schema Therapy – that I have taken from a modality I use in my consulting rooms.

The psychologist reflects – Schema Therapy

Schema Therapy was developed by Jeffrey Young and colleagues after understanding that classic Cognitive-Behaviour Therapy could not always offer healing at a deeper level, that something more was needed. In their seminal text, *Schema Therapy: A Practitioner's Guide* (2003), Young, J. S. Klosko and M. E. Weishaar state that schema therapy 'significantly expands on traditional cognitive-behavioural treatments and concepts. The therapy blends elements from cognitive-behavioural, attachment, Gestalt, object relations, constructivist and psychoanalytic schools into a rich, unifying, conceptual and treatment model'.[14]

Young proposed that for children and youth to grow into psychologically healthy adults, certain conditions must be present during the formative years. He postulated the following five needs that he views as universal:

1. 'Secure attachments to others (includes safety, stability, nurturance, and acceptance);
2. Autonomy, competence, and sense of identity;
3. Freedom to express valid needs and emotions;
4. Spontaneity and play;
5. Realistic limits and self-control.'[15]

When these needs are not met or are violated, *early maladaptive schemas*, or schemas for short, are set up and become neurally entrenched with repeated use. These schemas, dysfunctional filters if you will, comprising thoughts, emotions, physical sensations and memories, are then activated in adult life by triggering events that have the power to make us feel as we did as children when the schemas were first activated.

Through research, Young and colleagues identified eighteen early maladaptive schemas across five broad domains:

Domain 1 Disconnection and Rejection
Domain 2 Impaired Autonomy and Performance
Domain 3 Impaired Limits
Domain 4 Other-Directedness
Domain 5 Over-Vigilance and Inhibition[16]

Space forbids an explication of each of the eighteen schemas, but given that they are essentially unmet childhood needs, they are typically experienced in adult life as unpleasant and creating physical and psychic tension. Over the years, Young and others have moved the model along to capture 'right now', 'in the moment' behaviour that is unconscious and automatic. He called these behaviours, *modes*.

Mode work

E. Roediger, B. A. Stevens and R. Brockman state that the model Schema Therapy uses, sees us acting from different modes of behaviour and feeling, either when a schema is activated or to prevent a schema from being activated.[17] They discuss three types of modes:

1. child modes
2. parent/critic modes
3. coping modes

– all of which become activated as adults by the same triggers that would activate schemas.

Child modes

Common child modes, although there are many more than the three I list here, include:

- *vulnerable child* where fear, confusion, loneliness and anxiety reign
- *angry child* where unmet needs are expressed through anger, sometimes rage
- *impulsive child* where impulse control is negligible, and people live in a moment-to-moment existence that can be seen as selfish

The child modes can be activated across any of the above schemas but are especially active in the Domain 1 schemas. Those schemas tend to have their origin in early childhood, say over the first ten years of life. They are particularly debilitating and distressing, tend to be the most presented, and are typically seen in diagnosable personality disorders.[18]

There is also a *healthy child mode* where the five childhood needs as elucidated above are for the most part met.

Parent/critic modes

The two most common parent/critic modes are:

1. *punitive parent/critic* where the authority figure is cruel and
   insensitive, critical and harsh
2. *demanding parent/critic* where the authority figure is never satisfied,
   always wanting more.

Both are extremely unpleasant to experience and often engender fear.
Again, most of the schemas above can activate a parent/critic mode.

There is also a *healthy adult mode* where the adult figure is kind,
compassionate, sensible, wise, caring, thoughtful and emotionally
mature.

Coping modes

Coping modes manifest as three different types:

1. Surrender Coping Modes: where the *compliant surrenderer*
   acquiesces to the schema and goes along with it.
2. Avoidant Coping Modes: where the *detached protector* emotionally
   detaches from the pain of the schema; where the *detached self-
   soother* retreats into addictive behaviours like alcohol, drugs or
   work, gambling, sex, pornography, video games; where the *angry
   protector* uses anger to defend against pain or anxiety designed to
   keep people at a distance.
3. Overcompensation Coping Modes: the *self-aggrandizer* where the
   person behaves in an entitled, competitive or abusive way; the
   overcontrolling where the individual tries to allay anxiety by
   exercising control over what they can; *bully and attack* where the
   person seeks to harm others; *predator* where the individual seeks to
   eliminate a threat or rival.

The schema model and psychopathology

Many researchers over the years have investigated the nature of the
relationship between Young's schemas and levels of psychopathology.

People with psychopathologies such as personality disorders, eating disorders, alcohol and drug abuse, anxiety, and depression have all been found to report higher scores on the Young Schema Questionnaire (YSQ), designed to identify schemas, compared to healthy controls.[19] Furthermore, other studies have found a relationship between higher levels of schemas and past episodes of Major Depressive Disorder.[20] And also eating disorders.[21] 'These findings are in line with assumptions within cognitive theory on the dimensionality of the schema concept, on the positive association of maladaptive schemas and psychopathology, and on maladaptive schemas as a vulnerability factor for the development of psychological symptoms.'[22] The authors note importantly that:

> Depression was uniquely associated with schemas referring to incompetence (Failure to Achieve, Defectiveness/Shame, Dependence/Incompetence) and deprivation (Emotional Deprivation). Depressed adolescents perceive themselves as defective, inferior and inadequate in important aspects relative to peers, as unlovable and as unable to handle everyday responsibilities. Further, they have the expectation that their need for emotional support will not be adequately met by significant others.[23]

The schema model and conversion

Early maladaptive schemas typically become activated in childhood. However, the teen years, with the advent of high school and its concomitant challenges, can also be a source of schema activation. Deficiencies in the 'nuclear' family, typically in parenting, occasioning the violation of all or some of the five core emotional childhood needs, frequently lead to schemas like *Abandonment* and *Emotional Deprivation*. Traumatization typically leads to schemas such as *Mistrust/Abuse, Defectiveness/Shame* and *Vulnerability to Harm*.

In schema mode work, we know that the parent/critic figure does not necessarily have to be a parent. It can be an older sibling, a school bully, a teacher, a family member, a member of the conservative wing of the Christian Church. People who are 'churched' from childhood, that is, indoctrinated into the teachings and culture of the Christian Church, both universal and local, have already been told they are children of God, namely, a child role in the relationship to God and the Church. In strict churches of any denomination, there will be dogmatic teachings about God, humanity, sin, salvation, the end times and sex.

When we add to the mix strict fundamentalist teachings about gay sexuality and gender, as I described above, we have all the makings of a child indoctrinated into a human and cosmic worldview that sees them as inadequate and broken and outside the gates of God's camp. This young post-pubescent, churched LGBT+ person buys into a model that objectively sees the pastor, priest or elders as the authority/parent figure, the person themselves as the child figure, and where the treatment of them and message to them are abusive. Let me elucidate by way of example. Our young person we will call Tom.

Tom is a young man of seventeen years of age. He is a Christian and has been going to church all his life. He now goes to his youth group every Friday night with other older teens in a local Bible-believing church that holds with modern day miracles and belief in the supernatural in the everyday lives of its parishioners. Tom has known he is gay since about the age of thirteen. The ensuing years have confirmed it for him. He has a clear and assertive same-sex attraction that has become the dominant drive in his life.

Being in church forbids his having a boyfriend, holding hands or kissing another boy, let alone being sexually active with another boy. During high school, he was bullied from time to time for being different. The bullies called him 'gay' as a pejorative and a 'faggot'. Tom did everything he could to advertise his 'straightness' including going out with girls, which he found distressing and empty. School has already given him the message that he is not good enough, and that for him to be acceptable, he realizes he must live a life of striving to be someone he is not.

When he came out to his Christian parents, they showed great concern but scared him with stories of future failure and life-long challenge. They talked about how it was not God's way and that if he wanted help, they would send him to a ministry that assisted with this kind of thing. They added that they would really like him to go. Tom agrees. Powerful psychological, social and relational forces are already operating on Tom. At this point, he is hardly a free moral agent.

Tom has heard traditional teaching on sex and sexuality in church and youth group ever since he can remember. The ministry people are very nice, but it does not take long until he starts to hear that he is broken, there is something inside him that is wrong, that he has a failed relationship with his father, maybe too close a bond with his mother, that he must not give in to occasions of sin, either in thought or in deed, and that his same-sex attraction is against the natural order that God has designed. Almost turning eighteen, Tom is a young gay man now being torn in two. He is strongly attracted to one of the other boys in the programme but knows he cannot and should not do anything about it. His eternal soul may depend on it. He is drowning in cognitive dissonance and maladaptive schemas have been activated.

The dominant schema associated with conversion is the Domain 1 schema *Defectiveness/Shame*. Young describes *Defectiveness/Shame* this way:

> The feeling that one is defective, bad, unwanted, inferior, or invalid in important respects, or that one would be unlovable to significant others if exposed. May involve insecurity around others; or a sense of shame regarding one's perceived flaws. These flaws may be private (e.g. selfishness, angry impulses, unacceptable sexual desires) or public (e.g. undesirable physical appearance, social awkwardness).[24]

The whole point of conversion practices is to tell Tom that his life is not good enough, to augment the message of the school-yard bullies, that as he is now, he is insufficient and inadequate. He is broken, he needs fixing, he must change, he must reject his gay identity and suppress it. When you are a young person and being told that you are defective, enormous harm is done to the psyche. Shame is activated, a debilitating state that wears away self-worth like water on a stone.

Acting in the present moment hearing these things, the *Vulnerable Child* mode is automatically activated, where Tom is to listen to the parent figures in this ministry and do what they say. They are wise and godly, and they know much better than him. *Vulnerable Child* is characterized by sadness, grief, pain, confusion, powerlessness, and acquiescence.

The *Parent/Critic* mode that Tom introjects is both the *Punitive Parent* and the *Demanding Parent*. The *Punitive Parent* offers punishment to Tom when he inevitably does not meet programme expectations. He calls himself names: sinner; dirty; filthy; selfish; immoral. Maybe there is public confession of sins before forgiveness is offered. Further shaming. Like his parents, there appears here to be only conditional love. Do and be as we say, otherwise there are very unpleasant relational consequences. Another punishment, the threat of separation from God is readily proffered as Tom's sexuality is framed as aberrant, deviant, sick and sinful.

The *Demanding Parent* mode sees the authority figures as demanding more and more of Tom. It is never enough. Not having sex with another boy is not enough. He also must not think of the other boy in this way. After all, he is reminded: 'And if your right hand is causing you to sin, cut it off and throw it away from you; for it is better for you to lose one of the parts of your body, than for your whole body to go into hell.'[25] He must read his Bible and pray every day. However, Tom's sexuality is not a *behaviour* as the conversion programme leaders would have him believe. No, it is an integral part of his *identity*, and he is being coerced to suppress it every day and for the rest of his life.

The Coping Mode for *Defectiveness/Shame* might be *surrender* strategies, and probably will be while Tom continues to buy into the conversion model, in that *Compliant Surrender* mode will be his daily way of life; surrendering to the defectiveness message and accepting it as truth, behaving in the way they want him to. But there may also be some *avoidance* strategies in that *Detached Protector* mode that may be the only way Tom can cope with the defectiveness message; being detached from life and emotions and other people, withdrawn into himself. Then there is the *Detached Self-Soothing* mode, where Tom may eventually turn to maladaptive coping strategies like alcohol, drugs, gambling, spending money, risky behaviour, anything to anaesthetize himself against the oppressive message that he is broken and defective on the inside, which he interprets as being a worthless human being.

It is also possible that an *overcompensation* strategy might be activated. The only one I can see germane to *Defectiveness/Shame* is *Overcontroller* mode where Tom tries through strict routine to control his world to keep at bay the shocking 'truth' of him being defective. *Overcontroller* mode is what I used in my own attempts to turn straight via spiritual processes. The *Defectiveness/Shame* schema in this context is a gateway for major depression that routinely includes suicidal ideation among its symptoms and utterly destroys any sense of self-worth and sense of personal value.

However, *Defectiveness/Shame* is not the only schema involved in conversion therapy. *Subjugation* is also a powerful schema that is activated in these ministries. This is where I am forced or pressured to conform to the other's wishes, leaving me feeling helpless and powerless. Young describes it as a submission to avoid anger, retaliation or abandonment, and suggests there can be both a *subjugation of needs* (one's preferences, decisions and desires) and a *subjugation of emotions* (one's emotions, especially anger).[26] No one could possibly argue that young people or indeed even older adults have free agency inside these ministries. The coercion is transparent and overwhelming.

I believe at least twelve of the eighteen identified schemas may be activated in young people in conversion ministries where you have (a) a harmful and abusive message, (b) delivered by a divinely anointed authority figure, (c) to a vulnerable and idealistic person. A perfect storm.

Final words

Like all participants before him, when Tom finishes the conversion programme, he will either have bought into the model, leading to a temporary state of self-belief that he can live as a straight man, only to be disheartened when his sexuality inevitably reasserts itself, and where he then finds himself drowning in guilt, shame and sin-consciousness. This was me. It will see Tom a seriously damaged young man who, to remove the cognitive dissonance, will have to take a long journey of real therapy, healing and self-discovery, a journey hopefully he will survive. Alternately, he will leave the programme repudiating the model and knowing that he cannot live as a straight man. He will either abandon his faith, or if he wants to retain it, he will be forced to re-visit the interface between his sexuality and that faith. One way or another, he will have to reduce the extent of cognitive dissonance. This is the life of the gay Christian.

Since the publication of *Being Gay, Being Christian*, I have seen countless hundreds of LGBT+ people in my consulting rooms, some gay Christians, others just gay or transgender people who might also feel the need to bring up spiritual matters as they pertain to their personal journey, and many others of the LGBT+ community, just happy to talk to someone whom they feel will understand them. As part of what I do with all my clients, I regularly use Schema Therapy as a way to assist those with deeper needs. Should someone present with schemas of *Defectiveness/Shame* and/or *Subjugation*, I would do everything in my power to reduce and diminish those schemas, reassuring the person that they are not broken and not remotely defective, and to work to empower them to live their own life journey in confidence and self-worth. This would be done compassionately and at a pace the individual could manage.

Conversion 'therapy' does the exact reverse of what I do. Not only does it not work in turning gay people straight, not only is it unethical to hold out such promise to LGBT+ people, but its practices harm people by destroying the self, the sense of personal power, freedom of agency and self-worth. The immersion of a person into a complex religious worldview that is somehow transgressed by the individual's very identity, is incredibly injurious. Rather than removing early maladaptive schemas, that action actively induces and perpetuates them. This is not therapy. This is anti-therapy. Offering vulnerable people such mendacity and harming them in the name of God is obscene. It has no place in modern society.

Notes

1   S. J. Edser, *Being Gay, Being Christian* (Wollombi: Exisle Publishing, 2012).

2   Gen. 19. 1-29, Lev. 18. 22-24, Lev. 20. 13, Rom. 1. 18-32, 1 Cor. 6. 9-10, 1 Tim 1. 10.

3   See P. Catt and S. Edser, 'Christian Australia is Ready for Marriage Equality,' *Sydney Morning Herald*, 16 August 2015, www.smh.com.au/opinion/ christian-australia-is-ready-for-marriage-equality-20150816-gj0dcf.html (accessed 11 April 2023).

4   This was covered by the media: M. Koziol, '"Vote No to Fags": Outbreak of Homophobic Violence, Vandalism in Same-Sex Marriage Campaign,' *Sydney Morning Herald*, 25 September 2017, https://www.smh.com.au/politics/ federal/vote-no-to-fags-outbreak-of-homophobic-violence-vandalism-in-samesex-marriage-campaign-20170925-gyo9ri.html (accessed 11 April 2023); C. Tilley and N. Hoad, '"A respectful debate": The Same-Sex Marriage Debate has been Marred by Hate Speech, Vandalism and Bullying. Keep Track of the Incivilities,' *ABC News*, 26 October 2017, https://www.abc.net. au/news/2017-10-11/ssm-same-sex-marriage-respectful-debate-ugly-side/8996500 (accessed 11 April 2023). It has also been covered in scholarly journals: O. Mazel, 'Violence in the Name of Equality: The Postal Survey on Same-Sex Marriage, LGBTQIA+ Activism and Legal Redemption,' *Australian Feminist Law Journal*, 48, no.1 (2022): 137–63.

5   S. Verrelli, F. White, L. Harvey and M. Pulciani, 'Minority Stress, Social Support, and the Mental Health of Lesbian, Gay, and Bisexual Australians during the Australian Marriage Law Postal Survey,' *Australian Psychologist*, 54, no. 4 (2019): 336–46.

6   On this point, see D. Betts and J. Bennett, 'Resurgent Prejudice: Responses to Marriage Equality in Australia,' *Australian Journal of Social Issues*, 58, no. 4 (2023): 732–46 http://doi.org/10.1002/ajs4.279

7   J. Power, T. W. Jones, T. Jones, N. Despott, M. Pallotta-Chiarolli and J. Anderson, 'Better Understanding of the Scope and Nature of LGBTQA+

Religious Conversion Practices Will Support Recovery,' *Medical Journal of Australia*, 217, no. 3 (2022): 119–22.

8   S. Edser, *Being Gay, Being Christian*, 123–56.

9   T. Erzen, *Straight to Jesus* (Berkeley: University of California Press, 2006).

10 L. Festinger, *A Theory of Cognitive Dissonance* (Stanford: Stanford University Press, 1957).

11 S. Kagerer, T. Klucken, S. Wehrum, M. Zimmermann, A. Schienle, B. Walter, D. Vaitl and R. Stark, 'Neural Activation Toward Erotic Stimuli in Homosexual and Heterosexual Males,' *Journal of Sexual Medicine*, 8, no. 11 (2011): 3132–43.

12 A. D'Argembeau, H. Cassol, C. Phillips, E. Balteau, E. Salmon and M. Van der Linden, 'Brains Creating Stories of Selves: The Neural Basis of Autobiographical Reasoning,' *Social Cognitive and Affective Neuroscience*, 9, no. 5 M. (2014): 646–52.

13 S. Harris, J. T. Kaplan, A. Curiel, S. Y. Bookheimer, M. Iacoboni and M. S. Cohen, 'The Neural Correlates of Religious and Nonreligious Belief,' *PLoS one* 4, no.10 (2009): e7272.

14 J. E. Young, J. S. Klosko and M. E. Weishaar, *Schema Therapy: A Practitioner's Guide* (New York: The Guilford Press, 2003).

15 Young, et al., *Schema Therapy*, 10.

16 Young, et al., *Schema Therapy*, 13–21.

17 E. Roediger, B. A. Stevens and R. Brockman, *Contextual Schema Therapy: An Integrative Approach to Personality Disorders, Emotional Dysregulation, and Interpersonal Functioning* (Oakland CA: Context Press, 2018).

18 A. Arntz and H. van Genderen, *Schema Therapy for Borderline Personality Disorder*, 2nd ed. (Chichester, West Sussex: John Wiley & Sons Ltd, 2021), 13–15.

19 L. V. Vlierberghe, C. Braet, G. Bosmans, Y. Rosseel and S. Bögels, 'Maladaptive Schemas and Psychopathology in Adolescence: On the Utility of Young's Schema Theory in Youth,' *Cognitive Therapy and Research* 34 (2010): 316–32.

20 J. R. Z. Abela, R. P. Auerbach, S. Sarin and Z. Lakdawalla, 'Beck's Cognitive Theory of Depression: An Examination of the Schematic Content in the Life Stories of University Students,' *Cognitive Therapy and Research* 33 (2009): 50–8.

21 S. Sarin and J. R. Z. Abela, 'The Relationship between Core Beliefs and a History of Eating Disorders: An Examination of the Life Stories of University Students,' *Journal of Cognitive Psychotherapy* 17 (2003): 359–74.

22 Vlierberghe, et al., 'Maladaptive Schemas,' 317.

23 Vlierberghe, et al., 'Maladaptive Schemas,' 328.

24 Young, et al., *Schema Therapy*, 14.

25 Matthew 5. 30 New American Standard Bible.

26 Young, et al., *Schema Therapy*, 16.

Bibliography

Abela, J. R. Z., R. P. Auerbach, S. Sarin and Z. Lakdawalla. 'Beck's Cognitive Theory of Depression: An Examination of the Schematic Content in the Life Stories of University Students.' *Cognitive Therapy and Research* 33 (2009): 50–8.

Arntz, A. and H. van Genderen. *Schema Therapy for Borderline Personality Disorder*, 2nd ed. Chichester, West Sussex: John Wiley & Sons Ltd (2021): 13–15.

Betts, D. and J. Bennett, 'Resurgent Prejudice: Responses to Marriage Equality in Australia.' *Journal of Australian Social Issues* 58, no. 4 (2023): 732–46. http://doi.org/10.1002/ajs4.279

Catt, P. and S. Edser. 'Christian Australia is Ready for Marriage Equality.' *Sydney Morning Herald*, 16 August 2015, https://www.smh.com.au/opinion/christian-australia-is-ready-for-marriage-equality-20150816-gj0dcf.html

D'Argembeau A., H. Cassol, C. Phillips, E. Balteau, E. Salmon and M. Van der Linden. 'Brains Creating Stories of Selves: The Neural Basis of Autobiographical Reasoning.' *Social Cognitive and Affective Neuroscience*. 9 no. 5 (2014): 646–52.

Edser, S. J. *Being Gay, Being Christian*. Wollombi: Exisle Publishing, 2012.

Erzen, T. *Straight to Jesus*. Berkeley: University of California Press, 2006.

Festinger, L. *A Theory of Cognitive Dissonance*. Stanford: Stanford University Press, 1957.

Harris S., J. T. Kaplan, A. Curiel, S. Y. Bookheimer, M. Iacoboni and M. S. Cohen. 'The Neural Correlates of Religious and Nonreligious Belief.' *PLoS one* 4, no.10 (2009): e7272.

Kagerer S., T. Klucken, S. Wehrum, M. Zimmermann, A. Schienle, B. Walter, D. Vaitl and R. Stark. 'Neural Activation toward Erotic Stimuli in Homosexual and Heterosexual Males.' *Journal of Sexual Medicine* 8, no. 11 (2011): 3132–43.

Koziol, M., '"Vote no to Fags": Outbreak of Homophobic Violence, Vandalism in Same-Sex Marriage Campaign.' *Sydney Morning Herald*, 25 September 2017. https://www.smh.com.au/politics/federal/vote-no-to-fags-outbreak-of-homophobic-violence-vandalism-in-samesex-marriage-campaign-20170925-gyo9ri.html.

Mazel, O. 'Violence in the Name of Equality: The Postal Survey on Same-Sex Marriage, LGBTQIA+ Activism and Legal Redemption.' *Australian Feminist Law Journal*, 48, no.1 (2022): 137–63.

New American Standard Bible®, Copyright © 1960, 1971, 1977, 1995, 2020 by The Lockman Foundation.

Power, J., T. W. Jones, T. Jones, N. Despott, M. Pallotta-Chiarolli and J. Anderson. 'Better Understanding of the Scope and Nature of LGBTQA+ Religious Conversion Practices will Support Recovery.' *Medical Journal of Australia* 217, no. 3 (2022): 119–22.

Roediger, E., B. A. Stevens and R. Brockman. *Contextual Schema Therapy: An Integrative Approach to Personality Disorders, Emotional Dysregulation, and Interpersonal Functioning.* Oakland CA: Context Press, 2018.

Sarin, S. and J. R. Z. Abela. 'The Relationship between Core Beliefs and a History of Eating Disorders: An Examination of the Life Stories of University Students.' *Journal of Cognitive Psychotherapy* 17 (2003): 359–74.

Tilley, C. and N. Hoad. '"A Respectful Debate": The Same-sex Marriage Debate has been Marred by Hate Speech, Vandalism and Bullying. Keep Track of the Incivilities.' *ABC News*, 26 October 2017, https://www.abc.net.au/news/2017-10-11/ssm-same-sex-marriage-respectful-debate-ugly-side/8996500.

Verrelli, S., F. White, L. Harvey and M. Pulciani. 'Minority Stress, Social Support, and the Mental Health of Lesbian, Gay, and Bisexual Australians during the Australian Marriage Law Postal Survey.' *Australian Psychologist*, 54, no. 4 (2019): 336–46.

Vlierberghe, L. V., C. Braet, G. Bosmans, Y. Rosseel and S. Bögels. 'Maladaptive Schemas and Psychopathology in Adolescence: On the Utility of Young's Schema Theory in Youth.' *Cognitive Therapy and Research* 34 (2010): 316–32.

Young, J. E., J. S. Klosko and M. E. Weishaar. *Schema Therapy: A Practitioner's Guide.* New York: The Guilford Press, 2003.

Part Two

Stories of Repentance and Defiance in Documentaries and Biopics

3

'I Remember Feeling Like I was Sitting on the Wrong Side of the Circle': Documentary Film and the Exposition of Conversion Practices

James E. Bennett

A politics of injury and pain must formulate an address to the audience that emphasizes the relationship between pain and systems of power.[1]

In the opening sequences of *For They Know Not What They Do* (hereafter *For They Know Not*) (2019), the viewer is presented with an arresting montage portraying a collision between the religious and secular worlds. All the images selected, ranging from traditional church sacraments to a wedding ring, are designed to highlight the social, political, legal and religious battleground symbolized by the United States Supreme Court's landmark decision to legalize same-sex marriage in 2015. The segment ends with a pointed comment from key talking head, Reverend Dr Mel White of Soulforce, an organization dedicated to ending religious oppression of LGBT+ people.[2] White, an openly gay Christian minister who trained in the evangelical tradition, situates the opponents of LGBT+ equality as 'part of a great tradition of Christian history' that has placed it at the rear-guard of acceptance.[3] In his closing commentary towards the end of the documentary, White loops back to this umbrella statement about the traditional stance of Christian churches on these issues when he declares: 'my enemies are confused about homosexuality and gender identity'. Drawing on a vital Christian tradition, he references the moment when Christ looks down on his persecutors and utters the words: 'Father forgive them, for they know not what they do.'

Promoted as a documentary that explores the intersection of religion, sexual orientation and gender identity in America, *For They Know Not* does not address conversion practices per se, although it does feature prominently in one family story, ending tragically for Ryan Robertson, son of evangelical parents, Rob and Linda.[4] Rather, this is a production that considers the manifestation of conversion practices in a broader intersectional context that addresses the overlapping concerns of religion, race, gender identity and sexual orientation. Such an approach envisions conversion as one part of an underlying and interconnected ideology that links it to other phenomena in the socio-historical world, including attacks on marriage equality, battles over religious 'freedom', religiously inspired bigotry, and hate crime. Together with *Pray Away* (2021), a widely viewed Netflix production that

Figure 3.1 Ryan Robertson praying with his father Rob in *For They Know Not What They Do*.

approaches its subject through a narrower lens focused on the relationship between the ex-gay movement and conversion practices, as agents of social change these documentaries offer 'a particularly fruitful site for the exploration of filmic narrativization of … pain'. But more than this, they both gesture towards the possibility of a transformed future.[5]

This chapter explores the pain and trauma of conversion experiences through the lens of documentary practice. All four titles selected are examples of what documentary theorist Bill Nichols identifies as the expository mode; that is, an argument based on evidence presented by individual witnesses, usually referred to as talking heads, accompanied by supporting archival images from the socio-historical world.[6] Whether fiction or non-fiction, all film is a cultural artefact of the period in which it is made.[7] And while religiously mediated attempts to change or suppress same-sex attraction have been practised for over half a century, most documentaries shining a light on the phenomenon have been produced in the twenty-first century. To narrow the field further, a series of key developments in the 2010s and their significant implications – including the closure of Exodus International in 2013, the wide dissemination of powerful survivor testimony highlighting the trauma and serious harms of these practices as well as sustained media reporting – are embodied in the most recently-made documentaries on the subject. Moreover, the 2010s saw arguably the most profound shift ever in LGBT+ progress with the enactment of marriage equality legislation in an ever-growing number of jurisdictions around the world. Concurrently, this decade witnessed a fracturing of the liberal consensus and rise of populist right-wing governments in the United States and other domains (including Australia) where campaigns for LGBT+ rights were in sharp discord with the remonstrations of religious conservatives who reacted stridently to secular change. This political volatility is captured in both *Pray Away* and *For They Know Not*.

Less than a decade earlier in 2011–12, trans people and gender diversity barely registered in mainstream consciousness and few popular accounts had emerged of gay people's experiences in conversion programmes. The chapter therefore extends the temporal and spatial analysis to include two documentaries made in that period, one American, the other Australian. The American production, *This is What Love in Action Looks Like* (hereafter *Love in Action*) (2011), addresses the story of sixteen-year-old Zach Stark, a youth based in Tennessee who was forced by his parents to attend a Love in Action (LIA) conversion camp as a response to his coming out. The intense media scrutiny of the case brought the issues involved to national attention.[8] *The Cure* (2012) on the other hand provides us with the only documentary production on conversion practices in Australian society. Among others, this title explores the personal testimony of former evangelical preacher and conversion survivor, Anthony Venn-Brown, whose narrative is presented more fully in Chapter 1 of this book.

Religious belief and biblical interpretation

The documentarians who produced *Pray Away* and *For They Know Not* draw the viewer's attention to the religious beliefs behind most conversion experiences, not only through testimony from expert witnesses but also by means of various sequences highlighting the iconography of evangelical congregations, symbolized by outstretched arms. This vision is most prominently displayed in *Pray Away* through a focus on Jeffrey McCall who preaches his 'Trans 2 Christ' testimony to anyone willing to listen. He is re-introduced to the audience towards the film's conclusion as representative of the new leadership that has taken the movement away from the bricks and mortar of established ministries to the streets, however the techniques – highlighting emotion and bodily 'agitation' – remain broadly familiar: the use of charismatic speakers; a resort to repetitive use of buzz words and phrases such as 'freedom' and a cult-like response from followers.[9] The close relationship between evangelical thinking and conversion practice established in these films is largely validated by experience in the socio-historical world. This is not to say that the largest mainstream Christian organization, the Catholic Church and its adherents, by any means have an irreproachable record in this area, but it does hold true that Catholic theology is focused more on not *acting* on feelings deemed to be sinful rather than change.[10]

The author of Chapter 2 of this book, Stuart Edser, a gay Christian and clinician, writes elsewhere on a critical distinction between two fundamentally opposing knowledge systems: a classical world view emphasizing truth, immutability and universal concepts grounded in scriptural literalism on the one hand, and a post-Enlightenment modern world view underpinned by science and reason on the other. Importantly, the latter system, which prevails in our time, is based on the contingent nature of scientific knowledge, including an evolving understanding of human sexuality in all its complexity.[11] Edser further notes that selected passages of the Old Testament and New Testament have been used as a 'sledgehammer' by literalists against gay people, as McCall illuminates in *Pray Away* with the following assertion: 'When you know the truth, the truth sets you free. These people [LGBT+] will not inherit the Kingdom of God.'[12] This point aligns with the argument made by the Reverend Dr Delman Coates, a Bible scholar and Senior Minister based at Mt Ennon Baptist Church in Maryland, who appears as a talking head in *For They Know Not*. Coates asserts that most Christians are not trying to be homophobic, rather they are striving to be faithful to scripture. As he explains, there lies the rub; the biblical passages traditionally used to condemn homosexuality are, in truth, condemnations of sexual violence, rape and exploitation in the ancient world.[13] This discussion supports a key underlying message that the filmmaker is aiming to convey to his audience; namely, that 'misunderstanding and mistranslation of the Bible' is a foundational source of conflict in religious reception of non-normative sexuality and gender identity.[14] Indeed, this awareness raising sits in stark contrast with outpourings of hateful invective informed by fundamentalist Bible teaching, examples of which are interspersed throughout the documentary. The point takes on added significance in the light of evangelical faith in biblical infallibility and its status as 'the sole authority for theological doctrines'.[15]

Ex-gay ministries, conversion programmes and personal testimony

Following the opening sequence featuring Jeffrey McCall, the viewer of *Pray Away* is introduced to an assemblage of talking heads – Michael Bussee, Randy Thomas, Yvette Cantu Schneider and John Paulk – all former leading lights in the ex-gay movement who subsequently renounced their belief in conversion ideology and practice. The point of departure in tracing the evolution of their thinking from early gay lives to repudiation of ex-gay belief systems is why conversion appealed to them as an apparent solution to their 'unwanted sexuality'. The camera alternates between the speakers as we learn that their thinking aligned with the logic of scriptural literalism (and fringe psychoanalysis), namely, being gay was wrong, something must have happened to cause that, and if you did not want to be gay there was a pathway to salvation – or *change* in the mindset of reorientation therapists.

Michael Bussee's personal narrative intersects closely with the birth and rise of the ex-gay movement in the early 1970s. As a young man at the time deeply troubled by his feelings of same-sex attraction, Bussee desperately sought change, becoming a 'fervent Christian' in 1971 at a time when American Protestantism was experiencing the tumult of the Jesus Revolution.[16] Motivated by 'what we thought God wanted us to do', Bussee was instrumental in setting up counselling for same sex-attracted people within his own local church in California, significantly easing the burden of isolation on these parishioners. With time, it emerged that similar support groups had also sprung up in ministries around the country, inspiring Bussee and others to organize what became the first ex-gay conference, leading to the birth of Exodus International in 1976. Another Exodus co-founder, Frank Worthen, had established the prototype ex-gay ministry, Love in Action, three years earlier, an organization later led by Jon Smid when it became the subject of a national controversy sketched out in *Love in Action*. As both co-founder of Exodus – the interdenominational umbrella ex-gay organization synonymous with conversion practices – and its first luminary to defect in perhaps the most sensational circumstances imaginable, Bussee's evidence is central to an appreciation of key shifts in the movement and its fortunes over time.[17]

A key strategy of the ex-gay movement has been to make maximum use of 'public personal testimony' of those men and women seeking conversion.[18] Public testimony – and its concomitant, confession – is a powerful tool for it invites the scrutiny (and judgement) not only of God but of staff in ex-gay facilities and the peers of programme participants.[19] Foucault observes that confession has long been a key ritual in Western societies designed to enforce the production of truth, and that 'sex was a privileged theme of confession'. The myriad interconnections between sex, power relationships and salvation are powerfully articulated here by the French theorist and philosopher:

> The confession is a ritual of discourse in which the speaking subject is also the subject of the statement; it is also a ritual that unfolds within a power relationship, for one does not confess without the presence (or virtual presence) of a partner who is not simply the interlocutor but the authority who requires the confession, prescribes and appreciates it, and intervenes in order to judge, punish, forgive, console, and reconcile; a ritual in which the truth is corroborated by the obstacles and resistances it has had to surmount in order to be formulated; and finally, a ritual in which the expression alone, independently of its external consequences, produces intrinsic modifications in the person who articulates it: it exonerates, redeems, and purifies him; it unburdens him of his wrongs, liberates him, and promises him salvation.[20]

In her ethnographic study of subjects in the New Hope Ministry, one of the longest running residential ex-gay programmes in the United States, American scholar Tanya Erzen offers some valuable insights into the ideological rationale, operation, political utility as well as the limitations of testimony. Its function in the ex-gay psyche is both redemptive and healing, and at New Hope personal testimony and confession are woven into the fabric of the organization both at the public level and in 'small accountability groups' to deal with sexual 'falls' and other lapses by programme members. As Erzen further explains:

> The culture of ex-gay ministries involves constantly sifting through the past for crisis points and familial dysfunction as the causes of homosexuality. These become important devices within a larger testimonial narrative. Some people at the ministries relied on the idea of recovered memories to discover traumatic experiences from childhoods.[21]

Over time, personal testimonies also became 'evidence' that was central to the political arsenal of the Christian Right in the United States, allowing the expansion of its repertoire by moving away from sole reliance on anti-gay rhetoric and legislative tactics.[22]

The political exploitation of one conversion survivor's testimony, Julie Rodgers, is foregrounded in *Pray Away*. Rodgers is introduced to the audience in the company of her lover, Amanda. In the initial scenes of Rodgers's on-screen story, both are caught up in the excitement of wedding plans. The marriage narrative is rounded out when the two women exchange marriage vows in a moving ceremony towards the end of the production. Former Vice President of Exodus and talking head Randy Thomas makes an incisive political observation about the powerful symbolism of same sex marriage: it represented an 'existential threat' to ex-gay ministries for it defied every precept of their raison d'être. To that extent, the act of marriage by the two symbolizes the full circle journey of Rodgers from her early conversion experiences at Living Hope Ministry under the leadership of Ricky Chelette, to her elevation as a poster child for Exodus where she became a keynote speaker, framing her talks around personal testimony. It transpires that Rodgers had been working on a book about her experiences over the past year, and in some of *Pray Away*'s most painful moments on screen she reads aloud selected passages of the manuscript revealing, among other things, her self-harm practices as a teenager.[23] We also learn that she was pressured by the movement to incorporate into her testimony details of a sexual assault incident early in life that could be conveniently leveraged in support of a simplistic narrative that purportedly explained her same-sex attraction. Rodgers's visceral response to the deep pain engendered by survivor testimony in 2013 was another decisive moment in her journey as we shall see later in this chapter.

A seminal moment in public consciousness about conversion programmes came in 2005 through the reporting of events surrounding Tennessee teenager Zach Stark, who came out to his evangelical parents and was forced by them to attend a residential Love in Action camp, an ex-gay ministry that came under the Exodus umbrella. Led by executive director Jon Smid whose name is indelibly connected to Garrard Conley's personal narrative explored by Scott McKinnon in Chapter 8, the Stark case threw a spotlight on vulnerable minors forced into programmes by parents and guardians against their will and with no obvious way out. As gay activist Wayne Besen notes in his searing expose of the ex-gay movement, the new executive director of Exodus from 2001, Alan Chambers, embarked on a new wave by expanding the organization's reach to include youth. Besen, whose frank summation of the ex-gay movement is that it amounts to a fraudulent enterprise, concludes that the 'amplified focus' on adolescents was driven by the business model of endless 'therapy' administered to subjects who had been robbed of any agency.[24] Not only did the Stark controversy inspire Emily Danforth's coming of age novel, *The Miseducation of Cameron Post* – discussed in Chapter 7 by Jessica Ford and Annika Herb – it also generated a documentary in its own right, released six years later and directed by activist filmmaker, Morgan Jon Fox.[25]

Love in Action (2011) documents the events that opened up a national debate about the forced exposure of adolescents to conversion practices. Its engagement with multiple subjects affected by these practices and its coverage of the issues extending years after the initial events eclipse the story of a single individual's crisis notwithstanding the ostensible focus on him. The teenager at the centre of the controversy was by no means the only youth whose story came to light in this period. In an attempt to discredit ex-gay programmes, the National

Gay and Lesbian Task Force published a trenchant report in 2006 documenting the case of another teen, D. J. Butler, who was dramatically taken in handcuffs to an LIA facility.[26] However, it was the nature of Stark's story, his reaction to the experience and above all his dissemination of the narrative to the outside world that explains why it took on a life of its own.

The starting point for this story was Stark's blogging on his Myspace account – the first truly global social networking site. The computer screen – his means of communication for the period of confinement in camp – is deployed by the filmmaker as a key part of the visual imagery of the documentary. Myspace is where Danforth first encountered Stark after being contacted by friends.[27] He blogged initially that he had been sent to 'de-gaying camp' by his parents and later posted the highly restrictive rules of the facility including a bar on access to the secular world lest its opinions contradict the motivations and rules of the LIA programme. At the outset, these blogs were circulated among friends and later sent on to community activists, some of whom are interviewed in the production. Both bloggers and local Memphis activists, who picketed the LIA site as part of an ongoing protest, provided the initial momentum for a story that soon leapt to national attention. The events of 2005 were not only fuelled by anti-conversion activists: Jon Smid gave a public defence of his ministry's objectives; Alan Chambers was invited to speak about the Exodus youth programme on a major television network, while Stark's father, Joe, was interviewed on the Christian Broadcast Network, defending his right under the veil of religious 'freedom' to send his son to conversion camp. Significantly, the high-profile media coverage of the issues – including CNN and *Good Morning America* – was interested in probing the ethics of forcing minors into conversion programmes.[28]

Gender, sexual orientation and psychotherapy

As the Introduction to this book makes clear, efforts to change or suppress sexual orientation or gender identity are not the sole preserve of ex-gay ministries. Indeed, there is a substantial literature dealing with the many treatment modalities used historically in the service of a medical 'cure'. The accumulating weight of scientific evidence has long discredited many of the psychiatric methods that were at their peak in the mid-twentieth century due to ineffectiveness and long-term harms inflicted on patients. However, as Marshall Forstein, MD notes, 'psychoanalytically informed approaches' to reorienting homoerotic desire have remained remarkably persistent in the United States where a fringe group of psychotherapists clung to the theory postulated originally by Hungarian-born American psychologist, Sandor Rado, that homosexual orientation is 'at best, an entrenched adaptation to the failure to achieve normative heterosexual orientation'.[29] These fringe reorientation therapists split from the American Psychoanalytic Association in 1992 when that peak body adopted the normalizing view of same-sex attraction passed by the American Psychiatric Association in its landmark decision of 1973. The result was the National Association for Research & Therapy of Homosexuality (NARTH) – co-founded by Los Angeles-based Catholic psychologist Joseph Nicolosi, whose name is synonymous with advocacy of 'reparative therapy'. Nicolosi's two key published works – *Reparative Therapy of Male Homosexuality* (1991) and *Healing Homosexuality* (1993), considered to be the bible of 'secular' reorientation – situate psychotherapy as a means to 'free men' from the 'gender conflict' he claims underpins most same-sex attraction. His remedy for the 'gender identity deficit' is 'friendship and brotherly love', not sexual relations.[30] Their essentialist view of 'anti-homosexual morality', the compromised ethics of (ostensibly) secular reorientation therapists and their ties with the ex-gay movement, critically implicate them in the politics of pain and systems of power explored in these documentaries.[31]

The role of Nicolosi as the face of reorientation 'therapy' and the linking of him to Exodus is foregrounded in *Pray Away* while a connection between them is also established in *Love in Action* and *For They Know Not*. In a scene from *Pray Away*, we see an anguished man in therapy who, in line with traditional psychoanalytic theory, is pushed by Nicolosi to admit to his sexual 'brokenness'. The vision aligns with Waidzunas's account of reparative therapy in which 'men in therapy ordinarily view themselves on-screen as a form of biofeedback when they talk about their lives and their same-sex attractions', amounting to shame therapy focused on the identification of gender deficits.[32] In another scene from this production, Nicolosi is introduced to the stage as a messiah-like figure to Exodus movement followers at the 2009 annual conference. Here the politics of Exodus is on full display; Nicolosi is presented as the embattled maverick who had the courage to take on the mental health establishment and treat 'unwanted' same-sex attraction in clients for the past thirty years.[33] As Randy Thomas and Michael Bussee acknowledge, the therapeutic approach conferred both credibility and respectability on Exodus at the same time as science was increasingly challenging its shaky foundations. The director employs juxtaposition to make a key point: we see Nicolosi in the frame with microphone in hand addressing his audience while we listen to Bussee's voice over condemn conversion practices as 'awful pseudo psychology'.

In an earlier sequence employing historical footage of an Exodus support group in action, Bussee indicts the old medical model of homosexuality from the perspective of modern psychology and states candidly that, with few exceptions, ex-gay leaders had 'no qualification' in psychology, counselling, human sexuality or any other discipline relevant to conversion practices. This important point speaks centrally to contemporary concerns articulated by critics of faith-based conversion, namely that major mental health harms are linked to these practices, most of which are undertaken by untrained counsellors. One prominent conversion critic, New York-based psychiatrist and psychoanalyst, Dr Jack Drescher, points to the religious fundamentalism inspiring NARTH, an organization that cloaks its objectives in scientific and pseudo-scientific discourse.[34] Drescher further argues that '[r]eparative therapists, at least in their published works, do not accept or respect any religious view that affirms homosexuality'. The cognitive dissonance likely to be induced in individuals with same-sex attractions who do not accept scriptural literalism is discussed at length by Edser in Chapter 2 and, as Drescher and others observe, contravenes one of the oldest ethical dictums of medicine, viz. 'First, do no harm.'[35]

Made before the 'mea culpa' delivered by ex-gay leaders who figure so prominently in *Pray Away*, *Love in Action* draws instead on evidence advanced by mental health experts – including Drescher – in putting the case against conversion practices. Associate Professor Sharon Horne from the University of Memphis readily concedes that despite the ethical principle of 'do no harm', psychologists and psychiatrists had tried for decades to change the sexuality of same-sex attracted people and failed, in the process inflicting harms. Additionally, Dr Roy Gilbert-Higginson, Deputy Director of Field Policy, PLAG, critiques the approach of reparative therapists who cling to traditional psychoanalytic theory, trade in stereotypes and opinions rather than facts, all the while ignoring current scientific developments. The statements of these talking heads align closely with numerous position statements issued by peak body medical and mental health associations in the United States and many other Western jurisdictions, a trend that peaked in America in the 1990s.[36] In the contemporaneous Australian production, *The Cure*, that foregrounds the professional experience of psychologist and former Exodus co-leader, Paul Martin, the documentarians concerned provide one such example from the Australian Psychological Society in June 2000 using text on screen that reads: 'APS recommends that ethical practitioners refrain from attempts to change individuals' sexual orientation.'

As this chapter has already established, gender identity is central to psychoanalytic theory and, by definition, conversion practices. In *Love in Action*, former LIA clients, Peterson Toscano and Brandon Tidwell, draw on their own anecdotal experiences in highlighting the rigidity of messages about gender roles and practices. Any clothing, behaviour or mode of expression that spoke of clients' earlier (read, same-sex attracted) lives was deemed to be a 'false image' and therefore unacceptable under LIA regulations. The corollary to this idea was that same-sex attracted people were limited to expressing sexual desires only, not emotion and love. 'Love' in this world view could only ever amount to 'false love'.

This obsessive preoccupation with gender is updated in the more contemporary, *For They Know Not* through a focus on transgender people as new targets of the Religious Right and their political allies in the culture wars. Politically savvy and trailblazing transwoman, Sarah McBride, and her friend, Episcopal Bishop Gene Robinson, are both central to explaining this turbulent narrative. The culture wars manifested most visibly in the political domain through a 'long and cruel campaign against trans students' rights, legislating bans on bathrooms and locker rooms, participation in sporting activities, and access to medical and psychological care'.[37] The political tone had already been established in 2015 shortly after the passage of marriage equality legislation by the Supreme Court when Donald Trump and almost all of his rivals in the Republican Presidential candidates' debate made 'vociferously violent' statements about LGBT+ people.[38] In *Pray Away*, the resort to binaries in gender identity is evident in the emotive choice of language employed by Jeffrey McCall where he is shown delivering a sermon at the Love Revolution church. Schools, he claims, are promoting a false identity that results in children 'chopping up their bodies'.

The impact of these culture wars surrounding LGBT+ people in the United States can also be discerned in other parts of the world. A prominent example is Australia which has a long history of borrowing American-style political tactics and discourse.[39] Following very significant delays and in the wake of marriage equality legislation by majority vote in the federal parliament in 2017, former Prime Minister Scott Morrison, himself a Pentecostal, attempted to rush a long vaunted Religious Discrimination Bill through the House in early 2022. This was widely viewed as a means of pushback by opponents of the landmark 2017 legislation.[40] It also constitutes a prime example of what has been identified as *resurgent prejudice* in Australian post marriage equality politics.[41] Morrison's tactic of picking Liberal Party candidate Katherine

Deves for a key conservative Sydney electorate in the 2022 Australian federal election campaign became a central facet of the culture wars he promoted using LGBT+ people. Deves's candidature was highly controversial even within her own political party and she seriously overreached with various public utterances including the claim that transgender teenagers are 'surgically mutilated'.[42]

Not just in the USA

The reference to Australian political culture is a useful reminder that conversion practices are by no means an exclusively American problem, and yet it is also the case that narratives surrounding them have seldom been explored in screen culture outside the United States. As was the case for so many others, fictional narratives about the conversion phenomenon – above all *But I'm a Cheerleader*, explored by Tom Sharples in Chapter 5 – were the first reference point for Australian queer filmmakers, Heather Corkhill, Qingwen Huang and Helen Kelly, who also saw a short piece of reportage on the public broadcaster, ABC Television, about gay conversion survivor, Ben Gresham. Gresham would later appear as one of the talking heads featured in their documentary. This provoked their curiosity in the subject and led to conversations about making a film, ultimately resulting in production of *The Cure*, featuring a range of voices. What began as a work designed to expose the serious wrongs and harms of conversion practices later morphed into one with a focus on their mental health impacts. *The Cure* was thus a canvas for the filmmakers to address a serious issue in a format that allowed for in-depth coverage as well as a welcome opportunity to debunk the myth that Australia was immune from such practices.[43]

A similar pattern can be discerned between the United States and Australia in relation to the rise of faith-based conversion practices. Anthony Venn-Brown's experiences in 'rehab' at Paradise – an 'independent Pentecostal church in the southern suburbs of Sydney' –

in 1972 just before the emergence of the ex-gay movement in the United States (see Chapter 1) – is a clear indicator that this mindset about same-sex attraction was already present in conservative Christian communities in the early 1970s.[44] As in the US, mental health professionals, guided by position statements or clinical memoranda about same-sex attraction issued by professional bodies such as the Australian and New Zealand College of Psychiatrists in October 1973, began to vacate the field, a gap that was increasingly filled by religious organizations.[45] Although they emerged independently, these organizations affiliated in the 1980s with ideologically likeminded international bodies such as Exodus International, which had begun a process of expansion abroad to various countries including Australia.[46] Coloured by their local contexts, these affiliated organizations nevertheless made extensive use of ex-gay resources that originated in the United States, including, at times, human resources in the form of such ex-gay luminaries as Sy Rogers, a former Exodus president dedicated to nurturing local support groups, and who 'helped globalize the ex-gay movement'.[47]

A diverse group of talking head gay Christians, united by the lived experience of struggle and trauma in reconciling these two identities, are central to the case against conversion practices advanced in *The Cure*. Apart from Venn-Brown and Gresham, the audience is introduced to a Mormon man, Peter Williams; former Exodus co-leader turned psychologist, Paul Martin, and Filipino-born, former Living Waters co-leader in New Zealand, Hannah Pia Baral, now domiciled in Sydney. As with *Pray Away*'s Jeffrey McCall, the voice of a chief antagonist is embedded to symbolize the status quo and remind viewers that these practices are ongoing. Reverend Ron Brookman, director of Living Waters, is that voice in *The Cure*. Brookman speaks to his personal experience, attesting to reorientation from homosexuality as a youth to full-blown heterosexuality, marriage and family life via his deep relationship with God, but with some unconvincing provisos attached to that claim.[48] His insistent use of traditional terms such as 'sexual brokenness' and the quick resort to pop psychology explanations for same-sex attraction – notably the lurid expression 'cannibal compulsion' – locate Brookman as an unrepentant Australian ex-gay leader. He further denies mental harms or suicide were ever the outcome of a Living Waters programme all the while admitting he has no data to support his claims. Here the filmmakers deploy Venn-Brown as an oppositional voice – a conversion survivor himself who has extensive first-hand experience of the devastation wreaked on many lives by ex-gay programmes. He makes the essential point that no follow up or duty of care is exercised for individuals when they leave ex-gay programmes, accounting for the paucity of information held by Brookman and fellow ex-gay leaders on the outcomes of their programmes.

This segment – and the cumulative weight of survivor testimony provided by other talking heads – negates Brookman's claims and leaves the viewer pondering the ethics of such programmes and practices. The documentary concludes on an optimistic note, showing Venn-Brown leading a support group for gay Christians – many of whose members have survived ex-gay programmes – on the joyous occasion of the Sydney Gay and Lesbian Mardi Gras.

Figure 3.2 Anthony Venn-Brown presenting his point of view in *The Cure*.

Damascene conversion moments of ex-gay leaders

As a piece of expository filmmaking, *Pray Away* explores the origins, trajectory and impacts of the 'pray the gay away movement' using the testimony of prominent American ex-gay leaders as the centrepiece of its evidence. The chief argument is clear from screen text in opening frames of the documentary: conversion practices are ongoing; they are often religiously mediated and, in the professional view of numerous medical and mental health organizations, are innately harmful. More than this, however, the documentary can be read as a vehicle for these now ex-ex-gay eyewitnesses to offer repentance; to atone for the wrongs they have committed in the name of God.

Perhaps the clearest expression of contrition comes from former Exodus Vice President Randy Thomas who reflects sorrowfully on an encounter in which an accusation of 'blood on his hands' was levelled at him. Acknowledging impacts including suicide and, in a more general sense, the social and psychological devastation inflicted on many lives, Thomas concedes painfully: 'What I did was so wrong.' According to his testimony, Thomas's epiphany occurred during the divisive Proposition 8, a California ballot proposition and amendment to the state constitution designed to disallow marriage outside the traditional contract between a man and a woman. Passed in the 2008 state elections, the amendment was subsequently overturned in court. His tearful response on screen is triggered by the painful memory of LGBT+ protesters and vision of their traumatized response to the passage of Proposition 8. As a side note, Thomas is also recruited as a talking head – the only prominent ex-gay leader to so appear – in *For They Know Not* where his role is less overtly expiative. Here he concedes that conversion practices have exacerbated the religious stigmatization of LGBT+ people, advancing the overall argument of this documentary that conversion is merely one part of a cultural process conditioning bigotry against a minority group. The cathartic journey of Randy Thomas from unapologetic Exodus leader to a deeply reflective and repentant version of himself is but one of the ex-gay leadership narratives featured in *Pray Away*.

A bisexual woman with an Hispanic surname, once employed by the prominent right-wing Christian organization Family Research Council (FRC) and later Exodus, Yvette Cantu Schneider offers some compelling insights on the politics of the pro-conversion movement. Following an establishing shot of Reno, Nevada and her neighbourhood, the viewer first encounters Schneider in a domestic scene, cooking with her daughter. From there, the camera oscillates between past and present, incorporating archival footage of her earlier life via a recorded interview in which she is asked to 'talk from the heart to those who are trapped in the lifestyle'. These initial sequences of Schneider establish the context of her early life surrounded by the loss of many gay friends to the AIDS pandemic, a crisis frequently weaponized by the Religious Right against men who had sex with other men. Religious faith presented a means of salvation at that time in her life.

In subsequent scenes she makes the transition from private to public domain through her role as policy analyst and media spokesperson for the FRC, which was dominated by white heterosexual men who saw an advantage in recruiting her to broaden the lobby group's political appeal.[49] We see footage of her on Fox News attacking the 'aggressive homosexual agenda' that purportedly sought to 'destroy marriage' and bring about gay adoption – issues that touched at the core of FRC's political creed whose promotional video loudly proclaims: 'Family, faith and freedom'. Schneider's present self also reflects on her years of work as an Exodus speaker, beginning around the time of Proposition 8 in California. An admission is forthcoming that her rhetorical strategies – notably, the 'slippery slope argument' against marriage equality – were designed to play to the fears of ambivalent voters. Seated at her dining table surrounded by videotapes – artefacts from a former working life – her past and present once again collide as she concedes that these objects are now hard to look at and yet also important *not* to forget. It transpires that like Thomas, Schneider was traumatized by the experience of Proposition 8, feelings that were later triggered by any work she undertook for Exodus and the ex-gay movement. The therapy she underwent for nine years leads her to the conclusion that her feelings of same-sex attraction never disappeared; only her behaviour changed as she sought to conform to the prescripts of a model ex-gay life.

As will be recalled from earlier in the chapter, Julie Rodgers served in a leadership position with Exodus for some years. A singularly transformative moment in both her journey and the entire Exodus organization occurred in 2013 when she, President of the day, Alan Chambers, and a group of conversion survivors guided by Michael Bussee, confronted each other in a talking circle located in a church basement. The directors of *Pray Away* provide the broader social and political context to this cathartic moment using footage from 'God and Gays', a special episode of the documentary television series, *Our America with Lisa Ling*. Airing on the Oprah Winfrey Network in June 2013, this episode along with its precursors in 2011 and 2012 signalled a growing spotlight on conversion practices. The camera focuses on a political demonstration outside the US Capitol Building in Washington, DC, zooming in on placards carrying such messages as: 'Ex-gay, No way'; 'Exodus is a fraud', and, à la Foucault's theory of reverse discourse, 'Bigots need reparative therapy'. In this climate, including growing media interest in survivor testimony, stories of harm became harder to ignore – and plausibly deny. Rodgers then proceeds to narrate her seminal experience, culminating with the encounter beneath the house of prayer. In contact with two survivors on Facebook, she indicated her hope that she might one day hear their stories. As an educator and mentor to conversion survivors, Bussee acted as the intermediary, offering to create a secret Facebook group to facilitate exchange of survivor stories. Hearing about this development, Lisa Ling approached Bussee, inviting group members to have the exchange televised. As then head of Exodus, Chambers felt it important to hear survivor stories, so he too agreed to participate.[50]

What unfolded on that day, and the consequences it unleashed, was nothing short of profound. Exodus had long been accustomed to denying harms caused by conversion practices, explaining away departures from ex-gay programmes with various forms of sophistry. A barely contained rage and deep sense of pain is etched on the faces of survivors who openly confront their tormentors for the first time. One young woman gives vent to her emotions, levelling the accusation that 'you've had opportunities to see our wounds before, but you haven't done anything about it', while another, expressing her deep pain, declares: 'these kids are killing themselves and I can't be silent any longer'. There is a visceral rage in one young man who states bluntly: 'I lost my soul because I did the right thing'. The camera captures intense distress registered on Bussee's face in response to the devastating testimony disclosed in this intense and brutally honest group encounter. Chambers and Rodgers also appear visibly upset and all are deeply moved by what they hear.[51] Rodgers, who later confessed that the experience shook her to the core, declares: 'I remember feeling like I was sitting on the wrong side of the circle ... I can't do this any more, I can't be a part of it. This is just so toxic'. Randy Thomas concedes that when the Lisa Ling show aired, he knew the writing was on the wall. Sure enough, in June 2013 the closure of Exodus International was announced, accompanied by a written statement and apology from Chambers.[52]

Past, present and future

In the extratextual online resources created to accompany *Pray Away*, director Kristine Stolakis attributes her initial interest in the subject of conversion practices to her own religious background and to a close relative who came out as a trans child, survived their conversion experience, and later died unexpectedly. When embarking on the research she assumed – as so many others have – that her uncle's experience was 'a thing of the past'. What she in fact discovered is that the '"pray the gay away movement" is alive and well today'. The continuation of such practices in the era of marriage equality is indeed jarring to many as it appears to sit in stark contradiction with some of the powerful shifts in the socio-political landscape that have occurred across much of the Western world, particularly in the second decade of the twenty-first century. The ongoing presence of this phenomenon also speaks to the changing tactics and discourse used by conversion organizations to better conceal their anachronistic nature to an evolving wider world. To this end, Stolakis announces that the film and its accompanying resources are intended to be shared as widely as possible to assist anyone who may be struggling to accept their authentic self.[53] In so doing, she reflects a social justice commitment held by many documentarians to not only represent the world as it is but to change it for the better.[54]

Bussee and Thomas's repudiation of the entire belief system underpinning ex-gay programmes offers a compelling viewing experience. At the same time, the directors of both contemporary productions, Daniel Karslake and Kristine Stolakis, are very aware that the phenomenon is far from over. To illustrate the point, *Pray Away* features a clip of an interview with Anne Paulk, Executive Director of Restored Hope Network, successor organization of Exodus and defiant holdout to many residual ex-gay leaders. This scene segues to a married opposite-sex couple on stage, including an ex-gay man who offers emotional testimony relating to his former life. The camera zooms out to reveal Schneider viewing the scene on her laptop computer. She proceeds to deconstruct the couple's performance, noting all the elements of this 'indoctrination': the 'lingo' used; 'the pattern of the testimony and even the pattern of their lives'. She takes a deep sigh and concedes: 'it's not dying the way that we thought it would. I think it should'. As part of their shared commitment to transforming the future, the producers of *Pray Away* then invite Schneider to speak to camera and appeal to her former colleagues:

> Well, I used to be a true believer, just like you did. I absolutely thought what we were doing was right. But all it does is crush souls. It crushes people's lives. I can't stand that I was a part of it, and I would hope you have the empathy and compassion to see that all it does is damage.

The decision to speak out strongly by ex-gay leaders is paralleled by the determination of the Robertsons to share their story in *For They Know*

Not. Having endured the agony of losing a son, Ryan, because 'we made him believe he was unacceptable to God', their changed understanding of Jesus leads them to launch a life group for gay Christians in the Seattle area, which they see as a 'redemptive' act in the light of Ryan's tragic experience. In the closing scenes, the couple embrace each other with visible heartache in the cemetery grounds as the camera segues to a final shot of Ryan's headstone and epitaph.

Notes

1   B. Smaill, *The Documentary: Politics, Emotion, Culture* (Basingstoke and New York: Palgrave Macmillan, 2010), 70.

2   For further details, see www.soulforce.org (accessed 6 February 2024).

3   For a similar historical perspective, see A. Venn-Brown, *A Life of Unlearning – A Preacher's Struggle with his Homosexuality, Church and Faith*. 3rd edn rev. (Sydney: Personal Success Australia, 2015), 269.

4   www.fortheyknow.org (accessed 6 February 2024).

5   Smaill, *The Documentary*, 56 and 59–60.

6   B. Nichols, *Representing Reality: Issues and Concepts in Documentary* (Bloomington: Indiana University Press, 1991), 17–18.

7   See, for example, R. A. Rosenstone and C. Parvulescu, 'Introduction.' In *A Companion to the Historical Film*, eds Robert Rosenstone and Constantin Parvulescu (Chichester: Wiley-Blackwell, 2013), 1.

8   See, for example, A. Williams, 'Gay Teenager Stirs a Storm,' *New York Times*, 17 July 2005. https://www.nytimes.com/2005/07/17/fashion/sundaystyles/gay-teenager-stirs-a-storm.html (accessed 23 August 2023), R. Palazzolo, '"Ex-Gay" Camps, Therapy Programs Attract Controversy,' ABC News, 28 July 2005, www.abcnews.go.com/GMA/Health/story?id=983209 (accessed 23 August 2023). J. Borger, 'Straight and Narrow: Church's Gay Cure,' *The Guardian*, 26 August 2005, https://www.theguardian.com/world/2005/aug/26/gayrights.usa (accessed 23 August 2023).

9   For a discussion of devotional practice, see for example, G. Pfeil, 'Imperfect Vessels: Emotion and Rituals of Anti-Ritual in American Pentecostal and Charismatic Devotional Life.' In *Practicing the Faith: The Ritual Life of Pentecostal-Charismatic Christians*, ed M. Lindhardt (New York and

Oxford: Berghahn Books, 2011). McCall's credibility as founder of ex-gay organization Freedom March has been called into question. See 'Founder of Ex-Gay Group Admits to Having Sex with Multiple Men,' 22 December 2021, https://www.starobserver.com.au/news/founder-of-ex-gay-group-admits-to-having-sex-with-multiple-men/208094 (accessed 27 February 2023).

10 Zoom meeting with A. Venn-Brown, 23 November 2022. For details of conservative Catholics who contradict this general proposition, see S. Edser, *Being Gay, Being Christian* (Wollombi, NSW and Auckland: Exisle Publishing Ltd, 2012), especially 192–3. Other examples include the Catholic psychologist, Joseph Nicolosi, the most prominent advocate of reparative therapy, and the conversion documentary *The Sunday Sessions* (2019), featuring the young Catholic man Nathan who is desirous of conversion by his therapist.

11 Edser, *Being Gay*, 30–1.

12 Edser, *Being Gay*, see 123–52.

13 Also see Rev. Dr. Delman Coates, 'A Letter to the National Baptist Fellowship of Concerned Pastors,' 9 April 2015, www.manyvoices.org/blog/2015/04/a-letter-to-the-national-baptist-fellowship-of-concerned-pastors/ (accessed 27 February 2023).

14 Email, Dan Karslake to author, 25 November 2022.

15 A. M. Sánchez Walsh, *Pentecostals in America* (New York: Columbia University Press, 2018), 1.

16 T. Erzen, *Straight to Jesus: Sexual and Christian Conversions in the Ex-Gay Movement* (Berkeley: University of California Press, 2006), 29. Venn-Brown, *A Life of Unlearning*, 56.

17 Erzen, *Straight to Jesus*, 29–31 and 34. Venn-Brown, *A Life of Unlearning*, 169. Also see J. Kirkland, 'What is Exodus International, the Ex-Gay Christian Group at the Centre of Netflix's *Pray Away*?' *Esquire*, 4 August 2021, www.esquire.com/entertainment/movies/a37210531/netflix-pray-away-exodus-international-true-story-explained/ (accessed 22 January 2023).

18 T. Waidzunas, *Sexual and Christian Conversions in the Ex-Gay Movement* (Berkeley: University of California Press, 2006), 14.

19 See A. Aranjuez, 'Change of Heart: *Boy Erased, The Miseducation of Cameron Post* and Gay Conversion Therapy,' *Screen Education*, 94 (2019): 59.

20 M. Foucault, *The History of Sexuality*, vol. 1: *An Introduction* (New York: Pantheon Books, 1978), 60, 63–4.

21 Erzen, *Straight to Jesus*, 116, 122 and 134. On the highly contentious nature of recovered memory in reparative therapy, see W. Throckmorton, 'Reparative Therapy and Confirmation Bias: An Illustration,' 31 January 2012, www.wthrockmorton.com/2012/01/31/reparative-therapy-and-confirmation-bias-an-illustration/ (accessed 11 May 2023) and W. Besen, *Anything but Straight: Unmasking the Scandals and Lies Behind the Ex-Gay Myth* (New York: Harrington Park Press, 2003), especially 185.

22 Erzen, *Straight to Jesus*, 139.

23 The published version is J. Rodgers, *Outlove: A Queer Christian Survival Story* (Minneapolis: Broadleaf Books, 2021).

24 Besen, *Anything but Straight,* 242, 246 and 249.

25 C. Sittenfeld, 'The Best Novel About a "De-Gaying Camp" Ever Written,' interview with Emily Danforth, *Slate*, 8 February 2012, https://slate.com/human-interest/2012/02/the-miseducation-of-cameron-post-by-emily-danforth-a-conversation-between-the-writer-and-novelist-curtis-sittenfeld.html (accessed 22 December 2022).

26 Waidzunas, *The Straight Line*, 118.

27 Sittenfeld, 'The Best Novel About a "De-Gaying Camp".'

28 Waidzunas, *The Straight Line*, 118. Erzen, *Straight to Jesus*, 42.

29 M. Forstein, MD, 'Overview of Ethical and Research Issues in Sexual Orientation Therapy.' In *Sexual Conversion Therapy: Ethical, Clinical and Research Perspectives*, eds A. Shidlo, M. Schroeder and J. Drescher (New York: Haworth Press, 2001), 168–9.

30 J. Terry, *An American Obsession: Science, Medicine and Homosexuality in Modern Society* (Chicago: University of Chicago Press, 1999), 381. On the growing ties between anti-gay religious and secular arguments in 1990s America, see Terry, *An American Obsession*, 2.

31 See D. C. Haldeman, 'Sexual Orientation Conversion Therapy for Gay Men and Lesbians: A Scientific Examination,' in *Homosexuality: Research Implications for Public Policy*, eds J. C. Gonsiorek and J. D. Weinrich (Sage, 1991), 149–60, especially 156, and J. Drescher, 'Ethical Concerns Raised When Patients Seek to Change Same-Sex Attractions.' In Shidlo, Schroeder and Drescher, *Sexual Conversion Therapy: Ethical, Clinical and Research Perspectives*, 181–210, especially 181–2.

32 Waidzunas, *The Straight Line*, 2–3.

33 For assessments of Nicolosi and his controversial legacy in the wake of his death in 2017, see R. Sandomir, 'Joseph Nicolosi, Advocate of Conversion Therapy for Gays, Dies at 70,' *New York Times*, 16 March 2017, www.nytimes.com/2017/03/16/us/joseph-nicolosi-dead-gay-conversion-therapist.html (accessed 11 May 2023); B. Denizet-Lewis, 'Joseph Nicolosi,' *New York Times Magazine*, 28 December 2017, www.nytimes.com/interactive/2017/12/28/magazine/the-lives-they-lived-joseph-nicolosi.html (accessed 11 May 2023); and S. Brydum, '"He Got Away With It": Conversion Therapy Survivor on Dr. Joseph Nicolosi's Legacy,' *Religion Dispatches*, 10 March 2017, www.religiondispatches.org/he-got-away-with-it-reparative-therapy-survivor-on-dr-joseph-nicolosis-legacy/ (accessed 11 May 2023).

34 J. Drescher, 'I'm Your Handyman: A History of Reparative Therapies,' *Journal of Gay and Lesbian Psychotherapy*, 5, nos. 3–4 (2002): 21.

35 Drescher, 'Ethical Concerns,' 191–2.

36 Waidzunas, *The Straight Line*, 89–90.

37 M. Secombe, 'How the Religious Freedom Bill Fell Apart,' *The Saturday Paper*, No. 386, 12–18 February 2022, 8.

38 Email, Dan Karslake to author, 4 January 2023.

39 Secombe, 'How the Religious Freedom Bill Fell Apart,' 8.

40 See C. Brickell and J. Bennett, 'Marriage Equality in Australia and New Zealand: A Trans-Tasman Politics of Difference,' *Australian Journal of Politics and History*, 67, no. 2 (2021): 276–94, https://doi.org/10.1111/ajph.12752

41 See D. Betts and J. Bennett, 'Resurgent Prejudice: Responses to Marriage Equality in Australia,' *Australian Journal of Social Issues*, 58:4 (2023): 732–46, http://doi.org/10.1002/ajs4.279

42 N. Savva, *Bulldozed: Scott Morrison's Fall and Anthony Albanese's Rise* (Melbourne: Scribe, 2022), 223.

43 Email, Heather Corkhill to author, 16 December 2022.

44 Venn-Brown, *A Life of Unlearning*, 88.

45 See J. Bennett and C. Brickell, 'Surveilling the Mind and Body: Medicalising and Demedicalising Homosexuality in 1970s New Zealand,' *Medical History* 62, no. 2 (2018): 203. DOI 10.1017/mdh.2018.4

46 T. Jones, A. Brown, L. Carnie, G. Fletcher and W. Leonard, *Preventing Harm, Promoting Justice: Responding to LGBT Conversion Therapy in Australia*

(Melbourne: GLHV@ARCSHS and the Human Rights Law Centre, 2018), 4.

47 See Sy Rogers's obituary: D. Silliman, 'Died: Sy Rogers, Who Testified God Changed His Sexual Identity,' *Christianity Today*, 23 April 2020, https://www.christianitytoday.com/news/2020/april/sy-rogers-died-exgay-lgbt-exodus-conversion-therapy.html (accessed 27 February 2023).

48 On the political utility of Brookman's narrative to the Australian Christian Lobby, see A. Greenwich and S. Robinson, *Yes Yes Yes. Australia's Journey to Marriage Equality* (Sydney: NewSouth, 2018), 11.

49 On links between Joseph Nicolosi and the Family Research Council, see Terry, *An American Obsession*, 380–1.

50 Zoom meeting with A. Venn-Brown, 23 November 2022.

51 See L. Capretto, 'Michael Bussee, Exodus International Co-Founder, Recalls Painful Experiences in "Ex-Gay" Movement,' *HuffPost*, 24 June 2013, http://www.huffpost.com/entry/michael-bussee-exodus-international-ex-gay_n_3475243 (accessed 22 January 2023).

52 See A. Newcomb, 'Exodus International: Gay Cure Group Leader Shutting Down Ministry After Change of Heart,' ABC News, 21 June 2013, www.abcnews.go.com/US/exodus-international-gay-cure-group-leader-shutting-ministry/story?id=19446752 (accessed 22 January 2023).

53 See Director's Statement in www.prayawayfilm.com (accessed 22 January 2023).

54 A. Juhasz and A. Lebow, 'Introduction.' In *A Companion to Contemporary Documentary Film*, eds A. Juhasz and A. Lebow (Chichester and Malden, MA: Wiley Blackwell, 2015), 11.

Bibliography

Aranjuez, A. 'Change of Heart: *Boy Erased*, *The Miseducation of Cameron Post* and Gay Conversion Therapy.' *Screen Education*, 94 (2019): 54–61.

Bennett, J. and C. Brickell. 'Surveilling the Mind and Body: Medicalising and Demedicalising Homosexuality in 1970s New Zealand.' *Medical History*. 62, no. 2 (2018): 199–216. DOI 10.1017/mdh.2018.4.

Besen, W. *Anything but Straight: Unmasking the Scandals and Lies Behind the Ex-Gay Myth*. New York: Harrington Park Press, 2003.

Betts, D., and J. Bennett. 'Resurgent Prejudice: Responses to Marriage Equality in Australia.' *Australian Journal of Social Issues*, 58:4 (2023): 732–46. http://doi.org/10.1002/ajs4.279

Borger, J. 'Straight and Narrow: Church's Gay Cure.' *The Guardian*, 26 August 2005, www.theguardian.com/world/2005/aug/26/gayrights.usa

Brickell, C., and J. Bennett. 'Marriage Equality in Australia and New Zealand: A Trans-Tasman Politics of Difference.' *Australian Journal of Politics and History*, 67, no. 2 (2021): 276–94, https://doi.org/10.1111/ajph.12752

Brydum, S. '"He Got Away with It": Conversion Therapy Survivor on Dr. Joseph Nicolosi's Legacy.' *Religion Dispatches*, 10 March 2017, www.religiondispatches.org/he-got-away-with-it-reparative-therapy-survivor-on-dr-joseph-nicolosis-legacy/

Capretto, L. 'Michael Bussee, Exodus International Co-Founder, Recalls Painful Experiences in "Ex-Gay" Movement.' *HuffPost*, 24 June 2013, http://www.huffpost.com/entry/michael-bussee-exodus-international-ex-gay_n_3475243

Coates, Rev. Dr. D. 'A Letter to the National Baptist Fellowship of Concerned Pastors.' 9 April 2015, www.manyvoices.org/blog/2015/04/a-letter-to-the-national-baptist-fellowship-of-concerned-pastors/

Denizet-Lewis, B. 'Joseph Nicolosi.' *New York Times Magazine*, 28 December 2017, www.nytimes.com/interactive/2017/12/28/magazine/the-lives-they-lived-joseph-nicolosi.html

Drescher, J. 'I'm Your Handyman: A History of Reparative Therapies.' *Journal of Gay and Lesbian Psychotherapy*, 5, nos. 3–4 (2002): 5–24.

Drescher, J. 'Ethical Concerns Raised When Patients Seek to Change Same-Sex Attractions.' In *Sexual Conversion Therapy: Ethical, Clinical and Research Perspectives*, eds A. Shidlo, M. Schroeder and J. Drescher, 5–24. New York: Haworth Medical Press, 2001.

Edser, S. *Being Gay, Being Christian*. Wollombi, NSW and Auckland: Exisle Publishing Ltd, 2012.

Erzen, T. *Straight to Jesus: Sexual and Christian Conversions in the Ex-Gay Movement*. Berkeley: University of California Press, 2006.

Forstein, M. MD. 'Overview of Ethical and Research Issues in Sexual Orientation Therapy.' In *Sexual Conversion Therapy: Ethical, Clinical and Research Perspectives*, eds A. Shidlo, M. Schroeder and J. Drescher, 167–79. New York: Haworth Medical Press, 2001.

Foucault, M. *The History of Sexuality*, vol. 1: *An Introduction*. Pantheon Books, New York, 1978.

For They Know Not What They Do [Documentary] Dir. D. Karslake, USA: First Run Features, 2019.

'Founder of Ex-Gay Group Admits to Having Sex with Multiple Men.' *Star Observer*, 22 December 2021, https://www.starobserver.com.au/news/founder-of-ex-gay-group-admits-to-having-sex-with-multiple-men/208094

Greenwich, A. and S. Robinson. *Yes Yes Yes. Australia's Journey to Marriage Equality*. Sydney: NewSouth, 2018.

Haldeman D. C. 'Sexual Orientation Conversion Therapy for Gay Men and Lesbians: A Scientific Examination.' In *Homosexuality: Research Implications for Public Policy*, eds J. C. Gonsiorek and J.D. Weinrich. Sage, 1991.

Jones, T., A. Brown, L. Carnie, G. Fletcher and W. Leonard. *Preventing Harm, Promoting Justice: Responding to LGBT Conversion Therapy in Australia*. Melbourne: GLHV@ARCSHS and the Human Rights Law Centre, 2018.

Juhasz, A. and A. Lebow. 'Introduction.' In *A Companion to Contemporary Documentary Film*, eds A. Juhasz and A. Lebow, 1–17. Chichester, UK and Malden, MA: Wiley Blackwell, 2015.

Kirkland, J. 'What is Exodus International, the Ex-Gay Christian Group at the Centre of Netflix's *Pray Away*?' *Esquire*, 4 August 2021, www.esquire.com/entertainment/movies/a37210531/netflix-pray-away-exodus-international-true-story-explained/

Newcomb, A. 'Exodus International: Gay Cure Group Leader Shutting Down Ministry After Change of Heart.' ABC News, 21 June 2013, www.abcnews.go.com/US/exodus-international-gay-cure-group-leader-shutting-ministry/story?id=19446752

Nichols, B. *Representing Reality: Issues and Concepts in Documentary*. Bloomington: Indiana University Press, 1991.

Palazzolo, R. '"Ex-Gay" Camps, Therapy Programs Attract Controversy.' ABC News, 28 July 2005, www.abcnews.go.com/GMA/Health/story?id=983209

Pfeil, G. 'Imperfect Vessels: Emotion and Rituals of Anti-Ritual in American Pentecostal and Charismatic Devotional Life.' In *Practicing the Faith: The Ritual Life of Pentecostal-Charismatic Christians*, ed M. Lindhardt, 277–305. New York and Oxford: Berghahn Books, 2011.

Pray Away [Documentary] Dir. K. Stolakis, USA: Blumhouse TV and Ryan Murphy, 2021.

Rosenstone, R. A. and C. Parvulescu. 'Introduction.' In *A Companion to the Historical Film*, eds R. Rosenstone and C. Parvulescu, 1–8. Chichester: Wiley-Blackwell, 2013.

Sánchez Walsh, A. M. *Pentecostals in America*. New York: Columbia University Press, 2018.

Sandomir, R. 'Joseph Nicolosi, Advocate of Conversion Therapy for Gays, Dies at 70.' *New York Times*, 16 March 2017, www.nytimes.com/2017/03/16/us/joseph-nicolosi-dead-gay-conversion-therapist.html

Savva, N. *Bulldozed: Scott Morrison's Fall and Anthony Albanese's Rise*. Melbourne: Scribe, 2022.

Secombe, M. 'How the Religious Freedom Bill Fell Apart.' *The Saturday Paper*, No. 386, 12–18 February 2022: 8.

Silliman, D. Obituary: 'Died: Sy Rogers, Who Testified God Changed His Sexual Identity.' *Christianity Today*, 23 April 2020, https://www.christianitytoday.com/news/2020/april/sy-rogers-died-exgay-lgbt-exodus-conversion-therapy.html

Sittenfeld, C. 'The Best Novel About a "De-Gaying Camp" Ever Written.' Interview with Emily Danforth. *Slate*, 8 February 2012, https://slate.com/human-interest/2012/02/the-miseducation-of-cameron-post-by-emily-danforth-a-conversation-between-the-writer-and-novelist-curtis-sittenfeld.html

Smaill, B. *The Documentary: Politics, Emotion, Culture*. Basingstoke and New York: Palgrave Macmillan, 2010.

Terry, J. *An American Obsession: Science, Medicine and Homosexuality in Modern Society*. Chicago: University of Chicago Press, 1999.

The Cure [Documentary] Dir. H. Corkhill. Australia: Rambling Women Media, 2012.

This is What Love in Action Looks Like [Documentary] Dir. M.J. Fox. USA: TLA Releasing, 2011.

Venn-Brown, A. *A Life of Unlearning – A Preacher's Struggle with his Homosexuality, Church and Faith*. 3rd edn. rev. Sydney: Personal Success Australia, 2015.

Waidzunas, T. *Sexual and Christian Conversions in the Ex-Gay Movement*. Berkeley: University of California Press, 2006.

Williams, A. 'Gay Teenager Stirs a Storm.' *New York Times*, 17 July 2005, https://www.nytimes.com/2005/07/17/fashion/sundaystyles/gay-teenager-stirs-a-storm.html

4

Three Films, Conversion Practices and the Paratext: *I am Michael*, *Michael Lost and Found*, and *Once Gay – Matthew and Friends*

Marguerite Johnson

My focus is on the extensive paratext and transmedia storytelling, both of which are made possible through new media, in three films: *I am Michael* (2015), *Michael Lost and Found* (2017), and *Once Gay – Matthew and Friends* (2019) (hereafter, *Once Gay*). Each film tells a story but in distinct genres: *I am Michael* is a Hollywood biopic; *Michael Lost and Found* is a short bio made on a shoestring budget, and *Once Gay* is a bio-documentary. The films centre around two men: Michael Glatze, who is the subject of the first two films, and Matthew Grech who is the subject of the third film. Both men left the so-called gay lifestyle to embrace God, and both have been at the forefront of the ex-gay movement, Glatze in the United States and Grech in Malta (as well as in the United Kingdom through his connection with Core Issues Trust[1] based in Northern Ireland). Both men deny having undergone any form of conversion practice. By extension, my focus also engages with storytelling through what Ruth Tsuria and Jason Bartashius discuss as the shared, intwined and, indeed, complicated nexus between religion and the media, a relationship that has grown with the rise of new media.[2] This methodology ensures the themes of the ex-gay movement, conversion ideology and fundamentalist approaches to Christianity conjoin in an analysis that privileges film as cultural and social artefact.

Extending definitions of gay conversion practices, acknowledging conversion ideology

In response to both Glatze and Grech denying having undergone conversion 'therapy', I begin by posing a question that is integral to my methodology: how far can a definition of gay conversion 'therapy' be extended in order to dialogue with the content of the films under analysis? This is both an interesting and pressing question in view of each film conforming to the protagonists' position on the subject of conversion practices by avoiding any mention of well-known classifications of conversion practices. Instead, the films feature themes of conservative Christian tenets on the topic of same-sex attraction, and non-heteronormative, non-binary gender identities. This focus may, at a first viewing, suggest that the films offer nothing more than faith-based stories of queer individuals that stop short of the topic of mainstream ideas of conversion practices.[3] However, by approaching the three films and the paratexts around them with an eye to *extending* the definition of conversion practices to include 'prayer' or, more specifically, the 'pray the gay away' mantra, and by emphasizing an *environment* of conversion ideology, I suggest that the films engage with the topic of conversion practices that challenge the meanings behind their protagonists' insistence on a simple veneer of a personal, spiritual Road to Damascus experience.[4] In the two ex-gay stories, *I am Michael* and *Once Gay*, both protagonists advocate a personal faith-based epiphany, avoiding any notion of participation in conversion practices. And, in terms of the mainstream definitions of gay conversion practices and the images that come to mind – from conversion camps, intensive one-on-one 'healing' sessions, to medical interventions – both men's claims may be right.

Indeed, gay conversion practices, as discussed in this volume, are generally associated with specific and unambiguous interventions into an individual's private and sometimes public sexuality when that sexuality is deemed unnatural, ungodly, unclean and, essentially, deviant. Of the wide-ranging forms of gay conversion practices, the best recognized in the contemporary West include counselling and/or psychotherapy in faith-based settings.[5] An extension of the latter usually includes prayer, scripture readings, acts of repentance, spiritual retreats and, in more extreme forms, exorcism.[6] However, regularly lost in this paradigm is the essential tenet of conversion ideology, which is the lynchpin of conversion practices in fundamentalist-informed religions.[7]

Conversion ideology is the belief system and moral philosophy that informs and justifies conversion practices. In this case study, the focus is on the conversion ideology of evangelical and fundamentalist Christianity (see the Introduction for further discussion of these terms).[8] While a discussion of both types of Christianity is beyond the scope of this chapter, it is necessary to briefly address them, to better understand the place of some mutually held tenets as they inform the films under discussion. In general terms, their primary doctrine is biblical literalism; that is, the Bible is interpreted as the literal 'Word of God.' As Andrew F. Smith explains:

> Biblical literalists offer two key epistemological claims in defense of their position. The Bible is not only inerrant; it is also infallible. Inerrancy entails that the original copies of biblical documents – and copies of those copies up to the present – contain no mistakes, perhaps with the exception of minor inaccuracies associated with names and dates.[9]

Of course, in debates between biblical literalists and secular opponents from (liberal) Christian, agnostic and atheist perspectives, the hermeneutics of certain biblical passages are hotly contested. Accordingly: '*Yes*, indeed, the Bible condemns homosexuality versus *no*, in fact, the Bible does not condemn homosexuality.' Robert K. Gnuse has discussed the biblical passages regularly cited as evidence of the condemnation of same-sex union in the Bible, which clearly shows the inherent plasticity of meaning in several sections (see also, Edser herein: 72–73).[10]

What, then, are the ramifications of this biblical cornerstone of evangelical and fundamentalist Christianity for same-sex attracted individuals? What exactly is at stake for same-sex attracted people when confronted by those who advocate that their sexuality is a sin? In his memoir, *A Life of Unlearning*, Anthony Venn-Brown provides a succinct answer:

> Could I serve God and be in love with a man, or continue to preach and have an affair with Jason on the side? Could I stand up in front of crowds of people declaring God's power delivers from every sin and temptation? The answer to all these questions was a resounding 'No'.[11]

While Venn-Brown writes of a time in his life when he regarded his Christian faith as incompatible with his homosexuality, millions of same-sex attracted people who are agnostic, atheist or members of queer-friendly faiths and spiritualities are still confronted by a robust global community whose members express the belief that anyone outside the heteronormative model is destined for eternal damnation. Such a belief, inextricably bound with their faith, may not manifest in, or involve gay conversion practices. However, it does essentially entail a conversion ideology that, in the words of Mark Ward, is a 'culture' of 'biblical literalism' that is 'constructed through discourse'.[12] The discourse extends beyond the catechistic touchstone of biblical infallibility to the lived or experiential lifestyle of that sacred infallibility in which gender binarism and union between a male and a female are preached and embodied as performative exempla of a Christian life. Likewise, gender fluidity or non-binarism and so-called 'alternative' sexualities are condemned in various ways.

While the culture of conversion ideology is part of the whole that binds evangelical and fundamentalist Christian communities together, it is also unavoidable in relation to the broader community. In other words: conversion ideology seeps. It seeps because of the inherent nature of evangelism. Since the rise of the Christian Right from the 1970s, for example, the increase in mass-media and technology has enabled evangelism to become normalized as an embedded form of 'worldview' rhetoric.[13] One example on the theme of gay conversion practices as overt Christian signalling within a general conversion ideology is the advertisement campaigns, spanning as far back as the 1990s in the United States, which firmly embedded the topic of same-sex attraction in the culture wars.[14] Advertisements appeared in major newspapers, including the *New York Times*, and segued to billboards, broadcasting and even buses. This example is a powerful illustration of the intersection of religion and media, and as Tsuria and Bartashius stress, between 'religion, *sexuality*, and media',[15] to create an environment of conversion ideology. The new horizon that naturally followed the billboards, broadcasting and buses was the Internet and storytelling via new media.[16]

An example of conversion ideology in a broad sense is described by Bernadette Barton:[17]

> The social worlds within which I observed manifestations of Bible Belt Christianity included environments as diverse as grocery stores, neighborhood homes and shops, parties, public events, doctor's offices, gyms, small businesses, churches, and my workplace. . . . from bumper stickers, i.e., '1 CROSS + 3 NAILS = 4 GVN' and 'Jesus '08' to pamphlets, music, newspaper columns, yard signs, billboards, charity cups, and references to Christianity in daily conversations. I collected pamphlets and church announcements sent to our home. I jotted down bumper stickers. I counted churches. I noted references to Jesus in casual conversations. I listened to Christian programming. I went to church. In this way, expressions of Christianity – like the velvet painting of Jesus in boxing gloves for sale in a Christian store – intensely sprang into life. Christianity was literally everywhere I looked.

While Barton's words express an extreme example of conversion ideology, based as they are on the region generally termed the 'Bible Belt' in the United States, they nonetheless strike a chord in relation to the aforementioned concept of 'seepage'. As Barton acknowledges, the messages and the messaging of conversion ideology are ubiquitous, although their intensity depends on geography and demographics.[18] As a cultural rhetoric that preaches in its most basic form that 'homosexuality is a sin', conversion ideology, nevertheless, exists globally; it exists in overt forms as a scream, and it exists in other ways as a quiet hum. This interpretation is also addressed in Chapter 7 of this book in which Jessica Ford and Annika Herb discuss the novel and film versions of *The Miseducation of Cameron Post* as including depictions of 'the quiet violence and trauma of denying queerness' in a world that is often 'harsh' and characterized by an 'anti-queer sentiment'.[19]

I am Michael

In the American biographical drama, *I am Michael*, conversion ideology registers somewhere between a scream and a hum. The story of Michael Glatze, a gay activist and publisher who rejects his sexuality and converts to Christianity, ultimately becoming a pastor, *I am Michael* is underscored by a surprisingly low-key representation of conversion ideology. Stripped of a narrative of any overt conversion practices, which some viewers may have anticipated as a feature theme, the film is characterized by an interiority that dramatizes the psychology and spiritual journey of Michael as he rejects his sexuality and embraces God. The enigma that is Michael's journey and what prompts it, tempts the viewer into engaging in their own journey to find answers.

The paratext surrounding the film reveals that *I am Michael* was based on an article in the *New York Times Magazine* by Benoit Denizet-Lewis, 'My Ex-Gay Friend' (2011).[20] This information, along with many other sub-texts around the film, including how actor James Franco responded to playing Michael, to interviews with Michael Glatze himself, to reviews and various media coverage of screenings provide a paratext that, in the words of Gérard Genette, takes the 'text' from its 'naked state' and places it among 'the discourse of the world on the text'.[21]

I am Michael can stand alone as a single text. The film opens in 2008 with a short scene in which the converted Michael talks with a young man, Paul. Michael states: 'I hear you're having some trouble.' The 'trouble' is Paul's same-sex attraction conflicts with his belief in God; he does not understand 'why God made me like this'. Michael's responses include: 'He [God] didn't, trust me. . . . Gay doesn't exist. It's a false identity. . . . You want to go to heaven, right? . . . If you're a moral person, then you'll choose heterosexuality in order to be with God.' The film then takes its audience into the past, ten years earlier, and Michael's life in San Francisco with his partner, Benji Nycum. Two young men wake up in bed, ready to begin their day. The routine of Michael and Benji is summarized in a series of montages, particularly images from the national magazine, *XY*, based in San Francisco and where Michael worked as managing editor for several years. In the film, *XY* symbolizes Michael's 'gay life' or his 'gay past': it was where he met Benji; where he advocated for the rights, education and safety of young gay men; and ultimately the platform from which he became a leader in the LGBT+ community. The film includes a scene in which the team at *XY* discuss how they should cover the murder of Matthew Shepard, arguably the most infamous gay hate crime in the United States, and which also functions as a symbol of Michael's 'old life'.

As Michael is outspoken in his criticism of Christianity during his years as a campaigner for LGBT+ rights – 'They killed him [Shepard] because they are afraid, and they're afraid because of what their churches tell them and because of what they see in movies . . .' – his moral and religious turnaround is not only surprising, but shocking. A close interaction with the film reveals or at least hints at some of the reasons for the dramatic reversal: his innate and almost emotionally debilitating grief at the loss of his parents at a young age; his desperate desire to see them again, his hypochondria that stems from intense anxiety, are all signposted as the reasons for Michael's conversion. In short: Michael is looking for a miracle. Yet, before we dismiss the role of conversion practices entirely, and in reference to the earlier statement that the biopic does not contain any suggestion of such overt activities, there is the need to consider what exactly is meant by the standard phrase, conversion 'therapy'. In a report by the Independent Forensic Expert Group, we are reminded:

> . . . practices that constitute conversion therapy are wide-ranging in nature, and may include psychotherapy, clinical and pharmaceutical interventions, self-help and counselling, or faith-based practices across

a wide range of religious traditions. Extreme measures of conversion therapy may include forced medication, electroconvulsive therapy, beatings and rape. Practitioners may include healthcare providers, psychologists, psychiatrists and counsellors, faith organisations or ministries, and state actors.[22]

The sheer breadth of the above exempla is an important reminder or reality check that there are far more subtle forms of conversion practice than the sensationalist cases regularly reported by the media would suggest. The reference to 'self-help and counselling, or faith-based practices'[23] may well point to a conversion practice at play in the aforementioned opening scene of *I am Michael,* in which a converted Michael speaks with a young man about his same-sex attraction. Perhaps it would not be too extravagant an explanation to interpret Michael's counselling of young Paul as a filmic mimesis that re-enacts Michael's own faith-based counselling during his journey towards God. As the report further clarifies using an Australian context: 'conversion therapy is reported to occur most commonly in faith-based contexts. Typical practices tend to involve counselling, prayer, scripture reading, fasting, retreats or "spiritual healing".'[24]

Benoit Denizet-Lewis's 'My Ex-Gay Friend'

To return to the paratext of *I am Michael* in order to contextualize or better understand the biographical circumstances of Michael's path to conversion, Denizet-Lewis's article, 'My Ex-Gay Friend', which (as noted above) inspired the film, is not only insightful but also relevant to the theme of conversion ideology. At one point in the article, Denizet-Lewis quotes Benji:

> To me, Michael is a victim of this insane society we live in, where we grow up with all these conflicting messages and pressures around sexuality and religion, and where we divide into these camps where *we're* always right and the other side is always wrong. Some people are susceptible to buying into that, and I think Michael is one of them.[25]

Benji's statement links conversion ideology ('we grow up with all these conflicting messages and pressures around sexuality and religion')[26] with his view of Michael as a 'victim'. Extending outward into the reality of the multiple examples of the paratext around the film, such as Denizet-Lewis's article, including its quotation of Benji's words, brings into play a series of options for the viewer that shape and augment their interpretations and opinions. Such options are sometimes available and accessed before someone watches a film, such as Denizet-Lewis's article, although a curious viewer may search and access the material afterwards. This process of viewer engagement in the paratext of transmedia narratives can lead one down the proverbial 'rabbit hole'. As this particular study aims to explore and interrogate exactly what is at stake in Michael's story, it leans into the 'conflicting messages and pressures around sexuality and religion'[27] that drive the film and the article that inspired it, embracing the ancillary stories unfolding 'across multiple media platforms, with each new text making a distinctive and valuable contribution to the whole'.[28]

Indeed, the media hoopla attending the film constituted a paratext explosion, which catered to pre-viewers and post-viewers interested in learning more. Here new media reigns: a Google search for 'Michael Glatze' quickly locates information about conversion ideology (such as Benji's words in Denizet-Lewis) as well as conversion practices. Sometimes, the two topics converge, as illustrated by Internet publications such as the one at josephnicolosi.com, the website for Joseph Nicolosi, which has the homepage header, '*If gay doesn't define you:* YOU DON'T HAVE TO BE GAY', and the by-line, 'Offering Psychological Insight to Men with Same-Sex Attraction'.[29] Sometimes, what *is not* online or what has been removed is as informative as what *is* there. In the case of Nicolosi, founder and president of NARTH,[30] and the website, josephnicolosi. com, Denizet-Lewis's article includes a (now broken) link to a 2007 'published interview' between Nicolosi and Michael. Denizet-Lewis quotes from the interview – 'Michael said that he became "born again" in that moment and that "every concept that my mind had ever entertained – my whole existence – was completely re-evaluated"'[31] – which leaves the curious wanting more. While a case of what is *no longer* online, what *is* online is a 2009 interview involving the two men, which Nicolosi introduces as follows:

> In 2007, I first interviewed Michael Glatze for an article posted on the NARTH (www.narth.com) website. A leader in the gay-activist movement, Michael had just gone public about leaving his lifestyle and rejecting the gay movement. Homosexuality is not life-giving, he said, and 'I choose life.'[32]

The interview progresses in a manner that readers familiar with Nicolosi, Michael and conversion practices would expect. Nicolosi, one of the best-known proponents and practitioners of gay conversion practices and devout Catholic, prompts Michael with succinct questions and comments that create the conversational space for him to fill in the blanks:

> **JN**   I want to reiterate the point you said a few minutes ago – that natural sexuality is heterosexual … that to deny this, is to deny reality.
>
> **MG**   That's right. Heterosexuality is what's natural, human, normal and real. Same-sex activity isn't good for either person involved. On the part of gay activists and even the culture at large, there's been a 'waving of the magic wand' – that is, a using of all kinds of wonderful words which blind people from seeing what is actually going on in gay sex.
>
> **JN**   What kind of 'wonderful words' are being used in the culture?
>
> **MG**   You know, in recent months, I've tried to pay attention to things that are healthy and not focus on that aspect. As somebody told me, 'where the attention goes, the energy flows'. When I focus on all this negativity, I just get really frustrated.
>
> **JN**   That happens to all of us who are in this culture war. It's really toxic.

As evident in the above quotations, advocates and practitioners of conversion practices such as Nicolosi were quick to court Michael after his online conversion, and viewers can still access some of the material contemporaneous with this time in his life. However, Michael also acted independently, as briefly touched on in the film in scenes in which his public story, vitriolic, hateful, self-loathing and Christian, are referenced. These point to another paratext – Michael's blog (no longer available) – in which he railed against the LGBT+ community and enunciated conservative Christian tenets reflecting biblical literalism. The Internet has been scrubbed clean of Michael's sole-authored blogs and articles, though they are still referenced, including his 2007 column, 'How a "Gay Rights" Leader Became Straight',[33] which outlines his transformation from gay to straight.

Michael Lost and Found

Those who remember Michael when he identified as a gay man continue to fill in the gaps that are increasingly present where online content used to be. In addition to Denizet-Lewis's article, there is the short homemade documentary film, *Michael Lost and Found*, which is a fascinating sequel to the Hollywood biopic, *I am Michael.* Made by ex-partner, Benji Nycum and directed by Daniel J. Wilner, *Michael Lost and Found* is a mere nineteen minutes of footage filmed on a phone. It was released by Netflix in the same year as the biopic and has since found a home online via YouTube. The documentary features the two ex-partners along with Michael's wife, Rebekah Glatze, discussing Michael's radical change of life and his then life as a pastor in Wyoming.

This short documentary opens with a quotation from Michael from WorldNetDaily: 'It wasn't internal homophobia that caused my "hatred" of my own homosexuality. It was God.' What is telling and poignant here is the active use of the word 'hatred' and Michael's refusal to disassociate it from his God. For Michael and his God, same-sex attraction is hateworthy. Throughout the film, this position or tenet of faith, is never reconsidered by Michael. What is particularly noteworthy about Michael's silence on the position of evangelical and fundamentalist Christianity on homosexuality is the cognitive dissonance (see Chapter

2) on display over other biblical tenets, particularly on the topic of women and the history of female repression, which he and Rebekah passionately reject.

At the beginning of this chapter, I posed the following questions: What are the ramifications of biblical literalism on homosexuality for same-sex attracted individuals? What exactly is at stake for same-sex attracted people when confronted by those who call their sexuality a sin? I quoted Venn-Brown's succinct answer to these questions. Considering these questions once more in the context of this short film, it is evident that in the context of conversion ideology – even without reference to any form of conversion practices having taken place during Michael's epiphany – a conservative Christian has no recourse but to reject any alternatives to heterosexuality and gender binarism. What is evident, therefore, is that the stakes are exceedingly high for same-sex attracted people when confronted by those who advocate that their sexuality is a sin.

Michael Lost and Found provides little by way of answers to the conversion of Michael Glatze. However, as a paratext and transmedia adjunct to the biopic film, *I am Michael*, *Michael Lost and Found* the documentary sheds light on the toll conversion ideology takes on individuals. The title of Nycum's film – *Michael Lost and Found* – is compellingly ironic and thought-provoking for the viewer who has watched it *and* the Hollywood biopic. Nycum lost his partner, he finds him, yet the understated and unstated end of the documentary prompts the question: has Michael (really) found himself?

Once Gay – Matthew and Friends

Once Gay is a documentary directed by Frederick Williams and produced by Core Issues Trust and Icontowers Media. It is the story of Matthew Grech, a contestant on X Factor Malta in 2018 who, like Michael Glatze, renounced his homosexuality and embraced Christianity. *Once Gay*, like *I am Michael*, can stand alone as a single filmic text, but like the Hollywood biopic, the documentary tells a story that does not (or cannot) remain contained within the bounds of the initial film that seeks to tell it. Returning briefly to Jenkins on the 'transmedia story', the audience witnesses Grech's story unfolding 'across multiple media platforms, with each new text making a distinctive and valuable contribution to the whole'.[34]

In 2018, as a contestant on X Factor Malta, Matthew undertook a pre-audition interview in which he proselytized about finding God and rejecting his previous gay identity: 'For a long time, I stopped following my passions to follow Jesus. There can be love between two men and two women, yes – but only friendship love. Everything else is a sin.'[35]

The interview was aired by state broadcaster, Television Malta. It also aired on Facebook and YouTube but was removed after complaints, including criticisms voiced by the (then) Minister for European Affairs and Equality, Dr Helena Dalli, exemplifying the power of new media, not only to communicate 'religious heteropatriarchy'[36] but to fight against it (online). As the Minister for Social Dialogue, Consumer Affairs and Civil Liberties between 2013 and 2017, Dalli was particularly opposed to the screentime allocated to Grech. During her time in Parliament, for example, Dalli was a leading figure in the outlawing of conversion practices in Malta in 2016, introducing the *Civil Unions Act*[37] and the *Gender Identity, Gender Expression and Sex Characteristics Act*.[38] Perhaps, most pertinently, Dalli was instrumental in introducing a Bill (Act No. LV of 2016) to ban conversion practices in Malta in 2016, making it the first European country to do so.[39] The reasons behind the Bill highlight the intersections between sexual and gender identities and expressions, emphasizing the imperative of protecting all members of the LGBT+ community from conversion practices, including trans people and gender diverse people who, as Bennett discusses in Chapter 3 of this book, 'barely registered in mainstream consciousness'[40] less than a decade ago. The justification for the Bill reads:

> The main object of this Bill is to affirm that all persons have a sexual orientation, a gender identity and a gender expression, and that no particular combination of these three characteristics constitutes a

disorder, disease, illness, deficiency, disability and, or shortcoming. This Bill provides for a ban on conversion practices offered and, or performed by both professionals and individuals against variations of sexual orientation, gender identity and, or gender expression, particularly on vulnerable persons. This Bill also prohibits the pathologisation of any sexual orientation, gender identity and, or gender expression.[41]

The opposition to Matthew Grech's televised evangelism, particularly by Dalli, sparked a culture war in Malta, the reverberations of which are still being felt. The documentary *Once Gay* plays a crucial role in providing a powerful rebuff to Malta's progressive stance on LGBT+ rights through its free access screening options online and its promotion of Core Issues Trust (one of the two production companies behind the documentary). Grech has become the Christian darling of Irish organization Core Issues Trust, in much the same way as Glatze became the poster child for individuals like Joseph Nicolosi and the organizations they fronted. Like Nicolosi's practice and associated enterprises, Core Issues Trust is unapologetic about their members' views of the sins of the LGBT+ community and their active promotion of conversion practices:

> CORE seeks to provide support for relationally and sexually damaged and wounded adults who seek wholeness, and desire to walk in obedience to the Gospel of Christ. Grieving for those whose sense of rejection and abandonment is increased through the well-intentioned, but often misinformed acts of Christians seeking to uphold the Biblical prohibition on homosexual acts, CORE seeks to explore appropriate patterns of relating in both singleness and in marriage. It takes seriously the Biblical injunction to 'love one another deeply, from the heart' (1 Peter 1:22), and promotes the idea that change is possible.[42]

This extract from the Mission Statement promotes Core as a Christian organization built on the bedrock of biblical literalism, which, in the words of the previously discussed scholarship of Andrew F. Smith, venerates the Bible as both 'inerrant' and 'infallible'.[43] While Core is a slippery business, appearing not to directly provide access to conversion practices on its website, it does have clearly marked contact details and a slew of PDF files and eBooks available to download for free that include titles such as, 'Ten Good Reasons Not to Restrict Therapy for Unwanted Same-sex Attraction' and 'Personal Accounts of Counselling Interventions for Unwanted Same-sex Attractions'. In the case of these two documents, emphases are placed on terminology, such as 'freedom' and 'therapy', and messages of human rights and religious autonomy. As such, Core's extensive website and its multimedia industry, producing films such as *Once Gay*, exemplify the power of new media to 'educate and regulate traditional religious norms' that casts the Internet as a 'conserving force', a phenomenon 'theorized by Boellstorff [on anti-LGBT+ new media rhetoric in Indonesia] … as "digital heterosexism."'[44]

Once Gay begins with easy listening music, a beach scene and a quotation from Corinthians 6:11: 'You were washed, you were sanctified, you were justified in the name of the Lord Jesus Christ and by the Spirit of our God.' The first words are spoken by Pastor Gordon-John Manché of the River of Love Church to Mike Davidson, CEO of Core Issues Trust, and address the fallout around Matthew's X Factor controversy. Through a series of individual witnesses or, as Bennett refers to them via Bill Nichols, 'talking heads',[45] the documentary is littered with overt political messages, including the promotion of a right-wing Christian agenda and the active and vocal opposition to Malta's changes in legislation relating to LGBT+ rights. This propagandist documentary is mostly fixated on promoting resistance to the recent changes to Maltese law on conversion practices.

The early inclusion of Dr Ivan Grech Mintoff, leader of the now defunct Alleanza Bidla (Alliance for Change), a conservative democratic party, sets the scene for the rhetoric of conversion ideology that appropriates the language of equality and social justice for a fundamentalist Christian message. For example, Mintoff speaks of supporters of Matthew, and Matthew himself, as having had their right to free speech restrained and their basic human rights violated in general. Matthew testifies to Mike Davidson that rather than members of the LGBT+ community being the targets of vitriol, hatred and abuse, people such as himself – ex-gay advocates – are those who suffer:

> … unfortunately, in society right now in Malta, you are celebrated if you come out as LGBT, as a homosexual, but if you come out as an ex-gay, you are very frowned upon, in a very obscene and vulgar way. And also, it expresses a lot of hatred and a lot of intolerance.

This particular political voice situates advocates of the ex-gay movement and conversion practices as the victims of an oppressive liberal or 'woke' programme via 'the weaponization of language'.[46]

Interestingly, while Matthew strongly supports conversion practices in the documentary, he has consistently stated that he personally never underwent any form of conversion 'therapy'.[47] This echoes the experience of Michael Glatze who has also consistently denied exposure to any form of conversion practice, and yet advocated for it during the early years of his ex-gay life. Yet, despite Matthew's protestation against the suggestion that any form of conversion practice took place, as posited herein in relation to Michael, it may not be too farfetched to consider that it was a faith-based counselling program that led Matthew to an ex-gay lifestyle. This suggestion opens up new avenues to explore the multiplicity of meanings behind the expression, 'pray the gay away'.

What is meant, exactly, by this expression? Personal prayer? Congregational prayer? 'Therapy' in the form of a prayer? The ominous ambiguity of the 'pray the gay away' slogan points to the endless possibilities that can be undertaken under the umbrella of conversion practices, including prayer and spiritual intervention as equally as electroshock and hormone 'therapies'. The term may seem cutely safe or even silly, private and intimate between the individual and their God, but it is still predicated on a faith-based attempt to reverse sexual or gendered orientations and identities stigmatized by the Christian Right. An example of the murky boundaries between prayer and conversion practices was disclosed by a former patient of one of the Christian 'counselling' clinics owned by United States high profile Republicans,

Michele and Marcus Bachmann, Bachmann & Associates. Andrew Ramirez, who was seventeen years old when he went to Bachmann & Associates, reported he was advised that prayer would ensure an end to his homosexual desires:

> [One counsellor's] path for my therapy would be to read the Bible, pray to God that I would no longer be gay . . . And God would forgive me if I were straight.[48]

And again:

> Ramirez told *The Nation* that his counsellor said 'being gay was not an acceptable lifestyle in God's eyes' and prescribed prayer and reading the Bible as part of a 'cure'.[49]

Likewise, when an undercover investigation was conducted in 2011 by John Becker from Truth Wins Out, the gay rights activist group founded by Wayne Besen, the report was similar:

> The basic notion put forward by my therapist was that strains in my relationship with my father transformed into same-sex desire years later. I could shed these sinful desires through the formation of healthy, platonic same-sex relationships and healthy doses of prayer.[50]

Statements such as these recall the words of both Michael and Matthew in the many interviews in which they both consistently deny any form of conversion practices. However, in the context of the 'counselling' experienced by Andrew Ramirez and John Becker, the advice recommends prayer and biblical readings as a 'cure' for homosexual desire, which surely places such activities among recognized faith-based conversion practices.

Breaking news: Matthew Grech pleads 'not guilty' in court

Paratexts and transmedia narratives open many doors and remain ongoing addenda to the original stories. In the case of Matthew Grech

Figure 4.1 Mathew Grech prosecution order redacted (20 June 2022).

from *Once Gay*, he was once again in the news when, in 2023, he and two other individuals (Public Media News Malta founders, Mario Camilleri and Rita Bonnici), appeared in court on the charge of breaching the ban on the practice of gay conversion 'therapy'[51] under Malta's Act No. LV of 2016.

Grech was accompanied by two of the talking heads from the documentary, Pastor Gordon-John Manché and Ivan Grech Mintoff.[52] In relation to the discussion above on the issue of what constitutes conversion practices – including prayer – it is an important point that Matthew Grech and his co-accused were charged on the basis that the conversion discussed was conversion achieved through prayer.[53] Mike Davidson, CEO of Core Issues Trust, and interviewer and host of *Once Gay* is part of the case, publicly supporting Matthew, stating: '[this is] probably a test case where the freedoms of speech, conscience and religion are being attacked'.[54] Matthew has the notorious honour of being the first person in the world known to be charged with the crime.

Conclusion

As an analysis of extensive paratext and transmedia narratives, this chapter has no ending because the narratives will continue to grow. In this sense, this chapter may be considered the first in a sequel in the lives and loves of both Michael Glatze and Matthew Grech. This forecast is predicated on the ecology of new digital media that continually transforms and transposes through the process of content augmentation. In terms of the theme at hand – gay conversion practices – this theoretical and methodological approach to filmic texts refuses to permit a narrative monologue or, in other words, a single perspective, but instead subjects the works to 'a multiplicity of voices' (a term Tom Abba adopts as the digital equivalent to 'Mikhail Bakhtin's notion of 'multivocality').[55] Therefore, the challenge that this model of interpretation presents, ensures that the conversion practices and, perhaps more urgently, the conversion ideology that underscore *I am Michael*, *Michael Lost and Found* and *Once Gay – Matthew and Friends* – expressly the first and the third of these films – do not go uncontested but are open to a form of interrogation that presents their sole visions as more than a sum of their parts and lays them bare for the naïve and inherently damaging narratives they are.

Notes

1   See *Core Issues Trust*: https://core-issues.org/about-us/ (accessed 29 August 2023). The website states: 'Core Issues Trust is a registered charity in Northern Ireland operating throughout the UK and beyond. We support those leaving LGBT identities, behaviours, attractions and life choices. We campaign for the freedom to access pastoral care, counselling and therapeutic choice, now under threat, internationally, by 'conversion therapy' bans. Its trustees and projects are advised by a range of like-minded individuals from Anglican, Roman Catholic, Pentecostal and Reformed traditions.'

2   R. Tsuria and J. Bartashius, 'The Sex–Religion Matrix.' In *The Handbook on Religion and Communication*, eds Y. Cohen and P. A. Soukup (Oxford: Wiley-Blackwell, 2023), 453–68.

3   'The issue of repressing homosexuality is by no means limited to Christianity – it exists in most of the world's religions. Therefore, media representations of these issues in Judaism, Islam, Hinduism, etc. can be found' (Tsuria and Bartashius, 458).

4   See also, Chapter 8 and the political-cultural contexts around the memoir, *Boy Erased*, which also considers the broader evangelical environment of conversion ideologies; Scott McKinnon, 'Defined by their Abjection: *Boy Erased* and the Limits of Queer Victimhood in Activist Cinema.' In *Gay Conversion Practices in Memoir, Film and Fiction: Stories of Repentance and Defiance*, eds J. E. Bennett and M. Johnson (London: Bloomsbury, 2024), 237–59.

5   This is not to marginalize or diminish the historical and, at times, ongoing realities of more extreme and overtly violent forms of gay conversion 'therapy', which have and/or continue to include chemical 'treatments', 'medical' 'cures', bodily deprivations', and 'corrective' rape. Nor is it to deny the role of state interventions in 'correcting' sexuality and/or gender identity. For a clear distinction in terminology between faith-based practices and historical medical interventions, see A. Venn-Brown, 'Tasmania to ban conversion "therapy"', *The Big Smoke*, 16 September 2022, https://thebigsmoke.com.au/2022/09/16/tasmania-to-ban-conversion-therapy/ (accessed 31 March 2023).

6   See Jones et al. on this point: 'Spiritual practices – such as prayer, scripture reading, pastoral counselling, pilgrimage and spiritual deliverance or exorcism – were the most common types of LGBTQA + conversion practice reported by our participants. Other conversion practices reported included formal psychological counselling, peer support groups, 'ex-gay' programs, coerced heterosexual marriage and rape' (4). T. W. Jones, J. Power and T. M. Jones, 'Religious Trauma and Moral Injury from LGBTQA+ Conversion Practices,' *Social Science and Medicine*, 305 (2022): 1–9.

7   In non-Christian contexts, see, for example: M. Yadegarfard, 'How are Iranian Gay Men Coping with Systematic Suppression under Islamic Law? A Qualitative Study,' *Sexuality & Culture* 23, no. 4 (2019): 1250–73; A. Kabir and I. Nazareth, 'Conversion Therapy: A Violation of Human Rights in Iranian Gay Men,' *The Lancet Psychiatry* 9, no. 4 (2022): e19;

A. Ogunbajo, T. Oke, K. Okanlawon, G. M. Abubakari and O. Oginni, 'Religiosity and Conversion Therapy is Associated with Psychosocial Health Problems among Sexual Minority Men (SMM) in Nigeria,' *Journal of Religion and Health* 61, no. 4 (2022): 3098–128. See also *Homosexuality, Transsexuality, Psychoanalysis and Traditional Judaism*, eds A. Slomowitz and A. Feit (New York: Routledge, 2019), especially, J. Drescher, 'Moving the Conversation Along,' 3–7; R. Lesser, 'Discussion of "Does God Make Referrals?": Orthodox Judaism and Homosexuality,' 45–8.

8 See, B. Barton, *Pray the Gay Away: The Extraordinary Lives of Bible Belt Gays* (New York: New York University Press, 2012), 10–13. The term 'fundamentalist' herein extends to ultra-conservative sects within, for example, the Catholic Church. See A. Hennig, 'Political Genderphobia in Europe: Accounting for Right-Wing Political-Religious Alliances against Gender-sensitive Education Reforms since 2012,' *Zeitschrift für Religion, Gesellschaft und Politik* 2 no. 2 (2018): 193–219; M. Cornejo-Valle and J. Ramme, '"We Don't Want Rainbow Terror": Religious and Far-Right Sexual Politics in Poland and Spain.' In *Paradoxical Right-Wing Sexual Politics in Europe*, eds C. Möser, J. Ramme and J. Takács (London: Palgrave Macmillan, 2022): 25–60; D. Wetzel, 'The Rise of the Catholic Alt-Right,' *Journal of Labor and Society* 23 no. 1 (2020): 31–55.

9 A. F. Smith, 'Secularity and Biblical Literalism: Confronting the Case for Epistemological Diversity,' *International Journal for Philosophy of Religion* 71 (2012): 208.

10 R. K. Gnuse, 'Seven Gay Texts: Biblical Passages Used to Condemn Homosexuality,' *Biblical Theology Bulletin: Journal of Theology and Culture* 45 (2015): 68. The passages are: Genesis 9:20-7, 19:1-11; Leviticus 18:22, 20:13); 1 Corinthians 6:9-10; 1 Timothy 1:10; Romans 1:26-27. At the time of writing this article, Gnuse was a 'clergyperson' at the Texas-Louisiana Gulf Coast Synod of the Evangelical Lutheran Church of America. See also, M. Ward Sr., '"All Scripture Is Inspired by God": The Culture of Biblical Literalism in an Evangelical Church,' *Journal of Communication and Religion* 45 no. 1 (2022): 86–110; Ward writes: 'Three in ten Americans believe that the Bible is the Word of God and should be taken literally, word for word. Surveys and studies show this contingent of literalists is composed primarily of evangelicals and, for White evangelicals in particular, that biblical literalism is a strong predictor of their conservative politics' (86).

11 A. Venn-Brown, *A Life of Unlearning: A Preacher's Struggle with his Homosexuality, Church and Faith*, 3rd edn rev. (Sydney: Personal Success Australia, 2015). Kindle Edition. Chapter 15, 'Turmoil'. Also see Chapter 1 herein.

12 Ward, '"All Scripture Is Inspired by God"', 87.

13 See *The Electronic Church in the Digital Age: Cultural Impacts of Evangelical Mass Media*, 2 vols., ed M. Ward Sr. (Santa Barbara: ABC-CLIO, 2015).

14 T. Fetner, 'Ex-Gay Rhetoric and the Politics of Sexuality: The Christian Antigay/Pro-Family Movement's "Truth in Love" Ad Campaign', *Journal of Homosexuality* 50 no. 1 (2005): 71–95; S. Lund and C. Renna, 'An Analysis of the Media Response to the Spitzer Study', *Journal of Gay & Lesbian Psychotherapy*, 7, no. 3 (2003); C. O. Stewart, 'Social Cognition and Discourse Processing Goals in the Analysis of Ex-Gay Rhetoric', *Discourse & Society*, 19, no.1, 2008.

15 Tsuria and Bartashius, 'The Sex–Religion Matrix', 453. Emphasis mine.

16 W. Via and H. Beirich, *A Report from the Global Project Against Hate and Extremism*, https://globalextremism.org/wp-content/uploads/2022/01/Conversion-Therapy-Online-The-Ecosystem.pdf (accessed 9 December 2022). See also, Tsuria and Bartashius, 'The Sex–Religion Matrix'.

17 Barton, *Pray the Gay Away*, 15.

18 Barton, *Pray the Gay Away*, 9–10.

19 J. Ford and A. Herb, 'The Quiet Violence of Denying Queerness in the Novel and Film, *The Miseducation of Cameron Post*.' In *Gay Conversion Practices in Memoir, Film and Fiction: Stories of Repentance and Defiance*, eds J. E. Bennett and M. Johnson (London: Bloomsbury, 2024), 212.

20 B. Denizet-Lewis, 'My Ex-Gay Friend', *New York Times Magazine* (2011), https://www.nytimes.com/2011/06/19/magazine/my-ex-gay-friend.html (accessed 12 March 2023). A version of the article appeared in print on June 19, 2011, with the headline, 'GOING STRAIGHT' in *Sunday Magazine*: 36.

21 G. Genette and M. Maclean, 'Introduction to the Paratext', *New Literary History* 22 no. 2 (1991): 261–72. Genette's original theory of paratext, while applied to literary texts, has been extended to filmic texts, including in the studies by Jenkins and Gray; see H. Jenkins, *Convergence Culture: Where Old and New Media Collide* (New York: New York University Press, 2006); J. Gray, *Show Sold Separately: Promos, Spoilers, and Other Media Paratexts* (New York: New York University Press, 2010).

22 Independent Forensic Expert Group, *Statement on Conversion Therapy*, https://www.ohchr.org/sites/default/files/Documents/Issues/Sexual Orientation/IESOGI/CSOsAJ/IFEG_Statement_on_C.T._for_ publication.pdf (accessed 8 November 2022).

23 Independent Forensic Expert Group, *Statement on Conversion Therapy*.

24 Independent Forensic Expert Group, *Statement on Conversion Therapy*.

25 Denizet-Lewis, 'My Ex-Gay Friend.'

26 Denizet-Lewis, 'My Ex-Gay Friend.'

27 Denizet-Lewis, 'My Ex-Gay Friend.'

28 Jenkins, *Convergence Culture*, 95–6.

29 *Joseph Nicolosi – Reparative Therapy*®, https://www.josephnicolosi.com/ (accessed 4 December 2022).

30 National Association for Research and Therapy of Homosexuality. The website, www.narth.com, is no longer available, and links to it from josephnicolosi.com are broken. Joseph Nicolosi (1947–2017).

31 Denizet-Lewis, 'My Ex-Gay Friend.'

32 'Interview with Michael Glatze: Two-Year Follow-Up,' https://www.josephnicolosi.com/collection/interview-with-michael-glatze-two-year-follow-up (accessed 27 August 2022).

33 See, G. Meeks, 'Former Gay Activist Responds to Critics After Marrying a Woman,' *CHARISMANEWS* (17 December 2013), https://www.charismanews.com/us/42135-former-gay-activist-responds-to-critics-after-marrying-a-woman (accessed 28 August 2022).

34 Jenkins, *Convergence Culture*, 95–6.

35 A. Galea, 'X Factor Judges Had Not Seen Matthew Grech Interview Clip before Audition,' *Malta Business Weekly*, 29 October 2019, https://www.independent.com.mt/articles/2018-10-29/local-news/X-Factor-judges-had-not-seen-Matthew-Grech-interview-clip-before-audition-6736198515 (accessed 8 March 2023).

36 Tsuria and Bartashius, 'The Sex–Religion Matrix,' 454.

37 Civil Unions Act, 2014 (Act No. IX of 2014), https://www.ilo.org/dyn/natlex/natlex4.detail?p_lang=&p_isn=97242 (accessed 28 August 2023)

38 Act No. X of 2014 – Constitution of Malta (Amendment) Act. https://parlament.mt/12th-leg/acts-12th/act-x-of-2014/ (accessed 28 August 2023).

39 Act No. LV of 2016 – Sexual Orientation, Gender Identity and Gender Expression Act, http://url.au.m.mimecastprotect.com/s/yKFWCVARD0Ty vj8PiExO8X?domain=parlament.mt (accessed 28 August 2023).

40 J. E. Bennett, '"I Remember Feeling Like I was Sitting on the Wrong Side of the Circle": Documentary Film and the Exposition of Conversion Practices.' In *Gay Conversion Practices in Memoir, Film and Fiction: Stories of Repentance and Defiance*, eds J. E. Bennett and M. Johnson (London: Bloomsbury, 2024), 97.

41 Act No. LV of 2016 – Sexual Orientation, Gender Identity and Gender Expression Act.

42 'Vision and Ethics,' *Core Issues Trust*, https://www.core-issues.org/vision-and-ethics (accessed 19 September 2022). The statement quoted in n. 1 above is more overt in its support of conversion practices.

43 'Vision and Ethics,' *Core Issues Trust.*

44 Tsuria and Bartashius, 'The Sex–Religion Matrix,' 462. See T. Boellstorf, 'Om toleran Om: Four Indonesian Reflections on Digital Heterosexism,' *Media, Culture & Society*, 42 no. 1 (2020): 7–24.

45 B. Nichols, *Representing Reality: Issues and Concepts in Documentary* (Bloomington: Indiana University Press, 1991), 17–18.

46 C.-M. Pascale, 'The Weaponization of Language: Discourses of Rising Right-Wing Authoritarianism,' *Current Sociology*, 67, no. 6 (2019): 898–917.

47 'I Didn't Have Gay Therapy, Says Christian Convert Matthew Grech,' *NewsLetter*, 13 February 2019, https://www.newsletter.co.uk/news/i-didnt-have-gay-therapy-says-christian-convert-matthew-grech-111795 (accessed 2 March 2023).

48 B. Ross, R. Schwartz, M. Mosk and M. Chuchmach, 'Michele Bachmann Clinic: Where You Can Pray Away the Gay?' *ABC News*, 12 July 2011, https://abcnews.go.com/Blotter/michele-bachmann-exclusive-pray-gay-candidates-clinic/story?id=14048691 (accessed 3 March 2022).

49 L. Grindley, 'Hidden Camera Finds Reparative Therapy at Bachmann's Clinics,' *The Advocate*, 9 July 2011, https://www.advocate.com/health/2011/07/09/hidden-camera-sting-finds-reparative-therapy-bachmann39s-clinics (accessed 3 March 2023).

50 M. Benjamin, 'The Truth Behind Marcus Bachmann's Controversial Christian Therapy Clinic,' *Time* 15 July 2011, https://swampland.time.com/2011/07/15/the-truth-behind-marcus-bachmanns-controversial-christian-therapy-clinic/ (accessed 1 March 2023).

51 As this was the term used by the Court in Malta, I have maintained the phrase, 'gay conversion "therapy"'.

52 M. P. Camilleri, 'Matthew Grech Pleads Not Guilty to Promoting Gay Conversion Therapy,' *Newsbook*. 4 February 2023, https://newsbook.com.mt/en/matthew-grech-pleads-not-guilty-to-promoting-gay-conversion-therapy/ (accessed 10 March 2023).

53 M. Agius, 'Matthew Grech and Website Directors Charged with Promoting Illegal Gay Conversion Therapy,' *Malta Today*, 3 February 2023, https://www.maltatoday.com.mt/news/court_and_police/121091/matthew_grech_and_website_directors_charged_with_promoting_illegal_gay_conversion_therapy#.ZAGcMnZBy5c (accessed 1 March 2023).

54 P. Bradfield, 'Matthew Grech Malta: Trustee of Co Down Ex-Gay Charity Core Issues Trust to be "First in World" Charged with Promoting "Gay Conversion Therapy",' *News Letter* 24 January 2023, https://www.newsletter.co.uk/health/matthew-grech-malta-trustee-of-co-down-ex-gay-charity-core-issues-trust-to-be-first-in-world-charged-with-promoting-gay-conversion-therapy-3999040 (accessed 15 March 2023).

55 T. Abba, 'Hybrid Stories Examining the Future of Transmedia Narrative,' *Science Fiction Film & Television* 2 no. 2 (2009): 61.

Bibliography

Abba, T. 'Hybrid Stories Examining the Future of Transmedia Narrative.' *Science Fiction Film & Television*, 2 no. 2 (2009): 59–76.

Agius, M. 'Matthew Grech and Website Directors Charged with Promoting Illegal Gay Conversion Therapy.' *Malta Today*, 3 February 2023, https://www.maltatoday.com.mt/news/court_and_police/121091/matthew_grech_and_website_directors_charged_with_promoting_illegal_gay_conversion_therapy#.ZAGcMnZBy5c

Barton, B. *Pray the Gay Away: The Extraordinary Lives of Bible Belt Gays.* New York: New York University Press, 2012.

Bennett, J. E. '"I Remember Feeling Like I was Sitting on the Wrong Side of the Circle": Documentary Film and the Exposition of Conversion Practices.' In *Gay Conversion Practices in Memoir, Film and Fiction: Stories of Repentance and Defiance*, eds J. E. Bennett and Marguerite Johnson. 95–124. London: Bloomsbury, 2024.

Benjamin, M. 'The Truth Behind Marcus Bachmann's Controversial Christian Therapy Clinic.' *Time*, 15 July 2011, https://swampland.time.

com/2011/07/15/the-truth-behind-marcus-bachmanns-controversial-christian-therapy-clinic/

Boellstorf, T. 'Om toleran Om: Four Indonesian Reflections on Digital Heterosexism.' *Media, Culture & Society*, 42 no. 1 (2020): 7–24.

Bradfield, P. 'Matthew Grech Malta: Trustee of Co Down Ex-Gay Charity Core Issues Trust to be "First in World" Charged with Promoting "Gay Conversion Therapy".' *News Letter*, 24 January 2023, https://www.newsletter.co.uk/health/matthew-grech-malta-trustee-of-co-down-ex-gay-charity-core-issues-trust-to-be-first-in-world-charged-with-promoting-gay-conversion-therapy-3999040

Camilleri, M. P. 'Matthew Grech Pleads Not Guilty to Promoting Gay Conversion Therapy.' *Newsbook*, 4 February 2023, https://newsbook.com.mt/en/matthew-grech-pleads-not-guilty-to-promoting-gay-conversion-therapy/

Core Issues Trust, https://core-issues.org/about-us/

Cornejo-V., M. and J. Ramme. '"We Don't Want Rainbow Terror": Religious and Far-Right Sexual Politics in Poland and Spain.' In *Paradoxical Right-Wing Sexual Politics in Europe*, eds C. Möser, J. Ramme and J. Takács, 25–60. London: Palgrave Macmillan, 2022.

Denizet-Lewis, B. 'My Ex-Gay Friend.' *New York Times Magazine*, 16 June 2011, https://www.nytimes.com/2011/06/19/magazine/my-ex-gay-friend.html

Drescher, J. 'Moving the Conversation Along.' In *Homosexuality, Transsexuality, Psychoanalysis and Traditional Judaism*, eds A. Slomowitz and A. Feit, 3–7. New York: Routledge, 2019.

Fetner, T. 'Ex-Gay Rhetoric and the Politics of Sexuality: The Christian Antigay/Pro-Family Movement's "Truth in Love" Ad Campaign.' *Journal of Homosexuality*, 50, no. 1 (2005): 71–95.

Ford, J. and A. Herb. 'The Quiet Violence of Denying Queerness in the Novel and Film, *The Miseducation of Cameron Post*.' In *Gay Conversion Practices in Memoir, Film and Fiction: Stories of Repentance and Defiance*, eds J. E. Bennett and M. Johnson. 211–35. London: Bloomsbury, 2024.

Galea, A. 'X Factor Judges had not Seen Matthew Grech Interview Clip before Audition.' *Malta Business Weekly*, 29 October 2019. https://www.independent.com.mt/articles/2018-10-29/local-news/X-Factor-judges-had-not-seen-Matthew-Grech-interview-clip-before-audition-6736198515

Genette, G. and M. Maclean. 'Introduction to the Paratext.' *New Literary History*, 22, no. 2 (1991): 261–72.

Gnuse, R. K. 'Seven Gay Texts: Biblical Passages Used to Condemn Homosexuality.' *Biblical Theology Bulletin: Journal of Theology and Culture*, 45 (2015): 68–87.

Gray, J. *Show Sold Separately: Promos, Spoilers, and Other Media Paratexts.* New York: New York University Press, 2010.

Grindley, L. 'Hidden Camera Finds Reparative Therapy at Bachmann's Clinics.' *The Advocate*, 9 July 2011, https://www.advocate.com/health/2011/07/09/hidden-camera-sting-finds-reparative-therapy-bachmann39s-clinics

Hennig, A. 'Political Genderphobia in Europe: Accounting for Right-Wing Political-Religious Alliances against Gender-Sensitive Education Reforms since 2012.' *Zeitschrift für Religion, Gesellschaft und Politik*, 2 no. 2 (2018): 193–219.

I am Michael [Film] Dir. Justin Kelly, USA: Brainstorm Media, 2015.

'I Didn't Have Gay Therapy, says Christian Convert Matthew Grech.' *NewsLetter*, 13 February 2019, https://www.newsletter.co.uk/news/i-didnt-have-gay-therapy-says-christian-convert-matthew-grech-111795

Independent Forensic Expert Group. *Statement on Conversion Therapy.* https://www.ohchr.org/sites/default/files/Documents/Issues/SexualOrientation/IESOGI/CSOsAJ/IFEG_Statement_on_C.T._for_publication.pdf

'Interview with Michael Glatze: Two-Year Follow-Up.' https://www.josephnicolosi.com/collection/interview-with-michael-glatze-two-year-follow-up

Jenkins, H. *Convergence Culture: Where Old and New Media Collide.* New York: New York University Press, 2006.

Jones, T. W., J. Power and T. M. Jones. 'Religious Trauma and Moral Injury from LGBTQA+ Conversion Practices.' *Social Science and Medicine*, 305 (2022): 1–9.

Jones, T., A. Brown, L. Carnie, G. Fletcher and W. Leonard. *Preventing Harm, Promoting Justice: Responding to LGBT Conversion Therapy in Australia.* Melbourne: GLHV@ARCSHS and the Human Rights Law Centre, 2018.

Joseph Nicolosi – Reparative Therapy®, https://www.josephnicolosi.com/

Kabir, A. and I. Nazareth. 'Conversion Therapy: A Violation of Human Rights in Iranian Gay Men.' *The Lancet Psychiatry*, 9, no. 4 (2022): e19.

Lesser, R. 'Discussion of "Does God make referrals?": Orthodox Judaism and Homosexuality.' In *Homosexuality, Transsexuality, Psychoanalysis and Traditional Judaism*, eds A. Slomowitz and A. Feit. 45–8. New York: Routledge, 2019.

Lund, S. and C. Renna. 'An Analysis of the Media Response to the Spitzer Study.' *Journal of Gay & Lesbian Psychotherapy*, 7, no. 3 (2003): 55–67.

McKinnon, S. 'Defined by their Abjection: Boy Erased and the Limits of Queer Victimhood in Activist Cinema.' In *Gay Conversion Practices in Memoir, Film and Fiction: Stories of Repentance and Defiance*, eds J. E. Bennett and M. Johnson. 237–59. London: Bloomsbury, 2024.

Meeks, G. 'Former Gay Activist Responds to Critics After Marrying a Woman.' *CHARISMANEWS*, 17 December 2013. https://www.charismanews.com/us/42135-former-gay-activist-responds-to-critics-after-marrying-a-woman

Michael Lost and Found [Documentary] Dir. Daniel J. Wilner, Canada, USA: Gillian Nycum, 2017.

Nichols, B. *Representing Reality: Issues and Concepts in Documentary.* Bloomington: Indiana University Press, 1991.

Ogunbajo, A., T. Oke, K. Okanlawon, G. M. Abubakari and O. Oginni. 'Religiosity and Conversion Therapy is Associated with Psychosocial Health Problems among Sexual Minority Men (SMM) in Nigeria.' *Journal of Religion and Health* 61, no. 4 (2022): 3098–128.

Once Gay – Matthew and Friends [Documentary] Dir. Frederick Williams, UK: Core Issues Trust and Icontowers Media, 2019.

Pascale, C.-M. 'The Weaponization of Language: Discourses of Rising Right-Wing Authoritarianism.' *Current Sociology*, 67, no. 6 (2019): 898–917.

Ross, B., R. Schwartz, M. Mosk and M. Chuchmach. 'Michele Bachmann Clinic: Where You Can Pray Away the Gay?' *ABC News*, 12 July 2011, https://abcnews.go.com/Blotter/michele-bachmann-exclusive-pray-gay-candidates-clinic/story?id=14048691

Slomowitz, A. and A. Feit, eds *Homosexuality, Transsexuality, Psychoanalysis and Traditional Judaism.* New York: Routledge, 2019.

Smith, A. F. 'Secularity and Biblical Literalism: Confronting the Case for Epistemological Diversity.' *International Journal for Philosophy of Religion*, 71 (2012): 205–19.

Stewart, C. O. 'A Rhetorical Approach to News Discourse: Media Representations of a Controversial Study on "Reparative Therapy".' *Western Journal of Communication*, 69, no. 2 (2005): 147–66.

Stewart, C. O. 'Social Cognition and Discourse Processing Goals in the Analysis of Ex-Gay Rhetoric.' *Discourse & Society*, 19, no.1 (2008): 63–83.

Tsuria, R. and Bartashius, J. 'The Sex–Religion Matrix.' In *The Handbook on Religion and Communication*, eds Y. Cohen and P. A. Soukup, 453–68. Oxford: Wiley-Blackwell, 2023.

Venn-Brown, A. *A Life of Unlearning: A Preacher's Struggle with his Homosexuality, Church and Faith*, 3rd rev edn, Sydney: Personal Success Australia, 2015.

Venn-Brown, A. 'Tasmania to ban conversion "therapy".' *The Big Smoke*, 16 September 2022, https://thebigsmoke.com.au/2022/09/16/tasmania-to-ban-conversion-therapy/

Venn-Brown, A. 'A Life of Unlearning': The Author Reflects.' In *Gay Conversion Practices in Memoir, Film and Fiction: Stories of Repentance and Defiance*, eds J. E. Bennett and M. Johnson. 41–66. London: Bloomsbury, 2024.

Via, W. and H. Beirich. *A Report from the Global Project Against Hate and Extremism,* https://globalextremism.org/wp-content/uploads/2022/01/Conversion-Therapy-Online-The-Ecosystem.pdf

'Vision and Ethics.' *Core Issues Trust*, https://www.core-issues.org/vision-and-ethics

Ward Sr., M., ed *The Electronic Church in the Digital Age: Cultural Impacts of Evangelical Mass Media*, 2 vols. Santa Barbara: ABC-CLIO, 2015.

Ward Sr., M. '"All Scripture Is Inspired by God": The Culture of Biblical Literalism in an Evangelical Church.' *Journal of Communication and Religion*, 45, no. 1 (2022): 86–110.

Wetzel, D. 'The Rise of the Catholic Alt-Right.' *Journal of Labor and Society*, 23, no. 1 (2020): 31–55.

Yadegarfard, M. 'How are Iranian Gay Men Coping with Systematic Suppression under Islamic Law? A qualitative study.' *Sexuality & Culture*, 23, no. 4 (2019): 1250–73.

Part Three

Memoir, Film and Fiction

5

But I'm a Cheerleader: Awkward and Flippant, Accurate and Ground-breaking

Tom Sharples

But I'm a Cheerleader (1999) (hereafter *Cheerleader*) is an oddity of a film. It tackles a harrowing subject, namely the use of conversion practices on same-sex attracted teens under the threat of parental abandonment, with an awkward and often flippant tone. But what makes *Cheerleader* even stranger is that it often portrays the techniques, viewpoints and ineffectiveness of fundamentalist Christian 'ex-gay' movements with impressive accuracy and attention to detail against the backdrop of a sweet love story between two young gay women that refuses a tragic ending. As such, it has become a cult classic, particularly among LGBT+ audiences.

The protagonist of the film, Megan (Natasha Lyonne) is a teenage cheerleader in her final year of high school. While her life appears conventional, Megan's boyfriend, close friend and family are so concerned by her lack of interest in heteronormative eroticism that they stage an intervention. Megan's 'vaginal motifs in artwork and decorating' and lack of pleasure when kissing her boyfriend are all used as examples of her lesbianism, with cartoon-style music amplifying the exaggerated and comical tone of the scene.[1] The outcome is that Megan is sent to be 'rehabilitated' by her Christian parents.

It is during the film's second act that its fictional conversion programme group, True Directions, is formally introduced. As with the intervention scene, it is handled with a camp aesthetic,[2] with the young women clothed in neon pink and young men in garish blue. The camp leaders Mary (Cathy Moriarty), and Mike (RuPaul Charles) are portrayed as caricatures of ex-gays, shouting and abusing their young victims in an overstated fashion. It becomes clear after the opening fifteen minutes that the director, Jamie Babbit, was not aiming for the dark, morbid or realistic tone featured in most mainstream films with a queer protagonist from the 1990s, but a flamboyant, over-the-top comedy about teen romance and sexuality that just happens to be set against the backdrop of an ex-gay camp. A love affair occurs between Megan and fellow attendee Graham (Clea Du Vall) and concludes with the two eventually escaping the True Directions graduation ceremony, driving off into the sunset to face an unknown future.

While *Cheerleader* portrays conversion practices as a suitable topic for comedy, it falls flat through its failure to embrace black comedy as a means through which a director/filmmaker can make a powerful social statement. Born from the evangelical Christian movement that grew to prominence in the 1970s, the ex-gay movement sought to take the place of psychiatry, which in the same decade began to move away from pathologizing and attempting to 'cure' same-sex attracted people.[3] This new phenomenon, a strange mix of outdated nineteenth-century psychiatry, substance abuse treatment models, and faith-based healing, morphed into the unregulated model of conversion practices that exist to this day.[4]

The film was largely panned by critics for its awkward presentation of both trauma and comedy (as discussed below), but very little has been said about *Cheerleader*'s depiction of conversion practices, nor how rare it was to have any mainstream media in the late 1990s/early 2000s portray the subject in any form. Notwithstanding its reception and modest financial returns, *Cheerleader* has experienced a renaissance two decades after its initial release, resulting in a director's cut and stage musical. However, reappraisals have focused more on its portrayal of gender stereotypes than the accuracy with which it presents its central theme.

The focus of this chapter is the qualities and value of *Cheerleader* as a film as well as its portrayal of conversion and those who are presented as the subjects (read, victims) of these practices. I begin with some background on both the director and the era of the film's production, then outline what the film gets correct about ex-gay conversion practices, followed by an examination of why this accuracy is at odds with the inherent nature of the film. I also briefly compare *Cheerleader* to later productions about conversion practices, namely *Boy Erased* (2019), discussed in Chapter 8 and *The Miseducation of Cameron Post* (2018), discussed in Chapter 7, not only to highlight that the film was a product of its time, but also to show how far mainstream knowledge of the harmful nature of conversion practices developed in the twenty years following the film's release. The place of *Cheerleader* as a queer cult classic, a cinematic work, and as a cultural artefact are also addressed.

Jamie Babbit's background

Unlike her characters, when Babbit came out as gay her educated, middle-class family was largely accepting.[5] She grew up in Cleveland, Ohio, attended the prestigious New York University Tisch School of the Arts, and was twenty-eight when she developed *Cheerleader*.[6] The fact that her mother was a nurse who treated people for drug and alcohol addiction gave Babbit an interest in examining the methods of ex-gay groups:

> I'd always wanted to do a comedy about growing up in rehab and the absurdity of that atmosphere. But I didn't want to make fun of twelve-step programs for alcoholism and drugs, because they really help people; but when you turn it into Homosexuals Anonymous, then I felt that was a situation I could have fun with.[7]

Those aware of the subject matter may initially find Babbit's words off-putting. It is an unsettling statement that making 'fun' of those going through rehabilitation was deemed 'off-limits' and yet young gay people subjected to conversion practices was deemed appropriate material for comedic satire.

In regard to filmic inspirations, despite critics noting that *Cheerleader* featured an exaggerated tone not dissimilar to the films of John Waters's,[8]

Babbit herself has stated that while she enjoys his films, and was interested in using a 'camp aesthetic', she felt that his style was 'too dark'.[9] She was also influenced by Tim Burton's 'hyperreality',[10] but as her goal was to make a positive film, she reverses Burton's often drab palette in films like *Edward Scissorhands* (1990), instead using garish bright pink and blue and materials such as polyester for the characters' uniforms.

Babbit's influences also included the political. The director has mentioned that the awareness group AIDS Coalition to Unleash Power (ACT UP) helped guide her approach to filmmaking, as they were famous for using outrageous stunts to bring mainstream attention to the epidemic that afflicted the gay community throughout the 1980s and 1990s. She felt that this approach could be applied to *Cheerleader* to highlight the plight of young gay people, and this is evidenced in the frequently confrontational dialogue featured throughout.[11]

Filmic context

The 1990s witnessed breakthroughs in the depiction of healthy gay characters, but often packaged as comedy. Significantly, a small budget film *Go Fish* (1995) 'was celebrated for changing the genre of lesbian romance from drama (and its implicit sense of anxiety or tragedy) to comedy',[12] while in the world of television the rising fame of the sitcom *Will and Grace* (1998–2006) introduced audiences to the relatable and functional life of its gay protagonist, Will Truman.[13] However, the portrayal of gay or trans protagonists in mainstream American cinema of the 1990s is slight, with *My Own Private Idaho* (1991), *Philadelphia* (1993) and *Boys Don't Cry* (1999) being three prominent examples.[14] These films largely depict trauma experienced by their LGBT+ characters at a time when the scourge of the HIV/AIDS epidemic was fresh in people's minds. At issue is the fetishization of the epidemic as the primary lens through which LGBT+ people could be examined by Hollywood. By contrast, this is the reason that productions such as *Go Fish* and *Will and Grace* appear to be comparatively refreshing.[15]

Coinciding with this tendency, the late 1990s/early 2000s also saw a revival of teen 'gross-out' comedies that examined the discovery of sexuality and sensuality, which included *American Pie* (1999) and *Road Trip* (2000).[16]

Another phenomenon at its zenith in the late 1990s was ex-gay conversion practices. During the production of *Cheerleader*, ex-gay groups, the largest being Exodus International, were boosting their profile on an unprecedented scale.[17] Wayne Besen, a journalist and gay rights campaigner who investigated conversion practices in the late-1990s, states:

> In 1998, a coalition of religious right organisations launched [an] ad campaign featuring ex-gays with headlines such as 'We're Standing for the Truth that Homosexuals can Change.' The full-page ads appeared in major daily newspapers such as the *New York Times* … [ex-gay John] Paulk and his wife, a self-described ex-lesbian, were prominently featured.[18]

Tanya Erzen gives broader context regarding the scale of these various ex-gay churches, claiming that there were hundreds of evangelical Christian ministries in the United States and abroad where 'men and women attend therapy sessions, Bible studies, twelve-step-style meetings, and regular church services as part of their 'journey out of homosexuality'.[19]

When considering this context, and the general lack of mainstream representation of healthy queer people on the big and small screen, the idea of a film parodying conversion 'therapy' must have seemed highly unusual and provocative. Yet, this probably also explains why the film is not wholly satisfying when depicting ex-gay conversion practices.

What the film gets right about conversion practices

Brian Wayne Peterson produced a script based on Babbit's story for *Cheerleader*,[20] with the result featuring evidence of extensive research, though it does mix many time periods and elements together, including inversion (late-nineteenth century), electro-shock therapy (mid-twentieth century) and ex-gay practices (late-twentieth century). Robert Rosenstone argues that in the historical world of cinema, depicting the past 'can contribute to our understanding as well as the discourse of history', but also asks: 'What might we learn from viewing a number of films devoted to … a major subject?'[21] By examining *Cheerleader*'s portrayal of conversion practices, we can examine what it adds to the discourse surrounding this topic.

The fictional programme of True Directions features group therapy, 'reorientating exercises', and family therapy on the weekends, all completed according to the following structure:

Step 1: Admitting you are a homosexual
Step 2: Rediscovering your gender identity
Step 3: Finding the root of your homosexuality
Step 4: Demystifying the opposite sex
Step 5: Simulated sexual lifestyle

This is similar to the twelve steps of Alcoholics Anonymous, with same-sex attraction treated as an addiction that requires techniques to 'cure', which is consistent with ex-gay strategies that are largely based on substance dependency treatment models. Many real ex-gay groups use similar philosophies, exemplified in the autobiographical *Boy Erased* by recovering drug user, Brandon at Love in Action,[22] who assists the participants in dealing with their 'homosexual addictions'.[23]

True Directions participants are constantly monitored by Mary, Mike and other attendees for possible sexual falls, with the constant threat of expulsion. Erzen describes a similar situation at the New Hope ex-gay ministry which she researched, stating that their programme was intended as a form of 'bodily discipline', and that monitoring and surveillance were key in preventing participants reverting to their prior expressions of same-sex attraction.[24] In the early-1980s, groups like Exodus International went from prayer-based 'healing' to the pseudo-psychiatric model depicted in *Cheerleader*, as fringe American psychologists such as Elizabeth Moberly began to develop techniques that were a 'rehash of dated psychoanalytic ideas [arguing that] people are homosexual because of their relationship with their parents.'[25] Besen claims that these ideas 'provided the ex-gay ministries with the psychological underpinnings they desperately needed to attract new members' and that 'Exodus now had a tangible plan ... that combined pseudo-psychology with divine intervention.'[26] In the True Directions programme, this is apparent in each of its steps, to the point where the religious foundations are largely neglected.

The key tenets were developed by Moberly and expanded upon by acolytes including Joseph Nicolosi. They remain central to ex-gay theory and are apparent throughout the film. The first precept is 'defensive attachment' in which a person becomes same-sex attracted because a disruption during adolescence creates an emotional detachment from the same-sex parent. This in turn triggers 'gender rejection' which causes a male to avoid masculine pastimes such as sport, while a female will shun her femininity and engage in activities such as fixing cars. The result is a greater distance from one's gender,

Figure 5.1 The True Directions counsellor Mike (RuPaul Charles) instructs the male camp members in the 'masculine' action of chopping wood. Positioned nearby is an ironically phallic tree silhouette, and a prime example of the film's attempt at humour.

and the person then gravitates towards homosexuality, which is also a constant theme mocked by Babbit and Peterson, with male participants engaged in wood chopping and war games, while the women are made to clean and simulate caring for an infant. Additionally, Moberly believes 'same-sex friendships' are the 'cure' for homosexuality, with homosocial relationships with same-sex peers demystifying them and allowing the same-sex attracted individual to develop heteronormative feelings.[27] This element is lampooned in the sleeping arrangements and activities featured in *Cheerleader*, with communal rooms and team pursuits intended to develop friendships that in several instances develop instead into intimacy.

The most effective scene parodying the pseudo-psychiatric elements of ex-gay practices is when Megan is made to examine her same-sex attraction. While attending family therapy, Mary prompts Megan to discuss the 'root' of her lesbianism. This component of the 'therapy' model encourages the 'patient' to identify an early event that influences sexuality (a clear parody of Moberly's 'defensive attachment'). Megan states that she believes her feelings stem from her parents: 'there was that one year where … Dad was unemployed and mom had to support us'. After her father offers an excuse, with Mary looking on sceptically, Megan continues: 'Maybe seeing Mom kind of being the dad, maybe I … maybe I got kind of the wrong idea about the roles of men and women'. Mary becomes excited, stating: 'Your father was emasculated. Your mother was domineering … You wanted to emulate your mother. You have no respect for men because you don't respect your father … Megan, you have found your root!' This is followed by applause. The revelation results from Mary pressuring Megan to scour her memory for an event that produced her sexuality, and Megan is made to feel that she cannot begin to heal unless she discovers it. For fringe psychotherapists, this is a key belief, with Nicolosi stating: 'the most common pathway to lesbianism is a life situation that creates a deeply ambivalent attitude toward femininity, conveying the internal message: "It's not safe or desirable to be a woman."'[28] The discovery scene very precisely mocks this key pseudo-psychiatric belief of a 'life situation' creating same-sex attraction.

Writing on the efficacy of ex-gay conversion practices after analysis of various statements and interviews of 'ex-ex-gays', Besen states: 'in general, ex-gay groups have a near total failure rate … and the very sex they forbid occurs on a frequent basis'.[29] *Cheerleader* appears to confirm this as only 60 per cent of the original class make it to graduation, and with Graham and Clayton escaping in the final act with their respective lovers only 40 per cent complete the entire programme. Even then, the graduating characters, Joel and Sinead, constantly refer to the 'act' of being straight with no genuine conviction, meaning that potentially only 20 per cent of the class genuinely feel they have been converted. Even Mike, who is a counsellor and whom we assume has successfully transitioned from the 'gay lifestyle', has constant latent desires for Mary's son Rock, suggesting that he will ultimately 'fall' as well.

Another aspect of fundamentalist conversion practices that *Cheerleader* captures accurately is familial pressure to attend and complete the programme. Megan is told that her parents will not allow her to return home unless she graduates from True Directions, while Graham's father threatens to cut her off financially unless she converts. The fear that successful completion is the only viable option to ensure peace and happiness among family and friends is reflected strongly in the story of survivors, and while this acknowledgement is never addressed directly by the characters, the film makes it clear that this is the case.[30]

Flippant and tonally awkward depictions of conversion practices

In an early scene, Megan finally acknowledges her same-sex attraction, dramatically announcing: 'I'm a homosexual!' Oddly light-hearted music plays and as the group embraces her, a fellow programme attendee, Andre, 'minces' forward. Megan then begins crying, with saliva streaming down her chin, with the overall drama presenting as surreal and confusing rather than humorous. This example of tonal whiplash illustrates instances that undermine the credibility of the scenes accurately portraying ex-gay practices.

One of the film's largest missteps occurs during Megan's first night at True Directions, when she hears electric shocks coming from one of her roommates:

Megan   What are you doing?
Sinead   Aversion therapy, stupid … When you have inappropriate fantasies about girls, you shock yourself with this shocker. So, every time you think of them, you feel that pain.
Megan   That's sick!
Sinead   No pain, no gain, baby. You want to like dick? You better start training yourself.

This scene is clearly aiming for the provocative, hypersexualized tone of *American Pie* that came out in the same year, but in this case the comedy falls flat, appearing crude and misleading. Unlike the scenes covered in the previous section, the electroshock sequence is poorly representative of the concept it is meant to satirize; in reality, the shocks were frequently administered with the patient strapped to a chair, and immense pain experienced.[31] *Cheerleader* portrays this treatment as a mild zap delivered by a cheap looking prop with a small red bulb at the end, suggesting that the filmmakers were unaware of aversion therapy's dark history, or were uninterested.

An equally jarring scene occurs during a faceoff between Graham and Mary about the nature of the True Directions programme:

Graham   Masculine, feminine, blah blah blah. I think after advanced calc[ulus] and Chaucer I can follow this psychobabble.
Mary   This psychobabble, young lady, is the only healthy alternative to the gay lifestyle. Other than … guzzling a bottle of tranquillizers or slashing your wrists. Now who's ready to have fun?

The film cuts to a montage in which Mary and Mike perform inadvertent provocative sexual gestures while the students look on with desire, and easy-listening rock music plays. Again, a serious topic, tied to high rates of self-harm and suicide among same-sex attracted people, is satirized but in a tonally awkward and flippant manner.

As discussed, the discovery of Megan's 'root' is portrayed in a satirically accurate way, but the same cannot be said for the other camp members. In a later scene, Andre explains in front of his parents that his same-sex attraction comes from changing in front of other boys during swimming lessons as a child. After being called a 'faggot' by Graham's abusive father, Andre says: '[it] is a stupid-ass root. I'm never going to know why I'm a … faggot'. Here, vicious homophobia is presented in a comical tone with no insight given as to its effects, with Andre seemingly indifferent, and if a hidden pain is felt, this is never explored. Such a hateful term is used for obvious shock and comedic value, but the theatrical and dismissive delivery results in the joke falling flat. Scenes such as these make it hard to understand the director's intention.

Further to this, when discussing Andre's 'root', Jan interrupts and says: 'I'm a heterosexual.'

Mike   Not yet honey, you're almost there.
Jan   No, I know I've never been gay. (*Looks of incredulity.*)
Mike   Jan, remember, uh, you were molested. (*Laughs.*) I mean, just take a look at yourself.
Jan (*starting to get emotional*)   I mean, everyone thinks I'm this big dyke, because I wear baggy pants, I play softball and … I'm not as pretty as other girls. That doesn't make me gay. I mean, I like guys. I can't help it. I just want a big fat wiener up my …
Andre   Amen, sister.

This immediately cuts to the following scene with the descriptive captions stating: 'SPRIGHTLY MUSIC'. Again, the script was aiming for provocative teen comedy while also channelling the provocative methods of ACT UP, but there is no follow up with Jan's character to explore their harsh reality, resulting in the film seeming cold rather than camp or satirical. A more experienced director may have been able to present these themes of homophobia and sexual assault in a comedic manner that had a purpose or payoff, but Babbit seems to have struggled with something beyond shock value and superficial camp.

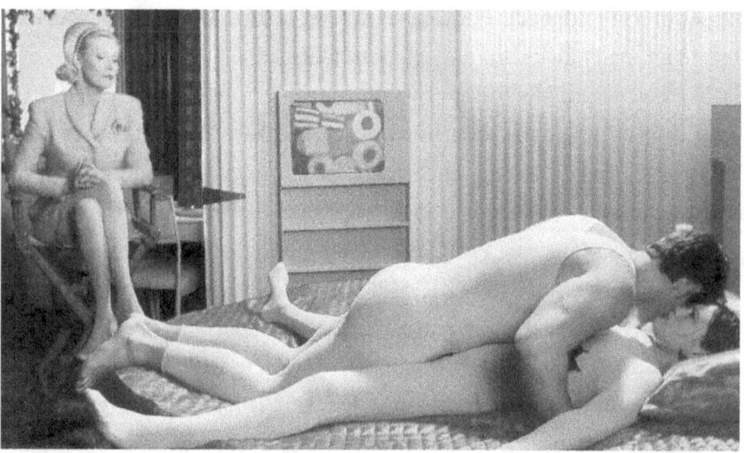

Figure 5.2 Another example of True Directions' method of conversion 'therapy': 'Straight' sex is enacted in front of the group with the programme's head Mary (Cathy Moriarty) looking on with approval. The scene is largely played for laughs despite the trauma felt by the participants.

A final but important flaw with *Cheerleader* is the absence of a narrative around internal religious conflicts. Megan is never clearly shown to express any anguish when removed from True Directions, while Graham briefly hesitates when Megan confesses her love during the graduation scene but is eventually happy to run away, with both abandoning their families and faith. In fact, apart from token references to God in the opening scenes, there is very little religious belief expressed by anyone in the film, and almost no spiritual struggle evident in the dramatization of anyone in the programme. This likely stems from Babbit's inability to understand and portray the trauma experienced by survivors of ex-gay programmes, with both the director and scriptwriter perhaps unaware of these important elements, or alternatively abandoning them for the sake of comedy (on religious struggle and same-sex attraction, see Chapters 1 and 2). As mentioned, Babbit believed that satirizing participants of ex-gay camps would be 'fun' in comparison to those suffering substance abuse issues. Her accepting and educated middle-class family background seems to distance her from the subject matter that lends a nasty tone to many scenes. While her attempts to replicate the shock tactics of ACT UP to depict the challenges of gay teens may have been well intentioned, they are particularly jarring when juxtaposed with the scenes in the film that contain carefully constructed depictions of the warped nature of ex-gay theory.

Critical reception

Cheerleader was largely panned by mainstream critics for its awkward and flippant tone, as well as its lack of a clear critique of conversion camps beyond slapstick. Matthew Leyland makes the following point:

> the film scarcely hints at the physical and psychological trauma such camps would visit on their inmates: . . . the camp's final test – in which male and female students must simulate straight sex – seems little more than an excuse to stage some handsomely stylised kitsch tableaux.[32]

Other critics make similar observations, that is, the film was attempting satire but was rather toothless when it came to making any clear and coherent attacks on conversion practices and those who administer them.[33]

However, Roger Ebert is more forgiving: 'It feels like an amateur night version of itself, awkward, heartfelt and sweet.'[34] But dismissing elements of the film as 'camp', 'amateurish' or 'satirical' only goes so far in explaining the odd tonal shifts, and the almost dismissive nature of how it tackles its traumatic subject matter. From various interviews at the time of the film's release and later to celebrate its twentieth anniversary, there is no mention from Babbit that she or the script writer consulted conversion survivors or had any interest in a realistic depiction of ex-gay conversion camps. The film was meant to be about queer romance that just happens to have a conversion camp as a convenient backdrop. A common interpretation is that this was done in poor taste, but I believe it is more likely a product of naivety from the director, with the good intentions of portraying a healthy queer teenage romance trumping tonal consistency and realism.

Comparisons with later cinematic depictions of conversion

In 1999, one may never have dreamt that there would be laws against conversion practices through many jurisdictions in the United States, Australia and beyond.[35] A decade later, there would also be a comprehensive report by the American Psychological Association stating unequivocally that conversion is not only harmful but ineffective.[36] Nonetheless, the strength of the ex-gay movement in the late-1990s perhaps explains Babbit's brightly coloured and over-acted counterreaction to the absurdity of what groups such as Exodus were peddling as well as all the moments where the film appears reluctant to go on the attack.

In comparison, the director of *Miseducation*, Desiree Akhavan, was clearly aiming for a muted, realistic tone rather than *Cheerleader*'s gaudy pinks and blues. In addition, *Miseducation* is not a comedy but more a coming-of-age film with satire thrown in. However, the major shift is the far more realistic, serious and melancholic tone of *Miseducation*. Moreover, the latter film embeds many more moments of levity in the form of jokes between the lead trio of Cameron, Adam and Jane, as well as Cameron's roommate, Erin. The jokes in these moments are often dark and could be designated 'gallows humour'.[37]

Despite this, the major story beats of *Miseducation* are uncannily similar to *Cheerleader*, with equivalent characters. Erin's 'iceberg' analysis matches the 'root' in *Cheerleader*; Dr Marsh is Mary's equivalent but far more controlled and predatory, while Rick is like a combination of Mike and Rock – related to Dr Marsh, maintaining a heterosexual façade, and a camp leader. Also, despite *Miseducation* aiming for the shock of personal trauma as opposed to *Cheerleader*'s provocation coming from tonal shifts, both have very similar endings, with their respective protagonists riding off in the back of a truck into the unknown. However, unlike Megan, Cameron has successfully portrayed the harshness of the conservative Christian world towards same-sex attracted people, so we have a better understanding of the challenges the characters face.

As mentioned, Megan very rarely appears conflicted, while in *Boy Erased*, Jared's sorrow is palpable; he just wants to live a normal life. When he attacks the advertisement with the shirtless man and screams 'Fuck you!', the anguish is heart-breaking, especially with the cut to his mother praying. The religious pressure is intense. In one scene, the pastor explains to Jared: 'God will not love you the way you are now, unless you really want to change.' The familial pressure is also palpable, with Jared's father telling him: 'Your mother and I cannot see a way that you can continue to live under this roof … if you're going to fundamentally go against the grain of our beliefs, and against God himself … in your heart, do you want to change?' These are all elements that are only glossed over in *Cheerleader* but are central to Jared's narrative – a result of the autobiographical nature of his story.

Cheerleader as a queer cult classic

Despite being superseded in quality and effectiveness in the depiction of conversion practices and those who have survived them, *Cheerleader* also needs to be considered as a piece of queer filmmaking. As most mainstream options for LGBT+ audience members in the late 1990s were films made by largely heteronormative directors with heteronormative actors playing gay characters, *Cheerleader* and its almost naïve depiction of gay love triumphing amidst the inherent homophobia of Megan's surroundings must have seemed a breath of fresh air.

As evidenced by the release of a director's cut, stage production and numerous articles claiming *Cheerleader* as a queer cult classic,[38] many LGBT+ viewers were able to overlook the tonal inconsistencies and the absence of a chronicle surrounding the trauma suffered by those exposed to conversion. Ultimately, in 1999 there were few other Hollywood films made by gay people for gay people, and the bright set design, costumes, overacting and flamboyant dialogue were seen as a positive rather than negative. Aimee Ferrier highlights the film's use of 'colour theory' to attack gender stereotypes, with Jon Mendelsohn agreeing, stating that straight audiences missed the concept that 'the bright colors represented how awkward and jarring the social construction of gender can be'.[39] Significantly, among these commentaries there is almost no mention of the conversion concepts surrounding the film, almost as if the backdrop of an ex-gay camp is inconsequential.

In fact, not maintaining the convention of a brooding, morbid atmosphere makes *Cheerleader* stand out; this, and its lack of contemporary peers are additional points to consider when appraising the film, and likely contribute to the nostalgia exhibited by many apologist reviewers. Babbit states in an interview in 2020: 'I wanted to make a fun, entertaining movie . . . I wanted people to feel joyful when they watched the film'.[40] Thus, the positivity of the film was a greater priority than realism or tonal consistency, and the rise of the survivor testimony which really grew in prominence in the 2010s was not yet visible.

Interestingly, when talking about *Cheerleader*, Akhavan states that while she 'loved it' and that it was discussed with her co-writer during pre-production, they did not rewatch it as they 'didn't want to have it in . . . [their] heads' when making *Miseducation*. While *Cheerleader* may have inspired the lighter moments of Akhavan's film, the lack of any naïve hope and romance suggests the tonal influence of *Cheerleader* was minimal. As Scott McKinnon suggests in Chapter 8 of this book, *Miseducation* followed the trend of gay protagonists being surrounded by tragedy, including a gruesomely described attempted suicide, whereas *Cheerleader* is ultimately hopeful. The former goes for the shock of personal trauma, whereas the latter aims for shock through tonal shifts. This helps explain why two decades later LGBT+ audiences continue to hold *Cheerleader* dear.

Cheerleader as a work of cinema

Babbit's goal of making a colourful, positive film employing the hyperreality of Tim Burton amid the morbid backdrop of an ex-gay camp, helps explain the confused tonal shifts of the film; even for an experienced filmmaker this would be highly ambitious. Despite its camp aesthetic, it has scenes more reminiscent of *American Pie* than classics of the genre; the electroshock scene has all the subtlety and nuance of a teenage boy sticking his penis in a warm pie. The result is that Babbit appears to have experienced genre confusion. Camp satire with a hopeful message can be done well, but master filmmakers such as John Waters's had decades of experience before tackling difficult subjects such as the Religious Right in *Polyester* (1981), and prejudice and classism in *Hairspray* (1988), and not against the challenging backdrop of an ex-gay camp. Babbit uses the pretext that critics did not understand her stylistic choices.[41] However, the acclaim of the equally flamboyant and sardonic films of Waters's challenges her explanation. Perhaps because Waters's films are tonally consistent whereas *Cheerleader* is not, lies at the heart of the matter. Thus, despite claiming that she was not pitching for the style of Waters's, perhaps Babbit should have drawn more on what makes an effective camp satire, rather than aiming too high on her debut.

In addition, Akhavan was also a young queer woman directing a film in an overwhelmingly male dominated field, on the same subject and with less funding but was able to achieve critical acclaim with *Miseducation*. She presented a tonally even, and at times humorous film while also displaying the trauma of those exposed to conversion practices. On the other hand, Babbit remains unapologetic about failing to depict this element, and when reflecting on these reviews twenty years later, she states:

[The critics] were so angry that I knew I had done something really audacious ... I think it upset people that I had made a comedy about a really serious subject matter. I also made the film when I was in my 20s, and ... I wanted to skewer not only my community, but also just the absurdity of gay conversion.[42]

It is noteworthy that even with hindsight and the increased prevalence of survivor testimonies, she still contends there is nothing wrong in making light of abuse (but feeling the need to excuse her youth) and that she includes those subjected to the camps as her 'community' when clearly ignorant of what many of them had suffered.

Despite stating that *Cheerleader* was simply meant to be a 'feel-good' comedy, Babbit chose to include often accurate depictions of a subject with both a long history and a very active present, with her film also inspiring other directors to address the subject on screen. This makes it ripe for historical analysis and to an extent must be examined as such, thus the director should not be surprised that critics chose to point out that the offhand tone with which she approached conversion programmes was often cinematically unsatisfying.

In the end, it appears Babbit was unable to reconcile the varied filmic styles she pursued, creating an uneven experience and as such it is more a cultural artefact of its time than a true classic in the manner of a *Hairspray*. Being the first mainstream conversion practice film that is nostalgically loved by many LGBT+ viewers does not make it a well-crafted film. Effective satire based on traumatic subjects can be achieved, as illustrated by *Four Lions* (2010) and *The Death of Stalin* (2017). *Cheerleader* on the other hand is largely inconsistent in humour and tone and is more of a cultural oddity than an underappreciated masterpiece, unless of course you were a same-sex attracted teen in the late 1990s with little countervailing mainstream media showing that your mind and actions were fundamentally healthy, and that gender expectations are a social construct.

Cheerleader as a cultural artefact

Just before the final credits in *Boy Erased*, text on screen indicates that a 2018 UCLA study disclosed 700,000 Americans have been affected by conversion practices. Here, a scale has been given to conversion practices, but studies such as this were not available during *Cheerleader's* gestation and production, and there were no equivalents to the since widely circulated survivor testimonies, including Garrard Conley's memoir, *Boy Erased* (2016), and Anthony Venn-Brown's *A Life of Unlearning* (2015), originally published in 2004. Consequently, Babbit was likely unaware of the trauma caused by conversion practices, and even though psychotherapists had increasingly distanced themselves from conversion practices since the 1970s, it was autobiographical accounts from conversion survivors that gained the public's attention. This explains the lack of exploration of religious conflict felt by Megan and her peers, and the dismissive tone with which concepts such as self-harming and abuse are handled. But despite this ignorance, Babbitt and Peterson were still able to accurately capture the methods and psychology behind ex-gay groups many years in advance of other filmmakers.

Babbit's own influence from ACT UP encouraged her to go down the provocative satire path[43] but, unlike the protest group, her ignorance of the subject matter made her attempt less effective. And as the reports and autobiographies of survivors were years away, lightly prodding ex-gay ministries may have seemed a better approach, particularly when wealthy and influential right-wing Christian churches were making an aggressive push to promote ex-gay 'therapy'. Indeed, many of the problems with the film would not be so significant had the first-time director decided not to critique such a politically and socially significant entity as the ex-gay movement. Though Rebecca Beirne suggests that it is inaccurate to label *Cheerleader* as 'more political than coming of age',[44] the fact that it is set against the backdrop of an ex-gay conversion camp instantly makes it highly political, yet it does not critique its target in a way that is satisfying. However, as discussed earlier, many aspects of *Cheerleader* that depict the 'coming of age' elements resonate with queer viewers, despite contemporary critics taking issue with the watered-down 'political' aspects.

In an intriguing development, the film has been reappraised by mainstream critics. Hillary Weston from *Criterion* makes the following point about the film:

it was entering a queer political landscape vastly different from the one we live in today. [Since then], we've witnessed the rise of LGBTQI representation in mainstream film and television . . . Babbitt's inclusive tale of love and self-discovery continues to feel . . . ahead of its time.[45]

Unlike *Miseducation* and *Boy Erased*, *Cheerleader* had no peers and can be seen almost by default as a trailblazing film. But it can also be considered to be part of (and limited by) the emerging trend of depicting gay lives and the issues they faced through comedy, with *Go Fish* and *Will and Grace* influencing and encouraging this path, as depictions of gay protagonists moved away from the Hollywood trend of tragedy.[46] In addition, packaging it with strong elements of provocative teen-comedy was a far easier sell to studios in the late 1990s due to their burgeoning popularity, with Babbit herself believing that the only way she got the funding to make a queer film was because of its genre, resulting in an awkward cocktail.[47]

However, the fact that *Will and Grace* tackled conversion practices with comedy only months after the release of *Cheerleader*, and was met with a far warmer critical reception, reinforces the argument that Babbit was ineffective in marrying the various strands contained within her film.[48] Despite this, Conley appraised *Cheerleader* himself and places it in the conversion practices genre:

> [The representation of conversion practices has had] a fun trajectory . . . It started with *But I'm a Cheerleader*, which is such a great movie. And then pop culture sort of sucked it up into *South Park*, and [*Saturday Night Live*] – most of the depictions were comedic. And then Miseducation is pretty great; it's an interesting balance between the drama of *Boy Erased* and the campiness of [*Cheerleader*].[49]

Conley clearly understands *Cheerleader* as the alpha conversion practices film, and conceivably the absence of predecessors and peers can also help to explain its inconsistencies. While it may not be completely satisfying when examined as an historical film, it has become part of the history of conversion practices and their assessment.

Conclusion

Cheerleader can be seen as both seminal for its portrayal of conversion practices, something that in the late 1990s had received no mainstream analysis, or alternately/simultaneously as an ineffective attempt to set a satirical romance against the harrowing setting of an ex-gay programme. Irrespective, *Cheerleader* has stayed relevant and remains a queer cult classic, despite the savaging the film received upon its premiere for the tonal inconsistencies and flippant representation of conversion practices. Regarding this, Babbit and many fans fend off reproach by claiming that critics at the time failed to understand just what *Cheerleader* was trying to achieve, while conveniently forgetting that films like *Polyester* and *Hairspray*, which feature camp and audacious characters dealing with dark topics, were critical darlings and enjoyed by audiences both gay and straight alike. Satire can be effective, but it is at its best when containing a clear message, while *Cheerleader* is very confused and inconsistent. Despite this, however, it is important to acknowledge that the film features a healthy queer romance that, unlike most films with same-sex attracted protagonists in the late 1990s, does not end in tragedy, and shows two young people simply in love.

Babbit said that she wanted to make a 'gay Clueless',[50] so from this regard it was unfortunate that the decision was made to have an ex-gay camp as the backdrop rather than a high school, making the attempts at humour far more awkward. *Cheerleader* hints at, but never satisfactorily conveys the trauma of conversion programmes. The very fact that the film decided to parody ex-gay groups in the late 1990s makes it unique, and yet its frequent clumsiness and lack of respect for the victims of conversion practices largely ruins the tone it was attempting. This makes the many accuracies of *Cheerleader*'s depiction of conversion practices stand out even more prominently. Can it be seen as a direct forebear of *Miseducation* and *Boy Erased*? Likely it was a notable step towards the increased awareness that we have today regarding the harmful nature of conversion practices.

Figure 5.3 The innocent budding same-sex romance between Megan (Natasha Lyonne) and Graham (Clea DuVall) would have been more appealing had the director Jamie Babbit not set it against the harrowing backdrop of a conversion 'therapy' camp.

In relation to the chapter's focus on the qualities and value of *Cheerleader* as a film as well as its portrayal of conversion and those who are presented as the subjects (read, victims) of these practices, the final assessment is nuanced. Its central love story is refreshing, and there are many moments of successful representation of the ridiculousness of ex-gay conversion practices. However, setting it against this scenario without full respect for the trauma experienced by survivors, and often puerile and flippant scenes, results in *Cheerleader* suffering from severe tonal inconsistency. While this can be partially explained by the director's distance from, and ignorance regarding aspects of the subject matter, it is also likely due to the director's inexperience. These elements are the costs and benefits to being an early proponent of a genre: the conversion practices survivor film.

Notes

1   The film was scored by Pat Irwin, who also provided very similar music for a 1990s children's show, *Rocko's Modern Life*.

2 When defining what makes a film 'camp', Paul McClure writing for the Australian Centre for the Moving Image draws on a 1964 article by Susan Sontag who stated that: 'The whole point of Camp is to dethrone the serious … One can be serious about the frivolous, frivolous about the serious … going against the grain of one's sex' and that 'alongside androgyny, camp seeks to expose the masculine inherent in the feminine, the feminine in the masculine', https://www.acmi.net.au/stories-and-ideas/camp-films/ (accessed 23 August 2023).

3 See J. Drescher, 'Out of DSM: Depathologizing Homosexuality,' *Behaviour Science*, Vol. 4 (2015): 565–75.

4 T. Erzen, *Straight to Jesus* (Berkeley: University of California Press, 2006), 13.

5 W. Dixon, *Film Talk: Directors at Work* (London: Rutgers University Press, 2007), 161.

6 Dixon, *Film Talk*, 162.

7 Dixon, *Film Talk*, 161.

8 For example, Matthew Leyland states in his 2001 review for *Sight and Sound* that the film is a 'a sub-John Waters's satire'.

9 Dixon, *Film Talk*, 173.

10 Dixon, *Film Talk*, 171.

11 M. Curby, 'Jamie Babbit Always Knew But I'm a Cheerleader Was Ahead of Its Time,' *them*, 8 December 2020, https://www.them.us/story/but-im-a-cheerleader-20th-anniversary-jaime-babbit-interview (accessed 25/02/2023). ACT UP used protest and public demonstration with challenging and aggressive language and concepts. See S. Schulman's *Let the Record Show: A Political History of ACT UP New York, 1987–1993* (New York: Farrar, Straus and Giroux, 2021).

12 L. Hilderbrand, 'Queer Cinema, Queer Writing, Queer Criticism,' in *The Cambridge Companion to American Gay and Lesbian Literature*, ed. S. Herring (Cambridge: Cambridge University Press, 2020), 80.

13 Will and Grace's impact has been deemed so significant that items from the show have been added to the Smithsonian Institute. See B. Zongker, 'Smithsonian adds LGBT history to museum collection,' AP, 20 August 2014, https://apnews.com/article/7c19401398684acca59e2445c6cb834a (accessed 25 February 2023).

14 'Mainstream' denotes that the film had a budget of greater than $1,000,000 USD, recognizable actors, and/or backing and release by a major studio or distributor.

15 Ruby Rich identified what she saw as a 1990s movement called 'New Queer Cinema', of which *Go Fish* was included, with all of the films identified not being what one would classify as mainstream or Hollywood; see 'Queer and Present Danger', *Sight and Sound*, 10 (2000): 23. In the introduction to *New Queer Cinema: A Critical Reader*, when referencing this article, Michele Aaron adds *Cheerleader* to a list of films that Rich saw as part of a later push of 'innocuous and often unremarkable films targeting a narrow, rather than all-inclusive, new queer audience'; see *New Queer Cinema: A Critical Reader* (Edinburgh: Edinburgh University Press, 2004), 8.

16 Natasha Lyonne also starred in *American Pie*.

17 W. Besen, *Anything but Straight* (New York: Harrington Park Press, 2003), 97.

18 Besen, *Anything but Straight*, 3.

19 T. Erzen, *Straight to Jesus*, 4.

20 Among existing articles/interviews, it is difficult to determine how much contribution to the story was made by Peterson, so I will include them both as writers and assume they collaborated.

21 R. A. Rosenstone, *History on Film/Film on History* (Sydney: Pearson Education, 2006), 134.

22 Love in Action was the oldest established member ministry of Exodus International but has been rebranded as Restoration Path after a lawsuit. See Smithsonian Institution, The Mattachine Society of Washington, 'Love in Action' Collection. Smithsonian Online Virtual Archives, 25 February 2023, https://sova.si.edu/record/NMAH.AC.1428 (accessed 25/02/2023) for details.

23 The author of *Boy Erased*, Garrard Conley, experienced ex-gay conversion practices only three years after the release of *Cheerleader*.

24 Erzen, *Straight to Jesus*, 17.

25 Besen, *Anything but Straight*, 100.

26 Besen, *Anything but Straight*, 100.

27 Besen, *Anything but Straight*, 100–3.

28 J. Nicolosi, *A Parent's Guide to Preventing Homosexuality* (Westmont: InterVarsity Press, 2002), 175.

29 Besen, *Anything but Straight*, 40.

30 Erzen states that: 'the men [of New Hope] acknowledged that their . . . crises . . . stemmed from familial and societal pressure and the psychological impact of living as a gay man or woman in a homophobic environment', *Straight to Jesus*, 69.

31 See K. Davison, 'Cold War Pavlov: Homosexual Aversion Therapy in the 1960s,' *History of the Human Sciences* 34 (2021): 89–119 for more details.

32 M. Leyland, 'But I'm a Cheerleader (review),' *Sight and Sound*, 11 (2001): 41.

33 See Emanual Levy's 2000 review in *Variety* and Peter Bradshaw's 2001 *Guardian* review for two prime examples.

34 R. Ebert, 'Reviews: But I'm a Cheerleader,' Rogerebert.com, 14 July 2000, https://www.rogerebert.com/reviews/but-im-a-cheerleader-2000 (accessed 25 February 2023).

35 It must be noted that many states in the USA have no such legislation, and many that do only protect minors, and only against psychotherapists administering conversion practices. See Movement, Advancement Project, 'Conversion Therapy Laws,' LGBTMAP.org, 25 February 2023, https://www.lgbtmap.org/equality-maps/conversion_therapy (accessed 25 February 2023). At the time of writing, Australia's position is equally complex, with some states having introduced legislation of varying effectiveness (Australian Capital Territory, Queensland and Victoria), while other states are considering a ban but currently have no protection of any kind. The United Kingdom committed to legislation in 2018 with no follow up, while countries like Brazil have already instigated trailblazing legal reforms. Stonewall, 'Which countries have already banned conversion therapy?' Stonewall.org.uk, 1 April 2022, https://www.stonewall.org.uk/about-us/news/which-countries-have-already-banned-conversion-therapy/ (accessed 25 February 2023).

36 See American Psychological Association, Task Force on Appropriate Therapeutic Responses to Sexual Orientation. (2009). 'Report of the American Psychological Association Task Force on Appropriate Therapeutic Responses to Sexual Orientation,' http://www.apa.org/pi/lgbc/publications/therapeutic-resp.html (accessed 25 February 2023).

37 One example is the scene where Adam is showing Cameron how she can 'bullshit' her way through the camp by using images from magazines during a collage exercise to interpret her same-sex attraction.

38 For example, https://pridecentre.org.au/event/but-im-a-cheerleader-directors-cut-melbourne-queer-film-festival/ and https://taggmagazine.com/but-im-a-cheerleader-rerelease/

39 A. Ferrier, 'Revisiting Jamie Babbit's Candy-coloured Queer Classic,' *Far Out*, 29 November 2022, https://faroutmagazine.co.uk/jamie-babbit-

classic-but-im-a-cheerleader/ (accessed 25/02/2023). Jon Mendelsohn,
18 July 2020, 'Why But I'm a Cheerleader Became a Cult Classic of Lesbian
Cinema,' https://www.cbr.com/why-but-im-cheerleader-became-cult-
classic/ (accessed 25 February 2023).

40 Team Cherry, 'An Interview with Director Jamie Babbit,' Cherry Picks,
8 December 2020, https://www.thecherrypicks.com/stories/interview-
jamie-babbit/ (accessed 25 February 2023).

41 R. Rubin, 'Director Jamie Babbit on the Queer Classic 20 Years Later,'
Variety, 5 December 2020, https://variety.com/2020/film/features/but-im-a-
cheerleader-director-jamie-babbit-20th-anniversary-1234842163/
(accessed 25 February 2023).

42 Rubin, 'Director Jamie Babbit,' 2020.

43 Katrien De Moor explains that: 'Amongst the diverse resistant strategies
that contest moralistic representations of HIV/AIDS and the
stigmatization of people with HIV/AIDS, two modes of resistance
frequently intersect within HIV/AIDS narratives: sick role subversions
and humour … The dark, black type of humour so prevalent in the age of
AIDS in turn functions as a potentially anti-sentimental, anti-redemptive
and anti-moralistic strategy', 'Diseased Pariahs and Difficult Patients:
Humour and Sick Role Subversions in Queer HIV/AIDS Narratives,'
Cultural Studies 19.6 (2005): 737–54. Babbit's exposure to ACT UP
undoubtedly encouraged her to attempt the second mode.

44 R. Beirne, 'Teen Lesbian Desires and Identities in International Cinema:
1931–2007,' *Journal of Lesbian Studies*, 16 (2012): 266.

45 H. Weston, 'But I'm a Cheerleader Turns Twenty,' The Criterion Collection,
June 18 2020, https://www.criterion.com/current/posts/6986-but-i-m-a-
cheerleader-turns-twenty-natasha-lyonne-and-clea-duvall-reminisce-on-
their-cult-classic (accessed 25 February 2023).

46 Dixon, *Film Talk*, 171.

47 Curby, https://www.them.us/story/but-im-a-cheerleader-20th-
anniversary-jaime-babbit-interview, 2020.

48 Internet Movie Database, 'Girl. Interrupted,' IMDb, 25 February, 2023,
https://www.imdb.com/title/tt0748792/ (accessed 25 February 2023).

49 A. Swartz, '"Boy Erased" Author Garrard Conley Talks Seeing his
Conversion Therapy Memoir Turned into a Film,' MIC, 26 July 2018,
https://www.mic.com/articles/190407/boy-erased-author-garrard-conley-

talks-seeing-his-conversion-therapy-memoir-turned-into-a-film (accessed 25 February 2023).

50 Rubin, 'Director Jamie Babbit,' 2020.

Bibliography

Aaron, M. *Queer Cinema: A Critical Reader*. Edinburgh: Edinburgh University Press, 2004.

American Psychological Association, Task Force on Appropriate Therapeutic Responses to Sexual Orientation. (2009). 'Report of the American Psychological Association Task Force on Appropriate Therapeutic Responses to Sexual Orientation.' http://www.apa.org/pi/lgbc/publications/therapeutic-resp.html

Beirne, R. 'Teen Lesbian Desires and Identities in International Cinema: 1931–2007.' *Journal of Lesbian Studies*, 16 (2012): 258–72.

Besen, W. *Anything but Straight: Unmasking the Scandals and Lies Behind the Ex-Gay Myth*. New York: Harrington Park Press, 2003.

Boy Erased [Film] Dir. J. Edgerton, USA: Focus Features, 2018.

But I'm a Cheerleader [Film] Dir. J. Babbit, USA: Lionsgate Pictures, 1999.

Curby, M. 'Jamie Babbit Always Knew *But I'm a Cheerleader* Was Ahead of its Time.' *them*, 8 December, 2020, https://www.them.us/story/but-im-a-cheerleader-20th-anniversary-jaime-babbit-interview

Davison, K. 'Cold War Pavlov: Homosexual Aversion Therapy in the 1960s.' *History of the Human Sciences* 34 (2021): 89–119.

De Moor, K. 'Diseased Pariahs and Difficult Patients: Humour and Sick Role Subversions in Queer HIV/AIDS Narratives.' *Cultural Studies* 19.6 (2005): 737–54.

Dixon, W. *Film Talk: Directors at Work*. London: Rutgers University Press, 2007.

Drescher, J. 'Out of DSM: Depathologizing Homosexuality.' *Behaviour Science*, Vol. 4 (2015): 565–75.

Ebert, R. 'Reviews: But I'm a Cheerleader.' *Rogerebert.com*, 14 July 2000, https://www.rogerebert.com/reviews/but-im-a-cheerleader-2000

Erzen, T. *Straight to Jesus*. Berkeley: University of California Press, 2006.

Ferrier, A. 'Revisiting Jamie Babbit's Candy-coloured Queer Classic.' *Far Out*, 29 November 2022, https://faroutmagazine.co.uk/jamie-babbit-classic-but-im-a-cheerleader/

Hilderbrand, L. 'Queer Cinema, Queer Writing, Queer Criticism.' In *The Cambridge Companion to American Gay and Lesbian Literature*, ed. S. Herring, 73–86. Cambridge: Cambridge University Press, 2020.

Leyland, M. 'But I'm a Cheerleader (review).' *Sight and Sound* 11 (2001): 41–2.

Mendelsohn, J. 'Why But I'm a Cheerleader Became a Cult Classic of Lesbian Cinema.' *CBR*, 18 July 2020, https://www.cbr.com/why-but-im-cheerleader-became-cult-classic/

Movement, Advancement Project, 'Conversion Therapy Laws.' *LGBTMAP.org*, 25 February 2023, https://www.lgbtmap.org/equality-maps/conversion_therapy

McClure, P. 'The evolution of camp cinema.' ACMI, 6 March 2023, https://www.acmi.net.au/stories-and-ideas/camp-films

Nicolosi, J. *A Parent's Guide to Preventing Homosexuality*. Westmont: InterVarsity Press USA, 2002.

Rich, B. R. 'Queer and Present Danger.' *Sight and Sound*, 10:3 (2000): 22–5.

Rosenstone, R. A. *History on Film/Film on History*. Sydney: Longman/Pearson, 2006.

Rubin, R. 'Director Jamie Babbit on the Queer Classic 20 Years Later.' *Variety*, 5 December 2020, https://variety.com/2020/film/features/but-im-a-cheerleader-director-jamie-babbit-20th-anniversary-1234842163/

Schulman, S. *Let the Record Show: A Political History of ACT UP New York, 1987–1993*. New York: Farrar, Straus and Giroux, 2021.

Smithsonian Institution. The Mattachine Society of Washington, 'Love in Action' Collection. Smithsonian Online Virtual Archives, 25 February 2023, https://sova.si.edu/record/NMAH.AC.1428

Stonewall, 'Which Countries Have Already Banned Conversion Therapy?' Stonewall.org.uk, 1 April 2022, https://www.stonewall.org.uk/about-us/news/which-countries-have-already-banned-conversion-therapy/

Swartz, A. '"Boy Erased" Author Garrard Conley Talks Seeing his Conversion Therapy Memoir Turned into a Film.' MIC, 26 July 2018, https://www.mic.com/articles/190407/boy-erased-author-garrard-conley-talks-seeing-his-conversion-therapy-memoir-turned-into-a-film

Team Cherry. 'An Interview with Director Jamie Babbit.' Cherry Picks, 8 December 2020, https://www.thecherrypicks.com/stories/interview-jamie-babbit/

The Miseducation of Cameron Post [Film] Dir. D. Akhavan, USA: Beachside Films, 2018.

Weston, H. 'But I'm a Cheerleader Turns Twenty.' The Criterion Collection, 18 June 2020, https://www.criterion.com/current/posts/6986-but-i-m-a-cheerleader-turns-twenty-natasha-lyonne-and-clea-duvall-reminisce-on-their-cult-classic
Zongker, B. 'Smithsonian adds LGBT history to museum collection.' AP, 20 August 2014, https://apnews.com/article/7c19401398684acca59e2445c6cb834a

Save Me: Reconciling Queerness and Christianity[1]

David R. Coon

The opening sequence of the 2007 film *Save Me* (Dir. Robert Cary) cuts back and forth between two seemingly unconnected scenes. One scene depicts two men kissing and taking drugs as they speed down the road in a beat-up car. They pull into a roadside motel and fumble their way into a room where they immediately have sex. This portion of the sequence includes POV shots out the window and many tight shots of the men in the car, often connected by disruptive jump cuts. The images are accompanied by aggressive rock music, which seems to originate from the car's radio, but then continues as non-diegetic music once the men leave the car and enter the motel room. The other scene plays out in a church, where the congregation is in the middle of a service, everyone standing and singing in unison. Visually dominated by wide shots and a few smooth dolly shots to capture many members of the congregation, this portion's soundtrack is provided by the hymn the churchgoers are singing.

This cross-cut opening sequence embodies the central conflict of *Save Me* and points toward its eventual resolution. By alternating abruptly between the two scenes, thus emphasizing their contrasting visual and sonic elements, the film immediately introduces tension between two key elements of the stories – homosexuality and Christianity. While the scenes initially seem to draw a clear line between the two stories and what they represent, the parallel editing pulls them together so that the audience experiences them as one sequence. Additionally, as the sequence reaches its climax, the hymn from the church carries over into the sex scene and combines with that scene's rock music, sonically linking the two stories as the men reach their sexual climax and the film's title appears on screen. The editing and sound design of the opening sequence thus create an overlap between homosexuality and Christianity, which becomes central to the film's development and conclusion.

Save Me tells the story of a young gay man named Mark (Chad Allen), who, after nearly dying from a drug overdose, reluctantly agrees to enrol in a Christian-run conversion programme led by married couple Gayle (Judith Light) and Ted (Stephen Lang). While in the programme, Mark befriends Scott (Robert Gant), another gay man seeking to become straight. The friendship develops into romance, forcing the two men to confront the apparent conflict between their feelings and their faith.

This chapter situates the film in its broader socio-political context regarding LGBT+ movements before examining the evolution of *Save Me* from its original screenplay to the completed film, paying particular attention to its exploration of the relationship between Christianity and homosexuality. I argue that by encouraging dialogue between opposing perspectives about conversion practices, *Save Me* makes a unique and valuable intervention into the debate about the compatibility of queer identities and Christian beliefs, ultimately supporting the LGBT+ movement by building understanding with a key opponent.

Storytelling, activism and social change

Save Me is one of many films made by and about queer people that uses a fictional narrative to highlight and critique social forces oppressing the LGBT+ population. Storytelling can be a valuable weapon in the fight against oppression because narratives have the power to challenge beliefs and reveal truths about human behaviour. Storytelling has played a significant role in the long evolution of LGBT+ rights, in ways both helpful and harmful. Historically, stories about LGBT+ people –

often generated by medical, government and religious institutions – have pathologized and criminalized them. Because of this, stories about non-normative sexualities and gender identities have long been associated with shame and embarrassment. Christopher Pullen explores the potential for out queer cultural producers to shape discourses by offering a new set of narratives. He argues that the self-reflective and honest practices of queer storytellers can reject the 'mythologies and histories of shame' that have enabled the oppression of queer people.[2] He also argues that storytelling allows people to 'challenge such subjugation through the production of discourse', ultimately creating opportunities for political visibility and community building.[3]

Storytelling can lead to additional personal benefits for individuals struggling with discrimination and oppression. Gloria Ladson-Billings argues that storytelling can help people to overcome internalized condemnation that often results from long-term exposure to discriminatory beliefs and practices. Although her work focuses on racial discrimination, her ideas also apply to anti-queer discrimination. She says: 'Historically, storytelling has been a kind of medicine to heal the wounds of pain caused by racial oppression. The story of one's condition leads to the realization of how one came to be oppressed and subjugated, thus allowing one to stop inflicting mental violence on oneself.'[4] Similarly, Richard Delgado and Jean Stefancic argue that, '[s]tories can name a type of discrimination …; once named, it can be combated.'[5] In this way, storytelling helps to demystify situations, enabling marginalized groups and individuals to understand the sources of their oppression and to identify clear targets and goals for social change efforts.

Cinematic storytelling has been a valuable way for filmmakers to address a variety of issues facing the LGBT+ population, and to expose specific sources of ongoing oppression. Although mainstream medical institutions have abandoned conversion practices, smaller organizations have persisted, usually citing religious beliefs as justification for their actions, as discussed in detail in the Introduction to this book. In the United States and much of the world, Bible passages and specific interpretations of Christian teachings form the backbone of conversion programmes. As a result, films about conversion practices, including *Save Me*, are uniquely positioned to examine the intersection of, and tension between queerness and Christianity. The broader rhetorical struggle between anti-gay conservative Christians and LGBT+ activists in the United States has a long history that provides an important context for understanding the intervention offered by *Save Me*.

LGBT+ liberation vs. conservative Christianity

The rhetoric of both pro-LGBT+ and anti-LGBT+ movements has fuelled the perception that non-heterosexual identities are incompatible with Christianity. In the 1960s and 1970s, the success and increased visibility of gay and lesbian activists in the United States generated backlash from those who opposed equal rights for LGBT+ people. In 1977, Anita Bryant, a singer, corporate spokesperson and born-again Christian, launched the Save Our Children campaign with the goal of repealing a gay rights ordinance in Dade County, Florida. Basing her anti-gay arguments on narrow interpretations of Bible passages and encouraging the belief that homosexuality stood in opposition to Christian beliefs, Bryant gained the support of many conservative Christians. After Bryant's campaign succeeded, she and other anti-gay activists continued the strategy of mobilizing conservative Christians to challenge the political gains of LGBT+ people.[6]

Gay and lesbian activists pushed back, identifying Christians like Bryant as their enemies and broadly painting Christianity as a source of oppression.[7] Anti-Christian sentiment became central to much gay rights activism, as epitomized by the ACT UP protests against Catholic churches during the height of the HIV/AIDS crisis. During these events, protestors stormed churches in New York and other large cities, publicly blaming church policies for the growing numbers of AIDS-related deaths.[8] As activists on both sides argued that homosexuality and Christianity were incompatible, Christians joining the gay and lesbian movements often chose to turn away from religion. Historian John D'Emilio, for example, describes how his entrance into the liberation movement led him to reject his religious affiliation (personal struggles explored in Chapters 1 and 2 of this book): 'Unlike some forms of oppression that required organized activism, such as that imposed by the state, its laws, and its police apparatus, the oppression of religious institutions could be ended, in my personal experience, simply by saying good-bye.'[9] Many activists made similar choices, partially agreeing with anti-gay Christians by accepting as truth the belief that homosexuality and Christianity are incompatible.

This perceived incompatibility has been reified over the years in part by activists' use of a rhetorical strategy known as polarization. A rhetoric of polarization is often used by leaders of social movements 'to transform relationships by creating clear distinctions between the evil other and the virtuous self.'[10] Presenting Christians and LGBT+ activists as diametrically opposed to one another can help both groups in their attempt to rally supporters, but the true relationship between the groups is far more complicated. During the 1970s, for example, a relatively quiet gay religious movement grew alongside the more visible liberation movement in the United States. Many gays and lesbians turned toward religious organizations rather than away from them during this tumultuous period. As historian Jim Downs notes: 'The unifying theme of the various strands of the gay religious movement was the belief that religion could and should offer shelter to gay people of faith, emboldening them to openly embrace both their sexuality and spirituality.'[11] Between 1973 and 1975, as LGBT+ Christians fought for change within their own churches, gay caucuses formed within every mainline Protestant denomination in the US.[12] Other queer Christians gravitated to the Metropolitan Community Church (MCC), a denomination founded in 1968 that provided a safe home for gay Christians and 'sought to demonstrate the compatibility between Christianity and homosexuality to the Christian world'.[13]

Although some conservative Christian leaders fought the rise of gay liberation, they did not represent the views of all Christians. Liberal Protestant clergy members regularly supported and participated in homophile organizations during the 1960s.[14] In 1972, the United Church of Christ became the first mainline denomination to approve the ordination of a minister who was openly gay.[15] In the 1980s, liberal Christian communities played a significant role in advancing gay rights, providing spaces of affirmation, and ministering to gays and lesbians with AIDS, pushing back against the conservative morality that dominated the United States during the Reagan era.[16]

Narratives that focus solely on conflict flatten the nuances of the relationship between queerness and Christianity. Films about conversion practices often continue that trend while also building on trends in the general portrayals of Christianity in Hollywood films. When Hollywood was regulated by the Motion Picture Production Code, filmmakers could not show religion or religious figures in a negative light, but in the decades following the code's demise, filmmakers frequently did just that. As Daniel S. Cutrara discusses, post-code Hollywood has regularly portrayed religious institutions as oppressive and believers as dangerous social 'others'. Cutrara notes that films rarely depict positive aspects of religion, and the focus on negative aspects 'has reinforced a dichotomy of secular/faith that sees the secular as life-giving and faith as enslavement'.[17] *Save Me* features Christian characters as antagonists, thus continuing, to a certain extent, the divide between queerness and Christianity as well as the general trend in Hollywood representations of religion. However, the film offers a more nuanced approach than most narratives exploring the subject. *Save Me* highlights the harms of conversion practices and rejects them while allowing characters and viewers to embrace positive aspects of Christianity. This approach was intentional on the part of the producers, and it reflects the general philosophy of Mythgarden, the independent production company responsible for *Save Me.*

Mythgarden

Mythgarden was formed in 2003 by Christopher Racster, Chad Allen and Robert Gant, all of whom are openly gay and had separately made names for themselves in the industry. Racster had worked in marketing and public relations before producing a string of short and feature films that made their way around the queer film festival circuit. Allen had been a working actor since he was a child, with prominent roles in television programmes such as *St Elsewhere* (1983–8), *Our House* (1986–8) and *Dr Quinn, Medicine Woman* (1993–8). Gant had completed a law degree before he began acting and co-starred in seasons two through five of *Queer as Folk* (2000–5). The three men knew each other socially but had not previously worked together. As part of his work with a small theatre company, Allen recruited Gant and actor/LGBT+ ally Judith Light to participate in a staged reading of an unproduced script about two men who find love at a Christian ex-gay ministry centre. The three felt the script had potential, and they wanted to develop it into a feature film. They took the idea to Racster, since they knew of his track record producing successful queer-oriented films, and also invited Light's manager, Herb Hamsher, to join the project. The team of five acquired and developed the script to produce what would become *Save Me*. Racster, Allen and Gant wanted to establish a production company that could produce additional LGBT+ films after *Save Me* was complete, so they formed Mythgarden.

According to its founders, the mission of Mythgarden was to tell important stories that would advance queer communities and raise the quality of LGBT+ filmmaking. They regularly characterized the work of Mythgarden as 'turning the page' on LGBT+ filmmaking, both in terms of message and quality. They wanted to emphasize aesthetic and technical excellence while moving beyond the coming out stories and AIDS dramas that had become common in queer filmmaking. Racster notes that the filmmakers were committed to 'telling stories that no one else was telling ... turning the page on what was considered LGBT content'.[18] Allen says that his interest in Mythgarden was 'born out of a desire to find good stories and find a way to tell them', adding that the company was primarily trying to 'provide an outlet and a voice for LGBT storytellers'.[19] The mission of Mythgarden was also rooted in the social justice efforts of its founders. All three men had been active in queer-focused political and charitable organizations such as the Human Rights Campaign, the Matthew Shepard Foundation, Point Foundation, Lambda Legal and GLEH (Gay and Lesbian Elder Housing). Explaining the connection between his own philanthropic work and the goals of Mythgarden, Gant says: 'I appreciate the opportunity to be of service and to be a part of the solution.'[20] Racster, Allen and Gant recognized the political and social value of queer storytelling, and they saw Mythgarden as an opportunity to continue their social justice work within the context of queer filmmaking.

From *The Lifestyle* to *Save Me*

With the production company's framework established, the producers moved forward with the script they had acquired. The original screenplay was, as Allen describes it, an 'over the top comedy about the ex-gay movement'.[21] Racster explains that the original script had a camp sensibility similar to the film *But I'm a Cheerleader* (1999), noting that Mythgarden 'saw a kernel of a very important message in there and [they] beat the comedy out of it' to turn it into a more sensitive and honest portrayal of the issue.[22] The partners of Mythgarden believed that changing the tone of the film from comedic to dramatic increased the story's potential to bring gays and Christians together rather than pitting them against one another and portraying them as incompatible. As men who identified as both gay and Christian, and who had seen and felt discrimination from both sides, they were personally invested in the need to reconcile the perceived divide between homosexuality and Christianity. Racster says:

> We wanted to really reach out and talk about the ex-gay issue in a way
> that was not being talked about. Normally it is the gay community

throwing rocks over a wall at the Christian right and the Christian right throwing rocks over a wall at the gay community ... There was no conversation. There was no listening. And we knew that had to be part of our purpose and drive with *Save Me* ... There's wrong people on both sides of the ex-gay argument. The gay community is not perfect. The religious right are not all our enemy. You can have God and you can have gay and you can have a conversation about this in a loving and honest manner.[23]

This desire to bring people together rather than pushing them apart (potentially enhanced by the economic goal of attracting both LGBT+ and Christian audiences) led to changes in the story and its tone, which dramatically reshaped the film.[24] Comparing the original script, the revised screenplay and the completed film reveals how the story was transformed based on the goals of the producers.

The first version of the screenplay was written by Craig Chester and titled *The Lifestyle*. In this version, a young gay man named Mark finds himself caught up in a world of drug abuse and prostitution. When he hits rock bottom and becomes convinced that the FBI and CIA are after him, his brother takes him to a hospital to detox and then delivers him to an organization called Broken Yoke Ministries, a Christian ex-gay group run by a married couple named Brenda and Bob. While Mark is staying at the organization's group home, Broken House, a man named Luke moves in. Unbeknownst to Mark or the leaders of the ministry, Luke is a reporter for a gay magazine, working undercover to write an exposé about ex-gay ministry programmes. As Mark attempts to turn his back on homosexuality and Luke pretends to do the same, the two begin to fall in love. When Luke's true intentions are discovered, he is kicked out of the house and moves back to New York, and Mark tries even harder to become heterosexual. Mark and Luke are reunited at a gay pride parade, where Luke is participating and Mark is protesting, and after some apologies and brief soul searching, the two decide to run off together.

Many of the major plot points remain in the finished film, but there are some notable changes. Mark still hits rock bottom, and his brother takes him to an ex-gay ministry, but the ministry is called Genesis House, and it is run by a couple named Gayle and Ted, who become much more prominent and developed characters in the final version. Mark still meets another man, but his name is Scott, and rather than being an undercover reporter, he is just another man seeking recovery from what he initially believes is a destructive gay lifestyle. While much of the original script's storyline is preserved in the final film, the producers' desire to shift the tone of the film from mocking ex-gay ministries through comedy to examining both sides of the issue with a more dramatic approach is visible in many details of the film's development.

In some cases, the final screenplay and film contain scenes or moments that appeared in another form in the original version – demonstrating how the comedic tone was removed from individual elements. For example, both the original screenplay and the film use the phrase 'Progress, not perfection', which is part of the teachings associated with ex-gay ministries. The context in which the phrase appears, however, changes significantly from one version to the next. In the original screenplay by Craig Chester, the phrase appears just after Brenda brings Mark to Broken House, only to discover smoke coming out of the kitchen windows. The screenplay reads as follows:

> MARK and BRENDA enter into the foyer. There is a ton of smoke pouring out of the kitchen in the back. In the living room, five very effeminate gay men sit watching a football game with BOB, all of them coughing and waving the air. TRISH, a large, very butch lesbian with badly applied makeup, comes running out of the kitchen in an apron that is too small for her. She enters the living room holding a spatula, wiping sweat from her brow.[25]

Trish apologizes for her failed attempt at cooking, and Brenda responds with, 'That's okay, honey … progress, not perfection!'[26] In the revised version, the line is used when Mark tries to sneak out of the house during his first night. He runs into Scott, who is sitting on the porch smoking a cigarette. Upon seeing this, Mark asks: 'What happened to "no nicotine"?' Scott replies: 'Progress, not perfection. I won't say anything if you won't.'[27]

In the original version, the line points to the absurd attempts to force Trish to conform to expected gender roles. With its references to Trish as a 'very butch lesbian with badly applied makeup', and to the men in the living room as 'five very effeminate gay men … watching a football game', the script seeks humour in the apparent clash between gays and lesbians and the socially expected gender performances of men and women. The revised version uses the phrase in a very different way, as it works to develop significant characters and relationships. Mark's initial impression is that Scott is a golden child at Genesis House, following all the rules and modelling perfect behaviour. When he finds Scott breaking a rule, he learns that Scott is also struggling with vices, opening the door for both Mark and the audience to see Scott as more relatable and human.

While this change shows how the tonal shift desired by producers was accomplished through slight screenplay adjustments, other changes are more drastic – adding or removing entire scenes or storylines to help shift the tone of the film. Chester's original screenplay features several scenes that use broad, sometimes raunchy humour to ridicule the ex-gay movement and its participants. An example of this begins when Mark and Luke attend a conference session called 'Appropriate Touch in Male Relationships'. The leader of the seminar claims that men should never hug in such a way that their torsos touch and encourages men to use a side hug by putting only one arm around the other man's shoulder. He says: 'This way you can greet your friend and at the same time, check out the pretty ladies in your church!' He goes on to tell the men that 'Slapping butts is also appropriate … as long as it's a hard slap. Caressing butts, I'm sure I don't have to tell you, is inappropriate … Generally, it's not good to look at the butt as your [sic] slapping it. Remember, keep your eyes on the ladies … never on your guy friends!"[28] Later, as Mark and Luke are browsing the conference book exhibit, the screenplay indicates that 'Behind them, several EX-GAYS who attended the "Male Touch" class greet each other by hugging from the side and slapping each other's asses.'[29] The original screenplay is not all butt-slapping sight gags, but this example gives an indication of the tone of the piece as it was first written. The outrageous verbal, visual and physical humour would have entertained some viewers, but it was at odds with Mythgarden's goal of generating sincere and thoughtful engagement from those on both sides of the ex-gay issue.

The revised screenplay by Robert Desiderio took the subject matter in a different direction, not only eliminating the broad comedy but also introducing some very emotional, even tragic scenes. The character of Lester, for example, is transformed from one who quietly celebrates the budding relationship between Mark and Luke to a much more pivotal and thought-provoking character who provides an indication of the consequences of denying same-sex attraction in the name of religion. In the completed film, Lester watches Mark and Scott grow very close, and he becomes extremely distraught when it looks like the two men will not be able to be together because of their faith. He confesses that he saw the relationship between Mark and Scott as proof that two men could really find love with one another, which is something that Lester wanted for himself. Recognizing that such a relationship is 'not the Lord's design', he says: 'I just don't think I can be any other way.' He is so upset by this turn of events and the resulting realizations about himself that he attempts suicide, and Mark finds him unconscious in a bathtub full of bloody water. Lester's suicide attempt serves as a wake-up call for Mark and a turning point in his journey, while highlighting one of the outcomes that critics of conversion practices and ex-gay ministries warn is a potential consequence of such programmes.[30] The emotional weight of scenes such as Lester's attempted suicide contribute to the serious tone present in the final screenplay and film as opposed to the original, more comedic script, thus enhancing the sincerity of the film's engagement with both sides of the issue.

Queerness and Christianity in *Save Me*

In addition to the shift in the film's tone, *Save Me*'s evolution also included a revised presentation of the relationship between queerness and Christianity, as conveyed, in part, by the interplay between the protagonists and antagonists in the story. Discussing how leaders of social movements use narratives to create and present their collective identities, Robert Benford notes that the creation of opposing sides is a common narrative strategy. He observes: 'In the course of imputing traits about their own group, which they typically frame as the narrative's "protagonists," they also make negative attributions regarding movement opponents, the story's "antagonists."'[31] As previously discussed, supporters of gay rights have often presented narratives in which conservative Christians are portrayed not only as antagonists whose beliefs are in conflict with the push for gay rights, but as villains out to punish or eliminate LGBT+ people. Any narrative needs protagonists and antagonists to generate the conflict that propels a story, and all versions of *Save Me* do present the leaders of the ex-gay ministries as antagonists within the narrative. But the development and treatment of those characters changes from the original draft to the completed film.

In the original screenplay, Brenda and Bob are introduced as 'a loud, relentlessly concerned woman of forty with a man-ish haircut,' and 'an overweight, crass, detached man with a beard and big, tinted glasses.'[32] The characters are never given a backstory or any significant development beyond the initial unflattering descriptions. As described above, they and their ministry are regularly sources of humour, making them and their beliefs seem outrageous and ridiculous. This makes it easier for an audience member to root for the young men in love and against the 'crazy Christians.'

The revised screenplay and completed film present Gayle and Ted in a much more sympathetic light, offering enough details to create them as fully developed, round characters, as opposed to the flat, stock characters presented in the original screenplay. The initial description of the couple in the revised screenplay immediately sets a more sympathetic tone. 'Gayle is early fifties. Salt-of-the-earth and air of a queen. Ted is a year or two younger. Street-wise and sensitive.'[33] Although the audience first glimpses the two in church in the film's opening sequence, a more complete introduction occurs a couple of scenes later, in their home. When Ted informs Gayle that a new resident (Mark) will be joining their programme, they both express excitement over his arrival, but Gayle also shares her concern about Mark's drug addiction. Ted notes that they are 'all God's children', and Gayle nods and says, 'Praise the Lord!' After Ted admits to feeling some jealousy when Gayle puts on a bracelet given to her by her previous husband, Gayle says: 'He had good taste ... but I love you.' She then wraps her arms around his neck and the two kiss. This introductory scene establishes Gayle and Ted as loving people with a commitment to helping others that is rooted in their Christian faith. Later, when a reluctant and stubborn Mark is dropped off by his brother, he clashes with Gayle as she firmly reviews ground rules. Were it not for Gayle's previous introduction, it would be easier for a viewer to see her only as Mark sees her in this scene, and thus read her as a villain.

As the story develops, elements of Gayle's and Ted's backstories are introduced to help explain and clarify their current behaviours and beliefs, and both characters are shown connecting emotionally with Mark as they try to help him. The film includes multiple scenes that reveal the losses and regrets that motivate Gayle's behaviours. For example, after getting off to a difficult start, Gayle and Mark have a breakthrough heart-to-heart conversation while running some errands. After Mark opens up to Gayle about attempting suicide, she tells him that she had a son who died of a drug overdose when he was seventeen years old. She also mentions that he was gay and indicates her belief that his involvement with 'that lifestyle' led to his drug use and eventual overdose. She gets choked up while sharing her story and Mark is clearly moved by it. While some of Gayle's beliefs are rooted in myths about LGBT+ people (such as her suggestion that drug abuse is an inevitable aspect of gay life), the pain and vulnerability she displays begins to endear her to Mark, and the scene suggests that her work with Genesis House may be an attempt to cope with the loss of her son.

Near the film's conclusion, as Mark decides to leave Genesis House with Scott, rather than focusing solely on the happiness of the two men, the film gives equal weight to Gayle's response and the pain she feels. When Mark tells Gayle that he loves Scott, she makes a final attempt to convince him to stay, clutching him and crying before collapsing in Ted's arms. In the following scene, Gayle asks her pastor for money to support Genesis House. She tells him about her son, mentioning specifically that he died a few months after she kicked him out of the house for being gay. After describing the pain, regret and helplessness she has felt since losing her son, she tries to end on a hopeful note by saying: 'But now I have the chance to save others . . . and to save me.' She delivers her story as a monologue, shot in one long take that lasts almost two minutes without a cut. As she speaks, the camera pushes in very slowly, almost imperceptibly, from a medium close-up to a close-up, emphasizing the quiver in her lip and the tears in her eyes. By drawing the viewer in to share Gayle's pain, the scene helps to solidify her presentation not as a villain, but as a wounded woman coping with a terrible loss.

Ted is not as prominent in the story as Gayle, but he is also shown to be a complicated and caring person. Ted is a recovering addict who regularly turns to the Lord and other Christians for support as he fights his addictions. After some vague references to drugs early in the film, Ted is shown participating in a support group, where he mentions that he had been sober for six months when he first met Gayle, who helped

Figure 6.1 A tearful Gayle recounting the painful loss of her son.

him get back on his feet before the two fell in love. He draws on his own experience to help those residents of Genesis House who struggle with drug and alcohol dependency. Both Ted and Gayle help Mark with his addictions, and while they do sometimes mistakenly conflate substance abuse with same-sex attraction (something that is common in many conversion programmes), their work does pay off. After some time at Genesis House, Mark proudly proclaims that he is 'ninety days sober' and says he feels that 'Jesus made all this possible'. While Gayle and Ted continue to provide obstacles to Mark and Scott's happiness and try to repress the men's true feelings and identities, they are depicted as people motivated by love, loss, struggle and faith, and are not easily dismissed as cruel or ridiculous. Additionally, the love and commitment they show to the residents of Genesis House, which is clearly rooted in their Christian beliefs, does have some positive outcomes, particularly with respect to helping the men manage chemical dependencies.

The generally positive portrayal of Christianity in *Save Me* is emphasized by the visual treatment of Genesis House, particularly in comparison with other spaces in the film. Scenes at Genesis House are frequently bathed in late afternoon or morning sunlight that gives everything a warm glow. Transitions and montage sequences emphasize landscape shots that situate the facility among lush trees, colourful rock formations and a picturesque pond. These visual details help to present Genesis House as a warm and inviting place, in stark contrast to the seedy motels, dimly lit bars, and sterile hospital rooms that define life outside Genesis House.

The contrast is highlighted in a handful of scenes early in the film. After Mark overdoses and is found on the floor of his motel room, he winds up in the hospital with an IV tube in his arm. The room is lit by harsh, overhead fluorescent lights, which give the space a blue-green tint and cast unflattering shadows that exaggerate Mark's sickly appearance. After Mark fights with his brother and tries to follow him down the hall, the scene ends with a high angle shot of Mark writhing on the floor of the hospital room as a worker tries to comfort him. As Mark lies on the floor, the diegetic sound of his cries is gradually replaced by nondiegetic music featuring gentle strings and piano, which continues as the image cuts to an exterior shot of a driveway in the country. The driveway is lined with trees and a wooden fence, and the end of the driveway is marked by an old, slightly rusty mailbox that says 'Genesis House'. The trees cast long shadows, as the scene is lit by the early morning sun. This shot is followed by a tracking shot moving along the driveway towards the house, then a shot of Scott working on a birdhouse in the side yard, and eventually an interior shot of Gayle watching Scott through her bedroom window as Ted walks in to tell her that Mark will be coming to stay with them. The shots all share the same golden glow from the rising sun. In addition to visually and temporally connecting the film's four main characters, this sequence immediately presents Genesis House as a warm and inviting alternative to the cold and lonely existence that has come to define Mark's life.

This is not to say that the film ignores the harmful ways Christianity has been used to oppress and belittle LGBT+ people. Gayle does use the Bible as the justification for the harmful practices that form the core of Genesis House (a topic addressed in Chapter 4), and when Scott's father lies dying in a hospital bed, Scott tries desperately to make a final emotional connection with him. Scott is instead met with condemnation, as his father uses his last breaths to recite Bible passages that have been used repeatedly over the years to denounce homosexuality as a sin. *Save Me* demonstrates some of the ways that the Bible and Christianity have been mobilized to hurt LGBT+ people but suggests that these specific actions run contrary to the love and acceptance that Christians tout as a central tenet of their faith.

Presenting Ted and particularly Gayle as sympathetic and nuanced characters – a significant change from the original screenplay and much of the rhetoric around the ex-gay issue – helps to present the two sides of the issue in dialogue with one another rather than at each other's throats. Similarly, the visual presentation of Genesis House as warm and inviting helps to convey the idea that even though Mark and Scott reject Gayle and Ted's attempts to 'heal' them, Genesis House, and by extension, Christianity, can still be a potential source of love and compassion. This is further emphasized by the fact that neither Mark nor Scott abandons their Christian faith even when they choose to leave the conversion programme behind. Scott, for example, cites Bible passages in his final argument with Gayle, noting that 'Jesus never said anything about homosexuality.' He argues against Gayle's interpretation of the Bible's teachings without entirely dismissing the Bible or Christianity. And when Mark and Gayle have their final goodbye, she quietly says to him 'May the Lord be with you,' to which he replies, 'Oh he is . . . he is!' before giving her a firm hug. These words, along with the cross that he continues to wear around his neck, suggest that Mark still finds comfort in his Christian faith even as he embraces his identity as a gay man.

By engaging with characters representing both sides of the ex-gay argument and doing so in a relatively balanced way, *Save Me* attempts to offer an alternative to the narratives that have circulated among both conservative Christians and the gay rights movement. Strategic 'counter-storytelling' is used in social movements when a marginalized group provides narratives that challenge the stories of a dominant group to destabilize the ideological viewpoints embedded in those stories.[34] *Save Me* provides a double counter-narrative, since it challenges not only Christian stories that demonize queer people but also queer stories that vilify Christians.

In relation to Christian stories, *Save Me* counters the stories offered by ex-gay ministries, which present homosexuality as a problem that can be overcome through prayer and spiritual guidance. As Benford points out, a common narrative strategy for social movements is to tell a story that begins in the same way as the dominant story, but then offer an alternative middle and ending that challenges the status quo. He says: 'Movement actors seek to insert themselves, individually and collectively, into an extant narrative (the status quo story) to bring about change, to create a new narrative.'[35] *Save Me* follows this approach, initially showing men who enter the ex-gay ministry programme, discover the apparent roots of their problems, and then take steps toward sexual recovery. Part way through the film, however, the story diverges from those told by ex-gay ministry leaders. Rather than 'overcoming' their 'sexual brokenness', Scott and Mark find love and happiness and decide to pursue a life together as a gay couple. This is certainly not the outcome included in the stories told by ex-gay leaders, unless it is part of a cautionary tale of what happens to those who abandon the programme. However, in such a case, the decision to leave the programme and pursue a relationship with another man would result in heartbreak and misery, rather than any sense of happiness, which the film offers.

Save Me provides a counter-story not only to the narratives presented by ex-gay ministries, but also to the stories told by some gay rights advocates and critics of ex-gay programmes. For example, in his book *Anything but Straight: Unmasking the Scandals and Lies Behind the Ex-Gay Myth*, Wayne R. Besen attacks ex-gay ministries and supporters of reparative therapy, portraying them as greedy hypocrites and liars, and taking great pleasure in catching an ex-gay leader in a gay bar.[36] Essentially, proponents of the ex-gay movement are cast as hate-filled villains and enemies to be defeated. As discussed above, the producers of *Save Me* go to great lengths to present Gayle, Ted and their programme in a sympathetic light, showing that their actions and beliefs are rooted in love rather than hate. And while Mark and Scott decide to leave the ministry, they do not turn their backs on Christianity. In this way, *Save Me* provides a reconciling counter-narrative that is an alternative to those presented on both sides of the ex-gay argument, and which seeks to advance the LGBT+ movements by making allies out of enemies.

The evolution of *Save Me* from a comedic attack on the Christian ex-gay movement to a sincere examination of the values that inform both sides of the ex-gay debate led to a film that seeks common ground between opposing perspectives as a way of encouraging dialogue. *Save Me* still emphasizes the failures and dangers of conversion programmes, but the film does so in a way that places the blame on the specific practice rather than on the religion that is often used to justify that practice. The filmmakers' efforts to understand and sympathize with characters who contribute to the oppression of LGBT+ people may not appeal to all viewers. Those who prefer to have clear villains who are soundly defeated, or who have experienced anti-queer discrimination at the hands of conservative Christians, are likely to find the film unsatisfying or even frustrating. The rhetorical strategy employed by the film's narrative, however, makes space for queer people, Christians, and perhaps most importantly, queer Christians to reconcile some of the differences that have been created and sustained by both pro- and anti-LGTB+ activists over the years. In this way, *Save Me* uses a fictional narrative to encourage and advance productive dialogue in support of ongoing efforts to end the oppression of LGBT+ people.

Notes

1   This chapter includes and expands on excerpts from an article originally published in the *Journal of Film and Video*. See D. R. Coon, 'Mythgarden: Collaborative Authorship and Counter-Storytelling in Queer Independent Film,' *Journal of Film and Video* 70, no. 3–4 (2018): 44–62.

2   C. Pullen, *Gay Identity, New Storytelling, and the Media* (New York: Palgrave Macmillan, 2009), 13.

3   C. Pullen, *Documenting Gay Men: Identity and Performance in Reality Television and Documentary Film* (London: McFarland, 2007), 10.

4   G. Ladson-Billings, 'Just What is Critical Race Theory, and What's it Doing in a Nice Field Like Education?' in *Race Is . . . Race Isn't: Critical Race Theory and Qualitative Studies in Education*, L. Parker, D. Deyhle and S. Villenas eds (Boulder, CO: Westview Press, 1999), 16.

5   R. Delgado and J. Stefancic, *Critical Race Theory: An Introduction* (New York: New York University Press, 2012), 49.

6   C. A. Rimmerman, *The Lesbian and Gay Movements: Assimilation or Liberation?* 2nd edn (Boulder, CO: Westview Press, 2014), 28–9.

7   T. Fetner, 'Working Anita Bryant: The Impact of Christian Anti-Gay Activism on Lesbian and Gay Movement Claims,' *Social Problems* 48, no. 3 (2001): 419.

8   P. Jenkins, *The New Anti-Catholicism: The Last Acceptable Prejudice* (New York: Oxford University Press, 2003), 101.

9 J. D'Emilio, 'Afterword', in *Devotions and Desires: Histories of Sexuality and Religion in the Twentieth-Century United States*, G. Frank, B. Moreton and H. R. White eds (Chapel Hill: University of North Carolina Press, 2018), 278.

10 C. J. Stewart, C. A. Smith and R. E. Denton, Jr., *Persuasion and Social Movements*, 6th edn (Long Grove, IL: Waveland Press, 2012), 149.

11 J. Downs, *Stand by Me: The Forgotten History of Gay Liberation* (New York: Basic Books, 2016), 48.

12 H. R. White, *Reforming Sodom: Protestants and the Rise of Gay Rights* (Chapel Hill: University of North Carolina Press, 2015), 165.

13 L. Gerber, 'We Who Must Die Demand a Miracle: Christmas 1989 at the Metropolitan Community Church of San Francisco', in *Devotions and Desires: Histories of Sexuality and Religion in the Twentieth-Century United States*, G. Frank, B. Moreton and H.R. White eds (Chapel Hill: University of North Carolina Press, 2015), 254.

14 White, *Reforming Sodom*, 105–6.

15 White, *Reforming Sodom*, 160.

16 J. I. Wenzel, 'A Different Christian Witness to Society: Christian Support for Gay Rights and Liberation in Minnesota, 1977–1993', *Church History* 88, no. 3 (2019): 750.

17 D. S. Cutrara, *Wicked Cinema: Sex and Religion on Screen* (Austin: University of Texas Press, 2014), 78.

18 C. Racster, phone interview with the author, 15 September 2009.

19 C. Allen, phone interview with the author, 21 October 2009.

20 R. Gant, phone interview with the author, 24 March 2010.

21 Allen, phone interview.

22 Racster, phone interview.

23 Racster, phone interview.

24 For a discussion of the popularity of independent films aimed at Christian audiences, see J. Russell, 'In Hollywood, But Not of Hollywood: Independent Christian Filmmaking', in *American Independent Cinema: Indie, Indiewood and Beyond*, eds G. King, C. Mollow and Y. Tzioumakis (New York: Routledge, 2013), 185–97.

25 C. Chester, *The Lifestyle* (unpublished screenplay, 1996), 18.

26 Chester, *The Lifestyle*, 18.

27 R. Desiderio, *Save Me* (revised shooting script, 2006), 26.

28 Chester, *The Lifestyle*, 71.

29 Chester, *The Lifestyle*, 73.

208   *Gay Conversion Practices in Memoir, Film and Fiction*

30 J. G. Ford, 'Healing Homosexuals: A Psychologist's Journey Through the Ex-Gay Movement and the Pseudo-Science of Reparative Therapy', *Journal of Gay and Lesbian Psychotherapy* 5, no. 3–4 (2002): 69–86.

31 R. Benford, 'Controlling Narratives and Narratives as Control Within Social Movements', in *Stories of Change: Narrative and Social Movements*, ed J.E. Davis (Albany, NY: State University of New York Press, 2002), 71.

32 Chester, *The Lifestyle*, 12.

33 Desiderio, *Save Me*, 2.

34 R. Delgado, 'Storytelling for Oppositionists and Others: A Plea for Narrative', in *Critical Race Theory: The Cutting Edge*, 2nd edn, R. Delgado and J. Stefancic eds (Philadelphia: Temple University Press, 2000), 61.

35 Benford, 'Controlling Narratives', 55.

36 W. R. Besen, *Anything but Straight: Unmasking the Scandals and Lies Behind the Ex-Gay Myth* (New York: Harrington Park Press, 2003).

Bibliography

Allen, C. Personal interview. 21 October 2009.

Benford, R. D. 'Controlling Narratives and Narratives as Control within Social Movements'. In *Stories of Change: Narrative and Social Movements*, ed J. E. Davis, 53–75. Albany, NY: State University of New York Press, 2002.

Besen, W. R. *Anything but Straight: Unmasking the Scandals and Lies Behind the Ex-Gay Myth*. New York: Harrington Park Press, 2003.

Chester, C. *The Lifestyle*. Unpublished screenplay, 1996.

Coon, D. R. 'Mythgarden: Collaborative Authorship and Counter-Storytelling in Queer Independent Film'. *Journal of Film and Video* 70, no. 3–4 (2018): 44–62.

Cutrara, D. *Wicked Cinema: Sex and Religion on Screen*. Austin: University of Texas Press, 2014.

Delgado, R. 'Storytelling for Oppositionists and Others: A Plea for Narrative'. In *Critical Race Theory: The Cutting Edge*, eds R. Delgado and J. Stefancic. Philadelphia: Temple University Press, 2000.

Delgado, R. and J. Stefancic. *Critical Race Theory: An Introduction*. New York: New York University Press, 2012.

D'Emilio, J. 'Afterword'. In *Devotions and Desires: Histories of Sexuality and Religion in the Twentieth-Century United States*, eds G. Frank, B. Moreton and H. R. White, 277–82. Chapel Hill: University of North Carolina Press, 2018.

Desiderio, R. *Save Me*. Revised shooting script, 2006.

Downs, J. *Stand by Me: The Forgotten History of Gay Liberation*. New York: Basic Books, 2016.

Fetner, T. 'Working Anita Bryant: The Impact of Christian Anti-Gay Activism on Lesbian and Gay Movement Claims.' *Social Problems* 48, no. 3 (2001): 411–28.

Ford, J. G. 'Healing Homosexuals: A Psychologist's Journey through the Ex-Gay Movement and the Pseudo-Science of Reparative Therapy.' *Journal of Gay and Lesbian Psychotherapy* 5, no. 3–4 (2002): 69–85.

Gant, R. Personal interview. 24 March 2010.

Gerber, L. 'We Who Must Die Demand a Miracle: Christmas 1989 as the Metropolitan Community Church of San Francisco.' In *Devotions and Desires: Histories of Sexuality and Religion in the Twentieth-Century United States*, eds G. Frank, B. Moreton and H. R. White, 253–76. Chapel Hill: University of North Carolina Press, 2015.

Jenkins, P. *The New Anti-Catholicism: The Last Acceptable Prejudice*. New York: Oxford University Press, 2003.

Ladson-Billings, G. 'Just What Is Critical Race Theory, and What's It Doing in a Nice Field Like Education?' In *Race Is . . . Race Isn't: Critical Race Theory and Qualitative Studies in Education*, eds L. Parker, D. Deyhle and S. Villenas, 7–30. Boulder, CO: Westview Press, 1999.

Pullen, C. *Documenting Gay Men: Identity and Performance in Reality Television and Documentary Film*. London: McFarland, 2007.

Pullen, C. *Gay Identity, New Storytelling, and the Media*. New York: Palgrave Macmillan, 2009.

Racster, C. Personal interview. 15 September 2009.

Rimmerman, C. A. *The Lesbian and Gay Movements: Assimilation or Liberation?* 2nd edn. Boulder, CO: Westview Press, 2014.

Russell, J. 'In Hollywood, but Not of Hollywood: Independent Christian Filmmaking.' In *American Independent Cinema: Indie, Indiewood, and Beyond*, eds G. King, C. Mollow and Y. Tzioumakis, 185–97. New York: Routledge, 2013.

Save Me [Film] Dir. R. Cary, USA: Mythgarden, 2007.

Stewart, C. J., C. A. Smith and R. E. Denton. *Persuasion and Social Movements*. Long Grove, IL: Waveland Press, 2012.

Wenzel, J. I. 'A Different Christian Witness to Society: Christian Support for
Gay Rights and Liberation in Minnesota, 1977–1993.' *Church History* 88,
no. 3 (2019): 720–50.
White, H. R. *Reforming Sodom: Protestants and the Rise of Gay Rights.* Chapel
Hill: University of North Carolina Press, 2015.

The Quiet Violence of Denying Queerness in the Novel and Film, *The Miseducation of Cameron Post*

Jessica Ford and Annika Herb

Queer cinema plays a pivotal role in both the novel (2012) and film (2018) versions of *The Miseducation of Cameron Post* (henceforth *Miseducation*), as the titular Cameron comes into her queerness through watching films and finds a language for her desires using queer-coded cinema. The title of the novel refers to both Cameron's experience in conversion 'therapy', and her early immersion in queer cinema. Set in the 1990s, Emily M. Danforth's novel depicts Cameron renting VHS copies of what B. Ruby Rich calls 'New Queer Cinema', such as *Personal Best* (1982), *The Hunger* (1983) and *Desert Hearts* (1985).[1] These films, much to Cameron's delight, feature explicit depictions of same-sex sexual activity and relationships that reconfigure traditional heterosexual conceptions of marriage and family; however, New Queer Cinema is also inextricably tied to the HIV/AIDS crisis and the activists and communities that emerged during this era.[2] In *Miseducation*, New Queer Cinema is smuggled into bedrooms, becoming a private, quiet and intimate way of coming to queer desire.

In the novel, Cameron facilitates her first physical same-sex experience while watching *The Hunger*'s sex scene between Sarah (Susan Sarandon) and Miriam (Catherine Deneuve). Narrating her experience with partner Coley, Cameron says: 'We barely made it through *the scene*.'[3] Despite the salaciousness of the erotic thriller, the girls' experience together is tender, quiet and intimate. Cameron's narration deploys evocative, affective language describing 'cold sheets', 'shivering, laughing', 'goose-bumped skin' and 'the hot closeness of our bodies'.[4] The novel makes a clear distinction between the 'complicated' version of queer sex rendered in the movies, and the simple, low-key joy of Cameron and Coley's experience.

A similar moment is rendered in the film adaptation of *Miseducation*, when in a flashback Cameron (Chloë Grace Moretz) and Coley (Quinn Shepherd) are entangled in bed together watching *Desert Hearts*. Echoing the quiet intimacy of the novel, the camera observes Cameron and Coley from a distance with little dialogue, only intense glances and connected body language. New Queer Cinema plays a very different role in the film than the novel, in part because by the time the film adaption was in production, queerness was increasingly more mainstream, both culturally and on screen. As Stuart Richards highlights, the emergence of queer-themed films such as *Brokeback Mountain* (2005), *Milk* (2008) and *The Kids Are All Right* (2010) as popular hits moved queer cinema from the fringes to the mainstream.[5] Further, as a queer film itself, *Miseducation* has a less nostalgic and more ironic and knowing relationship to New Queer Cinema. For New Queer filmmakers like Todd Haynes, Laurie Lynd and Cheryl Duyne, their films operated on the margins, rejecting heteronormativity, and depicting queer sexuality as chaotic and destabilizing. In contrast, Desiree Akhavan's *Miseducation* renders queer desire as a natural, affirming, intimate experience that, despite the messaging of conversion therapy, unites the characters.

In this chapter we argue both the book and film versions of *Miseducation* depict the quiet violence and trauma of denying queerness. We consider how popular culture operates as a respite from the harsh, anti-queer sentiment of the world the characters inhabit, and offers a language and script for queerness. The radicality of *Miseducation* as both novel and film is in the mundanity of the torture and abuse endured by those in conversion camp. Neither the film nor the book render Cameron and her fellow queer teens in melodramatic or spectacular terms (contra, *But I'm A Cheerleader*; see Chapter 5); rather, their suffering is depicted in quiet, unspectacular terms. Instead, both texts offer a critical insight into the quiet violence experienced by queer teens in conversion therapy, or as Travis Webster redefines the practice, 'conversion violence', acknowledging the enduring trauma and insidious internalization of conversion camp values, and ultimately finding opportunities for resistance and survival in queer community, acceptance of the queer self, and popular culture.[6]

Situating *The Miseducation of Cameron Post*

The Miseducation of Cameron Post is at once a story of queerness, a teen text and a narrative of conversion practices. It sits at the intersection of different filmic and literary trends and categories, as it is both young adult literature and a teen film, while also drawing on and contributing to queer literature and queer cinema. To understand how the book and film operate within intersecting literary and filmic traditions, we begin this chapter by situating *Miseducation* within these broader histories. First, we consider how conversion narratives work within a larger tradition of 'camp' stories that bring together adolescents under the guise of 'fixing' them. We then unpack how both young adult literature and the teen film codify the expectations and norms of heterosexuality. Finally, we consider how *Miseducation* is both drawing on, and contributing to a history of queer narratives across literature and screen.

Narratives of conversion practices tend to follow similar logics and rationale, irrespective of their medium or form. The primary logic of this kind of traumatic narrative is that gender performance is directly correlated with sexuality, as satirized in *But I'm A Cheerleader* (1999), discussed by Tom Sharples in Chapter 5.[7] These narratives assume non-normative feminine or masculine gender performance result in homosexuality and queerness, and the path to 'converting' someone to heterosexuality involves adhering to the aesthetic norms of one's sex at birth.[8] This echoes studies of conversion practices more broadly, which emphasize the false equivalency rendered between gender performance and sexuality in the 'ex-gay' movement.[9] As Jeffrey A. Bennett writes, narratives about the 'success' of conversion practices rely on the assumption 'gay and lesbian identities are more unstable than those secured by heterosexuals'.[10] However, focusing on the outcome (or lack thereof) of conversion practices, whether real or fictional, does not erase the trauma of enduring this kind of 'therapy' or the anti-queer stigma it promotes. Webster suggests reorienting discussions of conversion practices to think about how the rhetoric offered by these institutions constitute a kind of 'conversion violence'.[11] For Webster, 'conversion violence' offers a way of understanding how 'material and metaphorical violence' is used to shame people into the closet.[12] The literary and filmic versions of *Miseducation* make a case for this in a fictional setting, by underlining the anti-queer violence of conversion practices.

Conversion camp may initially seem like a strange setting for a book or film about and aimed at teens; however, Adrian Martin argues the teen film facilitates the exploration of liminality, owing to its setting during 'the heightened moment of suspension between two conditions', namely, childhood and adulthood.[13] Conversion camp is also a liminal space, as its aim is to 'convert' teens from queer to heteronormative. While camps are designed to address the 'problems' of youth whether weight, sexuality, addiction or gender performance, they are narratively productive insofar as they group together teens who are otherwise marginalized, making them the dominant-hegemonic social grouping within the camp. So-called 'rehabilitation' camps aimed at 'fixing' children are vile, destructive and demeaning, but as a storytelling device they provide a setting to centre characters, bodies and expressions that are generally marginalized or erased from traditional teen cinema and literature. In bringing 'problem' adolescent characters together, characters are united by their perceived challenges, creating a space where they can bond, create community and embrace their similarities. *Miseducation* works within this paradigm, as it depicts characters coming together and bonding over their 'problematic' queer desires. Their 'problem' becomes a uniting force, around which the characters coalesce and find belonging.

Queerness as 'problem'

Both Young Adult (YA) literature and the teen film have a history of rendering adolescent characters and their lives, particularly queer adolescences, as a 'problem'. The 'problem' novel was popularized in the 1980s, although it takes its cues from the first YA novel, S. E. Hinton's *The Outsiders* (1967) and the first queer YA novel, John Donovan's *I'll Get There. It Better Be Worth the Trip* (1969). The problem YA novel includes texts that focus on issues such as drug use, teen sex, pregnancy and homosexuality through a moralizing, didactic lens. Depictions of homosexuality were intended to scandalize, and often act as a sign of a character's moral degradation.[14] In contrast, Donovan's *I'll Get There* offered a sympathetic look at a gay teenager's coming out experience, and established enduring tropes for queer YA novels, including the ever-looming threat of discovery, and themes of rejection, alienation and punishment, their sexuality a catalyst for internal and external conflict. It also heralded a dominant focus on gay, white, cisgender and able-bodied teenage boys. Following Donovan's precedent where the protagonist's beloved dog dies shortly after he is discovered with another boy, teen characters in YA problem novels are often punished, consciously or not, for their queerness. Later texts provide more hopeful endings, although the narrative structure that places a character's queerness as a source of conflict, even to provide commentary on a homophobic setting, nonetheless reinforces queerness as shameful, a cause for distress and ultimately a problem. *Miseducation* deviates from the standard conversion and coming out narratives, while drawing on historical conventions and tropes of the coming out narrative and 'queerness as problem' tendency in YA, illustrating the quiet trauma and violence of denying queerness.

Similarly, the teen film has a well-established subset of 'problem youth' films, like *Rebel Without a Cause* (1955) and *Breakfast Club* (1985), which depict 'troubled' teens who resist authority but are ultimately punished and contained. Catherine Driscoll contends 'youth as problem' is a thematic that runs through much of teen film, which includes films about teen delinquency, stories where teens must overcome an external problem like social exclusion or internal problems like self-doubt, and movies that figure teens as a social problem in need of fixing.[15] We can see the thematic of youth as problem in *Miseducation*, but while the adults may see the teens as problems in need of fixing, the teens and the film itself are not buying into this narrative. According to both Jane Feuer and Driscoll, the teen film is principally a 'sexual coming of age narrative', where the key narrative obstacle is maturity.[16] We can see this at work in *Miseducation*, however for Cameron and her fellow residents of the conversion therapy camp for teens called God's Promise, they must also come to terms with their queerness in a setting that teaches them it is a problem. Driscoll highlights how the 'teen film is less about growing up than about the expectation, difficulty, and social organization of growing up'.[17] It is not their queerness itself that is the problem, but rather how others understand and attempt to erase their queer desires. In *Miseducation*, the 'problem of youth' is a problem of conversion violence inflicted on youth.

Queer teens: from literature to film

Danforth's *Miseducation* highlights how the evolution of YA literature and queer YA literature are closely entwined. YA literature – a designation that acknowledges readership, rather than genre – is often defined for its depiction of the Bildungsroman or coming-of-age narrative. The coming out and coming-of-age narratives mirror one another, with the queer YA novel following a specific trajectory – discovery of identity, fear and shame, before coming out, either willingly or unwillingly, and facing acceptance or rejection. *Miseducation* engages with these tropes, including the threat of discovery, internalized and external homophobia, and coming of age, but subverts conventionality through Danforth's refusal of spectacle and deployment of narrative intimacy.[18] In mapping the evolution of queer YA literature, Christine A. Jenkins and Michael Cart classify *Miseducation* within Homosexual

Visibility (HV) narratives, a core group of novels where closeted characters come out or are outed.[19] They note Danforth's novel and its contemporaries bridge a liminal space in the field: 'unlike earlier HV novels where the coming out was the denouement – today's HV tends to follow the consequences of coming out; in this regard HV comes very close to being [Gay Assimilation]'.[20] The liminality of the text evokes Derritt Mason's exploration of queer anxieties in YA media, particularly the limitations of the 'It Gets Better' narrative, and the consequences Cameron faces after being outed.[21] Published in 2012, the novel is set between 1989 and 1993 in rural Midwest America, evoking a specific cultural and literary context in relation to the problem novel. By commenting on queer representation through popular culture, the YA novel and the quiet reality of Cameron's experience, Danforth rejects a sensationalist narrative and instead provides intimate insight to queer identity and the harmful nature of conversion practices.

Akhavan's *Miseducation* is not just a teen film, but it is also a queer film insofar as it is both a film about queerness and is queer in its approach and politics. *Miseducation* is the product of the mainstreaming of queerness and queer culture, to the extent that in much of the promotion of the film, its teen-focus is emphasized over its queerness. Akhavan repeatedly asserts her desire to adapt the book as a 'teen film', stating: 'Cameron's story is about her and her friends, it's a teen film. It's comedic, it's silly at times.'[22] The teen film has been around since the classical Hollywood era, but unlike other genres, it is defined by its youthful intended-audience and subjects, rather than any consistent style, narrative, or aesthetic. While the teen film is often dismissed owing to its 'reputation for triviality', as Timothy Shary writes, adolescence is frequently used to represent 'our deepest social and personal concerns'.[23] Part of the critical dismissal of the genre's aesthetic and narrative concerns can be traced to the teen movie's frequent designation as 'trash', but it is also tied to the dismissal of teen concerns as less important to an adult audience, a perspective echoed in the reception of YA literature.[24] *Miseducation* dismisses and subverts this tendency by taking the concerns and lives of their teens seriously, but it also resists many of the popular archetypes, settings and themes of the teen film. Before Cameron's arrival at God's Promise, we get glimpses of her going to school dances, hanging out with her friends and partaking in standard teen film activities, but once at God's Promise the film largely takes on the style of a quiet character-driven indie film. At the same time, Akhavan is adamant she 'wanted to make a John Hughes film [renowned for their stories featuring convincing adolescent characters]. I wanted to make a teen film that I wanted to see as a teen and craved all the time, that I hadn't seen in a while.'[25] In many ways, Akhavan succeeds, as the filmic adaptation eschews the melodrama-like emotionality that characterizes films like *Boy Erased* (2018) (see Chapter 8), in favour of oscillating between joy and quiet melancholy. However, the film's setting means it avoids many of the teen film touchstones like dating, parties and high school. While much of the film is set at God's Promise, these more typical teen movie moments are rendered through flashbacks shot with a warm, foggy filter.

The novel and its film adaptation are united in how they approach conversion violence and the trauma it inflicts on the teens subjected to it. While different in form and structure, in depicting the quiet violence and trauma of denying queerness both versions of *Miseducation* highlight the radical mundanity of the torture and abuse endured by those in conversion therapy.

The Miseducation of Cameron Post (2012) by Emily M. Danforth

Emily M. Danforth's debut YA novel *The Miseducation of Cameron Post* follows the titular character as she explores her sexuality in the wake of her parents' death. When her relationship with another girl is discovered, Cameron's born-again Christian aunt sends her to God's Promise. Set in the rural western American municipality of Miles City, Montana from 1989 to 1993, a time and a setting autobiographical to Danforth's youth,

Miseducation explores sexuality, queerness, trauma and popular culture as entry to, and expression of queer community and identity. The novel is not explicit or overt in its condemnation of conversion camps; as narrator, Cameron largely avoids judgement on the practice due to her sociocultural context and entangled feelings of grief and guilt over her sexuality and parents' death. The first-person focalization creates a degree of detached perspective that allows the reader to witness the reality and mundane horror of the practice and form their own perspectives. Danforth evokes a complex relationship between dissonance and Sara K. Day's concept of narrative intimacy, with Cameron's confessional address intimately connecting the reader while also emphasizing her disconnection from the self.[26] The novel avoids spectacle in its depiction of conversion practices, rejecting the neat Hollywood narrative Cameron is fluent in, or that is established in YA conversion narratives; instead, Danforth's characterization and narration establishes the quiet trauma and violence of denying queerness.[27]

The death of Cameron's parents coincides with her first kiss with her best friend, Irene; subsequently, her grief over their death collides with her guilt over her emerging queer desire. The girls' kiss is also conflated with their earlier theft of gum from a local store, emphasizing a strong sense of immorality in both actions, and Cameron's rejection of her queerness. This conflict is evident in Cameron's narration, as she proclaims: 'Everything in me wanted to kiss her, and at the same time it felt like everything in me was sick.'[28] The illicit kiss and her parents' death are clearly conflated in Cameron's mind; she remembers, 'The day she dared me to kiss her. And the very next day my parents' car has veered through the guardrail.'[29] Cameron has internalized the homophobia of her regional and social context, where 'rurality and heterosexuality are deeply intertwined', shaping her reaction to her same-sex desires and later acquiescence to attending conversion camp.[30] The chronal and geographical setting of the text isolates Cameron from queer community and spaces for hope, until her revelatory discovery of New Queer Cinema.

Finding queerness through movies

Cinema functions as a voice and avenue of exploration of sexuality for Cameron, affording her a language and visibility of queerness otherwise inaccessible. One of her first actions after her parents' deaths is to take their TV and VCR to her bedroom, placing a photo of her mother on the top of the TV. In the first instance of using film to navigate the world, Cameron rents the movie *Beaches* (1988), where she finds a connection to her mother and Irene, and the film's depiction of grief. In explaining the impact of the film, she discusses the death of 'Barbara Hershey's character … near the end of the movie' and her daughter's reaction as a script for how to perform grief.[31] Cameron is searching for 'something official to show me how all of this should feel, how I should be acting, what I should be saying' and she finds that through films, finding escape and refuge, as movies act as literal religious saviour for her, a 'higher power'.[32] She observes: 'my religion of choice became VHS rentals [...] There was more than just one other world beyond ours; there were hundreds and hundreds of them, and at 99 cents apiece I could rent them all.'[33] Cameron looks to popular culture for language, codes and scripts for how to engage in the world. Popular culture, in particular New Queer Cinema, provides Cameron with an armour and sense of solidarity in a world where queerness is marginalized and demonized.

Cameron's engagement with queer cinema emphasizes the power of visibility of identity in popular media. After kissing Irene, she notes:

> Even though no one had ever told me, specifically, not to kiss a girl before, nobody had to. It was guys and girls who kissed – in our grade, on TV, in the movies, in the world; and that's how it worked: guys and girls. Anything else was something weird.[34]

Even before she discovers New Queer Cinema, Cameron feels shame about her film-watching practices. She hides *Beaches* from her aunt, associating her affection for film with queerness, guilt and her immorality. Danforth emphasizes how Cameron's social context reinforces and monitors heteronormativity. Barbara Pini, Wendy Keys and Elizabeth Marshall argue the surveillance of small rural towns enforces heterosexuality: 'Cameron is fearful of being outed at the video store for renting films with (often very muted) lesbian content.'[35] This invokes conventions of the coming out problem novel, such as the threat of discovery and rejection of the self. All Cameron's partners acknowledge a tacit need for secrecy. This is echoed in Coley's reaction and Cameron's own internalization of guilt after their relationship is discovered. When she first rents *Personal Best*, the act is shrouded in secrecy and shame; she is uncomfortable at the clerk's knowledge of her rental history: 'I didn't like that he knew every movie I took out of that store, watching me, watching me pick them up and bring them back.'[36] For Cameron, her rental history is deeply personal information, the act an intimate, proto-religious experience.

New Queer Cinema provides important social and cultural function for Cameron, and narrative and thematic functions for the novel. For Cameron, New Queer Cinema functions as an entry point, providing insight into queerness and queer lives not otherwise accessible. She seeks out films with lesbian content, numbing her grief. Cameron increases her queer education through film, attaining a fluency and literacy in queer-coded language and imagery. She reviews the paratext on VHS tapes for clues, such as two female actors 'standing close to each other in dim light', or a blurb describing a relationship as '*more than friendship*'.[37] Cameron notes: 'I guess somewhere there was a part of me that had figured out how to get those codes for gay content, but it wasn't something I could name.'[38] Queer film gives Cameron access to queer ways of desiring and being, and informs her relationship to queerness as she compares her experiences with those depicted on screen. Cameron notes whenever she watches a film with 'even a hint of lesbianism' she imagines 'Coley is Jodie Foster in *Silence of the Lambs*, Coley is Sharon Stone in *Basic Instinct*'.[39] Her sense of queer community also stems from a shared language, such as when Lindsay, a lesbian from another town, informs her '*Personal Best* is good, but you need to rent *Desert Hearts*', and introduces her to *The Hunger*.[40] Film is a facilitator for Cameron's relationships with Irene, Lindsay, Coley and her own queerness, to the extent Cameron and Coley adopt a ritual of watching queer film as catalyst and cover for their sexual engagements.

God's Promise and queer personal theologies

Crucially, the filmic references that characterize Cameron's narration cut off abruptly when she arrives at God's Promise and her connection to movies is framed as an 'unhealthy obsession' contributing to her presumed perversion.[41] Her voice and expression of queer identity has been silenced, the invasiveness apparent within the shift in her narration, indicative of the sublimating violence of conversion therapy. This subtle, underlying and invasive conditioning echoes throughout the practices at camp, highlighting the quiet violence inherent in God's Promise. As Cameron notes, over time the anti-gay messaging seeps into her mind, camp director Lydia's 'voice, in my head, where it hadn't been before', weighing her down.[42] Danforth illustrates the difficulty and trauma in resisting conversion violence through its invasion into Cameron's intimate, stream-of-consciousness narration. Cameron's internalized grief over her parents' death and guilt over her sexuality are entangled, informing her approach to faith-based conversion violence. Without film to filter her queerness, grief and guilt, Cameron turns to God. When Aunt Ruth encourages Cameron to talk to God, she reflects: 'I felt like it could be that God had made this happen, had killed my parents, because I was living my life so wrong that I had to be punished.'[43] Ironically, Cameron finds clarity and acceptance through Lydia, who tells Cameron:

> You've so convinced yourself that God was punishing you for your sins with Irene that you're blind to any other assessment [...] You need to stop making yourself such an important figure, Cameron Post [...] Your parents did not die for your sins.[44]

With this permission Cameron feels 'ready to move on',[45] evoking Robert Bittner, Cody Miller and Summer Pennell's argument:

> As young people within these YA [conversion violence] novels work to create their own queer personal theologies, they become empowered to rebel and break free from the constraints of the institutions that police their bodies and attempt to forcibly reform them.[46]

Cameron finds a subversive sense of personal catharsis and clarity in her therapy sessions, affirming her own quiet sense of self in a moment of resilience and survival that enables her to leave the camp, finding hope and peace in the novel's final scene, and in the queer community she creates within the camp.

Narration, conversion violence and catharsis

The intimate yet detached, numbed narration distances the narrative from both the reader and Cameron herself, enabling the novel to reject binary understandings of Cameron's queerness and conversion violence for much of the text. Danforth encourages the reader to interrogate the nature of the conversion violence objectively, as Cameron does not express judgement. It is not until Mark self-harms that Cameron explicitly addresses the failings of the camp:

> 'You guys don't even know what you're doing here, do you? You're just like making it up as you go along and then something like this happens and you're gonna pretend like you have answers that you don't even have and it's completely fucking fake.'[47]

Mark's self-harm leads to a formal inspection of God's Promise, during which Cameron denounces the camp. She details the insidious trauma of denying queerness, realizing it to be the intent and purpose of the camp. The cruelty of God's Promise is mundane. The camp is not rendered as malicious or outrageous, but a space that clearly holds harmful values, which, as Danforth identifies, is the key danger in such institutions. This realization frees Cameron from the guilt and grief she associates with queer desire, allowing her to reject the camp and its values, leaving with the queer community she has made there and found solace in.

Miseducation does not end with Cameron's testimony closing the camp, as the reader may hope or expect, but rather, a quiet coming to terms and acceptance of her sexual identity and her parents' deaths, untangling her grief and guilt, and finding support in the queer community.[48] Danforth affirms the impossibility of conversion practices without undermining the significant trauma and harm the practice causes. By offering a more complex perspective on the conversion camp ethos, the novel provides a glimpse into the traumatic reality of conversion violence. Avoiding spectacle and a clear catharsis subverts the conversion, coming out and coming-of-age narrative expectations; however, in doing so, Cameron fulfils the Bildungsroman while simultaneously emphasizing a continual state of growth and coming of age, rejecting the expectation of finality otherwise associated with the YA novel.

The Miseducation of Cameron Post (2018) directed by Desiree Akhavan

The 2018 film adaptation of Danforth's novel is written by Desiree Akhavan and Cecilia Frugiuele and directed by Akhavan. Frugiuele and Akhavan enjoyed critical success with their debut indie film *Appropriate Behavior* (2014, dir. Akhavan), which depicts a young Persian American woman coming into her queerness despite her conservative family. The low-key aesthetic, meandering style and quiet tone of *Appropriate Behavior* is echoed in the film version of *Miseducation* starring Chloë Grace Moretz as Cameron. Adhering closely to the source material, the film adaptation follows Cameron's experience at Christian camp, God's Promise, which is devoted to 'converting' teens from homosexual to heterosexual. As in the novel, upon arrival at God's Promise, Cameron meets her roommate Erin (Emily Skeggs), cool sceptic Jane Fonda (Sasha Lane), two spirit Adam (Forest Goodluck) and 'ex-gay' Reverend Rick (John Gallagher Jr). The film primarily takes place at God's Promise with the events leading up to Cameron's residence at the camp rendered in flashback. Notably, Cameron's relationship with girlfriend Coley (Quinn Shephard) is largely told through flashbacks, memories and dream sequences rather than present tense, creating a distance (although a causal link) between the events of the past and present.

While the novel carefully traces the events leading to Cameron's forced residency at God's Promise, the film is very much anchored in the camp and its residents. In the short scenes leading up to Cameron being sent to undergo conversion practice, we see Cameron performing compulsory heterosexuality, posing with her male date for the pre-dance photographs. Gender performance is underlined, as we see young girls adjusting their dresses at school dance, both primping and anxiously fidgeting. This is contrasted with the freedom of movement enabled once the lights go down and the adults fade into the background. The teens dance with joy and abandon. The energy and excitement spills over as Cameron and Coley abscond to the car to smoke marijuana and have sex before they are caught by Cameron's date. The scene with Cameron and Coley is shot intimately, with the camera in the car with them, their writhing punctuated with heavy breathing and shadows, highlighting the intensity and thrill of their connection. All this occurs before the film's title card, styled as white scrawled handwriting, small on a black screen. This marks a clear juncture in the film, as before and after the discovery of Cameron's queerness, cutting immediately to the aftermath.

Miseducation as 'smart' indie film

While the decision to send Cameron to God's Promise is immensely consequential, the audience is not privy to the conversation. Instead, we see the events from Cameron's perspective, peering around the corner as she watches her Aunt Ruth (Kerry Butler) crying and talking with their pastor. We do not hear the conversation that ensues, or the decisions made. There is no rationale for inflicting this kind of trauma on a young person, and the film does not attempt to provide one.

Instead, it puts the audience in the experience with Cameron through affective aesthetics that create a sense of slowness and inevitability. *Miseducation* is an 'indie' film, deploying low-key settings and aesthetics, quiet, intimate storytelling, emotional spectacle and dialogue and character-driven narratives, akin to American indie cinema. Indie emerges out of the American independent cinema movement that developed acclaim and cultural capital from the 1990s onward. Emanuel Levy contends: 'ideally, an indie is a fresh, low-budget movie with a gritty style and offbeat subject matter that expresses the filmmaker's personal vision'.[49] We use indie to describe the aesthetic, tone and narrative of *Miseducation*, because independent is often tied to specific industrial conditions and production factors, whereas indie points to a non-mainstream culture and stance, rather than a specific set of production conditions.[50] As Levy writes:

> . . . [t]he artistic drive behind the indie movement continues to be born out of a creative need to explore new themes, new forms, and new styles, as well as a politically motivated need to render unfamiliar or 'hidden' experiences previously ignored.[51]

Miseducation embodies this at the level of narrative, character, theme and style, but also draws on a particular subset of indie cinema called 'smart' cinema, thanks to its use of blank style, irony and reflexivity.

Smart cinema is a stylistic tendency of 1990s American indie cinema identified by Jeffrey Sconce.[52] Smart cinema privileges tone, character and dialogue over plot or structure, largely depicting white middle-class protagonists, therapy culture and post-youth issues using irony, blank style and a low-key aesthetic. Claire Perkins contends smart cinema is a post-youth cinema largely interested in 'damaged individuals, whose dysfunction is rooted in a general lack of "adult" perspective'.[53] While *Miseducation* follows teenage characters rather than the adults who populate the films Perkins examines, there is a maturity and determination displayed by the characters to resist the anti-gay and self-loathing propaganda promoted by conversion practices. Depicting conversion practices in a low-key, blank, almost affectless way, Akhavan's

Miseducation is slow, quiet and character-driven with little to no exposition. For instance, we do not know how long Cameron and Coley have been in a relationship together, nor do we necessarily know Cameron's parental figure is not her mother but her aunt, as her parents are both deceased. We learn this later in the film, as Rick uses it to explain Cameron's lesbian desires. Further, we do not see Cameron, Jane and Adam planning to leave the camp, but see them hiking and considering their options, surveying the routes, before eventually leaving. The film is not propelled by a particular quest or goal, and it is not designed to provoke outrage or elicit strong emotional responses. Rather, it depicts the quiet, mundane horror of the dehumanizing experience of conversion violence. This is rendered through smart tropes of irony, intimacy, blank style and knowingness.

Irony, smart cinema and conversion violence

Importantly, the film version of *Miseducation* takes an ironic approach to conversion violence, as irony enables layered meanings to coexist. The world of God's Promise is created through irony, however the narrative hinges on the problems and lives of the residents being taken seriously. Sconce contends smart cinema deploys ironic address to align the characters with likeminded or sympathetic viewers, while simultaneously enabling the character to distance themselves from the 'other', which is the subject of the character's derision.[54] In *Miseducation* the camera takes an ironic stance towards the sincerity and earnestness displayed in relation to Christianity and the capacity to be 'de-gayed'. Cameron, Jane and Adam's cynical view of God's Promise is adopted by the camera, as it keeps its distance, observing, echoing Cameron's detached narration in the novel. This is particularly evident in scenes where close ups of Cameron, Jane and Adam's sceptical facial expressions are contrasted with the earnestness and seriousness of the rest of the residents. They are often visually centred in group scenes, as the chaos of God's Promise swirls around them. This approach echoes another key stylistic element of smart cinema – blank style – which Sconce coined to describe how smart film performs an idea of blankness.[55] While there is no such thing as a truly blank style, an idea of blankness is cultivated through minimalist patterns of framing and editing, including use of a stationary camera, tableau presentation and symmetrical framing.[56] Sconce describes blankness as 'an attempt to convey a film's story, no matter how sensationalistic, disturbing or bizarre, with a sense of *dampened affect*'.[57] Perhaps the best example of this is the sex scene between Cameron and Erin. The scene consists of one long take with no edits or cuts, Cameron and Erin's bodies move within the frame, and we hear heavy breathing. It is not eroticized or sensationalized but presented in a blank, matter-of-fact style. In contrast to earlier sex scenes between Cameron and Coley that are full of movement and joy, this scene is stilted and cold.

In addition to being ironic, *Miseducation* is also intimate, personal and introspective. There is no exposition, persuasive monologues or overwrought displays of emotion; instead, mundanity and resolved strength are at the centre of the film. The mode of irony deployed in *Miseducation* is best understood as part of a feminist indie film tradition identified by Perkins in her work on the films of Nicole Holofcener. Perkins complicates the role of irony in the smart film, arguing Holofcener's films 'depart from the masculinist irony that has come to brand the indie sector'.[58] Similarly, *Miseducation* sits with the emotional and psychic trauma of conversion practices, by depicting the slow, quiet violence through a low-key dampened approach, establishing the depiction is not an endorsement. The camera holds for an extra beat on Rick eating his cereal and the kids walking across the field. *Miseducation* is a film about abuse, but it is not a film about the abusers; it is about those who survive and endure abuse. While comparable films like *Boy Erased*, as discussed in Chapter 8, attempt to humanize and rationalize the actions and abuse of the adults, *Miseducation* takes a slow, underplayed approach.

Akhavan's *Miseducation* is not just about queerness; the film is a queer film itself in its approach to the teen film and conversion narratives. Using Levy's language, we could consider *Miseducation* as having a queer 'sensibility' which manifests in small, intimate moments. In his analysis of homosexuality in early Hollywood, Levy asserts:

> ... [t]he real issue is not so much gay content as gay sensibility, the 'gay look' – how gays and lesbians perceive and dissect Hollywood movies, how they read films against the grain, looking for meanings not just in the text but in the subtext.[59]

For Levy, more important than the depiction of queer acts, is the embodiment of an awareness of queer ways of being and thinking. We can see this in how the camera in *Miseducation* consistently catches same-sex characters in close physical proximity to one another, heightening the sexual tension and gay sensibility at work. When Cameron and Erin lie on the grass with their heads pressed close to one another talking about their same-sex attraction past, the bird's-eye shot is intercut with footage of Cameron and Coley's face also lingering intimately together.

Further, throughout the film there is an unnatural and natural dichotomy at work, as the scenes in the conversion camp appear

Figure 7.1 Cameron and Helen at God's Promise, lying on the grass with their heads pressed close to one another talking about their experiences of same-sex attraction.

artificial and stilted, whereas in the natural world Adam, Jane and Cameron are comfortable. It works to naturalize their queerness in a setting that deems same-sex attraction deviant and unnatural.

Conclusion

The style, aesthetics and tone of the novel and film adaptation of *The Miseducation of Cameron Post* underline the mundane horror endured, rather than overcome by characters subjected to conversion violence. Their suffering is not presented as spectacle for enjoyment or entertainment, and there is no overt catharsis or sense of triumph offered by either text in a deviation from the norms of the coming out narrative. The texts are united in how they depict the characters' relationship to queerness and the violence and trauma of denying queerness, with each explored in a quiet, intimate and unobtrusive manner. Perhaps more importantly, both the novel and film avoid overt moments of catharsis for the audience, instead finding quiet acceptance in Cameron's discovery of queer identity and community. While the novel subverts the tropes of the queer YA problem novel, using narrative intimacy and dissonance, the film uses smart cinema tendencies of irony, blankness and dampened affect. Each provide a framework to approach God's Promise, and understand the quiet trauma evoked in denying queerness, and the innate violence of conversion therapies. Even within this setting, *Miseducation* depicts queer teens coming together, forming community and embracing their queerness. In doing so, the characters reject the logic of the camp, instead privileging their own 'queerer' logic.

Notes

1   B. R. Rich, 'The New Queer Cinema.' In *Queer Cinema, The Film Reader*, eds H. Benshoff and S. Griffin (London: Routledge, 2004), 53–4.

2 Rich, 'The New Queer Cinema,' 55.

3 E. M. Danforth, *The Miseducation of Cameron Post* (New York: Balzar + Bray, 2012), 223.

4 Danforth, *Miseducation*, 223, original emphasis.

5 S. Richards, 'A New Queer Cinema Renaissance,' *Queer Studies in Media & Popular Culture* 1, no. 2 (2016): 216–17.

6 Travis Webster, 'Queer Rhetorics as Intervention Methods: The Curious Case of Conversion Violence.' In *The Routledge Handbook of Queer Rhetoric*, eds J. Rhodes and J. Alexander (London: Routledge, 2022), 382.

7 R. Beirne, 'Teen Lesbian Desires and Identities in International Cinema: 1931–2007,' *Journal of Lesbian Studies* 16, no. 3 (2012): 266.

8 R. Bittner, C. Miller and S. Pennell, 'We're Not Sick, We're Not Straight: Conversion Therapy and the Compulsory Body in YAL,' *The ALAN Review* 48, no. 3 (2021): 30–1.

9 See M. A. Abate, '"Learning How to Be the Boy or Girl You Are": *Me Tarzan, You Jane*, the Crusade to "Cure" Pre-homosexual Children, and the New Face of the Ex-Gay Movement in the United States,' *Journal of the History of Childhood and Youth* 7, no. 3 (2014): 534–55.

10 J. A. Bennett, 'Love Me Gender: Normative Homosexuality and "Ex-Gay" Performativity in Reparative Therapy Narratives,' *Text and Performance Quarterly* 23, no. 4 (2003): 335.

11 Webster, 'Queer Rhetorics,' 382.

12 Webster, 'Queer Rhetorics,' 382.

13 A. Martin, 'Live to Tell: Teen Movies Yesterday and Today,' *Lumina* 2 (2009): 8.

14 See B. Sparks' *Go Ask Alice*, the fictional novel publicized as the diary of a real teen, emblematic of the problem novel archetype. As the titular character descends into drug abuse, she expresses same-sex desire and attraction, a common theme in Sparks' novels of wayward teens.

15 C. Driscoll, *Teen Film: A Critical Introduction* (London: Bloomsbury Publishing, 2011).

16 J. Feuer, 'A Postscript for The Nineties.' In *Popular Music: Critical Concepts in Media and Cultural Studies*, ed Simon Frith (London: Routledge, 1993), 230. Driscoll, *Teen Film*, 66.

17 Driscoll, *Teen Film*, 66.

18 S. K. Day, *Reading Like a Girl: Narrative Intimacy in Contemporary American Young Adult Literature* (Jackson: University Press of Mississippi, 2013).

19 C. A. Jenkins and M. Cart, *Representing the Rainbow in Young Adult Literature: LGBTQ+ Content Since 1969* (Blue Ridge Summit: Rowman & Littlefield Publishers 2018), 130.

20 Jenkins and Cart, *Representing the Rainbow in Young Adult Literature,* 131.

21 D. Mason, 'Getting Better: Children's Literature Theory and the It Gets Better Project.' In *Queer Anxieties of Young Adult Literature and Culture* (Jackson: University Press of Mississippi, 2021), 135–52.

22 A. Swartz, 'Desiree Akhavan made "The Miseducation of Cameron Post" for "everybody"', *MIC*, 2 August 2018, available: https://www.mic.com/articles/190547/desiree-akhavan-the-miseducation-of-cameron-post-interview (accessed 15 December 2022).

23 T. Shary, 'The Nerdly Girl and Her Beautiful Sister.' In *Sugar, Spice, and Everything Nice: Cinemas of Girlhood,* F. Gatewood and M. Pomerance eds (Detroit: Wayne State University Press, 2002), 1.

24 F. Smith, *Rethinking the Hollywood Teen Movie: Gender, Genre and Identity* (Edinburgh: Edinburgh University Press, 2017), 2.

25 H. Cillis, 'Director Desiree Akhavan on *The Miseducation of Cameron Post* and Reimagining the Teen Movie,' *Jezebel,* 2 August 2018, available at https://jezebel.com/director-desiree-akhavan-on-the-miseducation-of-cameron-1828002801 (accessed 15 December 2022).

26 Day, *Reading Like a Girl.*

27 Bittner, Miller and Pennell, 'We're Not Sick, We're Not Straight.'

28 Danforth, *Miseducation,* 45.

29 Danforth, *Miseducation,* 45.

30 B. Pini, W. Keys and E. Marshall, 'Queering Rurality: Reading *The Miseducation of Cameron Post* Geographically,' *Children's Geographies* 15, no. 3 (2017): 366.

31 Danforth, *Miseducation,* 35.

32 Danforth, *Miseducation,* 35, 40.

33 Danforth, *Miseducation,* 40.

34 Danforth, *Miseducation,* 10–11.

35 Pini, Keys and Marshall, 'Queering Rurality,' 365.

36 Danforth, *Miseducation,* 42.

37 Danforth, *Miseducation,* 46, original emphasis.

38 Danforth, *Miseducation,* 47.

39 Danforth, *Miseducation,* 135.

40 Danforth, *Miseducation,* 89.

41 Danforth, *Miseducation*, 296.

42 Danforth, *Miseducation*, 361.

43 Danforth, *Miseducation*, 39.

44 Danforth, *Miseducation* 452.

45 Danforth, *Miseducation*, 453.

46 Bittner, Miller and Pennell, 'We're Not Sick,' 29.

47 Danforth, *Miseducation*, 382.

48 Pini, Keys and Marshall, 'Queering Rurality,' 370.

49 Emanuel Levy, *Cinema of Outsiders: The Rise of American Independent Film* (New York: NYU Press, 1999), 2.

50 G. King, *American Independent Cinema* (London: IB Tauris, 2005), 3; M. Z. Newman, *Indie: An American Film Culture* (New York: Columbia University Press, 2011), 6.

51 Levy, *Cinema of Outsiders*, 52.

52 Jeffrey Sconce, 'Irony, Nihilism and the New American "Smart" Film,' *Screen* 43, no. 4 (2002).

53 Claire Perkins, *American Smart Cinema* (Edinburgh: Edinburgh University Press, 2013), 10.

54 Sconce, 'Irony, Nihilism,' 352.

55 Sconce, 'Irony, Nihilism,' 359.

56 Perkins, *American Smart Cinema*, 95.

57 Sconce, 'Irony, Nihilism,' 359, original emphasis.

58 Claire Perkins, 'Beyond Indiewood: The Everyday Ethics of Nicole Holofcener,' *Camera Obscura: Feminism, Culture, and Media Studies* 29, no. 1 (2014): 142.

59 Levy, *Cinema of Outsiders*, 480.

Bibliography

Abate, M. A. '"Learning How to Be the Boy or Girl You Are": *Me Tarzan, You Jane*, the Crusade to "Cure" Pre-homosexual Children, and the New Face of the Ex-Gay Movement in the United States.' *Journal of the History of Childhood and Youth* 7:3 (2014): 534–55.

Beirne, R., 'Teen Lesbian Desires and Identities in International Cinema: 1931–2007.' *Journal of Lesbian Studies* 16:3 (2012): 258–72.

Bennett, J.A. 'Love Me Gender: Normative Homosexuality and "Ex-Gay" Performativity in Reparative Therapy Narratives.' *Text and Performance Quarterly* 23:4 (2003): 331–52.

Bittner, R., C. Miller and S. M. Pennell. 'We're Not Sick, We're Not Straight: Conversion Therapy and the Compulsory Body in YAL.' *The ALAN Review* 48:3 (2021): 27–36.

Cillis, H. 'Director Desiree Akhavan on *The Miseducation of Cameron Post* and Reimagining the Teen Movie.' *Jezebel,* 2 August 2018, available at https:// jezebel.com/director-desiree-akhavan-on-the-miseducation-of-cameron-1828002801

Danforth, E. M. *The Miseducation of Cameron Post*. New York: Balzar + Bray, 2012.

Day, S. K. *Reading Like a Girl: Narrative Intimacy in Contemporary American Young Adult Literature.* Jackson: University Press of Mississippi, 2013.

Driscoll, C. *Teen Film: A Critical Introduction.* London: Bloomsbury Publishing, 2011.

Feuer, J. 'A Postscript for The Nineties.' In *Popular Music: Critical Concepts in Media and Cultural Studies,* ed S. Firth, 228–40. London: Routledge, 1993.

Jenkins, C. A. and M. Cart. *Representing the Rainbow in Young Adult Literature: LGBTQ+ Content since 1969.* Maryland: Rowman & Littlefield Publishers, 2018.

King, G. *American Independent Cinema.* London: IB Tauris, 2005.

Levy, E. *Cinema of Outsiders: The Rise of American Independent Film.* New York: NYU Press, 1999.

Martin, A. 'Live to Tell: Teen Movies Yesterday and Today.' *Lumina* 2 (2009): 2–16.

Mason, D. 'Getting Better: Children's Literature Theory and the It Gets Better Project.' In *Queer Anxieties of Young Adult Literature and Culture,* 135–52, Jackson: University Press of Mississippi, 2021.

Newman, M. Z. *Indie: An American Film Culture.* New York: Columbia University Press, 2011.

Perkins, C. *American Smart Cinema.* Edinburgh: Edinburgh University Press, 2013.

Perkins, C. 'Beyond Indiewood: The Everyday Ethics of Nicole Holofcener.' *Camera Obscura: Feminism, Culture, and Media Studies* 29:1 (2014): 137–59.

Pini, B., W. Keys and E. Marshall. 'Queering Rurality: Reading the Miseducation of Cameron Post Geographically.' *Children's Geographies* 15:3 (2017): 362–73.

Rich, B. R. 'The New Queer Cinema.' In *Queer Cinema, The Film Reader*, eds H. Benshoff and S. Griffin, 53–60. London: Routledge, 2004.

Richards, S. 'A New Queer Cinema Renaissance.' *Queer Studies in Media & Popular Culture* 1:2 (2016): 215–29.

Sconce, J. 'Irony, Nihilism and the New American "Smart" Film.' *Screen* 43:4 (2002): 349–69.

Shary, T. 'The Nerdly Girl and Her Beautiful Sister.' In *Sugar, Spice, and Everything Nice: Cinemas of Girlhood*, eds F. Gatewood and M. Pomerance, 235–50. Detroit: Wayne State University Press, 2002.

Smith, F. *Rethinking the Hollywood Teen Movie: Gender, Genre and Identity*, Edinburgh: Edinburgh University Press, 2017.

Swartz, A. 'Desiree Akhavan Made 'The Miseducation of Cameron Post' for "Everybody".' MIC, 2 August 2018, available at: https://www.mic.com/articles/190547/desiree-akhavan-the-miseducation-of-cameron-post-interview

The Miseducation of Cameron Post [Film] Dir. D. Akhavan, USA: Beachside Films, 2018.

Webster, T. 'Queer Rhetorics as Intervention Methods: The Curious Case of Conversion Violence.' In *The Routledge Handbook of Queer Rhetoric*, eds J. Rhodes and J. Alexander, 382–8, London: Routledge, 2022.

Defined by their Abjection: *Boy Erased* and the Limits of Queer Victimhood in Activist Cinema

Scott McKinnon

Released in 2018, the American film *Boy Erased* tells the story of Jared Eamon, a white nineteen-year-old college student and son of a Christian pastor, who enters a conversion programme after being outed to his parents in traumatic circumstances. It is a deeply distressing story, made more so by its basis in truth, having been drawn from the memoir *Boy Erased: A Memoir of Identity, Faith and Family* by Garrard Conley. The film changes some key details but remains true to the book's clear condemnation of the conversion 'therapy' programme, Love in Action (LIA). As such, the film can be read as a work of activist cinema, created with the (entirely admirable) aims of, first, increasing awareness of the cruelty of conversion practices and, second, inspiring audiences to speak out against such programmes. Unfortunately, while *Boy Erased* certainly conveys the brutal abuses of conversion practices, the film mostly positions its young LGBT+ characters as unknowable victims. The failure to explore the lives of young queer people beyond their position as Love in Action victims limits the film's capacity to inform and inspire.

Boy Erased on-screen maintains a determinedly low-key style. Colours are muted, with dim lighting blurring into hazy blues and dull whites. The soundtrack begins with the lilting voice of folksinger Sufjan Stevens and the score rarely rises above gentle piano and soft choral voices. As Jared, Lucas Hedges's reserved and interior performance, which is mirrored by the performances of each of the actors playing

Love in Action participants, adheres to the film's subdued aesthetics. These film-making choices are admirable, perhaps, in that they avoid histrionics. The film displays homophobia not only through moments of high drama, but as a relentlessly quotidian element in the lives of these young people.

Yet these choices also create a certain distancing, keeping the viewer at arm's length for much of the narrative and never providing much of a sense of Jared's inner-life. He is presented as a well-behaved and kind young man trapped in an awful system, but the film is unable to convey the richer sense of Garrard's connections to friends, faith and family contained in the source material. These limitations are even more obvious when it comes to the film's minor characters, particularly Jared's fellow Love in Action participants. The viewer learns so little about their lives outside the programme that, rather than being presented as fully realized young people, they are defined only by their abjection.

The film's insularity and constrained worldmaking convey the degree to which Love in Action participants felt trapped within the programme, despairing at the possibility of finding peace and happiness elsewhere. These directorial choices also constrain, however, the film's activist potential. As argued by Barbara Baird and Robert Reynolds, in discourses focused on LGBT+ youth, the 'centring of suffering, vulnerability and harm, has ... partially erased a politics rooted in pleasure and radical challenge to sexual and gender norms'.[1] *Boy Erased* positions Jared's sexuality, with good reason, as a source of turmoil and anxiety. Yet, to only describe queer youth as vulnerable and at risk is to ignore – even to suppress – the joyful possibilities (and realities) of queer young people's lives.

In this chapter, I explore *Boy Erased's* activist potential, examining how the film's relationship to its source material, along with its representations of gender, reveal the cruel abuses of conversion but deny agency and complexity to conversion programme participants. Significantly, the text of the film does not represent the limits of its activist work. The *Boy Erased* promotional campaign provided an important platform through which Garrard Conley was able to share his survivor experience. The author was frequently featured alongside the film's actors and director in media interviews, during which he was able to discuss the devastating, and in some cases fatal, consequences of Love in Action's work. The extratextual activism linked to the film suggested broader possibilities for acknowledging and celebrating queer joy. Conley's interviews, as well as a podcast produced in conjunction with the film, provided accounts of conversion practices that were no less harrowing, but which also broke open the constrained world of *Boy Erased* on-screen.

From page to screen

Conley's memoir details his life growing up in rural Arkansas in the 1990s and early 2000s. His father, Marshall, was a car salesman and Christian pastor. The Conley family's life revolved around their faith and Garrard was imagined as the inheritor of his father's legacy as a man of God. Clear throughout his childhood is the entwining of faith and gender. If Garrard was to be a godly man, he needed to embody the 'traditional' form of masculinity so proudly demonstrated by his father. Conley describes a state of constant anxiety, aware that his most passionate interests were regarded as failures of gender, particularly his love of books and writing. Conley writes: 'Though he never said it outright, each summer [my father] required me to do the kind of manual labour that would help me turn out to be a normal red-blooded Southerner, the kind that would offset my more bookish, feminine qualities.'[2]

Throughout his childhood and youth, Conley would monitor his own behaviour for fear of giving something away. The concern that he would have failed his mother, his father, and his God if his feelings of same-sex attraction were ever discovered, let alone acted upon, dominated his life. Struggling to negotiate these inner conflicts, but nonetheless determined to pursue his love of literature, Conley left home to attend college at the age of nineteen. While there, he was raped in his dorm room by another male student. This traumatizing abuse was extended when the rapist, fearful that Garrard would report him, rang Conley's parents and told them their son was gay. They in turn give Garrard an ultimatum: attend a conversion programme or leave the family altogether.

Conley entered a two-week Love in Action programme, hoping but doubtful that it may be of use. He writes: 'I was here by my own choice, despite my growing scepticism … I had too much invested in my current life to leave it behind: in my family and in the increasingly blurry God I'd known since I was a toddler.'[3] The programme leader, John Smid, soon declared that Garrard may need a longer period of 'treatment', which would require dropping out of college. For an aspiring writer, this idea was devastating. Garrard's always fragile trust in the programme had quickly faded and he began to see the lies at its core. Smid promised the possibility of change, or a 'cure', but of course could not deliver on that promise. The programme revealed itself as increasingly cruel and absurd, as Garrard began to understand that he had no reason to change himself. He left Love in Action and reversed the demand his parents had earlier placed on him: they could love him as he was or lose him.

The film of *Boy Erased* was written and directed by Australian Joel Edgerton, who also co-stars as the Love in Action leader. The telling of this story by the straight and cisgender Edgerton drew criticism from some queer critics and filmmakers. Chloë Grace Moretz, star of another conversion programme drama, *The Miseducation of Cameron Post* (henceforth, *Cameron Post*), which was released the same year as Edgerton's film, described *Boy Erased* as 'shot through a straight male gaze'.[4] Moretz believed her film received less industry backing because it featured fewer big-name stars and because its director, Desiree Akhavan, is a bisexual woman of colour. Noting that *Boy Erased* had quickly been picked up by a distributor, Moretz stated: 'They're still backing first and foremost the straight white man who is going to be putting out the movie that's the safer bet.' The actor's argument pointed out both the unfairness of an industry still weighted towards white straight men, as well as the impacts this had on how stories are told, noting: 'Queer movies should be told through a queer lens and created by queer people.'[5]

In interviews about the film, Edgerton frequently noted that he too had been concerned about telling Conley's story, stating: 'I didn't feel like I had the *right* to make it, and it took a series of quick steps in order to convince myself otherwise.'[6] He described his attraction to the book as coming from his own childhood fear of being removed from his family and sent to some kind of institution. Equally, however, he acknowledged that, as a heterosexual and cisgender man, he had no real-life experience of anti-LGBT+ bigotry and its impacts on children. While his level of prior knowledge (if any) about conversion practices is unclear, Edgerton justified his role as writer and director by stating that he frequently consulted with Conley throughout the development of the screenplay.

Edgerton's self-professed uncertainty may well have produced the film's reserved, cautious style. *Boy Erased* at times sits in uncomfortable relationship to its source material, claiming authenticity from its basis in Conley's survivor experience, and yet simultaneously hesitant about its right to draw on that experience. Perhaps the key indicator of this is the use of different names for characters that are so clearly based on Conley and the people in his life. Garrard Conley becomes Jared Eamon. John Smid is renamed Victor Sykes. Garrard/Jared's parents, played by Nicole Kidman and Russell Crowe, keep their real-life first names of Nancy and Marshall, despite their new surname. The intention of these changes is unclear. The film ends with photographs of Conley and his parents, as well as text on-screen stating 'Garrard Conley currently lives in New York City with his husband' and 'The real Victor Sykes left LIA in 2008. He now lives in Texas, with his husband.' In extratextual material, the film was constantly linked to Conley and Smid. And yet, *Boy Erased* is about Jared and Victor, not Garrard and John.

An absent element of Conley's memoir is a regrettable loss to the narrative. Conley had a girlfriend, as does Eamon. Jared is a basketball player and his girlfriend, Sarah (Madelyn Cline), is a cheerleader. After a game, Jared's parents congratulate them on their win. Jared tells his parents that he, Sarah and some friends are going to go to the lake. Marshall and Nancy exchange knowing looks about what 'going to the lake' might entail and Marshall hands Jared the keys to a car so the teenagers are free to drive themselves there. The scene indicates how his parents, in their efforts to guide their son towards a heterosexual future, rewarded Jared for adhering to a 'traditional' pattern of teen sexual development. Later, in the car, Sarah wants to have sex, but Jared says he thinks they 'should wait'.

In the book, Garrard also has a girlfriend, named Chloe. Chloe asks Garrard to sleep over one night, with the intention that they will have sex for the first time. Garrard is in turmoil, distressed by the weight of expectation and confusion. He likes Chloe, but he does not want to have sex with her. At the sleepover, Garrard shares a room with Chloe's little brother, Brandon, a delightful young boy with a skill for impersonation and a penchant for dressing as his favourite film characters. Rather than sneaking into Chloe's room late at night as planned, Garrard plays video games with Brandon and an unspoken recognition forms between the two boys. Brandon tells Garrard that he thinks their game avatar is 'probably gay',[7] before quickly looking away. Conley writes: 'When he looked back at me, we both knew what we were.' After this brief moment of recognition, they return to their video game battle.

Garrard subsequently felt unable to see Chloe, given he felt no sexual desire for her. But he is distressed that he will also never see Brandon, and that 'the only person who seemed to know who I really was would never again be part of my life'.[8] Just weeks later, Garrard's mother received a distraught phone call from Brandon's mother. Her son had been caught in bed with another boy. Garrard's father was sent to offer religious counsel to Brandon, warning him away from this 'sin'.

Brandon symbolizes a moment of queer childhood camaraderie outside of the world of Love in Action. He indicates the value to Garrard of being recognized and of, perhaps, finding a queer friend; a friendship that carries potential for joy. Within their brief exchange is a world of possibility and a hint towards what might be if queer children were supported and validated. There is nothing sexual in their interaction, but instead the simple pleasure of being seen and acknowledged. Brandon's absence from the film means that Jared's only interactions with queer people outside the Love in Action programme are abusive (the rapist) or romantic/sexual (a brief interaction with an art student at college). It positions queer solidarity only within the dire circumstances of a conversion programme, in which queer friendships, if they can be formed at all, are defined as necessary to survive cruel oppression, rather than as joyful in their own right.

Performing masculinity

As seen in the film of *Boy Erased*, Love in Action centres heterosexuality and normative gender expression as the interwoven norms, from which any deviation is unacceptable (a topic discussed in the Introduction). The purported goal of the programme was to return participants to the natural heterosexual state from which they had chosen, prompted by a range of factors, to stray. In this light, homosexuality was understood, first, as a sinful choice; second, as a product of past family sins; and third, as a failure to appropriately embody and perform gender. Sykes compares being a homosexual to being a football player, in that no-one is born a footballer, but some people choose to play that sport. He states: 'You cannot be born a homosexual … It's behavioural. It's a choice" (a cliché that informs the film, *I am Michael*, as discussed in Chapter 4).

Yet, according to the programme, that choice is formed by sins within the family. Participants are required to complete a 'genogram'; a kind of family tree in which parents, grandparents and other family members are labelled with acronyms describing 'behavioural sins'. Letters 'SSA' or 'H' represent same-sex attraction or homosexuality; 'D' represents drugs; a dollar sign represents gambling; 'M' mental illness, and so on. Labelling those sins, participants are told, will allow the apportionment of blame to the relevant family members. Participants are then required to announce each sin to the group while expressing anger at their family's perceived failures. This, they are assured, will allow each participant to move beyond their same-sex desires.

Something the film conveys well is the constant pressure on participants to publicly describe sin and to publicly perform their supposed healing process through gendered self-expression. It is not enough to identify the 'behavioural sins' of family members; those sins must be announced and described before Love in Action staff and their fellow participants. Participants must also publicly confess their own sins by standing alone before the group and describing any past same-sex sexual experiences in graphic detail. As argued by Adolfo Aranjuez, drawing on Foucault, the programme intensifies 'the affective impact of confession by situating it in a public context'.[9] As a result, participants are opened up to scrutiny, not just by God, but by Love in Action staff '*and* by their peers'.[10] Described as an act of cleansing, these traumatic experiences are revealed by the film as a form of punishment, trapping participants in a cruel loop. Same-sex experiences are condemned as deeply shameful, yet any refusal to publicly describe these experiences is read as failure to adhere to the programme's requirements – or to truly seek forgiveness and healing – and therefore more time in the programme will be taken as necessary.

According to Love in Action's jumbled mixture of scripture, pseudo-science and confused psychology, confronting these past sins is one step in a process. Another crucial step involves training participants to reconfigure their gender performance, as a result of which they will, according to Sykes, naturally begin to feel heterosexual desires. He tells the participants: 'Fake it until you make it, until you become the man you are not.' Christine M. Robinson and Sue E. Spivey describe the concentration on gender performance within conversion therapy as a theory of 'healing by doing', arguing: 'Ex-gay therapies commonly encourage ex-gay men to simulate masculine mannerisms and engage in masculine-defined activities.'[11] Act like a man and you'll begin to desire women.

Sitting in drab meeting spaces and dressed in uniforms of white button up shirts and beige trousers, participants are relentlessly, at times

Figure 8.1 Constructing a hierarchy of masculinity at Love in Action.

angrily, forced to perform the programme's limited gender vision. The film's colour palette of muted hues symbolically constrains the participants, trapping them into a dull, normative world, the banality of which only enhances its cruelty. Participants are told to think of the shapes their bodies are forming when they stand and to ask themselves 'is this a manly shape I'm making or is it a girly or feminine shape?' For boys, standing with legs apart and hands on hips is described as ideal because 'triangles are the strongest shape.'

When a female Love in Action participant is tasked with placing her peers in order of most to least masculine, this activity is revealed as deeply cruel. For male participants, the fear they will be deemed the least masculine of the group is crushing.

In some ways, the character of Jared sits outside the worst of this cruelty. For one thing, he is good at sports, and his skill is applauded as an appropriately masculine achievement. In scenes set in and outside of the programme, there is nothing 'feminine' about his gender presentation. He is able to 'pass' as heterosexual and masculine in ways that many in the programme are not. Aside from his love of reading and his desire to be a writer, it is perhaps only his gentleness and kindness towards the other participants that are read as potential failures of masculinity.

Given Jared's gender presentation, the worst impacts of Love in Action's cruelty fall onto minor characters, about whom the viewer knows almost nothing other than their struggles in the programme. One slightly-built young boy is hurt while attempting to play baseball and is rescued from the programme by his father, who yells at Sykes for having placed his son in physical danger. The character of Cameron (Britton Sear) is positioned as the film's most tragic figure. He is tall and heavy-set, but gentle and 'effeminate' in his self-expression. He is mostly silent throughout the film but is at the centre of a bizarre ritual in which he is forced to attend a staging of his own funeral, where he is beaten with a Bible by his family members. Cameron hints at inner depths when he helps Jared flee the programme. When Jared is home, however, Nancy announces there was a phone call from Love in Action and that Cameron had died by suicide.

With this character, *Boy Erased* plays into cinematic tropes of the tragic queer, placing Cameron as the doomed 'other'. Positioning queer characters as figures of tragedy has been common through much of Hollywood history. Describing the doomed romance of *Brokeback Mountain*, for example, Thomas Piontek criticizes that film's 'inability to imagine love between two men as anything but a tragedy'.[12] In *Boy Erased*, Jared, who mostly embodies or, at least, is able to perform hetero- and cis-normative masculine ideals, survives the conversion programme and ends the movie as a happily married, openly gay man. Cameron, on the other hand, represents the tragedy of gender failure. The viewer learns almost nothing about him besides his sexuality and gender performance. He spends the movie quietly enduring cruel abuse and then he dies.

In highlighting Cameron's tragic fate, I am not arguing that *Boy Erased* positions his gender performance as deserving of punishment. Indeed, the film presents his treatment as unspeakably cruel and his death as proof of conversion 'therapy's' loathsome consequences. Yet, rather than being developed as a fully realized character, Cameron only serves as a collection of traits that make him, from the film's point of view, a victim: over-weight; quiet; gentle; effeminate; queer. And because

Boy Erased offers no alternate vision for a young man like Cameron, it also presents his death as somehow inevitable. We do not see possibilities for pleasure and joy in gendered difference, because for this character and, by extension those like him, the world outside Love in Action does not exist.

Humour as resistance

Unlike other conversion narratives, particularly *But I'm a Cheerleader*, and, to a lesser degree, *Cameron Post* (see Chapters 5 and 7, respectively), *Boy Erased* avoids any temptation to ridicule or to find humour in Love in Action's absurd ideas of gender and sexuality. In interviews, Conley argued that, although from the outside Love in Action looked ridiculous, its impacts were far from humorous. He told one journalist, 'Conversion therapy seems like a joke to anyone who hasn't been involved with it, yet it kills people every year.'[13] Although Conley expressed his admiration for movies that deployed humour in their telling of conversion therapy stories, he described Edgerton's relentless focus on horror and tragedy as serving a valuable purpose, arguing that the humour of a film like *Cameron Post* allowed the viewer to feel 'safe' in a way that *Boy Erased* did not.

In *Boy Erased*, the only jokes are cracked by Love in Action leaders and are offered by the film as further proof of the programme's cruelty. Sykes mocks, for example, the LGBT+ acronym as containing a ridiculous and unknowable number of identity labels, before stating, 'There's so much choice in that group, but what are the consequences of that choice?' The consequences he lists, which include rape and AIDS, are no joke at all. Mocking humour is deployed as a means of attacking queer people but, within the context of the film, queer people are never given the opportunity to respond in kind.

Edgerton's intent is admirable, certainly, and Conley's argument is valid. Conversion therapy is horrific and certain kinds of humour may detract from that horror. It is worth considering, however, how glimpses of humour or pleasure may have added two valuable and inter-related elements to the film: first, in providing examples of queer joy and, second, in giving some of the film's queer characters a degree of complexity and, most importantly, agency that they are otherwise lacking. Describing the politics of 'queerness' as the 'reworking of abjection into political agency', Judith Butler describes a necessary strategy, 'in which passion, injury, grief, aspiration become recognized without fixing the terms of that recognition in yet another conceptual order of lifelessness and rigid exclusion'.[14] Too often, the queer characters of *Boy Erased* are defined only by their abjection, becoming lifeless and passive victims in ways that other conversion narratives more successfully avoid, in part, by using humour as an agentic strategy.

But I'm a Cheerleader is perhaps an unlikely point of comparison, given that, apart from its exploration of a conversion programme, this broad 1999 comedy has little to nothing in common with a film like *Boy Erased*. The film's lead character, Megan (Natasha Lyonne), is somewhat surprised to find herself labelled a lesbian given that she is, as the title suggests, a cheerleader and therefore the embodiment of heteronormative femininity. The conversion programme to which she is sent is a cartoonish, brightly lit world of radiant pinks and blues, through which the film neatly identifies the campiness at the heart of heterosexual conformity. The programme leader, Mary Brown (Cathy Moriarty), is a monstrous clown figure, desperately attempting to prove that her handsome, muscular son Rock (Eddie Cibrian), is an archetype of heterosexual masculinity, despite all evidence to the contrary.

It is undoubtedly true that this over-the-top comedy fails to impart to the viewer the true impacts of conversion practices, as Tom Sharples argues in Chapter 5, and I am certainly not suggesting *But I'm a Cheerleader* acts as a more insightful portrayal than *Boy Erased*. I think the earlier film's value lies, however, in its displays of joyful queer sexual and romantic desire utterly missing from its more dramatic counterpart. While *Boy Erased* reveals, for example, the utter, crushing distress experienced by Sarah (Jesse LaTourette), a programme participant who is forced to publicly recount her same-sex sexual explorations as evidence of sinful failures, the film never provides any sense that such explorations may, in the moment in which they took place, have been affirming, thrilling and pleasurable. In contrast, *But I'm a Cheerleader* provides Megan with an object of lust in the sexy bad-girl form of Graham (Clea DuVall). Their desire for each other is presented as a rare moment of rationality and joy within the film's absurdist world of hypocrisy and repression.

In *Cameron Post*, humour offers moments of queer solidarity, in which conversion programme participants act out against their positioning as tragic victims by mocking the strictures of the programme to which they are subjected. As the titular character, Chloë Grace Moretz often surveys the conversion programme and its leaders with a sceptical, mocking look. Unlike *Boy Erased*, the film gives complexity and depth to participants beyond the central character. Cameron forms deep friendships with two other participants, Jane (Sasha Lane) and Adam (Forrest Goodluck). Her friends offer solidarity, resistance, and dark humour. Adam describes the programme leader, Lydia Marsh (Jennifer Ehle) as 'like having your own Disney villain, only this one won't let you jerk off'. When a straight young man, who is in the programme because of drug use, tells Cameron she 'looks like a dyke', her response is not tearful horror but shocked laughter.

The film ends with Cameron, Jane and Adam fleeing the programme together, happily huddled in the back of a pick-up truck, while Cameron and Jane encourage Adam to flirt with a passing motorbike rider. This is, in some ways, a fairy tale that allows a happy conclusion without considering the challenges that lie ahead for three queer teenagers with no money or homes to go to. The film also celebrates, however, queer collaboration and the joys of finding friendship. The three are not only positioned as abject victims of cruelty, but as drivers of their own story whose use of humour is affirming and celebratory.

Until Jared's dramatic rejection of the programme, the only form of resistance offered by Love in Action participants relies, as much as the programme itself, on gender performance. The programme's concentration on performance as restorative practice intercuts with the awareness of participants that they must perform a particular role in order to survive. The programme says, in effect, 'Act like a man and you'll become heterosexual'. Some participants are aware, however, that faking a newly constructed gender identity is their only way out of the programme. One participant tells Jared, 'Play the part, man. Then once you are home, you've got to figure out what to do next.' This is performance as passive resistance, in which a queer character's only means of rebelling is to outwardly enact a normative vision of gendered self-expression while denying any connection between those externalized actions and the interior self.

Boy Erased's extratextual activist cinema

As a form of activist cinema (that is, a film that 'aims to activate or generate an activist public'),[15] *Boy Erased* reveals the horrors of conversion 'therapy' with the hope that viewers will then help end these practices. This activism is produced, firstly, from within the film, using narrative, performance, soundtrack, and directorial choices that cohere into a condemnation of Love in Action and similar programmes. The film attempts to build empathy for Jared and his peers, placing the viewer within the constraining world of a conversion programme and asking us to feel anger and sorrow at what is being experienced. This on-screen condemnation was then reinforced through a range of extratextual media that aimed, first, to attract more viewers to the film and, second, to further educate viewers about the need to ban conversion practices (on paratext, see Johnson, Chapter 4, in this volume). This extratextual information likely also broadened the reach of the film's message beyond its viewers. In other words, some members of the activist public produced by *Boy Erased* (or which the film hoped to produce) may never have seen the film.

Central to the extratextual elements of the film's activism is the participation of Garrard Conley. Since the publication of his memoir, Conley has dedicated himself to activist work, fighting for the protection of children and young people from the traumatic abuse he endured. In interviews, Conley has stated that a career as an activist was never his intention when writing his memoir. It was the beginnings of the Trump administration that prompted him to embrace a more public activist role.[16] In particular, Conley was deeply concerned about Vice President Mike Pence's professed support for conversion programmes.

There is an intriguing interplay between Conley's embrace of the film as a valuable tool for his activism, and the film's embrace of Conley within its promotional campaign. It was, in part, the possibilities for amplifying his anti-conversion message that led Conley to support the film's creation. His doubts that a straight man could tell this story were overcome by Edgerton's professed determination to act as an LGBT+ ally and by the likelihood that the well-known actor/director could help spread Conley's activist message. Conley stated: 'The memoir is this very insular queer perspective – it's me – but I felt like Joel had the ability to translate that, especially with the actors he hired, and could reach the mainstream and make conversion therapy a topic in almost every household and really get some stuff done in terms of advocacy.'[17] The author believed, with good reason, that a movie starring Nicole Kidman and Russell Crowe would draw more media attention than a smaller, independent film unlikely to reach a similarly sized audience.

In return, the film's promoters clearly understood the value of including Conley as a key element of their promotional campaign. His support gave *Boy Erased* a degree of authenticity that a film directed by a heterosexual, cisgender man might otherwise have lacked. Handsome, funny and articulate, Conley sat alongside Edgerton in interview after interview, revealing a playful and admiring relationship between author and director. Together, they rejected ideas that this film would sit in opposition to *Cameron Post* as a competing take on the same story (one authentically queer and the other from a heterosexual viewpoint), instead arguing that multiple conversion narratives were necessary in order to educate and engage audiences.[18]

This is not to say that Conley was entirely uncritical of the film. In one interview he reflected on the challenges of communicating nuance and complexity on-screen, as well as on the page. Conley described his difficult but loving relationship with his father. He hoped that movie audiences would not view Marshall as evil or entirely cruel, nor come to understand the difficulties of their relationship as being fully resolved. Conley stated: 'That's one of the bad things about, you know, a film version. It's like, my book, I feel, had that complexity. I think Russell Crowe brings it to the performance because he actually met my dad and spent a lot of time with him. But you're just never going to capture the complete complexity of that, even in book form, but I tried.'[19]

Conley was also a co-producer of a podcast made 'in conjunction with' the film and developed as both a promotional strategy and activist tool. Titled *UnErased* and described as 'revealing the hidden history of conversion therapy', the four-episode series is book-ended by stories directly connected to the *Boy Erased* narrative, beginning with an interview with Conley and ending with an interview with the real-life John Smid. In between is an investigation of changes in the 'treatment' of homosexuality by American psychotherapists, and interviews with members of the Mama Bears, an organization made up of Christian mothers who provide support to LGBT+ people rejected by their families.

As a companion piece, *UnErased* adds valuable elements missing from the film, including evidence of playfulness and joy. Conley's interview is interspersed with laughter, suggesting the ways in which he often deploys humour as a means of communicating – and, perhaps, coping with – the trauma of his conversion experiences. Similarly, the Mama Bears' description of their advocacy for young queer people is joyful, generous, and immensely kind. These Christian mothers reveal how their acceptance of their LGBT+ children is not solely defined by trauma and turmoil, but also provides abundant pleasure, purpose, and happiness in their lives.

The podcast also reveals possibilities for the entwining of faith and sexuality beyond the worldview of Love in Action. *Boy Erased* follows a common narrative for conversion stories, in which the protagonist's key challenges are resolved through their escape from conversion practices and acceptance of their sexual or gender identity. Research into such programmes has revealed, however, the continued importance of faith in the lives of many survivors and the need for mental health providers to more actively engage with survivors' faith and their relationship to faith communities.[20]

Conley more fully explores the complexity of his ongoing relationship to faith in his memoir and in several promotional interviews for the film. A Catholic nun interviewed for *UnErased* adds to this conversation when she movingly suggests an alternate relationship between Christian churches and LGBT+ people. She states: 'I think the gay community is here to tell us something: that God has ideas that we wouldn't have dreamed of. And that neither I nor you is the model for everything there is. Look at the variety in creation.'[21] Although centring a heteronormative worldview (LGBT+ people are an idea that 'we' might not have imagined), this statement at least offers alternate possibilities beyond the need for LGTB+ people to escape religion in order to be free.

Conclusion: supporting queer kids in conversion programmes and beyond

Despite my obvious reservations about *Boy Erased*, I continue, even after several viewings, to find the film deeply moving. Growing up as a queer child, I was never subjected to a conversion programme, nor was my Catholic family as religiously conservative as the Conleys. And yet, in reading the book and watching the film, I have felt an ongoing kinship and solidarity with the protagonist. The powerful, yet deeply fragile forms of hegemonic masculinity that shaped Conley's childhood and youth also dominated mine. I failed in my attempts to be properly male in similar ways. The Love in Action programme is an absurdly heightened version of lessons about masculinity that are all too familiar to those of us who similarly spent our childhoods conscious of how our bodies, our stance, and our speech patterns were viewed and assessed by the men around us.

This leaves me hoping that conversion narratives like *Boy Erased* might prompt broader discussions, not only about the need for legislative action to ban such programmes, but also for the need to support queer children more broadly. This is not to deny the specificity of conversion practices, which have profoundly damaging impacts on survivors, nor to question the need for stories that reveal such cruel abuse.[22] Rather, I want to acknowledge that these programmes emerge from social structures that reach much further than the conservative Christian churches of the American South. Conversion 'therapy' is a product of contradictory ideas that arguably impact all young people. In public discourse, childhood and youth are often imagined as times in which young people can or should be shaped into ideal citizens with normative sexual and gender identities.[23] As Conley himself has argued, 'Conversion therapy doesn't have to be done in a facility. If you're taught to be a "certain type of man", to act a certain way, and you're taught by authority figures that being gay is evil, then that's conversion therapy too' (for a broader definition of conversion practices, see Johnson herein on conversion ideology).[24]

The process of supporting queer children therefore requires a broader and more radical project than protecting them from conversion therapy practices. The next step is to celebrate the joys and pleasures of queer childhood and youth. Sadly, any efforts to support LGBT+ children in this way are often framed as attacks on childhood innocence. In Australia, for example, a number of controversies have arisen over programmes providing school students with positive, age-appropriate information about LGBT+ lives, with accusations that support programmes 'prematurely sexualize' children and that LGBT+ adults are 'grooming' children for sex.[25] Republican politicians in the United States have recently introduced legislation banning any discussion of LGBT+ issues in primary schools, similarly positioning all children as innately heterosexual and cisgender, with their sexual and gender identities depicted as at risk of perversion by ill-intentioned adults.[26]

These controversies, which have been replicated in a range of other countries, reveal the need to consider Conley's story within broader contexts. The film of *Boy Erased* reveals the punishing consequences of conversion programmes. Indeed, as argued by Stuart Richards: 'It would be near impossible to leave this film without being aware of the fact that gay conversion therapy is tantamount to torture.'[27] In proving this fact, the filmmakers inspire anger and sorrow on behalf of young people trapped in dire circumstances. Yet, the film's insular vision places conversion practices as a product of a particular religious mindset, while imagining queer young people mostly as its passive victims. It is a film with admirable activist intent, but a limited political vision, which fails to consider the radical possibilities of celebrating – rather than just accepting – gender diversity.

Missing from *Boy Erased* is any acknowledgement that queer childhoods are defined, not only by abjection, but by camaraderie and pleasure. This does not mean that the brutal consequences of bigotry should be ignored. Rather, what is required is a more expansive worldview, in which queer children and teenagers are allowed agency and complexity. Conversion 'therapy' is a serious topic that deserves serious consideration. But queer young people are not products of, nor should they be defined by, the cruelty to which they are subjected. Supporting them requires a form of activism that makes space for joy.

Notes

1   B. Baird and R. Reynolds, 'Unsafe Subjects: The Constitution of Young LGBTQ Political Subjects in the Safe School Controversy,' *Australian Historical Studies* 52, no. 3 (2021): 418.

2   G. Conley, *Boy Erased: A Memoir of Identity, Faith, and Family* (New York, NY: Riverhead Books, 2016), 38.

3   Conley, *Boy Erased*, 5.

4   M. Olsen, '*The Miseducation of Cameron Post* and the lessons of the Sundance grand jury prize for Desiree Akhavan,' *Los Angeles Times*, 2 August 2018, 'The Miseducation of Cameron Post' and the lessons of the Sundance grand jury prize for Desiree Akhavan - *Los Angeles Times* https://www.latimes.com/entertainment/movies/la-ca-mn-desiree-

akhavan-the-miseducation-of-cameron-post-20180802-story.html (accessed 20 August 2023).

5   Olsen, '*The Miseducation*'.

6   M. Fagerholm, 'Silence That Says So Much: Joel Edgerton and Garrard Conley on *Boy Erased*', RogerEbert.com, 29 October, 2018, https://www. rogerebert.com/interviews/silence-that-says-so-much-joel-edgerton-and-garrard-conley-on-boy-erased (accessed 20 August 2023).

7   Conley, *Boy Erased*, 73.

8   Conley, *Boy Erased*, 77.

9   A. Aranjuez, 'Change of Heart: Boy Erased, The Miseducation of Cameron Post and Gay Conversion Therapy', *Screen Education* 94 (2019): 59.

10 Aranjuez, 'Change of Heart,' 59.

11 C. M. Robinson and S.E . Spivey, 'The Politics of Masculinity and the Ex-Gay Movement', *Gender & Society*, 21, no. 5 (2007): 659.

12 T. Piontek, 'Tears for Queer: Ang Lee's *Brokeback Mountain*, Hollywood, and American Attitudes toward Homosexuality', *Journal of American Culture*, 35, no. 2 (2012): 131.

13 'Book Erased: Garrard Conley', *Headlight Review*, 10 March, 2022, https:// www.theheadlightreview.com/interviews/book-erased (accessed 20 August 2023).

14 J. Butler, *Bodies That Matter: On the Discursive Limits of Sex* (Abingdon, Oxon: Taylor & Francis Group, 2011), xxix.

15 B. Bennett, 'Cinematic Perspectives on the "War on Terror": The Road to Guantánamo (2006) and Activist Cinema', *New Cinemas: Journal of Contemporary Film,* 6, no. 2 (2008): 124.

16 J. Fields, 'Garrard Conley: Boy Erased', January, 2019 in *Good Life Project,* podcast, https://podcasts.apple.com/us/podcast/garrard-conley-boy-erased/id647826736?i=1000427683712 (accessed 20 August 2023)

17 D. Canfield, 'How the Gay-Conversion Therapy Memoir Boy Erased Made it to the Big Screen', *Entertainment Weekly*, 29 October 2018, https://ew. com/movies/2018/10/29/boy-erased-edgerton-conley-interview/ (accessed 20 August 2023).

18 Canfield, 'How the gay-conversion therapy'.

19 Fields, 'Garrard Conley'.

20 T. W. Jones, J. Power and T. M. Jones, 'Religious Trauma and Moral Injury from LGBTQA+ Conversion Practices', *Social Science & Medicine*, 305 (2022), https://doi.org/10.1016/j.socscimed.2022.115040

21 J. Abumrad, K. Aaron, G. Conley, S. Oliaee and A. Quinlan, 'Garrard and the Story of Job,' 2 November 2018, in *UnErased: the History of Conversion Therapy in America*, podcast, https://www.focusfeatures.com/boy-erased/ podcasts (accessed 20 August 2023).

22 T. W. Jones, T. M. Jones, J. Power, N. Despott and M. Pallotta-Chiarolli, *Healing Spiritual Harms: Supporting Recovery from LGBTQA+ Change and Suppression Practices*, Melbourne: The Australian Research Centre in Sex, Health and Society, La Trobe University, 2021.

23 K. H. Robinson, 'In the Name of "Childhood Innocence": A Discursive Exploration of the Moral Panic Associated with Childhood and Sexuality,' *Cultural Studies Review* 14, no. 2 (2008): 113–29.

24 E. Hilton, 'The Author of Boy Erased Hopes his Experience in Conversion Therapy Makes People Angry,' *Esquire*, 2 November 2018, https://www. esquire.com/entertainment/movies/a24525600/boy-erased-garrard-conley-interview/ (accessed 20 August 2023).

25 B. Law, 'Moral panic 101: Equality, Acceptance and the Safe Schools Scandal,' *Quarterly Essay* 67 (2017): 1–80.

26 A. Mahdawi, 'Florida's "Don't Say Gay" Law May Sound Vague – but its Purpose is Clear,' *The Guardian*, 2 July 2022, https://www.theguardian.com/ commentisfree/2022/jul/02/dont-say-gay-florida-week-in-patriarchy (accessed 20 August 2023).

27 S. Richards, 'Boy Erased is a Safe and Predictable Take on the Horrors of Gay Conversion,' *The Conversation*, 24 October 2018, https:// theconversation.com/boy-erased-is-a-safe-and-predictable-take-on-the-horrors-of-gay-conversion-104841 (accessed 20 August 2023).

Bibliography

Abumrad, J., K. Aaron, G. Conley, S. Oliaee and A. Quinlan. 'Garrard and the Story of Job.' 2 November 2018. In *UnErased: the History of Conversion Therapy in America*, podcast, https://www.focusfeatures.com/boy-erased/podcasts

Aranjuez, A. 'Change of Heart: Boy Erased, The Miseducation of Cameron Post and Gay Conversion Therapy.' *Screen Education* 94 (2019): 54–61.

Baird, B. and R. Reynolds. 'Unsafe Subjects: The Constitution of Young LGBTQ Political Subjects in the Safe School Controversy.' *Australian Historical Studies* 52, no. 3 (2021): 402–19.

Bennett, B. 'Cinematic Perspectives on the "War on Terror": *The Road to Guantánamo* (2006) and Activist Cinema.' *New Cinemas: Journal of Contemporary Film* 6, no. 2 (2008): 111–26.

'Book Erased: Garrard Conley.' *Headlight Review*, 10 March, 2022, https://www.theheadlightreview.com/interviews/book-erased.

Boy Erased [Film] Dir. J. Edgerton, USA: Focus Features, 2018.

But I'm a Cheerleader [Film] Dir. J. Babbit, USA: Cheerleader LLC, 1999.

Butler, J. *Bodies That Matter: On the Discursive Limits of Sex.* Taylor & Francis Group, 2011.

Canfield, D. 'How the Gay-Conversion Therapy Memoir *Boy Erased* Made It to the Big Screen.' *Entertainment Weekly*, 29 October 2018, https://ew.com/movies/2018/10/29/boy-erased-edgerton-conley-interview/

Conley, G. *Boy Erased: A Memoir of Identity, Faith, and Family*, New York: Riverhead Books, 2016.

Fagerholm, M. 'Silence That Says So Much: Joel Edgerton and Garrard Conley on *Boy Erased.*' RogerEbert.com. 29 October 2018, https://www.rogerebert.com/interviews/silence-that-says-so-much-joel-edgerton-and-garrard-conley-on-boy-erased

Fields, J. 'Garrard Conley: Boy Erased.' Good Life Project. January 2019. Podcast, https://podcasts.apple.com/us/podcast/garrard-conley-boy-erased/id647826736?i=1000427683712

Hilton, E. 'The Author of Boy Erased Hopes His Experience in Conversion Therapy Makes People Angry.' *Esquire*, 2 November 2018, https://www.esquire.com/entertainment/movies/a24525600/boy-erased-garrard-conley-interview/

Jones, T. W., T.M. Jones, J. Power, N. Despott and M. Pallotta-Chiarolli. *Healing Spiritual Harms: Supporting Recovery from LGBTQA+ Change and Suppression Practices.* Melbourne: The Australian Research Centre in Sex, Health and Society, La Trobe University, 2021.

Jones, T. W., J. Power, T.M. Jones. 'Religious Trauma and Moral Injury from LGBTQA+ Conversion Practices.' *Social Science & Medicine*, 305 (2022): https://doi.org/10.1016/j.socscimed.2022.115040

Law, B. 'Moral Panic 101: Equality, Acceptance and the Safe Schools Scandal.' *Quarterly Essay* 67 (2017).

Mahdawi, A. 'Florida's "Don't Say Gay" Law May Sound Vague – but Its Purpose is Clear.' *The Guardian*, 2 July 2022, https://www.theguardian.com/commentisfree/2022/jul/02/dont-say-gay-florida-week-in-patriarchy

Olsen, Mark. 'The *Miseducation of Cameron Post* and the Lessons of the Sundance Grand Jury Prize for Desiree Akhavan.' *Los Angeles Times*, 2 August 2018, https://www.latimes.com/entertainment/movies/la-ca-mn-desiree-akhavan-the-miseducation-of-cameron-post-20180802-story.html

Piontek, T. 'Tears for Queer: Ang Lee's Brokeback Mountain, Hollywood, and American Attitudes toward Homosexuality.' *Journal of American Culture*, 35, no. 2 (2012): 123–34.

Richards, S. 'Boy Erased is a Safe and Predictable Take on the Horrors of Gay Conversion.' *The Conversation*, 24 October 2018, https://theconversation.com/boy-erased-is-a-safe-and-predictable-take-on-the-horrors-of-gay-conversion-104841

Robinson, C. M., and S.E. Spivey. 'The Politics of Masculinity and the Ex-Gay Movement.' *Gender & Society*, 21, no. 5 (2007): 650–75.

Robinson, K. H. 'In the Name of "Childhood Innocence": A Discursive Exploration of the Moral Panic Associated with Childhood and Sexuality.' *Cultural Studies Review* 14, no. 2 (2008): 113–29.

The Miseducation of Cameron Post [Film] Dir. D. Akhavan, USA: Beachside Films and Parkville Pictures, 2018.

Conclusion

At the time of finalizing this book, twenty-three nations had introduced bans on conversion practices. The strictures vary between countries and sometimes wildly between jurisdictions within a federalist system of government, as in the case of the United States; for example, several countries (and state jurisdictions) ban 'health professionals' only, whereas others have a blanket ban; some states and countries ban the practice for minors but not for adults; and most have concentrated on sexuality rather than gender identity. Other jurisdictions are in the process of preparing bills to ban the practice amid increasing pressure to ensure such measures are inclusive of the rights of all members of the LGBT+ community.[1] As scientific, medical, psychological, psychiatric and social research has demonstrated, the practices are inherently damaging on several fronts and, therefore, need to be outlawed globally.

Conversion practices today are predominantly faith-based in origin, but fringe psychoanalytical methods along the design model of the National Association for Research & Therapy of Homosexuality (NARTH), often mixing the Bible with the therapist's couch, persist.[2] Amid the increasing pressures to ban faith-based practices, pseudo-medical programmes akin to personal growth therapies and other forms of conversion, practitioners are going underground, slipping below the radar of detection through more subtle mission statements on websites and more insular congregational networks.[3] As survivor and author of a 2017 memoir on his experiences with conversion practices, *The Inheritance of Shame: A Memoir*,[4] Peter Gajdics discusses the increasing difficulties around detecting practitioners: 'Organizations will never advertise themselves as practicing conversion therapy … They'll use words like "achieving sexual purity" and "breaking bonds." That makes them hard to detect.'[5] Gajdics's words ring true in the context of his own six-year experience with conversion practices, during which time he was part of a cult-like 'family' in a home ominously nicknamed 'the Styx' in British Columbia under the aegis of a psychiatrist (referenced with the pseudonym, 'Dr Alfonzo').

Through exploring narratives of storytelling in various genres, the chapters in this collection have demonstrated the fundamentally harmful and ineffective nature of conversion practices that seek to change an individual's same-sex attraction and/or gender identity. Faith-based practitioners and supporters may believe that God is on their side – but the science is certainly not. However, there is a real risk – even in the face of increasing bans – that the practice will continue in various forms as long as same-sex attracted people and transgender people are considered 'broken', 'sick' or in need of some form of healing. The practices will continue as long as fundamentalist religious communities and individuals believe that same-sex attracted people and transgender people are shameful, deviant and unworthy of their God's love.

The memoirs included and discussed in this collection witness the failure of any form of conversion practices as well as the harm they cause. As discussed in the Introduction, these examples of new storytelling have played a vital role in the campaign to end conversion practices and have communicated important survivor testimonies.[6] Likewise, Don James McLaughlin, writing in 2018 on what he calls 'the gay conversion therapy memoir', states:

> In the last five years, the publication of several first-person accounts has opened a crucial front in the movement to end these practices. For those of us who came out and came of age in cultures of conversion therapy, these narratives have mobilized a process of collective liberation from the stigma and trauma survivors experience. They also make our stories legible to readers who may not encounter them otherwise.[7]

McLaughlin's words emphasize the need for more memoirs, novels, films and documentaries, and for more divergent voices to be heard, including those by same-sex attracted women or lesbians.

Currently, the voices of trans people have not been communicated in memoir, dramatic film (with the exception of the 2022 horror film, *They/Them*)[8] or fiction, yet research is beginning to address their experiences with conversion practices.[9] Likewise, to date (and using an Australian context), 'there is no data on the extent of transgender people's participation in conversion therapy' despite the rise of ex-trans ideology 'in public discourse'.[10] We also need to hear more stories from outside Australia and the United States – a topic discussed in the Introduction – as well as personal narratives beyond a white perspective.

Additionally, more needs to be known about the nature and impact of conversion practices outside of the Anglosphere, most pressingly in developing nations and those countries where Christianity is not the dominant religion. As with research and activism associated with conversion practices and transgender individuals, analyses of such practices on the African continent, for example, as well as in Russia[11] and the Middle East are nascent. While there have been and continues to be successful campaigns in the West to ban active interventions in an individual's choices in relation to sexuality and gender identification, this is not the case on a global scale. Many countries have been left behind, particularly the Global South, where evangelical Christian missionaries have expanded exponentially since the 1970s, bringing with them an ex-gay rhetoric increasingly challenged in the West. Sharon G. Horne and Mallaigh Mcginley describe the 'transnational ex-gay movement'[12] as 'the main purveyor of public antigay and lesbian rhetoric'[13] in non-Westernized regions outside Europe and North America, highlighting its culpability in the perpetration of conversion practices as well as 'conservative public policy agenda' designed to impinge upon the human rights of LGBT+ people. Horne and Mcginley cite Uganda, Ghana, Nigeria, Kenya and Cameroon as particularly 'connected with U.S.-based Evangelical Protestant denominations'.[14] An especially striking example of the latter dynamic is the invitation extended to Scott Lively, Don Schmierer and Caleb Lee Brundidge, all representatives of (then) current or defunct ex-gay movements, by the Family Life Network in Uganda, to attend a think-tank that led to the 2013 Ugandan Anti-Homosexuality Bill[15] (annulled in 2014 by Uganda's Constitutional Court but reversed in 2023 by the passage of an 'egregious' *Anti-Homosexuality Act*).[16]

In a 2022 report published by OutRight Action International[17] based on surveys and interviews of 2,891 LGBT+ people who had experienced conversion practices in Kenya, Nigeria and South Africa, participants reported beatings, kidnapping, exorcism, rape and other forms of sexual assault, physical deprivations and electroconvulsive 'treatment'. Most contexts for the practices were religious, familial and medical, or a combination of all three, with religious environments being by far the most common. The report includes the words of some of the interviewees – such as the two quoted below – which illustrate the power of survivors' testimonies[18] and reminds us that new storytelling can take many forms outside of memoir and film:

> Family members organized different sessions, firstly with the pastor, then traditional healer, then with a professional psychologist. None of it helped.[19]

> I was continually prayed and fasted over, and when that didn't work, they made my cousin sleep with me forcefully. Actually, my cousin raped me.[20]

While the OutRight Action International report shows the domination of Christianity in Kenya, Nigeria and South Africa, it is important to acknowledge the need for research on the use of conversion practice in other religious faiths and cultures, including Islam,[21] Judaism,[22] Buddhism and Hinduism.[23] Amir Kabir and Irwin Nazareth have reported on the dual threats to Iranian same-sex attracted men of 'the Islamic penal code (clauses 108 to 126)'[24] and 'the development of pseudoscientific therapies by health professionals'. This combination of faith (and religious law) and medical prejudice has resulted in the continued recourse to conversion practices that range from 'counselling, prayers, aversion therapies, drugs or hormone injections, electroconvulsive therapy' and 'at extremes, sex reassignment surgery'[25] (the latter carried out as a 'cure' for same-sex attracted men and women).[26]

Finally, we also need to know more about the spiritual or religious impacts of conversion practices on LGBT+ individuals with faith. How has exposure to faith-based conversion ideology and/or conversion practices affected people who wish to keep a relationship with their God/s? This struggle or challenge is an inherent part of the memoirs of both Anthony Venn-Brown and Stuart Edser, as related in their chapters herein. The 2018 research findings of Timothy Jones, A. Brown, L. Carnie, G. Fletcher and W. Leonard on conversion practices in Australia include important inroads into this very subject, illustrated with powerful testimonies of survey participants.[27]

To return to the title of this book, we understand conversion as a concept and practice with a dual meaning: the original proselytizing function used by religious groups to persuade subjects to adopt a new faith-based identity, and, through 'therapy', to induce individuals to adopt a new sexual or gender identity. As scholars such as Erzen have pointed out, sexual orientation in ex-gay ideology is responsive to *change* under the right conditions, making conversion in this mindset a process fusing both religious and sexual identities. To be 'born again' encapsulates this vision. The narratives of Stuart Edser, Anthony Venn Brown, Garrard Conley, Michael Bussee and others in this collection have demonstrated the necessity for *defiance* of this belief system and the institutional power structures that support it, requiring enormous courage that often comes at great personal cost. Following the argument of McLaughlin cited earlier, these acts of rebellion and sharing of survivor testimony have shone a powerful light on the many abuses and harms that accompany conversion practices. In the subtitle of the book, we deliberately invoke another religious term, namely *repentance*. The word has both a secular and moral dimension but is more commonly used in the Christian theological sense as an act of turning away from sin and seeking salvation from God. The Christian Right and ex-gay movement have of course historically used the concept as the basis of their justification for conversion of same-sex attracted people, and yet our narratives reveal the more recent quest of ex-gay leaders and parents such as Linda and Rob Robertson in *For They Know Not What They Do* to seek atonement for the harms that they caused. Now equipped with the truth and understanding they once lacked, their act of speaking out where silence had once prevailed is an act of contrition and a vital step forward.

Notes

1   J. Motmans, P. Cannoot and G. T'Sjoen, 'Banning conversion therapy for trans people,' *BMJ* 380 (2023): https://www.bmj.com/content/380/bmj. p341 (accessed 24 April 2023).

2   See J. E. Bennett and M. Johnson, 'Introduction,' in *Gay Conversion Practices in Memoir, Film and Fiction: Stories of Repentance and Defiance*, eds J. E. Bennett and M. Johnson (London: Bloomsbury, 2024), 3.

3   See L. Ta, 'Conversion Therapy is Happening Underground in Iowa, LGBT Advocates say. Some Lawmakers are Trying to Stop It,' *Iowa Capital Dispatch*, 19 February 2020, https://iowacapitaldispatch.com/2020/02/19/ conversion-therapy-is-happening-underground-in-iowa-lgbt-advocates- say-some-lawmakers-are-trying-to-stop-it/ (accessed 24 April 2023); D. Cariboni and J. Hess, 'US Christian Right group accused of promoting anti-LGBTQ "conversion therapy"', *openDemocracy*, 24 November 2021, https://www.opendemocracy.net/en/5050/us-christian-right-conversion- therapy-despite-bans/ (accessed 24 April 2023). Research is nascent on this challenge to ending conversion practices; see M. Jennings, *Happy: LGBTQ+ Experiences of Australian Pentecostal-Charismatic Christianity. Christianity and Renewal* (London: Palgrave Macmillan, 2023), 135–45.

4   P. Gajdics, *The Inheritance of Shame: A Memoir* (Long Beach, CA: Brown Paper Press, 2017).

5   P. Gajdics in M. Jones, 'In "Treatment"', *lstv*, 14 January 2019, https:// lezspreadtheword.com/en/in-treatment/ (accessed 25 April 2023).

6   See Bennett and Johnson, 'Introduction,' 17–18.

7 D. J. McLaughlin, 'The Gay Conversion Therapy Memoir', *Public Books*, 14 November 2018, https://www.publicbooks.org/the-gay-conversion-therapy-memoir/#fnref-24783-1 (accessed 26 April 2023).

8 See Bennett and Johnson, 'Introduction', especially 17–18.

9 See Bennett and Johnson, 'Introduction', 16–17. See also T. Jones, A. Brown, L. Carnie, G. Fletcher and W. Leonard, *Preventing Harm, Promoting Justice: Responding to LGBT conversion therapy in Australia*, Melbourne: GLHV@ ARCSHS and the Human Rights Law Centre, 2018. Jones et al. note that the 'religious conversion therapy model was extended to include activities directed at transgender people' (14) during the period characterized by the globalization of the ex-gay movement from, approximately, 1990. The research project of Jones et al. included two transgendered individuals out of fifteen participants. See also C. M. Robinson and S. E. Spivey, 'Ungodly Genders: Deconstructing Ex-Gay Movement Discourses of "Transgenderism" in the US', *Social Sciences* 8, no. 6 (2019): 1–28.

10 Jones et al., *Preventing Harm*, 18.

11 S. G. Horne and L. White, 'The return of repression: Mental Health Concerns of Lesbian, Gay, Bisexual, and Transgender People in Russia.' In *LGBTQ Mental Health: International Perspectives and Experiences*, eds N. Nakamura and C. H. Logie (USA: American Psychological Association, 2023): 75–88.

12 S. G. Horne and M. Mcginley, 'Sexual Orientation Change Efforts and Gender Identity Change Efforts in International Contexts: Global Exports, Local Commodities.' In *The Case Against Conversion "Therapy": Evidence, Ethics, and Alternatives*, ed D. C. Haldeman (USA: American Psychological Association, 2022), 226–7; see, as cited by Horne and Mcginley: C. M. Robinson and S. E. Spivey, 'Putting Lesbians in their Place: Deconstructing Ex-Gay Discourses of Female Homosexuality in a Global Context', *Social Sciences*, 4, no. 3 (2015): 879–908; S. E. Spivey and C. M. Robinson, 'Genocidal Intentions: Social Death and the Ex-Gay Movement', Genocide Studies and Prevention, 5, no. 1 (2010): 70.

13 Horne and Mcginley, 'Sexual Orientation Change Efforts'.

14 Horne and Mcginley, 'Sexual Orientation Change Efforts', 235.

15 Horne and Mcginley, 'Sexual Orientation Change Efforts', 235.

16 See Gregory Andrews, 'LGBTIQ+ Persecution in Africa; Australia's Responsibility to Protect', *Pearls and Irritations*, 2 June 2023, https:// johnmenadue.com/lgbtiq-persecution-in-africa-australias-responsibility-

to-protect/ (accessed 2 June 2023). Andrews notes that at the time of writing, Ghana was preparing to pass similar legislation criminalizing LGBT+ people based on their identities, punishable by goal sentence and enforced conversion 'therapy'.

17 OutRight Action International, 'Converting Mindsets, Not Our Identities: Summary of the Research Findings on the Nature, Extent, and Impact of Conversion Practices in Kenya, Nigeria, and South Africa,' July 2022, https://outrightinternational.org/sites/default/files/2022-09/SOGIEReport_July192022_2.pdf (accessed 21 April 2023).

18 Also, an important part of the methodology employed in Jones et al., *Preventing Harm*.

19 OutRight Action International, 'Converting Mindsets,' 23.

20 OutRight Action International, 'Converting Mindsets,' 23. Further on the power of survivors' testimonies outside the framework of published memoirs and the like, see S. Brydum, '"He Got Away with It": Conversion Therapy Survivor on Dr. Joseph Nicolosi's Legacy,' *Religion Dispatches*, 10 March 2017, https://religiondispatches.org/he-got-away-with-it-reparative-therapy-survivor-on-dr-joseph-nicolosis-legacy/ (accessed 27 April 2023), which tells the story of Ryan Kendall who, as a young teenager, was 'treated' by Joseph Nicolosi. Kendall has sought the release of the video recording of his testimony in the federal trial against Proposition 8, stating: 'The importance and power of our lived experiences is why the stories of real-life LGBT people move hearts and have the ability to change law'.

21 On Islam, see M. Alipour, 'Essentialism and Islamic Theology of Homosexuality: A Critical Reflection on an Essentialist Epistemology toward Same-Sex Desires and Acts in Islam,' *Journal of Homosexuality*, 64, no. 14 (2017): 1930–42; J. B. Jahangir and H. Abdul-Latif, 'Investigating the Islamic Perspective on Homosexuality,' *Journal of Homosexuality*, 63, no. 7 (2016): 925–54. The latest data (April 2022) from the LGBT+ news service, *Erasing 76 Crimes* reports that 'no Muslim-majority nation has repealed an anti-LGBT law,' see 'Nations with anti-LGBT laws: 49% Muslim, 44% Christian,' https://76crimes.com/nations-with-anti-lgbt-laws-49-muslim-44-christian/?gclid=CjwKCAjwl6OiBhA2EiwAuUwWZacLFkEPsocjp8uwLQw8FCFzSfRSzZ2itx9KfkWyaOr9OdLDFlihfhoC9H0QAvD_BwE (accessed 26 April 2023).

22 On Judaism, see: *Homosexuality, Transsexuality, Psychoanalysis and Traditional Judaism*, eds A. Slomowitz and A. Feit (New York: Routledge,

2019), especially, J. Drescher, 'Moving the Conversation Along,' 3–7; R. Lesser, 'Discussion of "Does God Make Referrals?": Orthodox Judaism and Homosexuality,' 45–8.

23 On Buddhism and Hinduism, see T. G. Plante, 'The Role of Religion in Sexual Orientation Change Efforts and Gender Identity Change Efforts.' In *LGBTQ Mental Health: International Perspectives and Experiences*, eds N. Nakamura and C. H. Logie (USA: American Psychological Association, 2023): 109–24.

24 As homosexuality is a crime punishable by death, 'it has been reported that somewhere in the range of 4,000–6,000 Iranians, both male and females, have been executed since 1979 for engaging in same-sex relationships based on estimations provided by human rights activists and opponents of the strict Iranian regime', see M. Yadegarfard, 'How are Iranian Gay Men Coping with Systematic Suppression under Islamic Law? A Qualitative Study,' *Sexuality & Culture* 23, no. 4 (2019): 1251. For a comparative study on Malaysia, see J.W. Liow, J. W. Chong and R. S. K. Ting, 'Constructing Gay Male Identity in a Multicultural Society: A Qualitative Grounded Theory Study in Malaysia,' *Sexuality & Culture*, 27 no. 4 (2023): 1456–80. Liow et al. state: 'Sections 377A and 377B of the Malaysian Penal Code and multiple components of the Sharia law frame same-sex sexual activities as "unnatural" with legal consequences of fines, imprisonment and whippings' (1458).

25 A. Kabir and I. Nazareth, 'Conversion Therapy: A Violation of Human Rights in Iranian Gay Men,' *The Lancet Psychiatry*, 9, no. 4 (2022): e19.

26 Indeed, 'reports indicate that almost half (45%) of all sex reassignment surgeries performed in Iran are carried out as a "cure" for homosexual men or lesbians,' see Yadegarfard, 'How are Iranian Gay Men Coping with Systematic Suppression,' 1251.

27 Jones et al., *Preventing Harm*, 20–8.

Bibliography

Alipour, M. 'Essentialism and Islamic Theology of Homosexuality: A Critical Reflection on an Essentialist Epistemology toward Same-Sex Desires and Acts in Islam.' *Journal of Homosexuality* 64, no. 14 (2017): 1930–42.

Andrews, G. 'LGBTIQ+ Persecution in Africa; Australia's Responsibility to Protect.' *Pearls and Irritations*, 2 June 2023, https://johnmenadue.com/lgbtiq-persecution-in-africa-australias-responsibility-to-protect/

Bennett, J. E. and M. Johnson. 'Introduction.' In *Gay Conversion Practices in Memoir, Film and Fiction: Stories of Repentance and Defiance*, eds J. E. Bennett and Marguerite Johnson. London: Bloomsbury, 2024). 1–37.

Brydum, S. '"He Got Away With It": Conversion Therapy Survivor On Dr. Joseph Nicolosi's Legacy.' *Religion Dispatches*, 10 March 2017, https://religiondispatches.org/he-got-away-with-it-reparative-therapy-survivor-on-dr-joseph-nicolosis-legacy/.

Cariboni, D. and J. Hess. 'US Christian Right Group Accused of Promoting Anti-LGBTQ "Conversion Therapy".' *openDemocracy*, 24 November 2021, https://www.opendemocracy.net/en/5050/us-christian-right-conversion-therapy-despite-bans/.

Drescher, J. 'Moving the Conversation Along.' In *Homosexuality, Transsexuality, Psychoanalysis and Traditional Judaism*, eds A. Slomowitz and A. Feit, 3–7. New York: Routledge, 2019.

Erasing 76 Crimes. 'Nations with anti-LGBT laws: 49% Muslim, 44% Christian.' https://76crimes.com/nations-with-anti-lgbt-laws-49-muslim-44-christian/?gclid=CjwKCAjwl6OiBhA2EiwAuUwWZacLFkEPsocjp8uwLQw8FCFzSfRSzZ2itx9KfkWyaOr9OdLDFlihfhoC9H0QAvD_BwE.

Gajdics, P. *The Inheritance of Shame: A Memoir.* Long Beach, CA, Brown Paper Press, 2017.

Horne, S. G. and M. Mcginley. 'Sexual Orientation Change Efforts and Gender Identity Change Efforts in International Contexts: Global Exports, Local Commodities.' In *The Case Against Conversion "Therapy": Evidence, Ethics, and Alternatives*, ed D. C. Haldeman, 221–46. USA: American Psychological Association, 2022.

Horne, S. G. and L. White. 'The return of repression: Mental Health Concerns of Lesbian, Gay, Bisexual, and Transgender People in Russia.' In *LGBTQ Mental Health: International Perspectives and Experiences*, eds N. Nakamura and C. H. Logie, 75–88. USA: American Psychological Association, 2023.

Jahangir J. B. and H. Abdul-Latif. 'Investigating the Islamic Perspective on Homosexuality.' *Journal of Homosexuality* 63, no. 7 (2016): 925–54.

Jennings, M. *Happy: LGBTQ+ Experiences of Australian Pentecostal-Charismatic Christianity. Christianity and Renewal.* London: Palgrave Macmillan, 2023.

Jones, T., A. Brown, L. Carnie, G. Fletcher and W. Leonard. *Preventing Harm, Promoting Justice: Responding to LGBT conversion therapy in Australia.* Melbourne: GLHV@ARCSHS and the Human Rights Law Centre, 2018.

Kabir A. and I. Nazareth. 'Conversion Therapy: A Violation of Human Rights in Iranian Gay Men.' *The Lancet Psychiatry* 9, no. 4 (2022): e19.

Lesser, R. 'Discussion of "Does God Make Referrals?": Orthodox Judaism and Homosexuality.' In *Homosexuality, Transsexuality, Psychoanalysis and Traditional Judaism*, eds A. Slomowitz and A. Feit, 45–8. New York: Routledge, 2019.

Liow, J. W., J. W. Chong and R. S. K. Ting. 'Constructing Gay Male Identity in a Multicultural Society: A Qualitative Grounded Theory Study in Malaysia.' *Sexuality & Culture* 27, no. 4 (2023): 1456–80.

McLaughlin, D. J. 'The Gay Conversion Therapy Memoir.' *Public Books*, 14 November 2018, https://www.publicbooks.org/the-gay-conversion-therapy-memoir/#fnref-24783-1.

Motmans, J., P. Cannoot and G. T'Sjoen. 'Banning Conversion Therapy for Trans People.' *BMJ* 80 (2023): https://www.bmj.com/content/380/bmj.p341.

OutRight Action International. 'Converting Mindsets, Not Our Identities: Summary of the Research Findings on the Nature, Extent, and Impact of Conversion Practices in Kenya, Nigeria, and South Africa.' July 2022, https://outrightinternational.org/sites/default/files/2022-09/SOGIEReport_July192022_2.pdf

Plante, T. G. 'The Role of Religion in Sexual Orientation Change Efforts and Gender Identity Change Efforts.' In *LGBTQ Mental Health: International Perspectives and Experiences*, eds N. Nakamura and C. H. Logie, 109–24. USA: American Psychological Association, 2023.

Robinson C. M. and S. E. Spivey. 'Putting Lesbians in their Place: Deconstructing Ex-Gay Discourses of Female Homosexuality in a Global Context.' *Social Sciences* 4, no. 3 (2015): 879–908.

Robinson, C. M. and S. E. Spivey. 'Ungodly Genders: Deconstructing Ex-Gay Movement Discourses of "Transgenderism" in the US.' *Social Sciences* 8, no. 6 (2019): 1–28. DOI: org/10.3390/socsci8060191

Spivey, S. E. and C. M. Robinson. 'Genocidal Intentions: Social Death and the Ex-Gay Movement.' *Genocide Studies and Prevention* 5, no. 1 (2010): 68–88.

Ta, L. 'Conversion Therapy is Happening Underground in Iowa, LGBT Advocates Say. Some Lawmakers are Trying to Stop It.' *Iowa Capital Dispatch*, 19 February 2020. https://iowacapitaldispatch.com/2020/02/19/conversion-therapy-is-happening-underground-in-iowa-lgbt-advocates-say-some-lawmakers-are-trying-to-stop-it/

Yadegarfard, M. 'How are Iranian Gay Men Coping with Systematic Suppression under Islamic Law? A Qualitative Study.' *Sexuality & Culture* 23, no. 4 (2019): 1250–73.

Select Bibliography

Aranjuez, A. 'Change of Heart: *Boy Erased, The Miseducation of Cameron Post* and Gay Conversion Therapy.' *Screen Education*, 94 (2019): 54–61.

Barton, B. *Pray the Gay Away: The Extraordinary Lives of Bible Belt Gays.* New York: New York University Press, 2012.

Beirne, R. 'Teen Lesbian Desires and Identities in International Cinema: 1931–2007.' *Journal of Lesbian Studies* 16:3 (2012): 258–72.

Besen, W. *Anything but Straight: Unmasking the Scandals and Lies Behind the Ex-Gay Myth.* New York: Harrington Park Press, 2003.

Betts, D. and J. Bennett, 'Resurgent Prejudice: Responses to Marriage Equality in Australia.' *Journal of Australian Social Issues*,58:4 (2023): 732–46. http://doi.org/10.1002/ajs4.279

Boy Erased [Film] Dir. Joel Edgerton, USA: Focus Features, 2018.

But I'm a Cheerleader [Film] Dir. Jamie Babbit, USA: Lionsgate Pictures, 1999.

Conley, G. *Boy Erased: A Memoir of Identity, Faith, and Family.* New York: Riverhead Books, 2016.

Danforth, E. M. *The Miseducation of Cameron Post.* New York: Balzar + Bray, 2012.

Drescher, J. 'Can Sexual Orientation Be Changed?' *Journal of Gay & Lesbian Mental Health*, 19 (2015): 84–93.

Edser, S. J. *Being Gay, Being Christian.* Wollombi: Exisle Publishing, 2012.

Erzen, T. *Straight to Jesus: Sexual and Christian Conversions in the Ex-Gay Movement.* Berkeley: University of California Press, 2006.

Forstein, M. 'Overview of Ethical and Research Issues in Sexual Orientation Therapy.' In *Sexual Conversion Therapy: Ethical, Clinical and Research Perspectives*, eds A. Shidlo, M. Schroeder and J. Drescher, 167–79. New York: Haworth Press, 2001.

Jones, T. W., J. Power, T. M. Jones. 'Religious Trauma and Moral Injury from LGBTQA+ Conversion Practices.' *Social Science and Medicine*, 305 (2022). DOI: 10.1016/j.socscimed.2022.115040.

Jones, T. W., A. Brown, L. Carnie, G. Fletcher and W. Leonard. *Preventing Harm, Promoting Justice: Responding to LGBT conversion therapy in Australia.* Melbourne, GLHV@ARCSHS and the Human Rights Law Centre, 2018. https://www.ohchr.org/sites/default/files/Documents/Issues/SexualOrientation/IESOGI/Academics/Equality_Australia_LGBTconversiontherapyinAustraliav2.pdf (accessed 12 March 2021).

King, G., C. Mollow and Y. Tzioumakis eds, *American Independent Cinema: Indie, Indiewood, and Beyond*. New York: Routledge, 2013.

McKinnon, S., G. Waitt and A. Gorman-Murray. 'The Safe Schools Program and Young People's Sexed and Gendered Geographies.' *Australian Geographer*, 48, no. 2 (2017): 145–52.

Nicolosi, J. *Reparative Therapy of Male Homosexuality: A New Clinical Approach*. Maryland: Jason Aronson Inc., 1991.

Piggin, S. *Evangelical Christianity in Australia: Spirit, Word and World*, 3rd edn. Melbourne: Acorn Press, 2012.

Plummer, K. *Telling Sexual Stories: Power, Change and Social Worlds*. London: Routledge, 1995.

Power, J., T. W. Jones, T. Jones, N. Despott, M. Pallotta-Chiarolli and J. Anderson. 'Better Understanding of the Scope and Nature of LGBTQA+ Religious Conversion Practices will Support Recovery.' *Medical Journal of Australia* 217, no. 3 (2022): 119–22.

Pullen, C. *Gay Identity, New Storytelling, and the Media*. New York: Palgrave Macmillan, 2009.

Rich, B. R. 'The New Queer Cinema.' In *Queer Cinema, The Film Reader*, eds H. Benshoff and S. Griffin, 53–60, London: Routledge, 2004.

Robinson, K. H. '"Difficult Citizenship": The Precarious Relationships between Childhood, Sexuality and Access to Knowledge.' *Sexualities* 15, no. 3–4 (2012): 257–76.

Robinson, C. M., and S. E. Spivey. 'The Politics of Masculinity and the Ex-Gay Movement.' *Gender & Society*, 21, no. 5 (2007): 650–75.

Robinson, C. M. and S. E. Spivey. 'Ungodly Genders: Deconstructing Ex-Gay Movement Discourses of "Transgenderism" in the US.' *Social Sciences* 8, no. 6 (2019): 1–28. DOI: org/10.3390/socsci8060191

Save Me [Film] Dir. Robert Cary, USA: Mythgarden, 2007.

Terry, J. *An American Obsession: Science, Medicine, and Homosexuality in Modern Society*. Chicago: University of Chicago Press, 2010.

The Miseducation of Cameron Post [Film] Dir. Desiree Akhavan, USA: Beachside Films, 2018.

Venn-Brown, A. *A Life of Unlearning: A Preacher's Struggle with His Homosexuality, Church and Faith*, 3rd rev edn. Sydney: Personal Success Australia, 2015.

Waidzunas, T. *Sexual and Christian Conversions in the Ex-Gay Movement*. Berkeley: University of California Press, 2006.

Index